D0392495

DECEPTION
BY
GASLIGHT

DECEPTION BY GASLIGHT

A GILDED GOTHAM MYSTERY

Kate Belli

CROOKED
LANE

NEW YORK

Published in the United States by Crooked Lane Books, an imprint of The Quick Brown Fox & Company LLC.

Crooked Lane Books and its logo are trademarks of The Quick Brown Fox & Company LLC.

Library of Congress Catalog-in-Publication data available upon request.

ISBN (hardcover): 978-1-64385-464-9
ISBN (ebook): 978-1-64385-465-6

Cover design by Nicole Lecht

Printed in the United States.

www.crookedlanebooks.com

Crooked Lane Books
34 West 27th St., 10th Floor
New York, NY 10001

First Edition: October 2020

10 9 8 7 6 5 4 3 2 1

For determined women everywhere who refuse to be gaslit

CHAPTER 1

New York City

February 1888

When the man in the pineapple-embroidered waistcoat landed in front of her with a soft thud, Genevieve knew it had been a mistake to turn down this particular alley.

He'd leapt, sleek and nimble as a cat, from a first-story fire escape and was now standing between her and the entrance to the street.

There was no other way out.

Genevieve bit her lip. Being trapped between a rock and a hard place, or between a brick wall and a man in a dirty and torn waistcoat in a darkening alley, was *unsettling*, to say the least. But the only way to be a real journalist was to get a good story, she reminded herself.

And she was chasing the best story in town.

Shoulders squared, Genevieve looked at the man planted in front of her. It was obvious his waistcoat had once been rather fine, and even in the deepening gloom the gold pineapples glinted and winked. His head was bowed low, and she couldn't make out his face under the shadows of his hat.

This was *exactly* the sort of situation in which the heroine of a penny dreadful might find herself. The thought galled her. Genevieve loathed, above all things, anything resembling stereotype.

"Lost, miss?"

A gruff male voice came from behind her. She wheeled around, but no one was there.

What game was being played here? She shot a quizzical glance at Mr. Pineapple Waistcoat, and as he raised his head, his face passed through a beam of lamplight shining from the street. Her breath caught. He was, quite simply, one of the most handsome men she'd ever seen. Her brain flashed a brief image of Michelangelo's marble *David*, which she'd visited in Florence. She had only a moment to ponder the incongruity of encountering such beauty in a place like Bottle Alley before the man offered her a wry little half smile and gestured upward with his brows.

Genevieve followed his gaze, and there, perched on the iron ledge of another fire escape, sat one of the men she'd been tailing, his legs dangling.

"You were following us," accused another voice. She whirled around again and almost collided with a third man, his scruffy, bearded face only inches from hers. He grabbed her elbow to help steady her. Genevieve pulled free and took a step backward.

Her heart thudded. No story was worth her life. She darted a quick glance back toward where the alley spilled open to Mulberry Street and to some promise of safety. Hands shoved deep in his pockets, Mr. Pineapple Waistcoat idly kicked at something on the dirty ground and subtly stepped to the right, freeing a narrow passage for her. Glancing up from under his hat again, he flashed the same half smile. *Go, if you like,* his look seemed to say.

"My associate there seems to think you were following us, miss," the man on the fire escape called down in a thick Bowery accent. "But me, I think you might be lost. Maybe you wanna let us know? Because Billy there, he don't like being followed, even by a lady as pretty as you. I don't think you'll mind me saying this, but it's obvious you're not from this part of town."

Genevieve stole a quick glance down at the plain blue dress and short woolen jacket she'd had made just for her investigative journeys into the city's less prosperous neighborhoods. She always dressed simply, but this was Spartan even for her.

"So which is it, miss?" asked the man from his metal perch. "Lost or following?"

Genevieve decided she'd better get to the point quickly. "My name is Polly Palmer," she explained, offering her pen name rather than her real name. "I am a journalist with the *New York City Globe*. I want to speak with you about Robin Hood."

At the mention of Robin Hood, the men went still. Genevieve waited, her heart in her throat, half terrified and half hopeful. All her years of thankless toil at the newspaper writing asinine stories comparing talcum powders, all her long, desperate efforts to write something meaningful, seemed to boil down to this moment.

A deep chuckle from above broke the silence in the alley; then came the grinding of metal on metal as the man lowered his considerable frame down a rusty ladder hanging from the edge of the fire escape.

"It's disgusting back here, isn't it?" Mr. Fire Escape asked, chuckling good-naturedly. He extended his hand. "Paddy, miss," he introduced himself. "I thought it'd be better if we could talk on the same level."

Genevieve felt a surge of relief; perhaps her boldness had paid off. "I am pleased to meet you, Paddy." She took his hand, but what she saw in his face made her blood run cold. Paddy might have been laughing, but there was absolutely nothing good-natured about the look in his eye.

"Now, what makes you think we know anything about the Hood?"

"I overheard you talking on Mulberry Street," Genevieve answered swiftly. "I know the articles in the press have been rather one-sided, and I want to write a story that does him justice. But I need your help."

Genevieve nervously took a small pad of paper and a pencil from the leather satchel slung over her shoulder. "Do you believe," she said, clearing her throat, "that Robin Hood stealing from the wealthy to give to the poor is a sign of the city's indifference to the lower classes, as some claim, or is it simply a publicity stunt on his part? Do you know anyone who has personally benefited from one of his forays? The police can't find a soul—either the man is lying about what he does with the loot, or the recipients are an extremely closemouthed lot." She nodded to herself as she squinted at her list of questions in the weak light, temporarily forgetting her fear. "I tend to believe the latter," she muttered, then looked toward her subjects and took a deep breath, pencil poised on pad. "But I'm here to find out what *you* think."

Paddy regarded her gravely. "Miss, I think you should have stayed lost."

Genevieve felt her heart sink in both disappointment and fear.

"Aw, c'mon, Paddy." It was the third man, who leaned toward her and pinched at the fabric of her sleeve. She pulled the wool from his fingers and took a step backward. She decided she needed to leave *right then*, but before she could take a step, Paddy seemed to come to some kind of decision.

"All right," he said. "We'll answer your questions."

Genevieve glanced past Mr. Pineapple Waistcoat, who was standing like a stoic sentry, and toward Mulberry Street, measuring her longing for the well-lit street against her longing for a lead. Contrary to her better judgment, her ambition won out, and she hesitantly put pencil to paper again, nodding at Paddy to continue.

"But we can't talk here, in the open." Genevieve followed Paddy's sweeping hand gesture around the claustrophobic space, marked only with indistinguishable piles of refuse. "Come back this way, into the building." With that, he disappeared into the closed end of the alley and a pool of deep, dark shadows.

"But there's nothing back that way," Genevieve called after him nervously, inching away from the third man, Billy, who seemed determined to get a good whiff of her hair.

Then a shaft of weak light shone from the end of the alley, lighting Paddy from behind. Genevieve could discern only his silhouette in an open doorway, gesturing her to follow.

Thin as it was, the light emanating from the building brightened the alley. Not by much, but just enough that the shadowy forms in the corners and the heaps against the walls began to coalesce and take shape. She started forward, then hesitated, her gaze catching on what looked like a pile of rags.

What she had assumed was another mound of garbage against the far wall had a face, its mouth stretched into an unnatural frozen grimace. The remainder of the body—for it was suddenly, undeniably obvious that the lumpish form in the corner consisted at least in part of a dead man—was impossible to fully distinguish, as it was partially buried under rubbish.

Genevieve froze, rooted to the spot with fear, her eyes locked on the milky ones staring back at her from the gray, mottled face of the corpse. Bile rose in the back of her throat, but as ghastly as the scene was, she found she could not look away. She'd seen dead bodies before—not in the street, but elderly relatives, respectfully cleaned and laid out for viewing—and knew enough to recognize that the man had been dead for many hours, if not a full day. He was middle-aged, she could see that now, and the dark shadow of his beard was evident, as was the large dent in the side of his skull that gave his head a misshapen, lopsided look.

Her trance was broken when Billy grabbed her upper arm, pulling her toward the open door.

"Hey!" Genevieve yelled, trying to wrench out of his grasp. Panic rose in her rib cage and fluttered there wildly. This had been a mistake, a horrible, wretched mistake, and if she could just get out of here, she swore she would never follow strange men into strange alleys or courtyards *ever again*. "Let me go!"

"That's enough," came a low voice. Mr. Pineapple Waistcoat was suddenly in front of them, blocking their way to the open door. Billy paused, looking at his comrade.

"Aw, Danny, c'mon," he whined.

"No," he answered quietly. "I said that's enough. Go on." He indicated his chin toward Paddy. "Both of you, get outa here."

Billy's eyes narrowed and his lips drew back in a snarl. "Why we gotta listen to you, Danny? She was following us!" He began to pull Genevieve toward the door again, wrapping his other arm around her waist to get a better hold of her struggling form. He progressed only a few steps before Mr. Pineapple Waistcoat grabbed him by the shoulder and pulled him off.

With her arms free now and barely able to think through the haze of her panic, Genevieve pulled back and swung out at the two men. Pain exploded in her hand as her fist collided with hard flesh, causing her to cry out. She lost her balance and stumbled to the dirty ground. She'd boxed with her brothers for years, but never without gloves, and marveled at how much it hurt.

"Dammit, woman!" yelled the handsome man, staggering back a few steps and rubbing his jaw.

Danny, not Mr. Pineapple Waistcoat, she told herself, now that she had a minute to think.

Billy was so surprised that for a moment he simply gaped; then he moved toward Danny, his own fists raised.

"Not worth it, Billy," Paddy noted dispassionately from the doorway. "The man said to leave her be. Let's go. We can finish our business with Danny another time."

Billy paused again, and Danny took the opportunity to grab hold of Genevieve himself. He stood before her in a protective manner. Heart pounding, Genevieve gratefully took refuge behind his broad back.

"Listen to your friend," Danny warned Billy. "Get outa here."

"But Danny." He cut his eyes toward the corpse. "She saw."

"Never mind that. We'll take care of it later. Go on."

Though she knew Billy had been dragging her toward certain harm, it killed Genevieve a little inside to watch him walk away. These men were the closest she'd come to finding a break in the Robin Hood story, and she doubted she'd ever come this close again.

★ ★ ★

Daniel watched Billy "the Breaker" Hanlon mope toward the tenement door, refusing to take his eyes off the other man's back until the dirty entrance shut with an air of finality. He sighed and flexed his jaw in annoyance, glancing at the blonde woman's face.

He hated being followed. Daniel had first become suspicious that the woman was tailing his group about four blocks uptown. For starters, she was far too clean for this neighborhood. There were plenty of pretty girls around here, but her simple, neat blue dress was not patched and worn from being passed from an aunt to an older sister and finally to its current owner, only to eventually go to a younger sister, friend, or niece; and her shiny, thick hair had fairly gleamed against the sooty walls of the tenements they passed, making her stand out like a sore thumb. He'd noticed that, then noticed how she bobbed along in their wake for several blocks, like a shiny toy caught in the muddy current of the East River. He'd abruptly stopped at a fishmonger's cart, startling Paddy and Billy, just to be sure. As predicted, the blonde girl had halted just as abruptly about half a block back, suddenly inspecting the wares of a fruit peddler who was about to close for the night.

Paddy had given Daniel a sideways look, catching on right away. Billy, never the sharpest knife in the block, had inquired loudly why they were stopping for fish. The fishwife had reopened her cart hopefully, eager to make one final sale.

Now he had a piece of bluefish wrapped in brown paper weighing down his coat pocket. He disliked bluefish. Not so much that he'd throw it out—he despised waste more than bluefish—but enough that it was annoying to have the package thumping against his leg. He hadn't wanted to waste the fishwife's time, though, and if there was any justice in the world the blonde was similarly burdened with wormy apples or a shriveled pear.

He *hated* being followed, recalling how the press had hounded him when he'd first inherited his fortune, popping out of shrubbery and from behind moving carriages, shouting questions or snaking along behind him silently. He'd learned to shake them early and well. After a few years, the commotion had died down and they'd moved on to fresh meat like the sharks they were. But every once in a while he would feel the skin prickle on the back of his neck and, sure enough, he would spot one of the buggers riding his coattails.

It didn't happen often anymore, but it still rankled. Didn't people have better things to do than read about his life, which was exceedingly dull?

Well, usually it was dull. The surprise of finding himself in an alley with both a journalist and a corpse meant things might become quite exciting, quite quickly.

Finding out this elegant-looking girl *was* press had been a surprise. She was a far cry from the bedraggled, ratty fellows he normally had to shake. His best guess had been a temperance worker, as she had appeared soon after they exited Mulligan's. In no mood for a lecture, he'd led his compatriots to Bottle Alley, one of the most notorious parts of the neighborhood.

He'd truly thought there was no way she'd follow them in here, especially since night was falling, and had watched in astonishment as the blonde gingerly picked her way through the garbage in the alley. He knew it wouldn't have ended well for her and could have written the scene that would have unfolded: Billy, who really should be behind bars, would let his damn lust get the better of him, and Paddy would have looked the other way, so to prevent it all Daniel had been forced to jump in, hoping against hope she was new to town and wouldn't recognize him.

But he hadn't planned on the body.

A reporter. A goddamn reporter.

So far, his gamble appeared to have paid off, as she seemed not to know who he was, but he wasn't taking any chances.

"Just what the hell do you think you're doing?" he demanded, deliberately keeping his Bowery accent thick. Hopefully she'd had enough of a scare for one day. He surreptitiously glanced toward the dead man.

The woman glared back at him, pulling toward the street. "Let me go," she hissed. "Or I'll hit you again."

Daniel stared at her incredulously. She apparently hadn't been scared enough. "I've seen grown men killed for less than the stunts you were pulling there," he yelled, resisting the urge to give her a little shake. Christ, the woman had just barely escaped two of the most notorious criminals in the Bend and was sharing Bottle Alley with a corpse. Most women he knew would have fainted by now.

"Just let me go and let me leave," she said, suddenly looking tired. "I assume you wouldn't have saved me from them if you wanted to harm me yourself, so please let me go." She tugged at her arm again, trying to release herself from his grasp.

"I'll let you go after I've put you in a cab," he responded, leading the woman toward the open end of the alley. He glanced at her again as they walked and shook his head, wondering at her foolishness. "You nearly got yourself killed tonight, and I wanna make sure you get out of here before you finish the job."

The woman pursed her lips but said nothing. They reached the alley's end. It was almost full night, and the gas lamps illuminated the area's run-down buildings with a soft light. Daniel scanned the street for an oncoming carriage.

"Who is he, or was he?" she asked quietly as she looked back over her shoulder.

He felt a slight tremor pass through her arm. He knew exactly who she meant, but he had no intention of answering. The sooner she forgot what she'd seen, the better. He tightened his grip on her arm and kept scanning the street for a carriage.

"What about Robin Hood? Do *you* know anything about him?" she probed again, her voice soft in the night. "I heard you talking about him with those men."

Daniel's irritation rose. "See, miss, these are *exactly* the kind of questions that could get you killed." He fixed her with his piercing stare. "People round here don't like talking to strangers. I need you to promise me I won't see you in this part of town no more."

She gazed at him levelly. "I want this story. I could do it justice, do it right. I know what I did tonight was rash, and really, thank you for helping me. But I have to pursue this, especially after tonight. It's the best story in the city right now." Her look changed to one of pleading. "Please, if you know anything, talk to me."

He shook his head at her. "Drop it, miss. None of you reporters is gonna find out anything about the Hood unless he wants to be found. Now promise me."

"I don't have to promise you anything," she replied angrily, looking down the street for a cab now herself. She tugged at her arm again and glared up at him. "Why can't you let me go?" She scowled, pulling harder.

At the sound of an oncoming carriage, both Daniel and the woman turned toward the noise. Quickly noting that it was someone's private conveyance and not a cab, Daniel turned back, only to find his face inches from the pretty reporter's.

She was tall enough that he wouldn't have to stoop to kiss her full, lovely mouth. Were he inclined to kiss her.

She blinked in surprise, breaking the fragile spell.

Daniel turned away to cover his unease and used two fingers of his free hand to sound a low, long whistle. Within a moment a cab clambered into view.

He paid the driver as the reporter stepped into the carriage with a surprising amount of dignity for someone so covered in muck.

"Where's she going?" the driver asked.

"I don't know," Daniel muttered. He didn't like this unhinged feeling he was having; he just wanted this troublesome female out of his sight. Reporters always brought rotten luck, and this one was no different. "Take her home, wherever that is." He peered into the cab's window at the girl, who stared stonily ahead. "He'll take you home, miss. Now please, do us both a favor and stay away from this part of town."

She favored him with an icy glare. "Not to worry, sir. I sincerely doubt we shall ever meet again." She rapped the roof of the cab sharply. "Washington Square, driver."

With a small lurch, the carriage pulled away. Daniel watched it go, absent-mindedly rubbing his jaw where he'd been hit. Whoever she was, that odd and pretty woman packed quite a punch.

"Washington Square," he said softly. Well, that address could mean any number of things; all kinds of people lived on the Square now. The girl was probably right about one thing, though. It was doubtful they'd ever cross paths again.

Still, he'd gotten damn lucky tonight. Had she known who he was, he'd probably have had to board the next steamer back to London. While he could cross the Atlantic in relative comfort, he'd just returned to his hometown a few months ago and would prefer to wait another year or so before heading abroad again. He had things to take care of here in New York.

Starting with what, or who, was waiting for him in the alley.

CHAPTER 2

The appearance of the blonde reporter in one of the city's most exclusive ballrooms the next evening was so unexpectedly jarring, Daniel choked on the sip of excellent champagne he'd just taken.

He managed to force down the swallow, but only barely, and his throat and lungs protested with a violent coughing fit—a condition *not* helped by repeated back thumping from his well-meaning friend Rupert.

"Egads, man, this champagne is meant to be sipped, not gulped. I thought you were among the few Americans who knew that kind of thing," Rupert drawled while continuing to pound.

Daniel shrugged his friend off his back with an irritated twitch of the shoulders, his breath easing slightly. Rupert raised his hands in mock surrender. "Fine, then, expire right here in the middle of Andrew and Sarah Huffington's ball. Everyone has seen that I have tried to help you and was rudely rebuffed. You will have no one to blame for your senseless death but yourself."

Daniel ignored his friend's typically ridiculous antics. His eyes had not once left the rose-silk-clad figure across the room.

The reporter. She's here.

What had she called herself? Polly Palmer? Surely a pseudonym. And what was she doing in the Huffingtons' ballroom?

"Are you quite recovered?" Rupert regarded him with his typical bland facade, but Daniel discerned actual concern in his friend's eyes. The jolt of seeing the reporter must be showing on his face. He quickly rearranged his features into what he hoped read as impassivity and straightened up.

"Fine now, thank you."

"Good, because my probable future mother-in-law is heading this way. Don't make me talk to her alone."

Mrs. Elmira Bradley, mother to Esmerelda Bradley, Rupert's almost-affianced, was indeed heading straight for them, in a gown so vividly purple it was almost eye-watering. Daniel rearranged his features yet again, this time into a polite smile aimed at Mrs. Bradley, though over her approaching shoulder he kept his attention on the woman in rose. The reporter was talking to some other young ladies, one of whom he vaguely recalled meeting at some function or other over the years. He searched his memory, hoping it would jar a connection, but came up short.

She didn't appear to have seen him yet.

"My dear Mr. McCaffrey, are you quite all right?" Mrs. Bradley had reached them and was fluttering around Daniel like a small, pesky bird.

"He is fine, Mrs. Bradley, absolutely fine," declared Rupert, as he plucked another glass of champagne from a nearby tray. The glass was pressed into Daniel's hand, and he grasped it automatically. "Simply drank this wonderful vintage too quickly, and is now in need of more."

Daniel took a dutiful sip, the bubbles unpleasantly tickling his irritated throat. A crowd of people had gathered in a small knot near the refreshment table, partially obscuring his view of the reporter. He shifted his body slightly to the left, pretending to nod to an acquaintance across the room, and got her back in his sights.

Mrs. Bradley beamed. "Ooh, you do like it, then? The sommelier is coming to work for us, you know. We had a devil of a time luring him away from ol' Huffington, but apparently he's the best, and I wanted the best. And you know I get what I want." She gestured with a lavender fan toward Rupert's chest to emphasize her point, before unfurling it and fanning herself. The numerous diamonds decorating her purple satin–gloved fingers winked furiously in the dim gaslight provided by lamps festooning the ballroom's walls, which had been hung with gold silk for the occasion.

Daniel resisted the urge to snort. Get what she wanted, indeed. Elmira Bradley, like many of the newly moneyed of New York, held a particular fondness for the British titled class, craving the perceived old-world glamour and entitlement that accompanied such aristocracy. She had been pushing for a match between Rupert, the sixth earl of Umberland, and her heiress daughter for months. The fact that Rupert's family had barely two pounds to rub together seemed not to matter a whit.

The cluster around the refreshment table loosened. He had a direct view of the reporter now, and if she looked his way, she would have an equally direct view of him. Her companions appeared engaged in animated conversation, but she seemed listless, barely contributing to whatever they were saying.

She was more attractive than he recalled. Her honey-colored hair was piled off her face, and her simple, dusky-pink gown draped over her perfectly.

Attractive, despite her obvious tiredness.

Should he leave? Daniel toyed with the idea, imagining himself making polite excuses to Rupert, who would be surprised and irritated and would later accuse him of reneging on his promise to attend the ball. His hostess Sarah Huffington would be gracious but disappointed. He didn't go out in society much; he knew his presence was a bit of a coup for her.

But he did want to go out *sometimes*. He would be in New York for several months and had no desire play the hermit during his stay. If this girl was part of the Astor 400—and she must be to have been invited—surely their paths would cross again sooner or later.

Mrs. Bradley beckoned to someone to her left, and a painfully thin, pallid girl with pale-blonde hair emerged from behind a potted palm. "And here is Miss Bradley!" she exclaimed, nudging the girl in Rupert's direction. "Though I think it might be appropriate for you to start call-ing her Esmie," she added with a wink.

The reporter had accepted a glass of her own champagne but wasn't drinking it. Daniel took a sip of his, this one going down easier, listening to the exchange between Mrs. Bradley and Rupert with half an ear.

Esmie offered Rupert a nervous flash of a smile, which quickly faded as she regarded him in what appeared to be utter terror, despite the fact that the couple had been courting—or going through the motions of courting—for some time. Mrs. Bradley nudged her daughter again, less gently this time. "Esmie, talk to his Lordship," she hissed in a loud whisper.

Who *was* the reporter, really? Daniel had assumed she was some scrappy transplant from another part of the country, perhaps boarding in the newly flourishing bohemian section on Washington Square's south side. She looked at her champagne as if surprised to find it there, and raised it toward her lips, but lowered it again.

Esmie opened her mouth, only to have her mother interject before she could speak. "Not about that horrid book you're reading." Esmie's mouth snapped shut, and she flushed a deep, unflattering red, fixing a stony stare to the right of Rupert's head.

"I quite like books," Rupert attempted helpfully, only to be cut off by Mrs. Bradley.

"You wouldn't like this one, your Lordship; it's about some horri-ble man who changes from good to evil in the blink of an eye. Not that my Esmie is some bluestocking, mind," she hastily added, apparently fearful of giving Rupert the wrong impression. Esmie closed her eyes briefly in what appeared to be abject humiliation.

Stay. A forceful thought, that. Surprising. He turned it over in his mind a few times.

Fine, he would stay. Let himself be seen.

Smiling gently at Esmie, who still looked pained, Rupert softly stated, "Mrs. Bradley, this marvelous band has just begun a waltz, and my evening simply would not be complete if I were denied the oppor-tunity to dance with lovely Esmerelda. May I?"

Esmie shyly took his hand, and Rupert led her toward the dance floor. Daniel idly followed their progress before shifting his focus back to the reporter.

What would she do if she saw him? Would she scream? Faint? Alert the authorities?

"O-of course," Mrs. Bradley stuttered after the couple, who were already on their way. Her chest puffed slightly in triumph as she watched the Earl of Umberland turn her spindly, pale daughter around the room. Looking around in glee, she spied a group of her cronies nearby and swept toward them without a word to Daniel.

He would deny everything, of course. A case of mistaken identity. While he hated to capitalize on the notion of womanly hysteria—the women he'd grown up with were tough as nails; by Daniel's reckoning they were by far the stronger sex—the popular belief could prove useful.

If she became hysterical.

The reporter's companions turned their attention to the dance floor. Daniel followed their gaze and was dubiously rewarded by the always terrifically odd sight of Rupert Milton and Esmerelda Bradley dancing. Someone had not dressed Esmie kindly. Her thin frame was nearly drowning in a voluminous gown adorned with an alarming amount of puffs, bows, and ribbons, and the gown's bright-pink color was extremely unflattering to Esmie's already pinkish complexion. In marked contrast, Rupert looked elegant and refined in his expertly tailored black evening clothes, his dark-blond hair swept back. He gracefully swooped Esmie around the dance floor, expertly navigating her frequent missteps and near falls.

Daniel's chest tightened slightly. It was a painful sight. His friend desperately needed a wife, a very rich one. Esmie's family craved a title and the respectability they believed it would bring. Rupert had already confided to Daniel that he would likely hold his nose and go through with the match.

But, Daniel mused, what of affection, attraction, or—hell, what of *love*? A quick, unwelcome vision flashed in Daniel's head: his mother sitting on his father's lap, throwing her pretty head back and laughing at some jest he'd made. God, they had been so very poor, destitute really, but he'd never seen two people love each other with such fierce devotion.

Daniel forced the memory of his happy parents, now long dead, out of his mind. Putting his glass on a nearby table, he turned away from the spectacle of Rupert and Esmie, his gaze immediately returning to the spot where the mysterious woman from the alley had been standing.

She was not watching the dancing but gazing toward a pair of French doors leading to a balcony, open in case any guests cared to brave the chilly temperatures for a breath of fresh air. At some point she'd relinquished her glass, and her gloved fingers twisted idly in front of her waist.

Daniel's thoughts, as they had so often over the past twenty-four hours, returned to their encounter in Bottle Alley. The girl did have backbone. Even if it had been remarkably poor judgment, he knew of no other woman—and very few men, for that matter—who would have been brave enough to enter that alley in pursuit of a story. Nor did he know of too many women with such a powerful left hook.

What if she *didn't* become hysterical?

Almost as if she'd read his thoughts, the blonde sharply turned her attention from the open doors and in his direction. Her gaze swept past the refreshment table, past the dancers, and past him, then snapped back, fixing on his face with shocked, unmistakable recognition.

Here we go, then.

* * *

Genevieve had never fainted in her life, but as the edges of her vision blurred and the constant, abrasive chatter of the ballroom became muffled and distant, as if she were hearing the sounds of the party from deep beneath the calm waters of a still lake, she realized she was on the verge of experiencing the phenomenon.

The world wavered as her knees began to buckle, and she instinctively grabbed on to the nearest solid object to steady herself, which luckily was Callie's shoulder.

"Genevieve! Are you quite all right?" Eliza had a sudden strong arm around her waist.

As quickly as it had come, the sensation vanished. Colors snapped back to vivid sharpness, and the sounds of high laughter, raised voices, and music reassaulted her hearing. She nodded in the direction of Eliza's concerned face, but her focus was centered across the room on the tall, dark-haired man with the profile that could have been sculpted from stone.

Mr. Pineapple Waistcoat was here. *Here.*

And he was staring straight at her.

"This is my fault," Callie fussed, waving her green fan at Genevieve's face. "I absolutely hounded you to come, though I knew it would be the worst sort of crush."

"Callie, stop that," Eliza commanded, swatting the fan away. "Genevieve, what is wrong?"

"I became a little dizzy for a moment. It's so loud in here, isn't it?" she replied faintly. Mr. Pineapple Waistcoat was speaking with someone she didn't recognize now, but his glance surreptitiously flicked in her direction every few seconds.

"About as loud as usual, I suppose." Callie looked around doubtfully. "Let's go outside, get a breath of air."

"No," Genevieve said, more forcibly than she intended. There was no way she was letting that man out of her sight. Callie and Eliza both blinked at her. "I'm fine, honestly."

She wasn't fine, though, and hadn't been all night. The crowd of pressing bodies combined with the competing scents of over a hundred different perfumes had been making her feel light-headed for hours. And Callie *had* hounded her to come, when she hadn't wanted to, but she had agreed that morning, hoping the party might distract her from memories of her encounter in the alley. But it was no use; while her eyes had been automatically noticing and cataloging the clashing colors of ladies' gowns, the brief flash of an acquaintance's face emerging from and then being swallowed by the crowd, the open mouths of a group of gentlemen laughing nearby, her brain had been constantly replaying the moment when the pile of rags in the alley suddenly merged into the recognizable shape of a dead human.

There wasn't a body, and then there was. Over and over and over. All it took was a slant of light.

Genevieve took a deep breath and managed a smile for her friends, watching identical expressions of cautious relief cross their faces. Callie offered to get them all some lemonade and squeezed through the crowd. Genevieve watched her friend's curvy figure, clad in green satin, draw admiring glances as she made her way to the refreshment table, then allowed her gaze to sweep across the expanse of the ballroom, over shiny bald pates and headpieces adorned with beads. The sights were so familiar, the same as at the dozens of similar balls she'd attended since coming out at the age of eighteen.

Her gaze inexorably returned to Mr. Pineapple Waistcoat, who seemed to stiffen slightly under its weight. What else *wasn't* she seeing? she suddenly wondered. What else would be revealed if the light shifted in the right way?

Who *was* he? What was he doing at the Huffingtons' ball?

"Why did I agree to this again?" Genevieve murmured to Eliza as they were severely jostled by the ample form of a passing matron dressed in a garish yellow taffeta. She scowled at the bouncing yellow feathers protruding from the oblivious woman's retreating coiffure.

"I know you hate these things as much as I do, Genevieve," her friend replied, taking her hand. "I am truly grateful you are here." Eliza peered at her anxiously. "Are you *sure* you're feeling well?"

Genevieve nodded absent-mindedly. "I was working late last night and am tired, that's all. I am sorry I don't come to parties more often," she managed, wishing to change the subject from her near faint. "I can't quite believe your father is still insisting you attend every social event of the season."

Eliza scrunched her face. "You'd think he'd have surrendered the idea of marrying me off by now, wouldn't you? I am twenty-four, after all; I've been coming to these parties since I was eighteen and still am not married. It's quite clear I'm destined to be an old maid."

"And you know you could marry half a dozen men in this room tomorrow, if you gave any of them the slightest bit of encouragement," Genevieve replied absently. It was true. Eliza, though beautiful and wealthy, was famously uninterested in suitors.

"But I don't want any of them, you know that," said Eliza, a bit sourly. "I know it breaks my father's heart every time I say it, but I can't wait until I am officially too old to participate in this silly charade anymore. Just declare me a spinster already and be done with it. You are lucky to be spared, Genevieve."

"Yes, I suppose I am fortunate my parents are not pressuring me to wed," Genevieve murmured, fanning herself and looking in vain for Callie with their drinks. She kept half an eye on Mr. Pineapple Waistcoat, though; he had moved slightly toward the entrance to the ballroom.

Don't you dare leave.

"Oh, I am sorry," Eliza began sincerely, looking stricken, but Genevieve cut her off with a wave of her hand.

"It's fine," she reassured her friend with a smile, even though a slight pang went through her. A softer and quieter pang than it used to be, true, but it was there all the same. Both women were dancing around the topic of Genevieve's broken engagement, now some six years ago, to Ted Beekman. Ted had ended their agreement largely because he disapproved of Genevieve's eccentric family. Her parents, perhaps out of guilt, had not broached the subject of matrimony with their only daughter again. When she insisted upon pursuing a career in journalism afterward, the Stewarts had used their influence to help her gain a position.

"Is he here?" Eliza queried as softly as she could in the din, as if reading her thoughts. For a moment Genevieve gaped at her, thinking she meant Mr. Pineapple Waistcoat. Then she realized that of course her friend was referring to Ted.

"I haven't seen him," Genevieve replied just as quietly. There was no use pretending she hadn't been looking, at least before she spotted the man from the alley. One of the reasons she avoided social events was the inevitable awkwardness of running into Ted and, of course, his wife. Amelia was a nice enough girl and had played no part in the breakup. She had become Ted's wife simply by virtue of being of appropriate social standing, appropriately staid, and available. Genevieve often privately thought that being completely empty-headed may have also worked in Amelia's favor; Ted disliked being challenged.

"The downside to having a family such as mine," she continued, attempting to make light of her past difficulties. "It often results in broken engagements." She raised her fan again and wished desperately for a cool drink.

Truthfully, a breath of fresh air would also be lovely, but she did not want to risk losing sight of the man from the alley. He was watching the dancers now with a dispassionate expression, but every few moments his eyes subtly slid in her direction.

He was keeping watch on her as well, then.

Eliza's eyes narrowed. "Your family is as Old New York as they come." It was true. The Stewarts were an old and venerable clan who traced their origins to the colonial era.

"Yes." Genevieve nodded. "But we're odd. And after my mother . . . well, there's no use in rehashing ancient history."

"Here you are, my darlings: lovely, cool refreshment." Callie emerged from the crowd, holding out two cut-crystal goblets, her brilliant emerald eyes sparkling. "And I have the most exciting news. How are you feeling, Genevieve?"

"Better, thank you. This is helping," she said, holding up the glass of lemonade. And it was. The tang of citrus on her tongue seemed to clear her head.

"More exciting than Rupert Milton and Esmie Bradley waltzing?" Eliza asked dryly.

"That is always a most unusual sight," Callie agreed, snagging a glass of champagne from a passing footman's nearly empty tray. "I don't know if I'll ever become accustomed to it. But didn't Rupert look handsome?" She sighed. "It is a shame he's only after a fortune. Ooh, but this is what I wanted to tell you. Just moments ago, I spied the Earl of Umberland and Mrs. Bradley speaking."

She paused dramatically.

"Yes, Callie?" Eliza prodded.

"With Daniel McCaffrey!" Callie finished triumphantly.

For a moment, Eliza and Genevieve simply gaped at Callie, who smiled back and took a satisfied sip of her champagne.

"*The* Daniel McCaffrey? He's here?" asked Eliza with wide eyes.

"The one and only," whispered Callie, leaning closer to them. "The man who inherited the Van Joost fortune! Can you imagine?"

Genevieve's eyes whipped back to Mr. Pineapple Waistcoat. He was speaking to Rupert Milton now, though Mrs. Bradley and Esmie were nowhere in sight.

Danny, Paddy and Billy had called him.

"Callie, is *that* him?" She gestured toward Mr. Pineapple Waistcoat with her brows. "Talking with Rupert Milton?"

"Isn't he handsome?" Callie murmured dreamily.

Genevieve closed her mouth, which she realized was hanging open like a carp's. Her mind struggled to wrap itself around the fact that her one possible lead on Robin Hood and the elusive Daniel McCaffrey, about whom she'd heard rumors and stories for years, were one and the same.

Eliza craned her neck slightly to get a better look. "You've never met him?"

"No," admitted Genevieve faintly. "He's been abroad for so long."

"He's close to the age of your brothers, isn't he?" Callie peeled her eyes away from Mr. Pineapple Waistcoat—Daniel McCaffrey, her brain corrected—long enough to shoot her a quizzical look.

Genevieve shook her head slightly, trying to remember if either of her older brothers, Gavin or Charles, had ever mentioned meeting the mysterious millionaire. "I think so. But they didn't go to school together, as far as I know." She swallowed hard, her mind swimming. "Does anyone know what his relationship to Jacob Van Joost actually was?"

He was smiling at something Lord Umberland was saying. That same wry half smile as the night before. It was so dislocating, Genevieve almost lost her breath.

"I heard from a reliable source he was from the San Francisco branch of the family," Eliza said promptly, exchanging her empty lemonade glass for one full of champagne. "One of the Van Joost cousins ran away when he was a teenager during the gold rush, and Mr. McCaffrey is supposedly the bastard child of this cousin's sister. He was the only family old man Van Joost could find before he died."

Callie was shaking her head. "No, no, no, I heard he grew up in India. Some of the original Dutch Van Joosts settled there, and the last daughter of that line married a semi-disgraced Scotsman. When the family's shipping company failed, they begged old man Van Joost to take in their only son. He only did so after both parents died of snake-bites," she finished dramatically.

"And I always heard that Daniel McCaffrey is Mr. Van Joost's actual nephew, the product of the oldest Van Joost brother and an Irish laundress." Genevieve could feel her temper rising. "That version says the couple ran away to Philadelphia, where they lived under the laundress's last name. But these are all ridiculous. Nobody knows anything for certain, do they?"

She stole another glance in his direction, catching his eyes sliding away from her and back toward Rupert.

Why hasn't he left? The thought popped into her mind, sudden and unbidden. He clearly recognized her from the alley and had seen her before she saw him.

It was almost as if he were goading her to expose him.

"And then, of course, there are the *other* rumors," Callie began delicately.

"Callie," warned Eliza, "can we not speak of such horrible things? No proof of foul play was ever discovered."

"It would be devastating for such a handsome man to have committed murder," Callie nodded, artfully arranging an errant curl over her left shoulder.

Eliza wrinkled her nose. "That was not my point."

The hairs on the back of Genevieve's neck prickled at the word *murder*. Her unruly brain again flashed the image of the body in the alley.

"If you'll excuse me," she began. The rest left her mouth almost before the thought had even formed. "I need to speak with Mr. McCaffrey." Her heart began to accelerate slightly. Was the light starting to shift?

"What?" Callie exclaimed, looking confused. "I thought you hadn't met."

"Genevieve, what is it?" Eliza, ever sensitive to anyone's mood variations, grabbed her hand again.

"Work," she said shortly. Which wasn't entirely a lie.

CHAPTER 3

"Mr. McCaffrey, I believe you owe me some answers."

Even though he'd been mentally preparing himself for this confrontation since he decided to stay at the ball, Daniel felt the muscles of his jaw tighten. God, he hated the press. And damn Billy's loud mouth. If he hadn't been expounding on Robin Hood so vocally, the reporter wouldn't have overheard them and he wouldn't be having to deal with a delicate situation in the middle of one of the most exclusive ballrooms in the city.

"Good evening, Miss . . . Palmer, isn't it?" Daniel replied, knowing the silly pen name wasn't really hers. She was obviously itching to pepper him with questions, not that he intended to give any satisfactory answers. "Would you like to tell me who you really are?"

"Not a trace of last night's accent, I see," the girl noted tartly. "And I told you who I was last night, which is more than I can say for you."

So, she doesn't want to make this easy, Daniel thought. *Well, two can play at that game.* "Young ladies who write for papers always use pen names. But if you don't care to tell me, I can always ask our hostess for an introduction. Because really, Miss Palmer, a formal introduction would be more proper." Daniel plucked a fresh glass of champagne from a passing tray as her eyes narrowed in annoyance.

"Proper?" she fairly hissed. "You were rolling around an alley in a perilous part of town, dressed *and* smelling like someone who hadn't bathed in a year, and now you're worried about being *proper*?"

"Of course," he replied smoothly. "It's all about context."

"What's about context?" Rupert had popped up next to Daniel's right shoulder like a jack-in-the-box. "Oh, hello Genevieve. Surprised to see you here. Where'd you find that champagne, McCaffrey?"

"Why is it so shocking I'm at a party?" the girl bristled. Daniel suppressed a small smile; Rupert was often a useful distraction.

"You rarely come out. Ever since it went south with what's-his-name. Always thought you were too good for him, you know. *Sir!*" Rupert attempted to flag down a footman several feet away, but the man's tray was emptied long before he was able to fight his way toward them. "Hell's bells," Rupert muttered.

The reporter—*Genevieve*, Daniel corrected himself—stood with her mouth gaping, seeming too stunned to speak. Whatever breakup Rupert had been alluding to was clearly a sore spot. Daniel mentally filed the information.

"Language, Rupert," came a mild reproach. Their hostess, Sarah Huffington, sleek as a seal in a steel-gray gown, sidled up on Daniel's left. He passed a speculative eye back toward Genevieve, wondering how willing she might be to discuss publicly what had transpired between them in Five Points.

Her mouth was set tight with anger, though she seemed to be regaining her composure. As he watched, she squared her shoulders and raised her chin a notch, a stance he recognized from the night before, when she'd similarly squared off against Paddy and Billy. She fixed him with a meaningful look, accompanied by the slightest raise of a delicate left brow. Her combined stance all but shouted *your move*.

Daniel took a slow, deliberate sip of champagne and weighed his options. Would she allow her reporter's instincts to outweigh social niceties and expose him?

No, he thought. If she had been invited to the Huffingtons' ball, she was high society, and social decorum had been drilled into her since birth. She wouldn't risk it.

He answered her raised brow with a gentle quirk of his own.

Go on, it said. *I call your bluff.*

Rupert's gaze bounced between the two of them as if he were watching a tennis match. Never able to abide silence for too long, he broke the increasingly tense moment.

"My apologies. Are the two of you not acquainted? Daniel McCaffrey, may I introduce Miss Genevieve Stewart?"

Her challenging gaze didn't alter as she leisurely extended a gloved hand for him to shake. He took it, unsurprised and satisfied by the firmness of her grip.

"Heavens, did I fail in my duties as hostess?" Sarah Huffington drawled, watching the exchange with avarice. "I rather thought we'd stumbled upon a lovers' quarrel. Rupert and I do enjoy a good scene."

"Well, if it's a scene you want, you're about to get one." Rupert dropped his voice to a mock whisper. "Elmira Bradley is heading this way."

"Oh, that odious woman," Sarah sighed, twitching her red curls briefly as she made a moue of distaste. "You know I wouldn't have them in the house, but Andrew insisted. He and Amos have made piles of money together, and are about to embark on some other new venture. I'm very fond of the money, but I find *her* most disagreeable."

Daniel kept his features neutral, casually glancing toward Mrs. Bradley, but out of the corner of his eye he saw Genevieve almost imperceptibly stiffen another degree.

"Let's take to the dance floor and avoid her, then." Rupert smiled persuasively, holding out his arm. "I've most certainly had my fill of Elmira Bradley for the night." Sarah treated him to a look of amused condescension but acquiesced, laying a delicate hand on his elbow.

"You lovebirds ought to follow suit," she advised over her shoulder.

Sarah Huffington's teasing didn't bother Daniel; the well-known socialite, recently married to a shipping magnate thrice her age, was a malicious gossip who enjoyed stirring up trouble, then stepping back to observe the results. Miss Stewart seemed to be having a different reaction, though, as she let out a small, frustrated huff.

Again Daniel found himself weighing his options. Mrs. Bradley had been waylaid by some acquaintances, and he and Genevieve were alone. Her light-brown eyes were assessing, and she appeared to be deciding whether there was enough privacy to speak. He could take his leave, but if she was as dogged as he suspected, she'd be hanging about his office doorstep soon enough, no doubt waving a notebook in his face and asking more of the kinds of questions that could get her killed.

Best to satisfy at least some of her curiosity now.

Depositing his glass on a small table nearby, he held out his elbow. "Dance with me."

She blinked at his offered arm as if he were presenting her with a poisonous viper, and for the barest of moments he thought she might refuse.

She nodded once, then tucked her gloved hand into his arm, and Daniel escorted her to the center of the room, where they joined a multitude of other couples swirling around the elegant dance floor.

They danced in silence for a few minutes. Daniel was surprised how well his dance partner fit into his arms, and inexplicably pleased to notice, as he had been last night in the alley, that she was nearly as tall as he was. His palm fit perfectly into the small of her back, and she matched his every step with an agile, natural ease. Daniel glanced at her face and found her looking distractedly beyond his shoulder. He risked a peek in that direction.

"Mrs. Bradley doesn't seem to have many friends here," he remarked, noting the subject of her gaze. "Are you among them?"

This snapped her attention back toward him, as he'd thought it might.

"No," she answered emphatically. "She doesn't like me, or my family, and the feeling is mutual."

Understanding clicked. *Stewart*. "You're Wilbur Stewart's daughter, aren't you?"

Genevieve looked surprised. "You remember the case?"

He was surprised in turn. "Of course. Mrs. Bradley on one side, willing to pay an ungodly sum to commission a hat with Koola bird feathers from the last of its species, and your father on the other, fighting tooth and nail to defend the *birds*." He gave a low, delighted chuckle. It made sense now, that she was the daughter of someone like Wilbur

Stewart. "It was a brilliant defense and set quite a legal precedent. Any lawyer worth his salt knows that case."

A fleeting smile passed over her lips. "Yes, that's the one. My father didn't believe the last surviving pair of that species should be slaughtered to adorn a stupid hat, no matter how much Mrs. Bradley was willing to spend. He's quite a naturalist."

"They're beautiful birds, and I quite agree with your father. It's a shame they've been hunted almost to extinction."

"Most people thought my father was mad," she noted with a rueful look. "Nobody could understand why he was making such a fuss over two small birds in a faraway jungle."

Daniel smiled. "I did."

A slight shift came over her features, unnoticeable unless one was watching closely.

"And does that care apply only to exotic birds, Mr. McCaffrey?" she asked with more than a touch of asperity. "Or does it extend to the local citizenry as well?"

Ah. It begins. "More than you could ever know."

"I see."

"You don't, actually."

"Enlighten me, then."

"I don't believe I owe you any explanations, Miss Stewart."

"And that's where you're incorrect, Mr. McCaffrey." Her voice dropped low, and he had to incline his head slightly to hear her. "Don't forget I saw you with a dead man."

"You were also sharing space with the deceased," Daniel reminded her.

A look of alarm crossed Genevieve's features. "That is not the same thing."

"No? You were only a few steps behind us on Mulberry Street. Do you really think we killed a man in the time it took you to catch up?"

She said nothing to this, but held his gaze speculatively as they continued to glide across the floor.

"The presence of that body was just as much a surprise to me as it was to you," he continued, dropping his voice slightly as well.

A few more beats of music passed.

"Who was he?" she asked softly.

He shook his head at her but did so gently. "Nobody of consequence."

The play of anger across her face was fascinating. "Surely his family would disagree with that sentiment. Or the police."

"He had no family, and the police were notified. His demise was ultimately the result of his sustained overconsumption of gin, Miss Stewart. Bottle Alley comes by its name honestly."

"His head had been struck." It came out in a furious whisper.

They swept past Rupert and Sarah, the former of whom raised an inquiring brow at Daniel over his hostess's shoulder. Daniel ignored him.

"And yet the police determined the cause of death was liver failure from alcohol."

"How are *you* in possession of this knowledge?"

"Who do you think alerted the authorities?"

Her brows nearly shot off her forehead. "And what did the police make of a millionaire's presence in Bottle Alley?" she asked archly.

He smiled slightly at her intuitiveness. "I did not say I remained in the alley. My associates did, and they informed me of the results."

He waited while she digested this. "Why is it called Bottle Alley when it doesn't lead anywhere?" she finally asked in a rather peevish tone. They were sweeping past the refreshment table again, where he observed her friends watching them with wide eyes. Hell, half the ballroom seemed to be staring.

"It used to be an alley that cut from Mulberry to Mott, but a tenement was erected within part of the space."

"That can't be true."

"Why not?"

"An alley does not offer enough space for a building. There wouldn't be enough light, or air," she trailed off, then set her mouth in a frustrated line. "You must think me terribly naïve."

He shook his head. "You'll forgive me for making assumptions, but my guess is your life has offered little opportunity to think of such things. Ignorance is not the same as naïvety. I advise you to stay away from the topic of Robin Hood, Miss Stewart, but you may wish to learn more about the conditions that led to his necessity."

Her gaze turned sharp. "Is that a threat?"

"No. It is simple advice not to waste your time. As I said when we last met, nobody will find Robin Hood unless he wants to be found."

Under the hand that rested on her back, Daniel felt rather than heard her sharp intake of breath.

"What do you know?" It was a fierce whisper, barely audible above the music and the din of voices floating up from the periphery of the dance floor.

Daniel shook his head at her again, just once. "Only that, whoever he is, Robin Hood has eluded capture by the police thus far, whose methods are far more brutal than those of journalists. You won't find him."

A few more beats passed as they continued to circle the floor. The music, a waltz, was winding its way toward its finish.

"So you were on a slumming tour," she stated matter-of-factly, before casting a look of disgust his way. "How dare you make me believe I was in actual danger!"

Anger, hot and fierce, slammed into him. "*What?*" For decades, it had been possible for the wealthy to take "slumming tours" of the city's poverty-stricken neighborhoods, paying to observe the less fortunate as if they were animals in Central Park's zoo.

"Did you have all the details worked out beforehand? Were those men paid extra for pretending to accost me so that you could play the hero?"

Daniel had to take a deep breath to calm the rage coursing through his body. There was no way she could know how offensive this accusation was to him. "Believe me, Miss Stewart, you were in just as much danger as you thought. Paddy and Billy are not men to be trifled with." His jaw was clenched so tight he could barely get the words out.

"That's the only possible explanation," she shot back. "How else would a man like you know men like Paddy and Billy? If those are even their real names." She looked at him accusingly. "Though how anyone could take part in such unfeeling and barbaric activities is beyond me, acting as though human beings were specimens under a jar."

"Which is why I would never do such a thing," he ground out.

"Then what *were* you doing there?"

Damn, damn, damn. So much for appeasing her curiosity, though he grudgingly admitted to himself it was likely an impossible task. Thankfully, the music was reaching its final crescendo, and Daniel swirled his dance partner through the last steps of their waltz.

They paused at the end of the dance, staring each other down in the middle of the ballroom floor, panting as if they'd run a race. Other couples ebbed and flowed around them, chatting easily. He caught her eyes with his and fixed her with an unwavering stare.

"I was *not* on a slumming tour," he breathed, surprised by the low ferocity of his own voice. "That is all I can tell you, Miss Stewart."

She stared at him intently, indecision clearly written on her face. For reasons he wasn't prepared to explore, Daniel needed her to know this. He could abide many, many misconceptions she might have about him, but not that he would pay to gawk at the impoverished.

"I. Was. Not." He waited, breath almost held, as the ballroom floor began to refill with a new set of dancers, many glancing at them quizzically.

Genevieve nodded almost imperceptibly, acknowledging his claim, and he felt his shoulders soften.

It was past time to leave. He escorted Genevieve to the periphery of the dance floor, murmured a polite good-night, and turned to go.

"Wait," she whispered urgently.

He faced her, rearranging his features into a look of bland politeness. Her mouth twisted slightly, and he could tell questions were tangling up inside her, fighting to get out.

"Who *are* you, really?"

What she finally asked was so unexpected, and so refreshingly honest, that a burst of laughter escaped before he could stop it.

At the sound of his laugh, she folded her hands in front of her and glanced away, seeming embarrassed.

"I know you won't answer," she muttered.

"Honestly, Miss Stewart, I'm not even sure I know how to answer," Daniel replied, growing serious. "I do thank you for asking it, however. From the day Jacob Van Joost made me his heir at the age of seventeen, I know it's foremost on every person's mind when they meet me. You are the first person to *ever* simply ask me outright. Again, I thank you."

"I doubt you'll be thanking me for long, Mr. McCaffrey." She extended her hand for a final shake.

"I would expect nothing less," he politely, but honestly, replied.

Despite his often nomadic ways, there were a few constants in his life he'd learned he could count on: the unquestioning loyalty of choice friends such as Rupert; the unwavering undercurrent of guilt he carried over his inherited wealth; and the relief he felt every time he disembarked at New York harbor, when the miasma of sea air and garbage combined with the bustle of commerce and the tangle of multiple languages being spoken on the docks all hit him squarely in the chest with a singular, blessed sensation: *I'm home.*

He had the sinking feeling now that, whether welcome or not, Miss Stewart was about to become another constant.

CHAPTER 4

Genevieve stood before her editor's desk, fuming. Arthur Horace looked back at her in exasperation. She could tell he was thinking what he often said aloud: Genevieve Stewart would be the death of him.

"Look, Genevieve," said Arthur, mopping his brow with a handkerchief, "I've already sent Clive to cover the latest Robin Hood burglary. He's at the Huffingtons' now. And I can't send two reporters; the police are reluctant enough to allow one on the scene."

"But Mr. Horace, why didn't you send me?" Genevieve began to pace the chief editor's small office in frustration. "I was at the ball on Saturday and Clive was not. I can provide all kinds of insight into Sarah Huffington's state of mind, the quality of the diamonds that were taken, and a detailed account of the refreshment table. Why on earth won't you give me this story?" She stopped pacing and glared at him, her hands on her hips.

Arthur sighed and wearily regarded his sole female reporter. "As I said, I've already given the story to Clive. I can't reassign it now." He cut off her protest with a raise of his hand. "I *won't* reassign it now. Clive is more suited to dealing with these types of situations, talking to the police and all that. I'm sorry, but the authorities simply won't give the same details to a woman." He frowned at Genevieve a final time, then hid his shiny, bespectacled face behind an open morning edition of the *Globe*, signaling the end to their conversation.

Genevieve nearly screamed. It was so, so unfair. *She* had been at that party, *she* should be the one writing about the crime that had occurred in the hostess's mansion. Instead, *Clive* was there right now, doubtless oozing false charm all over the housemaids. It was particularly humiliating that, of all the other journalists on staff, her rival had been assigned this story. Clive had made it perfectly clear on more than one occasion that he didn't think it was appropriate for women to work in newspapers. This would have been a perfect opportunity for Genevieve to finally best him, as she had actually attended the dratted ball and had a level of firsthand knowledge of the story—or the setting, at least—that Clive could not match.

Arthur's voice drifted out from behind his paper. "I would never have guessed you were at the Huffington ball, Genevieve. Everyone knows you never go to parties."

"I do go to parties, sometimes," Genevieve muttered in response, half listening.

Arthur rustled the paper and peered around at her. Genevieve briefly considered telling Mr. Horace about her encounters with Daniel McCaffrey, but dismissed the idea almost immediately. Her editor would be thrilled to have such a piece of juicy information about the reclusive millionaire, but Genevieve knew he'd simply assume the high-and-mighty Mr. McCaffrey had been caught on a slumming tour, and that would be the end of it. A minor scandal would flare and be forgotten almost immediately.

Despite her better judgment, she didn't believe Daniel had been slumming. Which was wildly inconvenient, as a slumming tour would have wrapped up the whole affair in a neat little bow. But Daniel was too familiar with that alley and its denizens for his presence to have been part of a tour; there was something deeper going on, and she wanted to get to the bottom of it.

Something that might have to do with a body whose head had clearly been bashed in, liver failure or no.

Arthur frowned at her and rattled his paper again, apparently mistaking her continued presence in his office for an attempt to sway him into letting her join Clive at the Huffingtons'. "I'm not changing my mind about this, Genevieve," he began warningly.

"Can I at least see the letter the Hood sent here?" she asked. Robin Hood had committed three burglaries so far, and after each he'd sent a letter to the *Globe*, claiming responsibility for the attack and professing why he'd chosen his victims. In a society that celebrated wealth but turned a blind eye to how it was obtained, Robin Hood's letters offered detailed accounts of his prey's abundant greed and avarice. At first, the police had been averse to having the Hood's letters printed in the *Globe*, but careful persuasion from Arthur had convinced them that public knowledge of the crimes might be helpful in catching the thief. So far all it had done was stir up gossip—and help sell newspapers.

"Clive has the letter with him." Arthur sounded surprised. "You know that."

Genevieve gritted her teeth in frustration. "Right, of course."

Arthur raised a furry eyebrow in her direction. "Never mind about the Robin Hood burglary. I want that piece on the flower show on my desk by noon."

"Yes, noon," Genevieve grumbled, as Arthur buried himself behind his paper again. She turned to go, but a list of names in an unfamiliar hand on the edge of Arthur's desk caught her eye. They were names she knew: her former fiancé, Ted Beekman; the host from Saturday's ball, Andrew Huffington; her father's friend Reginald Cotswold; and a few other familiar high-society New Yorkers.

"Mr. Horace, what's this?" She picked up the list by its corner. "'Mayoral Committee to Investigate Housing Reform'?" She gave her editor a puzzled look.

Arthur sighed, putting the paper down. "You saw the police commissioner leave earlier?"

Genevieve nodded and glanced toward the door, where she had indeed seen the smartly cut figure of Commissioner Simons making his exit as she entered for the day.

"He wanted me to know that, on his advice, the mayor is putting together a committee to explore the need for tenement reform. But he asked me as a favor to hold off on reporting it. They're afraid it will seem as though they're giving credence to this thief's letters, and they don't want to embolden the man."

Genevieve furrowed her brow. "But it's a simple fact that housing conditions for the impoverished are terrible. The mayor really needs a committee to explore the notion?" She thought of the run-down building jammed into the narrow confines of Bottle Alley. Criminals lurked in such alleys. And dead men. But children likely lived there as well.

"It's not the fact of bad conditions, Genevieve. It's the how of fixing them. Tear them all down and start anew? Renovate what exists? Who pays?" He took off his glasses and rubbed at his eyes wearily before waving her toward the door. "Never mind about this committee, and keep it to yourself. I promised the commissioner. You concentrate on the flower show."

Genevieve mulled over this secret mayoral committee as she made her way back to her desk. She pulled out her notes on the flower show but, glancing at the clock, decided she had enough time to spend a few minutes checking the paper's files on a different topic. Surely someone, somewhere, had been able to uncover something about Mr. McCaffrey over the years.

A half hour later, a disheartened Genevieve stared at her notes. It was as if Daniel McCaffrey had simply sprung out of Zeus's head at the age of seventeen, when he was publicly introduced as Jacob Van Joost's heir. There had been, of course, a flood of articles following the announcement, all rife with speculation as to his origins and his relationship with the venerated old Knickerbocker, many of them salacious in one way or another. And as Callie had darkly hinted at the ball, some subtly suggested foul play. Despite the best efforts of the journalists at the time, nobody had been able to uncover a thing.

She returned to her desk and pulled out her leather-bound notebook, examining the notes she'd made the morning after her encounter in Bottle Alley. Amending them, she began to write down everything she had discovered about Daniel McCaffrey: his elusive past, his frequent long stays abroad, his work as an attorney.

"What's the word, Genevieve? How's Monday treating you?" Luther Franklin perched on the edge of her desk, grinning amiably at her. Genevieve hurriedly closed her notebook and shoved it aside.

"Luther! Just the person I wanted to see." She leaned back in her chair and smiled broadly.

"Yeah? Little old me?" A slight blush crept up Luther's cheeks. Genevieve knew her fellow reporter was a trifle sweet on her, though she clearly didn't return the sentiment. She did like him, though. He was a nice man, and fair; the antithesis of Clive.

And she had been waiting for him to come in—Luther covered homicide for the paper. He appeared too young for the job, with a round, open face, giving him an almost boyish appearance, but he was one of the best journalists they had.

Genevieve leaned forward conspiratorially. "Any dead bodies of interest over the weekend?" She picked up her pencil and began to tap it against her desk idly. "In Five Points, say?"

Luther's genial brow furrowed. "Five Points, huh? Genevieve, people are always dying around there, you know that."

"What about Bottle Alley?" she pressed, tapping the pencil faster.

Looking thoughtful, Luther nodded. "Yeah, I did see something about an old lush who froze to death down there. Or his liver finally went kaput. But no murders."

"What if it *was* murder?" Genevieve asked, keeping her voice casual. "I heard that maybe his head was struck."

Luther raised his brows in surprise. "Where'd you hear that?"

Genevieve waved her pencil in a lazy circle. "Around."

"Around, huh? Well, I dunno. Maybe he fell and hit his head."

"Or maybe he was hit."

Luther nodded again, concern creeping into his features. "Maybe."

"Can you keep your ear to the ground for me? Maybe get your hands on the police report, see what it says?"

Now her friend looked alarmed. "Genevieve, what are you involved in?"

She managed a smile. "Probably nothing. But would you do it?" She cringed a bit internally, knowing full well she was exploiting his feelings for her.

"Okay, toots," he replied, still looking concerned.

Genevieve's smile turned more genuine; Luther was the only person in the newsroom she would allow to call her such a nickname, as she knew it stemmed from genuine affection.

"But be careful, all right?"

Glancing at the gilt clock mounted to the office wall as Luther made his way to his desk, Genevieve was startled by the time: ten forty-five already. She reluctantly reopened her notes on the flower show she'd unenthusiastically attended the previous Friday. *Resplendent gladioli reigned supreme at the 24th annual Flower Extravaganza sponsored by the Ladies' Auxiliary Horticulture Society . . .*

Five hundred words on flowers. That was it. Five hundred words before noon, and then she could tackle the real business of the day: uncovering whatever secrets Daniel McCaffrey thought fit to hide.

★ ★ ★

Daniel strolled down Irving Place toward Fourteenth Street, hat pulled low and hands in his pockets, enjoying the uncommonly warm February afternoon. He figured he'd walk over to First Avenue and catch the elevated train—or "el," as it was known—downtown rather than take his carriage. Being on foot was better for this errand anyway. The wind picked up slightly, and he turned his head to better coil the silk scarf at his neck. That's when he spotted her out of the corner of his eye: Miss Polly Palmer, hot on his heels. Or Miss Stewart, he supposed.

Genevieve, a low voice in the back of his mind whispered.

Amusement battled with annoyance at her presence. He had to give her credit. As he'd suspected, she was persistent. She was dressed suitably for skulking in a dull-gray woolen coat, and she'd hidden her bright hair under a black scarf, wrapping it in imitation of the recent immigrants. But her full mouth was unmistakable.

Daniel hopped across the busy intersection of Fourteenth and First, making his way toward the train's entrance. Somehow being followed by Genevieve Stewart wasn't as vexing as when it was the ratty fellows on his tail. Though he didn't want her knowing where he was headed—she was a reporter, after all, and obviously a very ambitious one—he was mildly curious to see how long she could keep up.

He noted with some satisfaction that she'd anticipated his move across Fourteenth and had managed not to get caught behind the hurtling traffic. *Attagirl.*

Bounding up the stairs two at a time, Daniel wondered why he was mentally cheering on a journalist bent on finding out . . . what? Why he had been in Five Points? How he knew Paddy and Billy? What had become of the dead man in Bottle Alley? How he'd inherited Jacob's money? He didn't know what she wanted but was surprised by how much he was enjoying the chase.

After flinging himself through the train's doors just before they closed, he settled on one of the long wooden benches lining the car and pulled a folded newspaper out of his pocket, pretending to read. Through the windowed door that led to the next car, he could see her black-scarfed head swaying in time with the motion of the rattling train as it noisily made its way downtown. She was studiously pretending to be engrossed in the rapidly passing scenery: shop windows, apartments, billboards. Every once in a while, though, she would casually glance at the window between their two cars.

Daniel wondered again why he was putting up with a shadow, even one as pretty as her. He'd bet his boots she was trying to break the Robin Hood story on her own, hoping to prove herself and move ahead. It was a gutsy and unusual move, he thought approvingly. If he understood anything, it was the ambition to succeed. He'd just rarely encountered it in the upper class, most of whom were content with their inherited piles of money.

Daniel deliberately folded his paper and put it away, silently signaling that he would detrain at the next stop. In response, he saw Genevieve stand near the doors, head bent to hide her face, ready to step off if he did. The clamorous rattling of the train slowed, brakes screeching in protest. Once the doors whooshed open, Daniel moved quickly again, out in a flash and down the stairs two at a time, joining the mass of moving humanity on Rivington Street.

A torrent of voices, many speaking German, washed over him from all sides. This was the heart of *Kleindeutschland*, or Little Germany: a vibrant, bustling neighborhood, full of restaurants, oyster houses, photographer's studios, and delicatessens, with brightly painted signs in English, Hebrew, and German. Daniel ducked down a side street and crossed toward the Bowery, leaving Little Germany and making his way uptown toward Houston Street, casually following the stream of pedestrian traffic.

It was midday, and the streets were terribly crowded, everyone eager to take advantage of the sparse winter sunshine. He wasn't certain Genevieve was keeping pace, but he had a feeling she was still back there. Sure enough, as he paused before the well-kept brick townhouse at Twenty-Five East Houston, he could see her several feet away, putting a coin into the can of an organ-grinder. He grinned, wondering idly if she'd try to follow him inside. After ringing the bell, a very large red-haired man pulled the door open a crack and peered at him, then opened it wider with a smile.

"Good afternoon, Mr. McCaffrey. I'll let Miss Dugan know you're here." Augustus closed the door behind them, and Daniel handed over his coat and hat to a nearby maid.

"Thanks, Augustus." He allowed the bouncer to Lead him to his cousin, who as usual had outdone herself in the meal she had waiting.

He peered out one of the front windows from behind a curtain, looking for his shadow.

She was standing on the sidewalk in front of the townhouse, open-mouthed, staring at the facade. She'd undoubtedly seen the red light shining next to the modest black door; less bright in daytime but still visible, it was an instant and obvious visual shorthand to passersby. Twenty-Five East Houston was an establishment where certain services could be purchased. *Female* services.

In short, it was a brothel. As he watched, she looked around confusedly for a moment, then dodged an oncoming fire engine to cross the street, eventually settling in a café across the way, her gaze fixed on the front of the house.

Daniel dropped the curtain back into place, feeling a curious mix of frustration, amusement, and intrigue surrounding the fact that Genevieve had not only managed to follow him but was now keeping vigil across Houston Street, presumably waiting for him to leave and ready to pick up his trail the moment he did.

Behind him, Kathleen shook her head. "You're losing your touch, Danny, if one of them was able to follow you here. Gone soft overseas?"

Daniel snorted. "I *let* her follow, Kathy."

His cousin's eyebrows rose high. "*Her?*" she exclaimed, her Irish brogue still distinct despite her years in New York. "What, you let a girlfriend follow you here? That's not very kind of you, Danny, if you don't mind me saying so. It's unlike you."

"She's a reporter, not a girlfriend," he replied, making his way back to the table.

Somehow Kathleen managed to look even more surprised. "What are you playing at, Danny? Why would you let a reporter follow you to my house? It'll be all over the papers."

"It hasn't yet."

"She's likely just biding her time," Kathleen pointed out. "And even though you won't take more than tea and toast from me, she'll be writing that you've got one of my girls hanging from the ceiling so you can have your way with her."

Daniel rolled his eyes at her. "First, this is hardly tea and toast," he began, gesturing toward the ornate table laid with roast pig, three kinds of vegetables, and a delectable French vintage.

Kathleen waved this off. "It's a figure of speech, and you know it."

"Second," Daniel continued, "the paper couldn't print that even if she wrote it."

Now it was Kathleen's turn to roll her eyes. "They could make it sound like such, and you know that too."

He did. The papers had intimated all kinds of things about him when he'd inherited Jacob Van Joost's fortune. Some had even come close to the truth.

"I can't put my finger on it, Kathy, but I trust her," he admitted softly, moving to look out the window again. He had a clear view of Genevieve across the street. She had removed her head scarf, and gaslight from the just-lit streetlamps reflected on her bright hair. A waiter set down a cup of tea in front of her, and she glanced at it in distaste.

Kathleen interrupted his train of thought. "More fool you, mark my words," she warned.

"I think she's sincere in what she's attempting. Misguided, perhaps, but sincere."

Kathleen snorted. "The same could be said of those religious types who give my girls hassle on the street for the way they earn their living."

He shook his head, still watching the café. "It's not the same."

Her small huff of breath made her opinion obvious, but she held her tongue on the matter. "She's still there?"

Daniel nodded mutely. He heard his cousin laugh behind him. "Well then, Danny, it looks like you'll finally be spending the night with us. She's got you trapped. Now, I'll ring Augustus to have a maid make up a room. Are you sure you don't want some company? You know my girls are the best in town. And sit, eat something."

"As always, I appreciate the offer, but no. You know I wish you'd get into a different line of work."

"I know it, Danny," Kathleen replied, "and I appreciate the financial help. It's because of your loan I can be discriminating about our clientele. My girls get to choose, not the other way around."

He shook his head. It was true: Kathleen's brothel, or Miss Dugan's as it was known, was one of the most high-end, discreet establishments in town. If a working girl didn't like the look of her client, or heaven forbid if he behaved badly, that man was unceremoniously ushered out by Augustus's large and capable hands.

"Girls want to work here," Kathleen continued proudly. "They know they'll be well fed, well paid, and not forced to do anything they don't like. I've built something good here, Danny. And the men are clamoring for more—we have to turn them away."

Daniel sighed. He'd studied different theories of economics at Harvard and didn't want to argue with his cousin that the young women in her employ typically came from such impoverished circumstances that of course Miss Dugan's seemed a luxurious option, but what would truly be luxurious would be other options: higher education and a job that didn't involve selling their bodies.

He rubbed his jaw. She wouldn't understand. Kathleen simply saw the larger social system in place, not how it needed to change. He was partially to blame, having loaned her the money to start the business in the first place. Daniel had been away at school when she arrived from Ireland, and when she showed up on his doorstep nearly three years later, destitute but asking for a loan instead of charity, he'd been so thrilled to find a relation that he'd have signed over his entire fortune if she'd asked.

As far as he knew, she was the only family he had left.

Daniel irritably stared out the window again. He knew he could probably disguise himself, as Genevieve had, and with the cover of night, give her the slip again. But she'd proved damn tenacious, and even if he eluded her now, she'd just pop up again like a jack-in-the-box sometime in the coming days.

No, best to get this over with, he told himself. If she wanted to talk, then fine, they could talk. It was probably the only way to get her out of his hair.

He settled into the magnificent meal Kathleen had presented. If she was still there by the time he finished, Genevieve Stewart was going to get an earful.

★ ★ ★

Genevieve shifted again in the seat of the wooden chair she'd been occupying for hours, trying to alleviate the ache that had developed in her tailbone. It was a perfectly ordinary café chair, but she'd never noticed before how devilishly hard they were. Probably because she'd never sat in one for so long.

She stared moodily at the lukewarm cup of tea in front of her. She'd drunk countless cups during this vigil and wasn't sure she could stomach another sip. Over the course of several hours she'd also consumed a bowl of oyster chowder and a satisfying plate of hot gingerbread, but now her stomach was starting to rumble restlessly from hunger again, adding to her discomfort.

Genevieve sighed and checked her timepiece. Should she order another meal? Or admit that her attempt to learn something useful about Daniel McCaffrey had been a failure and leave?

She glanced out the window at the establishment across the street, undecided. The discreet red light by the door had informed her instantly of the unassuming townhouse's function. Seeing Daniel walk into such a place had caused swift and unexpected disappointment, but she had found this café and settled in to await his departure, ready to resume the chase whenever he left. It was her first attempt to follow him, an effort she planned to continue until she learned *something* of note. Something about Robin Hood, or the dead man in the alley.

Something that settled the nagging, persistent suspicion that Daniel McCaffrey knew more than he was saying.

Something of greater interest than the fact that he apparently spent hours in a brothel upon occasion.

Genevieve tapped her pencil against the table, pondering, and consulted her notebook for what felt like the thousandth time, weighing the known facts against what was unknown.

On one side of an open page, she had listed what she knew: Robin Hood had begun his rash of thefts six weeks prior. Or at least his *known* thefts, the ones for which he had claimed responsibility in his letters to the *Globe*. Three families had been struck thus far: Winston and Bitsy Collins, Mrs. Pauline Jones, and now

Andrew and Sarah Huffington. In all three cases, jewelry had been taken.

According to ship passenger manifests in the newspaper's archives, Daniel had arrived in New York on Friday, November eighteenth.

The thefts had begun in early January.

Winston and Bitsy Collins had given a dinner party the first week of 1888 to celebrate the New Year, and the exclusive guest list, Genevieve had learned, included Caroline Schermerhorn Astor, Mr. and Mrs. Hamilton Fish, Mrs. Pauline Jones, and Daniel McCaffrey, among others. As far as she had been able to glean, both Bitsy Collins and Pauline Jones were wearing the jewels that night that would later be stolen: Bitsy a three-strand pearl choker necklace with a vast diamond at its center, surrounded by small emeralds, and the widowed Mrs. Jones a diamond bracelet containing a sapphire nearly the size of a robin's egg.

The necklace had gone missing the night following the dinner party, the bracelet almost three weeks later. Mrs. Jones had not worn the bracelet since the Collinses' dinner party, nor had she entertained at her own home in the duration.

Sarah and Andrew Huffington had not been invited to the dinner party.

Indeed, Genevieve was a little puzzled as to why Daniel had been included, as the guest list otherwise had been made up of a very particular elite crowd. Perhaps because Winston Collins and Jacob Van Joost had been friends?

Genevieve gazed meditatively at a passerby on the street, bundled against the dropping temperatures. The café was busier now, and she decided to wait a few more minutes before placing another order.

Sarah Huffington's ring had been stolen the very night of her own ball. It was her engagement ring, a diamond so large it made even the wealthiest of socialites blink. Indeed, Genevieve had never seen its like, though the one Mrs. Bradley sported came close. She wondered how either woman held her hand up, as the stones appeared awfully heavy.

None of the jewels had been recovered.

These were the facts. Then there were the letters.

Arthur's decision to publish Robin Hood's letters was wildly controversial. Each letter outlined the supposed sins of the victims as justification for the thefts, and the public outcry upon reading these sins was swift and at times substantial. The paper received letters and telegrams from readers daily, in ever-increasing numbers, some begging Arthur to cease giving Robin Hood a platform and an equal amount imploring him to continue.

Newspaper sales had increased by almost twenty percent.

The various misdeeds of the thief's victims ranged in severity. By far the most shocking were those of Winston Collins, a powerful railroad magnate, whom the thief accused of also running a lucrative prostitution ring. While some members of New York's elite had been aware of the family's side business (indeed, many gentlemen had been enthusiastic patrons), once the lurid truth was exposed so publicly, the rest of society and the general public turned on the family. There had been calls for their arrest in some of New York's other papers. Mud was thrown at the Collinses' frightened teenage daughters as they attempted to shop on Broadway, and rumors circulated that the Collins household might be set afire. The family had become so terrified that they'd packed their belongings and left town in the dead of night, presumably to Europe.

The letter regarding Mrs. Jones, on the other hand, elicited a modicum of sympathy from some. The thief detailed how Mrs. Jones's late husband, Matthew Jones, had made his fortune in textiles by aligning with Southern plantation owners both before and after the war. The letter accused the late Mr. Jones, and by extension Mrs. Jones, of having personally profited from the slave trade, despite the pro-Union stance they had maintained during the conflict a quarter of a century prior. At this, most of the Astor 400 rallied to Mrs. Jones's defense, likely knowing the majority of their fortunes couldn't withstand similar scrutiny. But while much of the general public disliked seeing an elderly widow the target of a thief, many others, particularly those who remembered relatives lost in the war, sided with Robin Hood.

The latest letter, published just yesterday, had been far more personal in nature. Robin Hood tore Sarah Huffington to shreds, recounting feuds she had begun, others' reputations she had maligned, and accused her of marital indiscretion with one of her husband's business partners, financier Ernest Clark (not named in full, of course, but anyone who was anyone knew what "E.C." meant). While Genevieve didn't particularly care for Sarah Huffington, née Alston, who had been two years below her at school and a horrid girl even then, it was still unsettling to see the details of her life spilled all over the newspaper in such a way. Also, she couldn't fathom Sarah, who regularly looked down her long nose at young (though very wealthy) social climbers like Ernest Clark, engaging in a dalliance with such a man.

Genevieve paused for a moment and looked around for the waiter, but he was busy at another table. Keeping half an eye on the window, she turned her attention back to her notes. Having glimpsed the original two letters before they were turned over to the police permanently for evidence, she knew they were composed in an educated hand, and the language and word choice also indicated someone with proper schooling.

These were the knowns. The unknowns were tangled, complicated questions. What did it all add up to? Some of the thief's complaints were political, some highly personal. The only connections between the victims seemed to be their social status and the fact that it was jewelry that had been taken.

And what of Daniel McCaffrey?

She didn't know how, or if, he was related to the thefts. Only that she'd heard him and his companions talking about Robin Hood, that the thefts had started a few weeks after he arrived in town, that he'd been present at both social events apparently related to the thefts, and that he seemed to have a disturbing familiarity with both unsavory parts of town and dead bodies.

Genevieve turned her full attention toward the window and shifted in her seat again, wondering if she could make Daniel appear by the sheer force of her will.

The waiter appeared at her table instead, but rather than requesting more chowder, Genevieve asked for the bill. Either Daniel would be staying at the brothel all night, or he'd already exited through the back door into an alley. Regardless, it was time to go home; after all, *she* could hardly stay out all night.

She rooted through her reticule for the proper change. It actually had been rather fascinating to observe the various men enter and exit the establishment. Most were well dressed, some even obviously upper class; she'd half expected to see someone she knew.

"If you're not overfull from the gingerbread, perhaps you would care to join me for dinner."

Her head snapped up.

Perhaps she *had* conjured him. For standing in front of her, wearing an entirely solicitous expression, was the very man she'd been waiting hours to see.

CHAPTER 5

Genevieve shifted on the hard seat of the hansom cab while she eyed the man across from her. While it was more comfortable than the café chair, it had been a long afternoon of sitting. Nothing today had gone as planned. Agreeing to dine with the target of her investigative pursuits after he'd spent the last several hours in a brothel was unexpected, to say the least.

Neither spoke as the cab lumbered downtown. Mr. McCaffrey folded his arms over his chest and regarded her mildly. She drew a breath to speak but paused, unsure of exactly how to begin. He quirked a brow at her, waiting.

She finally asked what seemed like the most pressing question. "Where are we going?"

"Delmonico's."

She waited for him to elaborate. When nothing else came, she asked the next most pressing question.

"Why?"

"Because I thought you might be hungry."

She was, actually. Her last bowl of chowder had been eaten a few hours prior; she was famished. The mere thought of the delicious dishes one could order at Delmonico's set her mouth watering.

But then her brow furrowed. "Which Delmonico's?"

One corner of his mouth lifted in a half smile, seeming to indicate approval. "The original. William Street."

Oh, good. She settled back in her seat, satisfied. The other three branches were new, and she preferred the first location.

As the cab wended its way through traffic, Genevieve pondered this unusual turn of events. She was now in a carriage, apparently headed to dinner, with the very man she'd been wanting to speak with all day.

A man who might or might not be responsible for a rash of thefts all over the city.

The social implications of being seen with Daniel McCaffrey at Delmonico's flashed before her, but she dismissed them before they had a chance to fester. She was a journalist, and journalists did not let opportunities like this pass them by.

They each watched the passing scenery for a few blocks. She stole an occasional glance at the hard, handsome lines of his face, sometimes brightly illuminated by the lights of theaters, music halls, or restaurants, sometimes softly accentuated by a gas streetlamp. She allowed the silence to unfold, knowing that sometimes a reporter's best strategy was to stay quiet.

When it became clear Daniel was disinclined to speak first, she asked another pressing question.

"How long did you know I was there?"

He turned his face toward hers, expression lost in the shadows of the carriage interior. "The whole time," he replied.

She briefly closed her eyes; she'd thought she'd been so careful. "I thought I was better at this."

"You're not bad, actually. I've just had lots of practice evading your kind."

She turned back, only to find his face was still hidden in shadow. "Why not evade me tonight, then?"

Daniel's face was turned toward hers, but she still couldn't make out his expression. The silence returned and unspooled, growing thick and warm in the close confines of the cab. He gestured out the window. They had arrived at their destination. "We'll talk inside."

Genevieve followed Daniel into the large, well-appointed main dining room of the Manhattan establishment. Though cafés and coffeehouses had abounded on the island for at least a century, Delmonico's had been the first true "fine dining" restaurant in the city, introducing concepts such as à la carte ordering and a wine list. Genevieve had eaten there since she was a child, her parents having been frequent patrons for years.

She had removed her black head scarf in the cab, and now gratefully handed it and her Drab, heavy coat to a waiting employee. Her red-plaid wool walking dress and jacket had been chosen for warmth rather than style that morning, but now she was glad she hadn't worn the dull-blue muslin. While not quite as dressy as she might have liked, the plaid was serviceable enough for Delmonico's.

Daniel appeared well known at the restaurant also, as the maître d' greeted him warmly and immediately responded to his request for a private room.

Oh dear, Genevieve thought. *A private room.* While not entirely improper, particularly given her age, dinner in a private room would still set tongues wagging.

Straightening her back, Genevieve put on her best Polly Palmer persona. Let the tongues wag; she was here on business. Nothing else.

Daniel nodded at a few acquaintances as they made their way toward the stairs that led to the private rooms, including, she noted with surprise, the Earl of Umberland and Esmie Bradley. As usual, Esmie was clad in an awful gown: bright pink again, this time with a high, ruffled neck that almost obscured her chin and covered in an alarming pattern of purple and green butterflies. The effect was somewhat dizzying. Sympathetically, Genevieve wondered how the poor girl could eat with the stiff fabric bunched around her neck, then wondered how Rupert would manage as well, being faced with such a blinding dress at the dinner table. They both looked miserable as they picked at their food in silence.

Once settled in the ornate, dimly lit room, Genevieve felt more at ease. The heavily clothed table could have sat up to six, but was small enough that two didn't feel overwhelmed. The lavish settings of china and crystal were as familiar to her as those in her parents' dining room, and she surveyed her menu happily. Spring lamb with mint sauce? Halibut in hollandaise sauce? Deciding that the cold night called for comforting food, she ordered squab chicken with a side of the restaurant's famous potatoes, while Daniel asked for a *terrine de foie gras* for them to share, and chose a French wine.

"You're not having an entrée?" she asked in surprise.

"I already ate."

She put down her menu in annoyance. "Then why ask me to dinner?"

"As I said, I thought *you* might be hungry. And it was past time we talked, don't you agree?"

Genevieve remained silent, pondering the questions she wanted to ask, until the wine and foie gras and her meal arrived. After the ritual of the wine being opened, tested, and poured, she settled back in her chair, eyeing her unexpected dinner companion over the edge of her glass. He offered her some of the pâté, then helped himself to a small portion.

"I thought you ate."

"I did." He smiled. "But I cannot resist their foie gras."

She smiled back uncertainly, a bit disconcerted at how pleasant this encounter was turning out to be, then shook her head slightly to clear it from any foolishness. It was time to get to business. Was she a good enough reporter to discern if he was, in fact, Robin Hood?

"Mr. McCaffrey," she began carefully, "why did you come find me tonight? You're apparently very good at evading journalists, as you've said. Why not let me lose you?" She focused on cutting her chicken, which was excellent, as usual.

Daniel leaned back in his own chair, swirling his wine. "Why were you following me?" he asked bluntly.

"I told you. I'm researching the Robin Hood thefts."

"And I told you, I don't know anything about Mr. Hood," he countered.

She shook her head at him slowly. "But I think you do."

He raised a brow at her. "And what makes you think that?"

"You and your associates were discussing Robin Hood in Five Points the night we met," she began, but Daniel interrupted her.

"Yes, we were talking about the thefts," he said. "Everyone talks about them. Neither I nor they have any specific information for you, Miss Stewart. Or should I say Miss *Palmer*."

She put down her fork. "Well, what about you? Is there anything about yourself you'd like to tell me?"

Daniel laughed, a rich, warm sound. "I haven't spoken to the press in seventeen years. What makes you think I'd tell you anything new?"

"Then why am I here?" she shot back. "As we've established, you could easily have evaded me tonight, and yet here we are at Delmonico's. Why? And for goodness' sake, call me Genevieve."

For a moment Daniel appeared slightly baffled, as if he didn't know himself why she was there. He seemed to consider her, his eyes glittering in the candlelight.

"Perhaps I simply enjoy your company," he said finally, swallowing the last of his wine. "Genevieve."

Pleased she appeared to have gotten under his skin, Genevieve sipped her own wine and waited. Maybe silence would be her friend this time.

She was rewarded when he nodded to himself, seeming to come to some kind of internal decision.

"I know there has been speculation as to why I returned to the city after such a prolonged absence," he began. Genevieve's pulse began to quicken. After years of avoiding the press, the elusive Daniel McCaffrey seemed to be consenting to an interview. She withdrew her notebook from her satchel and raised it at him questioningly.

Daniel nodded, and she put pencil to paper.

"The truth is," he continued, when it was clear she was ready, "I was hiding."

Genevieve was surprised. She didn't know what she had expected to hear, but that wasn't it.

"Hiding?" she repeated.

"Jacob's fortune brings with it a great deal of responsibility, Miss Palmer. And truthfully, I inherited at such a young age that I didn't know what to do with the money. I apprenticed in the law, as you know, and practiced here for a while. But I knew I wanted to do more. Could do more."

Genevieve wrote furiously. "Such as?" she prompted.

"Helping the city's less fortunate. Improving housing conditions, in particular."

"And why this cause? There are many ways to use a fortune to help the needy."

He raised a brow at her. "Because I was born in Five Points," he said.

Genevieve barely had time to stop her jaw from dropping open. She'd just been given the scoop of the year.

Of the decade.

"So how did you come to be Jacob's heir?"

Daniel smiled slightly and refilled their glasses, emptying the bottle. "That, Miss Palmer, will remain between me and Jacob."

That line of questioning was clearly a dead end. She switched back to a topic he seemed willing to discuss. "And you had to hide because . . ."

"Because for a long time, New York held too many memories. I needed to spend time out of the city to see it clearly. To see what I could do with the money, how I could maximize its use, without those memories crowding in on me."

"What kind of memories?" she asked softly.

The door swung open and a waiter entered, inquiring if they cared for any dessert. Daniel raised a brow at her.

"No thank you, but I would take coffee."

"And a chestnut Nesselrode," Daniel added. Genevieve raised a brow back at him.

"I enjoy sweets," he responded mildly.

She waited for the waiter to leave the room, then impatiently poised her pencil again, trying another tactic. "Can you give specifics on how you plan to aid in housing reform?"

"No," he answered. "That is all I am prepared to say for now."

Genevieve tapped her pencil on her pad once, thinking to herself. "Robin Hood is concerned with the housing conditions in Five Points," she ventured.

"So his letters to the newspaper state."

"The *Globe* has received countless missives about him," she continued. "Some expressing horror that he is still at large, an equal number cheering him on. The mayor seems quite determined. There's talk of replacing the police commissioner if he's not caught soon."

Daniel regarded her impassively. "Is that surprising to you?"

"I'm not sure it's entirely fair. Besides." Genevieve shifted in her seat, a little uncertain. *In for a penny*, she thought, and plunged on. "The mayor is forming a committee to assess the situation around housing in impoverished areas, to make recommendations." She kept a careful eye on Daniel's face and almost missed the fleeting expression of sharp interest that flared and just as quickly disappeared under an ironic smile.

"A committee," he dryly remarked. "Surely that will solve everything."

Genevieve felt herself flush, even though she had exactly zero involvement with said committee. "Isn't it better than nothing?"

Daniel took a sip of wine and looked thoughtful. "It depends on who is involved," he finally said.

"Andrew Huffington, Reginald Cotswold, Ernest Clark," she began. "Ted Beekman," she added. At her ex-fiancé's name, Daniel raised his brow again, but said nothing.

Rupert must have filled him in. Genevieve felt herself flush again.

"One of the Peter Stuyvesants, but I don't know if it is Junior or Senior; Commissioner Simons; the deputy mayor . . ." she forged ahead, then trailed off, uncertain. "Perhaps something will come of it," she finished lamely.

"It won't."

Anger flared. "Why mightn't it? If Robin Hood's actions are raising awareness—"

"No," he interrupted. "It's a sham." Something lit in his eyes, and he leaned toward her so abruptly that Genevieve had to stop herself from instinctively flinching backward.

"Who stands to gain from the development of these tenements, Genevieve? Who loses if housing reform passes? Why *these* men on the committee, when there are people doing work on housing reform?"

"People like you?"

"Not like me." The half smile, the one she remembered from the alley, lifted the corner of his mouth. "I prefer to stay behind the scenes. Those working publicly."

He leaned in a few inches closer, and this time she didn't have the urge to flinch back. Instead she leaned in too, closing the distance between them, mesmerized by the intensity of his voice.

"Follow the money, Genevieve. That's your story. That's *always* the story."

★ ★ ★

In a carriage bound for Washington Square, Genevieve held tightly to her satchel containing her notebook with its precious information. Scant though it was, it was still enough to earn her a major story. There was no way Mr. Horace could ignore her now. And Daniel being from Five Points . . . another piece of the puzzle toward the even bigger story: the possible unmasking of Robin Hood.

But her mind kept looping back to Daniel's words. *Follow the money.*

She knew most of the men on the mayor's committee. They ran in the same circles as her family. It was unsettling to think that people she'd known her whole life could be involved in something potentially immoral or illicit.

Including someone she'd almost married.

Despite her best efforts not to think about it, memories of her six-month engagement to Ted Beekman came flooding back. His sincere, ardent protestations of love for her. The long minutes they'd spent kissing in secluded gardens, behind half-closed doors, in cabs like this one. Behind the curtains in the darkened box of a theater.

She had given Ted her heart, freely and willingly, enjoying her status as an engaged young woman of means, enjoying the intricacies of planning a major society wedding. She was so caught up in the excitement of it all, thought she was so in love, happily would have given him her virtue before the wedding had the opportunity arisen, and it very nearly had.

She remembered the moment all too well: Ted had had her clasped in an enthusiastic embrace in the darkened sitting room of her parents' house after a late soiree. Her parents, oblivious to basic propriety as usual, had retired to bed, assuming their soon-to-be son-in-law was on his way home as well.

Ted's cool, smooth lips had pressed firmly against hers as he stroked her hair and back, occasionally breaking free to murmur "My darling" before reuniting their mouths. Genevieve had never felt so happy, so desired. Everything was so delightful until Ted lunged forward, pinning her down on the settee with his weight, and then began thrusting his tongue inside and around her mouth in vigorous strokes. Genevieve gave a little squeal of surprise, which quickly turned to one of dismay. It was like being licked by an overenthusiastic mastiff and left her feeling not desired but as though she was being overpowered. She was pushing on his chest, trying to wrest his heavy form off her body, when her brother Gavin walked in.

Ted jumped up quickly and smoothed his hair while Genevieve sat up, dazed and trembling slightly as she tried to make sense of the riot of emotions coursing through her. Gavin's gaze swept the room, quickly taking in the scene. "Beekman," Gavin greeted her fiancé coolly.

"Gavin, good to see you," Ted blustered, moving forward to shake her brother's hand. Gavin regarded it for a moment distastefully.

"You have exactly thirty seconds to leave this house," her brother responded, the menace in his voice very clear.

Ted drew himself up taller and tried to look affronted. "Now see here, Gavin, you know we're to be married next Saturday. Sometimes young couples get carried away."

If anything, Gavin's voice grew icier. "You're not married yet."

Giving Genevieve a quick peck on her flushed cheek, Ted quickly took his leave. Gavin then sat down and put his arm around her, giving his only sister a worried look.

"Are you all right?"

Genevieve wasn't sure why she was still trembling. Her fiancé had kissed her. A bit more roughly than she had liked, but it was just a kiss.

"Yes," she finally responded.

"You know, Muffy, you don't have to marry him." Muffy was the pet nickname her other brother, Charles, had given her when they were children, short for Little Miss Muffet. When she was four, Gavin had grown tired of his baby sister dogging their steps and had tried to scare her away from their games with an actual spider, held by one wriggling black leg and waved in her face. Genevieve had grabbed the spider in her own chubby fingers and deposited it into a glass jar that housed a toad she'd caught that morning in the park. She had intended for the toad and the spider to be friends, but the toad promptly ate its new tenant, much to the delight of her older brothers.

"Guess she ain't little Miss Muffet after all," Charles said admiringly, and the nickname stuck. From then on, her brothers had treated her as one of the boys.

Though unafraid of spiders, the adult Genevieve was shocked and, truthfully, a bit terrified at her brother's suggestion. Of course she had to marry Ted! Invitations had been sent, orange blossoms purchased that couldn't be unpurchased; bridesmaids' dresses had been designed and created specifically for the event. Three hundred fifty individual tulle bags filled with sugared almonds and each tied with a tangerine-colored ribbon were piled in boxes in her father's study, waiting to be distributed. If she didn't marry Ted, what would become of all those sugared almonds?

That was exactly one week before the wedding.

Four days later, her mother's highly publicized arrest and jailing during a march for women's rights and birth control caused a furor throughout New York society and escalated into a ridiculous scandal. The day after that, Ted claimed he had no choice but to succumb to pressure from his parents and break off their engagement.

Genevieve hadn't quite been left at the altar, but it was close enough. Three days before the wedding was close enough. Her wedding dress was still pristine, never worn after the final fitting, already slightly out of fashion in its box high on a shelf in her wardrobe. The public humiliation had been immediate and swift. Society sided with Ted, its collective opinion being he had done the right thing to not align himself with a family whose matriarch was clearly a bit unhinged, despite the old Stewart name. Even so, Genevieve had always wondered if the incident in the sitting room had been a factor.

Jilted at twenty years old, Genevieve hadn't known what to do with herself. Given that she'd always enjoyed reading and knew women were writing for papers, she'd told her parents she wanted to give it a try. They'd helped her find a position with the *Globe* and she had thrown herself into her chosen work, attempting to claw her way toward some kind of meaningful career.

It was all she had.

Well, that wasn't quite true. She had her family, whom she loved despite their oddities, and she had her friends. She avoided parties, avoided Ted, and time had mostly healed her heart.

Without risk, there is no reward, her father liked to tell his children. And look at what the Stewart children had done with that advice: Her oldest brother Gavin, jaunting off to the desert without a backward glance. Her brother Charles, designing beautiful buildings that were changing the face of the city.

She hugged her notebook tighter.

What was she willing to risk to unmask Robin Hood and break the story of the century?

Everything.

CHAPTER 6

"Reginald Cotswold is dead."

Genevieve sat down hard on the edge of a wooden chair facing her editor's desk. The seat was mostly crammed with papers, but her knees had buckled unexpectedly at the news. Mr. Horace regarded her with alarm.

"I'm sorry to be the one to tell you." He peered at her worriedly. "Shall I send Alice for some water?"

Her hand floated to her mouth, and she was surprised to find it trembling. "Murdered?" she managed.

Mr. Horace let out a bark of surprised laughter. "Heavens, no. Died peacefully in his sleep. He was ninety-one, after all. A good long life."

"But—wasn't he on that mayoral committee? The one on housing reform?"

Her editor's gaze turned sharp. "I told you to forget about that committee, Genevieve." He shook his head. "You weren't supposed to see that list; nobody was, until it was announced."

"Hasn't it been announced?"

"No, and I'm not sure it will be. The deputy mayor seems to want to keep it quiet, for reasons known only to him. Are you quite all right?" He glanced at his closed office door. "Let me get Alice." Mr. Horace clearly did not want to deal with whatever female vapors he assumed Genevieve was enduring.

She took a deep breath and firmed her voice. "No need. The news simply came as a bit of a shock. Mr. Cotswold was a great friend of my father's."

"Ninety-one, Genevieve," he remarked mildly. "His death can't be all that surprising."

"No," she agreed, though in truth it was surprising. Reginald Cotswold was one of those renowned pillars of Knickerbocker society, well known for his charitable deeds and for being continually appointed to various committees. One simply assumed he was a permanent fixture, and he had been in remarkably good health, including the last time she'd seen him.

Which, she recalled with a start, had been at the Huffingtons' ball.

"I'd like you to write a remembrance of him," Arthur said. "About his philanthropy, his habits, that kind of thing. He's rather a symbol of a certain type of citizen of this city that is rapidly disappearing, for better or worse."

Understanding grew: Arthur was referring to *her* kind of people, to the hushed, dignified, old-money set of New York, who until a decade or so ago had ruled the city with a collective iron fist. But vast, shiny piles of new money were being accumulated on a daily basis by newcomers, and power was starting to shift and erode older social barriers.

She herself felt no particular qualms about this shift; it was simply the way of the world. The new elbowed out the old, and whether the old were destroyed in the process or simply bruised about the edges mattered not. The old could make room or be plowed over as if by a racing streetcar.

"He hasn't any family left," Arthur continued, "but his housekeeper's been with him forever and said she'd be happy to speak to someone. Alice will locate the address if you need it. I don't know where I've placed it." He patted several nearby piles of paper, causing one to wobble precariously.

"It's fine. I know where he lives," Genevieve hastened to assure him, eyeing the stacks. "Or lived, I should say."

She stood to go, relieved that even though her mind was still unsettled, her legs seemed to have recovered.

"Wait, Genevieve. I need you to cover another story as well." Arthur pulled a sheet from the stack, almost toppling a teacup that had been balanced on the top. "Barnum Brothers Best Baby Contest. Yes, that's the one. I forgot to give it to you this morning."

She stared at the address. *A best baby contest?* "Mr. Horace," she began wearily, "I don't know anything about babies."

"I'm sure you'll do fine, Genevieve," Arthur said as he began rereading his editorial. "Noon tomorrow. On the nose. Barnum first, then Cotswold." He turned his attention fully to the piece on his desk, scratching out a word and replacing it, shaking his head.

Conflicting feelings battled within Genevieve as she shrugged into the tailored dark-blue jacket that matched her skirt. For the past week, logic had been telling her to approach Mr. Horace with her information about Daniel being from Five Points. The mere fact that he'd revealed his origins was huge news, answering a years-old question.

But the possibility of a bigger story kept holding her back. Daniel's cryptic advice about the mayoral committee had been unsettling, but now in light of Reginald Cotswold's death, it felt almost sinister. She tried to tell herself that surely her father's friend had died of natural causes associated with old age but couldn't shake the deeply disquieting notion that someway, somehow, his death was connected to larger events.

Hopefully her visit with the housekeeper would reveal more.

And there was still the unsettled matter of Robin Hood. It had been almost two weeks since his theft after the Huffingtons' ball.

As she placed a freshly sharpened pencil into her satchel, her mind groped to recall exactly when she'd seen Reginald at the ball. On the few occasions she attended parties, Genevieve often danced with him, as he was amusingly quick-witted and surprisingly spry for his age. But she hadn't that night. She paused, thinking. No, the only memory she had of him was seeing him deep in conversation with Ernest Clark in a dim corner of the ballroom. She'd meant to seek him out to say hello, but of course the whole evening had been upended by the appearance of Mr. Pineapple Waistcoat himself, Daniel McCaffrey.

"Off so soon?" came a low, nasally voice from behind her, interrupting her train of thought. Genevieve clenched her jaw in annoyance. *Clive.*

"Yes," she replied curtly, not bothering to turn around as she put her notebook into her satchel. "I'm leaving this second." She hoped to dart out of the office without having to reveal where she was going.

It didn't work. In a moment Clive was in front of her, perched on the edge of her desk.

"And just where is old Hoary sending you?" Clive smirked an oily grin, making Genevieve grimace. His diamond stickpin flashed in the early-afternoon sun.

"That is between me and Mr. Horace." Genevieve tried to scoot around her desk toward the door.

That didn't work either. Clive grabbed her hand as she tried to get past him, pulling her back toward the desk. "Really, Mr. Huxton!" Genevieve snapped, snatching her hand out of his grasp.

Clive let her go, looking unfazed. "Fine, Miss Stewart. Run away on your little mystery errand. You know I'll only read about it in tomorrow's edition with the rest of the city."

Genevieve's annoyance grew, and she crossed her arms over her chest. "As a matter of fact, I'm covering P. T. Barnum's Best Baby Contest," she informed Clive with as much dignity as she could muster. It was on the tip of her tongue to tell him about the piece on Mr. Cotswold too, but something made her hold back.

Let him read it in the paper when it's published.

To his credit, Clive didn't laugh, though the corners of his mouth twitched. "Good old P. T. Barnum. Well, he's colorful enough, and you're talented enough that you could probably wring a good story out of this."

Genevieve regarded Clive with surprise. Had he actually paid her a compliment? "What do you want, Clive?" she asked.

Clive smiled and looked down at the desktop. He fiddled with the pencil Genevieve had been chewing earlier. "Perhaps when you're finished with the babies, you'd join me at Delmonico's and tell me all about it."

Genevieve gaped. The mention of Delmonico's sent her thoughts instantly to Daniel McCaffrey. "Really, Mr. Huxton," she stammered in confusion, "I was under the distinct impression you disliked me."

Clive smiled and looked down at the desk again. Clive looking shy? Genevieve was flabbergasted.

"Come on, Genevieve," he said. "You know I only give you such a hard time because you're the only other reporter on staff with an ounce of skill."

Genevieve knew no such thing. In fact, Clive was fond of loudly stating, in her presence, that while it was perfectly acceptable for an unmarried young woman from the working class, such as Alice, to have employment, particularly secretarial or factory employment, any woman over the age of twenty-two was simply stealing a man's job.

As Genevieve was twenty-six, she took this rather personally.

And yet she hesitated. Could it be that Clive was threatened by her, causing his abominable behavior? Had he been harboring tender feelings for her this whole time? It seemed utterly implausible, yet he—oh dear—was actually trying to *gaze* into her eyes.

He wasn't so bad looking, Genevieve thought while trying to avoid gazing back. There was a reason Alice and the chambermaids giggled in his presence. He had thick dark-blond hair shot through with golden highlights, which might have been nice if he hadn't slicked it so prodigiously with hair oil. He had attractive light-blue eyes. Sneaking a peek at him while avoiding his searching gaze, however, Genevieve admitted to herself that there was something in his manner she didn't care for. His manicured hands. His ridiculous diamond stickpin. Why did he need to decorate himself? What was he trying to prove? A man like *Daniel McCaffrey* would never wear such a loud diamond, Genevieve thought, and he was one of the richest men in New York.

"Genevieve?" Clive interrupted her rambling train of thought. "Five o'clock, then?"

"Mr. Huxton . . . Clive . . . I'm sorry, but I can't have dinner with you."

"You already have plans, I take it? Perhaps later this week?"

This was going to be harder than she'd thought. "No, it's not that," she began. "I just don't think it is a good idea for us to get any closer than we are. You know, working together and all."

Clive's soft-eyed expression of encouragement began to shift into a sulky pout. "You don't think I'm good enough for you, do you?" he asked. "I know I'm not society, but I didn't think you Stewarts cared about that."

"Now, that's not it at all," Genevieve protested.

"Well, what then?" Clive stood up and looked down at her. "I've been to university too, you know," he sneered. "I know I'm just from the outskirts of Albany, but the gossips all say your laughingstock of a family doesn't care if you marry wealth."

Genevieve gasped at the insult to her family. "Marriage? Mr. Huxton, we were just speaking of a meal. And it has nothing to do with Albany."

"Oh, I know what you think," Clive interrupted her. "You've made yourself perfectly clear, Miss Stewart." He curled his lip and fixed her with one last, scornful look, then strode across the office back to his desk, where he began to angrily shuffle papers. Genevieve stared after him, baffled.

She shook her head and pulled on her yellow kid gloves. Clive had always been slightly unpredictable, but she had a bad feeling that her refusal did not bode well for any future interaction. Well, there was one positive aspect of the whole encounter, she thought to herself as she left the office the long way to avoid Clive's desk. After this, dealing with best babies was bound to be a snap.

★　★　★

"Watch where the hell you're going, mister!" The shrill shriek of the unknown woman's voice carried loudly over the din of traffic on Broadway as she bent to pick up her spilled packages. A few passersby turned to stare briefly, ascertained that nothing more exciting than the jostling of two fellow pedestrians had occurred, and kept moving.

Mortified, Daniel stooped to help her. "I'm so sorry, madam; allow me to assist you." He had been so busy staring at Genevieve's quickly moving form that he'd completely ignored his surroundings, a potentially life-threatening act on a street as busy as Broadway. While he'd managed not to walk into oncoming traffic, he had crashed into the poor woman in front of him, sending her many bundles flying.

Daniel quickly snatched a parcel wrapped in brown paper—bread from the feel of it—before it was squashed under a booted foot, then scurried after a hatbox that had rolled dangerously close to the edge of the sidewalk. Straightening up and cursing under his breath, he hurried back to the red-faced woman, who was waiting for him impatiently.

He piled the packages into her already-laden arms. "Are these all of them?" he asked politely. The woman responded by nastily telling him, in no uncertain terms, exactly where he could go. Daniel raised his brows at her retreating form, impressed; he hadn't heard cursing like that in years.

Turning southward again, he scanned the busy street for a sign of Genevieve's trim figure in her blue suit, but the pedestrian traffic had swallowed her up. He was near Park Row, though, where the city's newspaper buildings were housed. It was a bit after noon; perhaps she'd been returning to the office from lunch.

Daniel shoved his hands in his pockets and began walking again toward Gramercy Park. He'd been returning from a meeting with a client, and the crisp February day was so fine he'd sent his own carriage back to the office without him, preferring to walk. Ever since he'd been a child he'd enjoyed losing himself in the kaleidoscope of city life: to flow along with the bustle of the streets, to eavesdrop on bits of passing conversation, to casually glance in the shop windows, and to see what new wares were on display. He loved the energy and humanity of navigating the streets of New York; it made him feel invigorated and truly alive. And today, whose profile should emerge for a brief moment from the interchangeable flux of faces but that of the very person he'd been pondering as he walked: Miss Genevieve Stewart. Sidestepping a chattering trio of factory girls on a smoke break, his restless mind roamed over the issue of Genevieve.

He was clearly, oddly irrational where this problematic woman was concerned. He'd had no business inviting her to dinner, no business telling her anything about his past. And yet he found himself wanting to open up, to tell her everything: what had happened to his sister, to his other siblings, how he had become Jacob's heir.

What harm would it do if you told her the truth? His mind whispered persuasively. *Maggie is dead, Jacob is dead. After all these years, what does it matter?*

"Because I made a promise," he whispered back to himself, too low to startle his fellow pedestrians. And he kept his promises. He would protect those he loved, even after their deaths.

Besides, he hadn't returned to New York to socialize with a lady reporter, no matter how compelling he found her. He was there for one purpose, to finally use Jacob's money for some good. To help people in the neighborhood in which he'd been raised. Even if some of his methods were unorthodox.

Shaking his head free of the vexing Miss Stewart, Daniel turned his mind to the equally thorny problem of tenement reform. It was proving more difficult to enact changes than he'd anticipated, as corrupt landlords, police officers, and politicians all profited from the terrible living conditions of the less fortunate. He had upcoming meetings scheduled with the chief of police and several prominent members of City Hall, but so far he was meeting more resistance than expected.

And now there was this mayoral committee to contend with. Even though it was not meant to be public knowledge, it was a poorly kept secret. He'd heard about it from two other sources in the days following his dinner with Genevieve at Delmonico's.

Well. Hopefully he'd thrown Genevieve off the scent of Robin Hood, for a little while at least.

He breathed deeply and considered the upcoming evening. One of the great benefits of wealth was a good cook, and he wondered what his cook Mrs. Rafferty was making for dinner. Perhaps there was still some of that delicious roast lamb from Sunday; she could surely work marvels with that. Maybe a stew. Nothing went to waste in his house. He supposed that later, when he'd finished with work and was settled in his favorite chair with a book, he could have a whiskey. He had that wonderful single-malt that had just come in from Scotland. Another benefit—

Daniel grunted, his reverie interrupted by the impact of his shoulder on something solid. *Dammit. Have I knocked over another woman on the street?*

"I beg your pardon," he began, but stopped midsentence from pure surprise.

"Danny." Tommy Meade smiled his narrow smile, black eyes glittering.

Daniel returned the greeting mildly, though all his senses immediately snapped to attention. Tommy Meade never sought one out without a reason. And he never traveled alone.

"Fancy running into you here," Tommy commented, continuing to smile.

Yes, a remarkable coincidence.

"What can I do for you, Tommy?"

Tommy affected a look of deep hurt. "What, a guy can't run into another guy from the old neighborhood on Broadway?" The man took a half step closer, placing his whip-thin body only inches from Daniel's broader form. Daniel hadn't fought him for many years, but he was sure Tommy's slight frame encased the same rock-hard, wiry muscles it had when they were young. Besides, there were always Tommy's henchmen to consider. Daniel flicked his gaze to the right and spotted at least one, sallow faced and slouching in a doorway, pretending to read a paper but avidly watching the whole exchange through half-lidded eyes.

"You used to be friendlier, Danny," Tommy said sadly, shaking his head.

Daniel held the other man's gaze levelly. After a few moments of silence, Tommy laughed.

"Yeah, I guess that's right. Not really friends, were we? You insisted on running with those Bayard Toughs."

There was no point in answering. The Oyster Knifers, Tommy's gang, were the Bayard Toughs' rivals. Gang membership was serious, lifelong business where they were from.

"Look, Danny," Tommy began. "You know I've been on the city council for some time now. I've been a little disappointed that you haven't come to any of my rallies or meetings since you've been in town. I've sent messages."

"And as I responded to the first message, I have little interest in politics," Daniel replied curtly. He tried to sidestep Tommy, who neatly blocked his movement with a matching one. Out of the corner of his eye, Daniel saw the henchman straighten. Tommy didn't even look in the bodyguard's direction, but at the slightest shake of his head the thug settled back into his doorway.

"Just hear me out, Danny. For old time's sake. You say you have no interest in politics, but that's not what I hear." Tommy smiled his thin smile. "In fact, I hear you've been hanging round the Bend some nights, offering legal advice."

"Helping the less fortunate with their legal troubles is not necessarily political," Daniel replied.

"It is in this town, particularly when we're talking housing or labor conditions."

Daniel felt his insides clench with rage. He wondered briefly how many unscrupulous landlords, policemen, and city inspectors were in Tommy's pocket.

"Between you and that pesky Robin Hood," Tommy continued, pausing to send a meaningful look his way, "a lot of folks seem to be getting restless. People don't like having their own misfortune pointed out to them."

"People don't like realizing they've been the dupes of a corrupt system," Daniel corrected.

"We've been trying to clean up that area for a good spell now, you know. While you were off dallying with the crowned heads of Europe. Poor old Gerry, did you hear? Seems he got the wrong idea about our efforts." Tommy rocked back on his heels and fixed Danny with a hard look.

So that was how Gerry Knox had wound up with his head caved in under a pile of garbage in Bottle Alley. And how the police report would reflect a different story.

It had been so long, yet his body automatically began to prepare for what was starting to seem like an inevitable fight. His knees bent slightly in readiness to duck or feint, and the muscles in his shoulders and arms tensed.

Ever observant, Tommy took note of the subtle shifts in Daniel's form and held his hands up. "I didn't come here to argue with you, Danny," he said. "I came to ask personally for your support."

"For what?" Daniel ground out, refusing to relax.

"Why, for my candidacy! I'm running for mayor." Tommy's smile widened. "It would be such a boon to my campaign to have the support of someone as respectable as yourself, not tainted with the slightest hint of scandal."

Daniel stared at the man, incredulous. Tommy Meade, terror of the East Side, as *mayor* of New York?

"Don't look so stunned, Danny boy," Tommy sneered. "You always were so high-and-mighty. Must have been your sister's influence. Ah, but she was a beauty. Went to work for old man Van Joost, didn't she?" Tommy grinned wolfishly, and Daniel knew the other man had just played his trump card.

Tommy gave a slight nod, as if observing that Daniel had indeed gotten his message. He took a step back and stared at Daniel coldly. "You know I could win this, Danny. I'm exactly the pull-yourself-up-by-your-bootstraps kind of man they want, a survivor of the Draft Riots, the bad boy from the tenements made good. And besides," Tommy continued, spreading his hands wide and assuming the role of the benevolent politician, "I *am* for the people. I'm for reform."

Daniel felt cold rage envelop him. "You're interested in profiting off the people, not in making their way easier."

"Why, Danny," replied Tommy, smooth as a snake, "whoever said the two were mutually exclusive? Think about it."

With a quick wink, he turned and melted into the crowded street, his henchman disappearing along with him. Daniel stood alone for a few moments longer, forcing himself to breathe deeply until he felt he could move without punching an innocent passerby. Then, muttering a curse that caused a few startled stares, he too lost himself in the throngs of pedestrians.

CHAPTER 7

After her confusing encounter with Clive and an alarming after-noon navigating an exhibition hall full of crying babies (what made any of them "best," anyway? They all looked rather the same to her), a brisk walk in the crisp winter air did much to lift Genevieve's spirits. She had brooded during the entire carriage ride back to her home, where she had gone to change into something more suitable for visiting the house of the recently deceased, and once there decided to make her way north on Fifth Avenue to Mr. Cotswold's mansion by foot, despite the chilly temperatures.

It had been the right decision. With each passing block, her black mood improved, and by the time she arrived at the front steps of the Cotswold townhouse, her shoulders, which had been bunched up tight near her ears, were relaxed and her arms were loosely swinging by her sides. She felt so jaunty, in fact, that she had to forcibly slow herself down as she climbed the stone steps and remind her body that the home was in mourning.

Genevieve paused halfway up the steps, gazing at the dark-brown facade of the house with appreciation. It was a deceivingly simple exte-rior, its clean lines belying the lavishness of the interior. Reginald and his now-departed wife had built the house in the late 1860s, when wealthy families were beginning the march of mansions up Fifth Ave-nue, each more elaborate than the last. While many of the houses built then had already been torn down as society moved further north toward Central Park, the Cotswolds had stayed on. Genevieve had spent many happy hours here as a child, playing hide-and-seek in the vast house with her brothers. The Cotswolds, having no children of their own, had been surprisingly indulgent of the Stewart children's antics.

A pang went through her at the memory. Sally Cotswold had died over a decade prior, predeceasing her husband, and as far as Genevieve knew, the pair had no other family. She wondered what would become of the lovely house. Knowing Reginald, he likely had arranged for the proceeds from its sale to benefit any number of charities. Smiling sadly to herself, Genevieve made an internal vow to do her best to preserve his memory with her written remembrance.

The heavy front door creaked open, startling her out of her memories. Three police officers made their way out of the house and down the steps, the last one pausing as he passed her, his gaze briefly but appreciatively traveling down her figure. Genevieve felt her shoulders immediately begin to tense again.

He tipped his hat. "You have business at the house, miss?"

"Yes," she responded icily, tipping her chin up. "I'm a family friend, expected by Mrs. Dolan." What she said wasn't technically a lie, even though it wasn't the full truth—Arthur had cabled a message over that she would be arriving this afternoon. There was no reason for the police to know she was also a journalist.

But why were the *police* here at all? Reginald's death had been natural.

Or so she'd been told.

"Is aught amiss?" She dropped her haughty demeanor, exchanging it for a furrowed brow and a look of helpless concern. Better to catch flies with honey. She blinked her eyes a few times for good measure. "My father was a dear friend of Reginald's," she added, deliberately using Mr. Cotswold's Christian name, in essence reminding the officer that her family, being on such intimate terms with the Cotswolds, was also high society. Like the eye blinking, such tactics were unpleasant but sometimes useful.

"I don't like to say too much, miss, but seeing as you're a friend of the family . . ." The officer hesitated, glancing down at his companions, now impatiently waiting at the bottom of the stairs and stamping their feet in the cold. "Perhaps you can help Mrs. Dolan," he continued, smoothing his elaborate moustache. "She seems to be having a hard time coping with Mr. Cotswold's passing. She was in hysterics just now, insisting we treat the man's death as murder."

Something bright and unpleasant unfurled in Genevieve's stomach, and she did not have to feign an expression of horror.

"Whyever would she think such a terrible thing?" she asked.

"Apparently a bauble has gone missing," the officer confided, leaning a bit closer. Genevieve placed a hand lightly on his forearm, pressing her advantage.

"Not Robin Hood?" she gasped, rather impressed at her own performance. Perhaps journalism was the wrong calling; she would have excelled on the stage.

The officer puffed out his chest a bit and patted her gloved hand. "Not likely, miss. Robin Hood isn't a killer, far as we know. Meaning no disrespect, but with the piles of knickknacks in that house, Mrs. Dolan likely misplaced one in her grief. It'll turn up."

Genevieve allowed herself a few more eye blinks. "I'm sure you're right, Officer . . . ?" She paused and gazed at him inquiringly.

"Officer Jackson, miss." He smoothed his hands down the front of his uniform jacket and somehow managed to expand his chest a degree more.

"Officer Jackson, then. Thank you for letting me know. And thank you for being so helpful. I would have been quite alarmed to hear such an assertion from Mrs. Dolan, but now I feel most reassured."

A satisfied gleam lit Officer Jackson's eye, and he touched the brim of his cap as he moved to join his companions. Genevieve offered a smile, but it was immediately erased as the officer's eyes dropped to her bosom with a small leer as he passed. She watched his retreating back incredulously, fighting the urge to cover her chest with her arms, which was ridiculous, seeing as she was encased in a snug velvet jacket from chin to midthigh. Her own gaze dropped to her bosom doubtfully as the officers rounded the corner and she caught the sound of their retreating laughter.

Perhaps the jacket was *too* snug? It was quite new, the color and texture of tilled soil, trimmed with a bit of black rabbit's fur. She was fond of it.

Stop it, she scolded her own fretting mind as she rang the bell. It was a lovely jacket, and she wasn't about to let her pleasure in it be ruined by a rude man with ridiculous moustaches who happened to be a police officer.

A young maid with wide eyes and a black armband on her gray dress opened the door. She took Genevieve's hat, gloves, and jacket, then gestured toward the front drawing room. "Mrs. Dolan is in here, miss."

"Oh! Miss Stewart." The plump, gray-haired housekeeper bustled over to her, her black bombazine skirts rustling, and pulled her into an embrace. "I'm sure you'll forgive me being so forward, but it is good to see you. I have been quite beside myself." Mrs. Dolan waved a pink handkerchief in the air in a distracted gesture, then dabbed at her eyes.

"You must call me Genevieve," Genevieve insisted. "You've known me since I was born, Mrs. Dolan."

The housekeeper offered a watery smile. "You and your brothers were a handful. But the Cotswolds appreciated your high jinks; they believed children should be lively. Oh, there I go again." She patted at her wet eyes, then gestured for Genevieve to sit. "I'll have Letty bring in some tea. Or would you prefer coffee?"

"Tea is fine," Genevieve reassured her. The drawing room looked much the same as it had for the past two decades, with oversized paintings in heavy gilded frames dominating the walls and thick carpets blanketing the floors. But her comfort in the familiar surroundings was overshadowed by her concern for what the policeman had revealed on the townhouse's front steps. She leaned toward the woman she had known since childhood, who had often cared for her and her brothers while the adults dined and chatted the night away, recalling that Mrs. Dolan might have known another child.

"Mrs. Dolan, did you hear that Daniel McCaffrey is back in town?" she began, settling herself on an armchair that was surprisingly comfortable for so much gilding. "Do I remember correctly that Mr. Cotswold was friends with Jacob Van Joost?"

"He was indeed. And yes, Mr. McCaffrey came to visit me a few weeks ago."

This *was* news.

"You are that well acquainted?" She'd thought perhaps the house-keeper would have a distant memory of the man as a boy, not a recent one.

"Oh yes. I've known Mr. McCaffrey since he was a lad. He didn't accompany Mr. Van Joost here often, mind, perhaps about once a year. He spent so much time abroad at school when he was young, you know. Once Mr. Van Joost died and left his fortune to young Daniel, and the newspapers began to insinuate all kinds of terrible things—no offense to your current employers, dear—well, Mr. Cotswold brought Daniel around more, when he was home from university and the like. To encourage him, you know. The poor lad needed a guiding hand."

Genevieve had to fight to keep her mouth from dropping open in astonishment. All this time, society had wondered at Daniel McCaffrey's origins and whereabouts during his youth, and at least some of the answers had been right here all along, in the Cotswold drawing room.

"But . . . I never heard of any affiliation between Reginald and Mr. McCaffrey," she began.

"Oh no, you wouldn't have. Mr. Cotswold did like to keep things private, and he wanted Daniel to be able to make his own name. Which he has, hasn't he? Done quite well, I'd say." Mrs. Dolan sighed, looking around the room in a distracted manner.

Genevieve filed the information away in her brain to pick apart later. It was astonishing news, but she also wanted to know why officers had been at the home. "I saw some police officers leaving the house just now—" she began, but the housekeeper interrupted her.

"Those pups." Genevieve's surprise at Mrs. Dolan's uncharacteristic impertinence must have shown on her face, as the older woman drew herself taller in her armchair. "Yes, I said it. They are determined not to hear me. With your being out in the working world, my dear, I can tell you what I might not say to another young lady: I firmly believe Mr. Cotswold's life was taken from him." And with that, the housekeeper buried her face behind the pink handkerchief for some minutes.

Genevieve was patting Mrs. Dolan's back soothingly when Letty arrived with the tea. The young maid looked with alarm at her employer before setting the service down gingerly. Mrs. Dolan recovered herself enough to shoo the maid away and pour as Genevieve resumed her seat.

"Mrs. Dolan, why would you make such a claim? Mr. Cotswold was ninety-one," she said, parroting her editor. She knew what the ill-mannered officer had claimed but wanted to hear the tale from the housekeeper herself.

"A most valuable Russian jeweled box is missing," Mrs. Dolan confided with a sniff. "It was a gift from Emperor Alexander the Second himself, decorated with rubies, prized as much for its sentiment as for price. It went missing the very night Reginald passed." The pink swath of fabric came to her eyes again, but briefly this time.

"And why do you think the potential theft of the box has any relationship with Mr. Cotswold's passing?" Genevieve asked gently. "Could it not have been coincidence? Or perhaps it was simply misplaced? It's only been two days." The Cotswolds had been profligate art collectors, amassing objects from their frequent and extensive travels all over the world. One thing the officer had said on the steps was true: the vast house was crammed with an enormous number of paintings, sculptures, and all manner of bric-a-brac, ranging from the shockingly expensive to trinkets purchased from street vendors. It was altogether imaginable that one jeweled box had become lost in the mix.

Mrs. Dolan pursed her lips and shot Genevieve a scolding look. "You know me better than that, dear. I know where every object in this house belongs and make sure the staff does as well."

Genevieve ducked her head in acknowledgment and some shame, as she did in fact know this. She, Gavin, and Charles used to delight in the multitude of treasures to be found in the house, carefully palming and exclaiming over those they were allowed to handle, and no matter where they had found each object, Mrs. Dolan knew exactly what it was and exactly where it belonged.

"But I still don't understand why you assume the missing box is connected to Mr. Cotswold's death," she pressed, stirring a touch more sugar into her tea.

"Well, it has to be that Robin Hood character," Mrs. Dolan said definitively. She took a quavering breath but managed to keep her eyes dry. "Who else has been stealing valuables from houses such as these?"

"But Robin Hood has not committed murder," Genevieve replied with care. *Yet*, an inner voice instantly replied, causing a shiver to run down her spine.

"It is my belief that Reginald caught the ruffian in the act of pilfering the box and instantly expired from the shock of it." Again the handkerchief was applied, though only momentarily. At Genevieve's furrowed brow, the housekeeper sighed. "My guess is you assume your father's dear friend passed while asleep in his bed, yes?"

"I had assumed that, yes," Genevieve confirmed slowly. She searched her memory for the exact wording of her conversation with Arthur, and the shorter one she'd had with her father earlier that afternoon when she'd gone home to change clothes. "No, not assumed," she remembered. "It is what my editor told me."

Mrs. Dolan shook her head, taking another deep breath. "That is what is being said publicly. In truth, I found him . . . expired, in his bedclothes, on the floor of the upstairs study yesterday morning. The very room where the box was kept."

The icy shiver danced on Genevieve's spine again. "Was there any evidence of a break-in?"

"No, the house was locked tight as a drum, as always. But don't you see? Reginald was a very light sleeper, particularly since Sally passed. He must have heard a noise coming from the study and walked in to investigate . . ." The housekeeper was overcome again for a moment.

Genevieve put down her teacup and waited for Mrs. Dolan to compose herself, her mind swirling. The housekeeper removed the pink handkerchief from her face and continued. "The police say he was probably awake to get a drink of water or the like." She colored a little and Genevieve nodded, indicating that she understood. "But there was no reason for Reginald to be in the study if such were the case. The water closet is at the other end of the hall," she concluded with dignity.

Mrs. Dolan started fussing about with a lovely-looking lemon cake, noting that she had barely been able to eat since Mr. Cotswold's passing but pressing a slice upon Genevieve, who accepted it mutely. She barely knew what to make of this new information, but it did suggest that some kind of foul play had been involved in Reginald's death.

"I know your time is short, Genevieve," Mrs. Dolan said, "and you're here to gather information for the remembrance in the paper. I am so very glad it is you who is writing it, by the way. Reginald would be so pleased. But . . . I scarcely know how to ask this . . ."

"You want me to keep an ear out for anything that may have to do with the missing jeweled box, or any other news regarding Mr. Cotswold?" Genevieve guessed, keeping her voice soft.

Mrs. Dolan breathed a sigh of relief. "Yes. Yes, that would be welcome. I know you are not a police officer, but they do not seem inclined to help at present anyway. You are in a position to possibly hear of something, as the *Globe* receives the letters from Robin Hood." The housekeeper peered at Genevieve hopefully.

"I will do my best. And if something comes to my attention that might corroborate your theory, I shall let both you and the authorities know at once," she promised.

Seeming satisfied, Mrs. Dolan composed herself, and they proceeded to have a long, lovely chat around their shared memories of the Cotswolds, with Genevieve taking occasional notes and both of them shedding an occasional tear, until Mrs. Dolan noticed with surprise that dusk was falling.

"I've taken far too much of your time," said the older woman, bustling Genevieve to the door.

"No, it's I who have taken yours. Our discussion will be so helpful as I write my newspaper piece; I can't thank you enough."

"Of course, dear. And you're right to focus on his charitable and committee work. That man gave so much to this city." Mrs. Dolan sighed unhappily.

"Mrs. Dolan, we didn't speak of the most recent committee Mr. Cotswold was appointed to—I understand he was meant to serve on a mayoral task force on housing reform?"

The housekeeper pursed her lips again, then narrowed her eyes in a way that suggested she was rolling them without actually doing so. "Yes, and it pains me that his last act of kindness towards this town caused him such headaches."

Genevieve's heart skipped a beat. "Headaches?"

Before Mrs. Dolan could answer, a distant telephone rang, and the older woman excused herself to answer it after a hurried, distracted embrace, leaving Genevieve with the maid Letty, who had retrieved Genevieve's things.

"Miss," whispered Letty as she helped Genevieve into her jacket. "It was me."

Genevieve twisted around and regarded the young woman with an alarmed curiosity. Letty was wringing her hands in front of her waist, wearing an expression of acute misery.

"What was you?"

"It was my fault. Mr. Cotswold's death. I left the kitchen door unlocked that night on accident. I'd snuck out, you see. My young man, he wanted to take me to the theater, and Mrs. Dolan would have said no, but I went anyways, and in the morning discovered I'd plumb forgot to lock the back door. So if someone broke in to steal the box and . . ." Letty's eyes welled with tears. "They got in because of me."

The icy tendrils returned, now creeping their way up the back of Genevieve's neck. It was seeming more and more probable that Reginald Cotswold had suffered an unnatural death. "Didn't you tell Mrs. Dolan? Or the police?"

If anything, the poor girl looked even more miserable. "No, miss. I didn't want to get in trouble and lose my place, or worse. But I heard you and Mrs. Dolan talking, and maybe it's useful for you to know. Maybe it can help you catch whoever took the box." The tears spilled over and down Letty's face, and she wiped at her eyes with her sleeve. "But please don't tell, unless you must."

Letty would most certainly be sacked if Genevieve relayed the information to her employer, and it would only upset Mrs. Dolan more. She sighed. "Let me see what I can find out," she said.

"Thank you, miss." Letty bobbed her knees gratefully and opened the door, her relief palpable.

A great breath escaped Genevieve the moment the door closed behind her. Daniel not only knew Mr. Cotswold well, he had been a frequent visitor to the house. But what use would a millionaire have with one jeweled box? And according to Mrs. Dolan, Daniel's relationship with Mr. Cotswold had been friendly, perhaps even filial. Were Reginald's "headaches" with the mayoral committee why Daniel had directed her focus in that direction?

Mulling over these revelations as she made her way down the front steps with care, Genevieve clasped her hat, which was nearly yanked off by a sudden gust. The wind had increased in speed and the temperature had dropped during the hours she had spent at the Cotswold house, and the walk south down Fifth Avenue toward her home in Washington Square was decidedly less comfortable than her reverse journey had been earlier that afternoon. The few pedestrians she passed in this largely residential area were bundled to their eyebrows, walking with their heads bent against the wind, hurrying home in the deepening shadows.

Genevieve ducked her own head and picked up her pace. The Square was only a few blocks away, and it seemed silly to hail a hansom cab for such a short distance.

Silly, that is, until an uncomfortable chafing across the back of her left heel caused her to stop. Clicking her tongue in frustration, Genevieve ducked alongside the steps of another grand townhome, hoping their bulk would provide a modicum of shelter from the biting wind as she adjusted her boot. The laces had loosened, causing the leather to rub uncomfortably.

As she straightened back up, boot now tightly laced, she caught sight of a man about half a block behind her. He was too far away and it was too dark for her to make out any identifying details—he was just an outline of a figure in a hat, coat, and scarf, like every other man she'd seen on the street today—but what caught her attention was his movement.

Or lack thereof.

He was standing stock-still in the middle of the sidewalk, facing south, toward her.

Not ducking his head against the wind, not readjusting his scarf or clamping down his hat, not hastening home toward a warm fire. Just standing—and looking.

Uneasy dread began to prickle at her belly, then spread toward her limbs.

It's nothing, the rational part of her mind whispered.

Move. Now, another, more primal part of her whispered back.

The dreadful feeling circled and ticked her spine as she turned her back on the figure, walking south again. She forced herself to maintain an even pace, heart pounding, the rational and emotional sides of herself still warring with each other.

Crossing the busyness of Broadway provided some relief, as there were a few more pedestrians rushing down the thoroughfare, and Genevieve breathed a trifle easier. Only six blocks until home. Was he still behind her?

She paused at the corner of East Tenth Street and peered west, as if trying to decide whether or not she should turn right. Risking a peek over her shoulder, the dread blossomed into full panic. The figure was still there. And he had also stopped.

He was matching her movements.

Both sides of her brain were in agreement now: *Run.*

Heedless of whether she was making a fool of herself by running from a perfectly normal businessman on his way home or whether she was truly in danger, Genevieve hitched up her skirts and began sprinting toward the intersection where Fifth Avenue transformed into the park. Her family's house was just around the corner on the northeastern edge. If she could make it to that corner, surely she'd be safe.

Was it her imagination, or did she hear footsteps behind her quickening as well?

The discomfort in her left heel came roaring back as the dratted laces on her boot reloosened, but she dared not stop to fix them. She was almost there.

Why were the streets suddenly so empty? Where was a leering police officer when a girl needed one? The wind continued to pick up, the dry tree branches clicking together eerily as she raced beneath them toward home.

Almost there, almost there.

Boots thudding, heel chafing, she ran, then abruptly halted when she reached the corner of Fifth and Washington Square North. Her next-door neighbors, the Wellingtons, were alighting from their carriage in front of their townhouse. Emboldened by their presence, as well as by that of their sturdy groom, she whirled around, ready to face her pursuer.

Fifth Avenue was empty. It yawned northward in a seemingly endless trajectory, mansions and shop facades shuttered and still in the cold February night. A lone carriage crossed the Avenue about ten blocks up, but otherwise the street was almost preternaturally devoid of life.

If someone had been following her, he was gone.

"Miss Stewart? Genevieve?" Henry and Clara Wellington gathered around her, glancing from her face toward the Avenue. Heart pounding, she kept her eyes facing north, until a few shadowy figures of pedestrians emerged from side streets and houses, populating the Avenue once more. "Are you quite all right?" Mrs. Wellington pressed.

Her body was cooling from its exertions, and Genevieve shivered in the chilly air. Her jacket clung to her damply. Offering a distracted nod to her bewildered neighbors, Genevieve passed them without a word and climbed the front steps of her house, refusing to look back.

CHAPTER 8

"Oh, so he's not from India, then?" Callie appeared crestfallen at the news that Daniel did not hail from an exotic locale. She brightened as a new thought occurred to her. "That doesn't necessarily mean the part about his parents dying of snakebite isn't true!" she suggested, giving her shiny black curls a satisfied shake.

"Yes, because there are so many poisonous snakes creeping around the Lower East Side," remarked Eliza wryly. "Really, being hopeful that another person's parents might have died of snakebite is rather gruesome."

For weeks, Genevieve had resisted telling her friends about her unauthorized investigation into Robin Hood, but Callie, ever insistent, had pried out a portion of the story. There were many elements she still held back: the dead man in the alley with the misshapen head, Luther's promise to look into it, and her growing fears around the circumstances of Reginald Cotswold's death. Her friends could not be dissuaded from hearing a full accounting of her dance with Daniel McCaffrey, however, and she found herself revealing select details from their impromptu dinner as well, to the delight of Callie and the wary astonishment of Eliza.

In truth, it was a relief to unburden herself, even partially. The weight of the information she had recently uncovered had been gnawing at her, causing sleepless nights as her brain puzzled over each new revelation.

The trio had been walking through Washington Square Park, around which they all lived. The recent bitter winds had relented somewhat, and while the day was not quite warm, at least it was sunny. There was the barest hint of January's snow still covering the shrubbery, and patches of brown grass were being uncovered bit by bit as the crusty sheet of white that had blanketed the ground slowly melted. Despite the thin sunshine, Genevieve folded her arms around her chest, shuddering a bit as a brisk breeze stirred the still-bare branches of the park's trees, the clacking sound returning her instantly to the recent night she had been pursued—maybe—down Fifth Avenue.

Another detail she deliberately withheld from her friends.

"Are you too cold, Genevieve?" Eliza asked with concern. "Shall we go to my house? There's cake, I'm sure."

Callie perked up at the mention of cake. "Yes, let's!"

Genevieve shook her head. "I ought to be getting home."

"Perhaps you should rest," Eliza said, placing a hand on Genevieve's shoulder.

"You've got circles under your eyes," Callie added.

"Callie!" Eliza scolded. "That is not kind."

"I'm sure it's nothing she doesn't know."

"There is no need to be impolite."

The girls' familiar, friendly banter was giving Genevieve a headache. "Stop it, both of you. Can we please sit?" She sat hard on the nearest bench and rubbed at her temples.

"Genevieve," ventured Eliza, after both she and Callie had settled themselves, "may I ask something? Do you fear Daniel McCaffrey is Robin Hood?"

Genevieve sighed. She ought to have known her friends were clever enough to divine her thinking.

Callie was nodding in agreement. "It partially adds up. But it partially *doesn't*."

Genevieve sat on the open end of the bench and gazed contemplatively at the grand, crumbling gothic towers of the old university building that dominated the Square's east side. "Exactly." She smoothed the skirt of her pink wool dress. "It feels tied somehow to his being made the Van Joost heir. It's not as if the Van Joosts were known for their charity work, nor were they terribly kind to, um, outsiders," she finished lamely, looking apologetically at Eliza. While her family and Callie's could trace their origins to the early Dutch settlers of New York, Eliza's merchant father hailed from Massachusetts and had made his fortune in the war manufacturing Union uniforms, afterward turning to ladies' corsets. The Van Joosts, a terribly snobby clan, had refused to associate with that kind of "new money."

"No, certainly not," murmured Eliza. "One can't imagine the old man taking in a stray newsboy or the like out of the kindness of his heart."

"Do you recall how terrifying old man Van Joost was when we were children?" Callie interjected. "Eliza, you must consider yourself lucky that your family was not included in the annual Van Joost Christmas party, really. We children were made to stay in the main party with the adults, highly unusual and mind-numbingly dull."

Genevieve was surprised. "You remember those parties? You were so small then."

"I'm only four years younger than you. And yes, my fear of that house is among my earliest memories. My grandmother was such a crony of old man Van Joost's."

"I'd forgotten your grandmother had been close to him. Did she ever speculate as to why Mr. McCaffrey was made the heir?" Eliza asked.

"No." Callie shook her head. "She was just as bewildered as everyone else."

"I can't imagine attending such an awful party—and at Christmastime, no less!" exclaimed Eliza, reaching behind her to pluck a twig from a nearby shrub, shaking off the remaining snow before twirling it between her fingers. "Of course, my father would have expired of joy to receive an invitation."

A new thought occurred to Genevieve. "I don't ever recall seeing Daniel there."

"Nor do I," agreed Callie, shaking her head slowly. "I was a bit younger of course, but even then I'm sure I would have noticed someone as good-looking as Daniel McCaffrey."

Genevieve rolled her eyes at Callie. "Let us put aside the question of the man's handsomeness for now. Mr. Cotswold's housekeeper said Mr. McCaffrey spent part of his youth at school abroad. Why would Jacob Van Joost take an interest in a young boy from Five Points and pay for his education?"

Nobody had an answer for this. The tree branches clacked again in the breeze, and the friends almost unconsciously scooched closer together on the bench.

Eliza finally broke the silence. "I am glad of your new assignment, Genevieve. About Mr. Cotswold."

"Yes, a welcome change from writing about the size of bustles, I'm sure," Callie agreed.

"I've been a bit shaken by Mr. Cotswold's passing," Eliza confided. "He was one of the first to welcome my father into society. It made a tremendous difference to us."

"He was a nice man," Callie conceded. "But old as dirt. Even Grandmama is fairly sanguine about his death, and she'd known him forever."

"Your grandmother knew everyone," remarked Genevieve.

"They were all thick as thieves back in the sixties and early seventies," Callie said. "Jacob Van Joost, Reggie Cotswold, John Jacob Astor, my grandfather . . . they were in charge of this town." She smiled a bit sadly. "How times change."

Eliza and Genevieve fell uncomfortably silent, aware that Callie and her grandmother had fallen on hard times of late.

"Let us talk of the living rather than the dead," Callie declared in a firm voice. "You've now had a dance and a private supper with Daniel McCaffrey. Maybe you should allow him to court you," she said playfully.

Genevieve felt an unexpected blush begin to creep up her neck as she drew herself back in surprise. "*Court* me? I think my path as a spinster is set, thank you very much."

"That's not true," Eliza protested.

"It's been six years, darling," Callie said gently. "Ted Beekman is a pompous ass who didn't deserve you anyway. Perhaps you should take yourself off the shelf?"

"I'm not keeping myself on a shelf; it's simply where I've landed," Genevieve answered irritably. "And it's fine. Mr. McCaffrey has no interest in courting me, I'm sure."

"He knows you want to write a story," Callie remarked, turning her face toward the weak sunshine. "He took you to dinner and let you *interview* him, for goodness' sakes. It seems like he's plenty interested. And you *like* him, don't you?"

Do I like Daniel McCaffrey? It had not occurred to Genevieve to wonder whether she liked the man. Suddenly the whole topic annoyed her. "Don't we have something else to talk about?"

Eliza's mild look indicated that she knew Genevieve was holding something back, which annoyed Genevieve further.

"What do you want to talk about, then?" Callie asked, also wisely holding her tongue.

"Someone *else's* romantic possibilities. Don't you have a latest conquest?"

"I'm quite tired of men," Callie replied tartly, waving her hand through the air.

Genevieve felt her mouth drop open in shock. Men were Callie's favorite subject.

"Callie, are you well?" Eliza asked tentatively.

Callie's eyes were suddenly bright with tears. "I'm just tired of playing games," she said.

Genevieve, worried, pulled a handkerchief out of her flower-sprigged velvet reticule and leaned over to press it into Callie's unoccupied hand. Callie was always so joyful; something must be seriously wrong for her to behave in such a manner. Though Genevieve feared she knew what was coming, she asked, "What is it, darling?"

Callie heaved a mighty sigh. "Well, girls, it looks as though I am to be married." Her eyes filled with tears again and she quickly blotted them with the handkerchief. "Grandmama and I talked last night. We are quite without funds, and we simply can't afford another season." She gave her friends a stricken look, her red-rimmed eyes lost and sad. "In all honesty, we can't afford fuel for next winter." Callie bowed her head and began to cry in earnest.

That bad? Genevieve and Eliza shared a quick, shocked look over Callie's head. It was worse than either of them had realized. Genevieve jumped up and moved to the other side of the bench. Between Callie's sobs she made out the words "husband" and "freeze." She and Eliza surrounded Callie with their loving arms.

"Nonsense, sweetness, we'd never let you freeze!" Eliza insisted, stroking Callie's midnight-black hair soothingly.

"Of course not," agreed Genevieve. Privately she was fuming. Callie and her grandmother were two women, alone in the world. Who had mismanaged their fortune so completely? "You and your grandmother can live with us."

Callie looked up again and managed a watery smile, controlling herself. "I know I could, but Grandmama would never agree to such a thing. I can do this for her; I must do this for her. I get proposals all the time; I'll just . . . accept one."

Genevieve's heart panged at the thought of her friend in a tepid, loveless marriage.

"Men absolutely adore you; you'll have no trouble finding someone suitable," Eliza said stoutly. "Genevieve and I will help, won't we?"

"Of course!" Genevieve exclaimed, putting her reservations aside for the sake of her friend. She hugged Callie from her other side, accidentally knocking her pretty feathered hat askew. "We'll make sure he's kind, handsome, and swimming in money."

Callie straightened her hat and gently pulled free of her friends' arms, suddenly looking much older than her twenty-two years. "We shall see," she replied. She then brightened and lightly smacked her hand to her cheek. "I forgot the exciting part!"

Genevieve was heartened by the sudden shift. "There's an exciting part?"

"Well, a small bright spot. At any party of my choosing this season, Grandmama is going to allow me to wear the Maple diamonds!" Callie beamed at her friends.

Eliza gasped. "The ones smuggled from France during the revolution?"

"The very same. They haven't been worn since my parents married, though apparently Queen Victoria desperately tried to buy them from Papa."

Even Genevieve, who cared little for jewels, was stunned. Callie's grandmother kept the precious heirlooms in a vault at the bank at all times. "Gracious," she breathed. "Where shall you wear them?"

"Maybe the Porters' costume ball," mused Callie. "Speaking of, I was being fitted for my costume last week, and who do you think I saw at Mrs. Brown's? Esmie Bradley."

"Really?" Eliza looked thoughtful. "Perhaps she wriggled out from under her mother's thumb long enough to order a decent dress. They certainly have the money."

"That is my hope as well," Callie replied. "She's a pretty girl, under all those ruffles." She stood up and stretched her arms, looking around at the deepening shadows gathering in the barren park. "Come on, let's have some cake. It's starting to get dark."

Relieved that her friend seemed to be feeling better, Genevieve stood, and the three linked arms. Together they began to stroll down one of the winding paths that crisscrossed through the park.

"I've an idea about Mr. McCaffrey," ventured Eliza, peering around Callie.

Callie perked up. "Oh yes, let's talk about Mr. McCaffrey again!" she exclaimed.

"If you want to see him again, for your research, you should consider attending the Bradleys' ball this weekend." Eliza looked at Genevieve uncertainly. "You were invited, weren't you?"

"Of course," Genevieve said, a bit thunderstruck at the idea. Though her father had bested Mrs. Bradley in court, the Stewarts were part of the upper tier of New York society, which the Bradleys wished to join. They wouldn't dream of snubbing any old Knickerbocker family and consistently invited *all* of the Astor 400 to their functions.

The Stewart clan always declined.

"What makes you think he'll be there? He doesn't attend that many functions, from what I understand."

"Rupert Milton's engagement to Esmie Bradley will be announced, of course," Callie answered promptly. "He and Mr. McCaffrey are great friends; I can't imagine he wouldn't be there. It's a brilliant idea, Eliza."

"How do you know the engagement will be announced, if it hasn't happened yet?"

"Everyone knows. How do you *not* know?"

"I've been a trifle preoccupied," Genevieve answered. She didn't quite snap, but came close, and let out a small, vexed breath when she caught her friends exchanging a meaningful glance.

Why was she so irritable on the topic of Daniel McCaffrey? Eliza was right: if she wanted to get more information, the best way to do it was to interact with the man.

"I'm sorry," she sighed. "It is a good plan, Eliza. Now I just have to break the news to my parents that I'll be attending a function at the Bradley household." The three friends had reached the point where they would part ways, Genevieve north to her family townhome, Eliza and Callie west toward Eliza's. She bid her friends adieu, giving Callie a particularly long hug.

"Thank you," Callie whispered into her ear. "I'll be fine. Go on, best not delay letting them know."

Genevieve chose the most direct path home toward the Square's north side, but as she had parted from her friends on the southern edge, she still had to traverse the park's length, and the path wended its way through several areas not well lit. The tree branches continued their unpleasant song as the wind increased again, and she shivered and shoved her hands deeper into her white fur muff.

The unexpected sound of loud, boisterous singing made her start, and she spotted two men down the path far to her left, supporting each other and stumbling slightly. She accelerated her pace. The park was mostly safe, but vagabonds still sometimes frequented its paths.

Halfway there, a distinct tickling sensation at the back of her neck caused her to pause. Dusk had given way to a darker-hued sky, and the lamps scattered throughout the park provided little illumination against the deep pockets of gloom created by the shrubbery and towering, ancient trees. When she risked a peek over her shoulder, her heart stopped, then immediately resumed at triple its regular tempo.

A man was there. As on Fifth Avenue, he was far enough away that any details beyond his general form were obscured, but again he was immobile, facing her direction.

There was no one else in the park.

A breath that was part moan involuntarily escaped her, and Genevieve turned north, letting her muff dangle and picking up her skirts to facilitate a faster stride. Fear rippled through her, tingling her back, where she could almost feel the unknown man's gaze resting.

Blessedly, the distance was short. Though it felt like miles, she reached the front steps of her home in under two minutes, and flung herself through the heavy front door gratefully.

Leaning back against the door, Genevieve allowed her breath and heart to resume their regular pace before removing her jacket with trembling hands. She had no idea if her imagination was getting the better of her or if both incidents had represented actual danger.

Perhaps you're going mad, a sly internal voice insinuated. *Perhaps you're not up to the task of finding Robin Hood.*

She firmly pushed the thought away. That was the naysayer's voice, Clive's voice, and she refused to let it take root.

A moment in the water closet with a damp cloth pressed to her temples helped calm her shaking. She took a deep breath and ventured forth to find her parents.

The front drawing room was, like all the rooms in the Stewart house, an odd, ramshackle mix of elegance and clutter. A bit more of the residual tension from her walk home slipped away; she loved her slightly messy, eccentric house, and felt more comfortable here than anyplace on earth. The deep-blue wallpaper and dark, heavy furniture ought to have been oppressive but gave the room a cozy feel. Hung around the walls were delicate watercolor landscapes, portraits in oil paint, and framed photographs of family. Some of the paintings were by friends such as Eliza, or the Stewart children at various ages; some had been painted by local artists Genevieve's parents admired; and there were a few inherited works by old masters interspersed throughout. Tall windows overlooked the Stewarts' front garden and the wide expanse of park, keeping the room bathed in sunlight most of the day, though she was glad to see they were now shuttered against the early night. The opposite wall was lined with ceiling-high bookshelves, each crammed with volumes in no particular order.

"Hello, dear," said Anna, her mother, around a mouthful of chocolate biscuit. "Come sit and have some tea." Anna Stewart, tall and full of bustling energy, pushed a pile of pamphlets to one side to make room for Genevieve at the tea table.

"What are those?" Genevieve asked, settling herself onto the comfortable settee but refusing a biscuit. She was still too unsettled to eat.

"Leaflets about our rally next week," Anna said. "We're surrounding the mayor's house and demanding women be given the right to vote in the next mayoral election. It's very exciting; twelve ladies will dress as Lady Liberty and stand in formation blocking traffic at the front of the main gate." Anna stood up suddenly, scattering several pamphlets to the floor and holding her half-eaten biscuit aloft. She grabbed a nearby book and mimicked the new statue's pose. "Pretend the biscuit is a torch. Can't you see it, my dear? The artistic and political impact we'll make? All twelve of us?"

Genevieve decided she did need a biscuit and chose one, considering her mother's stance. "Will the torches have flames?"

Anna beamed at her briefly, then resumed her somber, statuelike face. "Of course," she replied, trying not to move her lips.

"I think you'll probably get arrested again," Genevieve said. Anna, along with several other well-known women, had been arrested two years prior while protesting women's exclusion from the statue's dedication.

Anna Stewart, in fact, was often being hauled away by the police during political protests over one cause or another. The arrest at the statue's dedication was not even the one that had ended Genevieve's engagement. *That* had been a protest over universal access to birth control outside City Hall. Genevieve had often wondered whether Ted— or really, Ted's family—had been so scandalized not because of the jailing but rather because Anna had been speaking publicly about the delicate issue of birth control.

Anna broke her stance and beamed again. "Oh, that would be quite fitting, wouldn't it?" She collected the fallen pamphlets and organized them into a small pile, then sat back and finished her biscuit with a contented air.

"Where is Charles?" Genevieve asked. Her brother kept his own separate bachelor residence a few blocks away but typically managed to appear whenever food was served. She glanced at the windows uneasily. Charles was, like all the Stewarts, tall and athletic; having him in the room would make her feel more at ease.

Genevieve's father answered from behind a stack of books at the corner desk. "I believe he had a meeting of the Architectural League this afternoon," floated Wilbur's deep, burly voice.

"What are you buried in back there, Papa?" asked Genevieve, straining her neck to catch a glimpse of her father around the precarious pile. "Come out before we finish the biscuits."

"Nellie brought me a plate back here, thank you very much. I knew I couldn't trust you ladies to leave me any." Wilbur's kindly, bearded face suddenly appeared above the small tower. "But I shall emerge nonetheless, to give you a kiss hello." Wilbur came out from behind his cluttered desk and leaned over to kiss Genevieve's cheek before settling into a deep leather armchair to her right.

"Here, darling," he said, handing Genevieve several pieces of folded paper. "I was buried in a letter from your brother."

"Gavin wrote?" Gavin was an archaeologist currently undertaking fieldwork in Egypt. In their correspondence, he frequently assured her that life in a tent was much less glamorous than she believed, primarily consisting of sand and bugs. While Genevieve knew this intellectually, she couldn't picture her brother's life without imagining him in scenes inspired by *1001 Arabian Nights*: Gavin drinking tea on a lavish silk cushion, Gavin being attended to by a gorgeous woman in wide, billowing pants, Gavin wearing a fez. Normally she would grab at the letter, but today she felt too drained. And she wanted was to get this business about the ball sorted.

"Mother, did you receive the usual invitations for the weekend?"

Anna glanced up from the pad upon which she'd been writing, undoubtedly a draft of the rousing speech she intended to give at the upcoming rally. "Yes, yes. I haven't answered them all yet," she replied distractedly.

"Might I look through them?" Genevieve hesitated, feeling a trifle unsure. She shot a quick glance at her mother, who had returned to scratching frantically upon her pad. Another glance confirmed that her father was now consulting one of their many volumes on Egyptian history, as he often did after receiving a letter from Gavin.

"I thought I might attend the Bradleys' ball on Saturday." She carefully studied her fingernails, pretending to be suddenly deeply concerned about her manicure. She fervently hoped her parents would remain engaged in their pursuits and give her the quick and distracted "Of course, darling" that typically accompanied any announcement of plans from their adult children.

Genevieve risked a peek up from her cuticles. No such luck. Both Anna and Wilbur were gaping at her, mouths slightly ajar, nearly identical looks of utter astonishment on their faces.

"Elmira and Amos Bradley?" asked Anna dubiously, blinking. "The *Koola bird* Bradleys?" She looked at her daughter as if she were a rare specimen of bug from Egypt come crawling out of Gavin's letter: with surprise bordering on shock, fascination, and an underlying vague, intellectual distaste.

Genevieve nodded. "Yes, and yes," she muttered, giving her fingernails her full attention again.

Her mother gave her own slow nod. "I see. And were you encouraged to attend by anyone in particular?" she asked delicately, seeming hesitant herself now.

After a slightly puzzled pause, Genevieve realized her mother was asking if a potential suitor wanted to accompany her to the ball. Her gaze flew back to her mother's face, which now held an expression of vague intellectual distaste mingled with slight apprehension.

"No," she said firmly. "It's for work." Which, she consoled herself, was not entirely a lie. "Someone will be in attendance with whom I ought to speak."

Genevieve felt her mother's keen eyes bore into her forehead as she carefully picked chocolate crumbs off her skirt.

The quiet moment seemed to drag on for years as Genevieve continued to inspect her skirt for stray biscuit, but probably lasted only fifteen seconds or so. Finally Anna answered, "Well, I suppose that's fine, if it's for work," and turned her attention back to her speech writing.

Genevieve exhaled quietly, relieved that part was complete. Now she just had to get through the ball itself.

★ ★ ★

Leaning appreciatively into his deep, red leather office chair, Daniel propped his booted feet onto his large mahogany desk and read Genevieve's article on a best-baby contest again. *Damn*, he thought admiringly. She was good. Very good. She'd caught the essence of the whole event: the alternating boastfulness and boredom of the show parents, the slight pathos of poor families in their barely clean best clothes hoping for a premium, the wild exuberance of the children, and the utter ridiculousness of the entire affair, with a subtle wit that was clever enough to be noticed by most readers but not so sharp that it was condescending.

Ah, Miss Palmer, he thought, folding the newspaper carefully and putting it aside. *Genevieve.* He'd thought of her more than he liked to admit in recent days.

Would she be an asset or a hindrance? Only time would tell.

A light knock sounded on his door, interrupting his train of thought. Daniel sighed and removed his boots from the furniture.

"Yes?"

Asher, his personal secretary, thumped into his office and handed him a note. "This just arrived." He glanced at the desk and frowned. Daniel followed Asher's disapproving gaze, guiltily noticing the dirt and scuff marks his boots had left behind on the expansive surface.

"I'm sure Mrs. Kelly will be able to get the scratches out," Daniel said, brushing some of the dirt away with his hand.

"Probably, but I'm the one that's gonna get an earful about it." Asher shook his head at Daniel and stalked out of the room. Daniel sighed. The majority of the people who worked for him were

people he'd known growing up in Five Points, and they had no reservations about informing him when he'd acted like an ass. Asher
had been a prizefighter in his younger days, and his enormous size,
scarred face, and often angry countenance had seriously frightened
several of his clients. But Asher, like all those in Daniel's employ,
was hardworking and exceedingly loyal. Daniel figured anyone who
couldn't handle his staff's often less-than-polished manners didn't
need to be a client of his. Another luxury of Jacob's money: he
could afford to be choosy.

Returning his attention to the newly arrived note, Daniel flipped it
over and noted it was from Rupert.

He read the missive quickly, and felt his mood, already made intro-
spective by the confounding Miss Stewart, plummet.

Cursing under his breath, Daniel tossed the note aside and leaned
back in his chair again, feeling his jaw clench in helplessness and
frustration.

It was done, then. Rupert reported he'd come close to not going
through with it, but in the end he had proposed to Esmie Bradley, and
she had accepted.

Daniel closed his eyes. His friend was deliberately choosing an
unhappy life for the sake of family duty.

Didn't you do the same? The thought floated into his mind and
lodged there stubbornly.

Daniel frowned, swiveling his chair to stare contemplatively
through the window at Gramercy Park's trim paths.

It wasn't the same. He wasn't forcing himself into a loveless union.

But you're forcing yourself to be alone, his mind whispered back.

He pushed back from the window more violently than he'd
intended. "Asher!" he bellowed.

Asher's scowling visage popped into view. "Yes?" he growled.

"My evening clothes are ready for this weekend?"

Asher nodded.

"Good. The engagement will be announced after all."

Asher grunted impassively, then turned to go.

"And Asher?"

"Yeah, boss?"

"Is the other matter I asked you to take care of finished?" he asked quietly.

Asher's homely, ravaged face softened into what was almost a smile. "Yeh, it's all set," he replied. "Paddy and Billy got that family outa Cherry Street and resettled uptown."

"Good," Daniel said, leaning back in his chair again. He folded his arms behind his head and stared up at the ceiling, brooding. It *was* good, a bright spot in what seemed like a dark, thankless world today. "Good."

CHAPTER 9

Daniel blinked at what was the most lavish ballroom he'd ever encountered. Outside of some royal palaces in Europe, that is.

Which was clearly the association Elmira Bradley sought to invoke.

The grand room was massive, two stories high, the walls decorated with paintings in the French Rococo manner. Though as Daniel peered at one more closely, he reassessed: they were originals, undoubtedly brought over from France, as were the majority of the furnishings and other decorations, he'd wager. Probably even the marble under his feet.

Where was Rupert? The sole reason he was at the Bradleys' monster of a house—and the elaborate exterior matched the opulence of the interior; there were pointed *towers* on the thing—was to support his friend through what undoubtedly would be a spectacle of an engagement announcement.

An added bonus, of course, was that this was a social event at which he was unlikely to run into Genevieve Stewart, given her family history with the Bradleys. For almost two weeks, he had expected his revelation about his origins to result in a story in the paper, but as with their encounter in the alley, she'd surprised him yet again.

Which was both impressive and disquieting, in equal measure. He wanted her to stay away from investigating Robin Hood, even if portions of his past had to be the proverbial sacrificial lambs. So far, she hadn't taken the bait.

Daniel delved deeper into the crush of bodies representing many of New York's most exclusive families. Except for the Astors, of course. The Bradleys were still new money, after all, and far too gauche for the likes of the closest thing New York had to royalty.

"Mr. McCaffrey," Mrs. Bradley trilled, emerging from the crowd in a blinding flash of peacock-blue silk and a headdress with matching feathers. "How wonderful to see you. It's so refreshing when gentlemen support our young ladies by attending functions. So many are too concerned with business matters to keep these late hours, you know," she added with a significant glance at the cigar-chewing man dutifully trailing in her wake. "I believe you know my husband?"

Amos Bradley clasped Daniel's hand in a shake so firm it was just short of uncomfortable. He had met the man on several other occasions, and liked him. Amos was, physically, everything his wife was not: a towering figure with a large, well-earned belly, in contrast to Elmira's diminutive, bony form. He moved and spoke slowly and with deliberation, while she darted and feinted among the crowd, her sharp eyes constantly roving, seeking the person or persons she believed could best advance her family's place in society.

True to form, Mrs. Bradley excused herself and flitted away, leaving the men to converse alone. Amos watched her disappear, then slid his heavy-lidded gaze back to Daniel, lazily chomping his unlit cigar.

Daniel wasn't fooled by Amos's somnolent manner. His indolent appearance and large size had initially lulled many of New York's businessmen into believing Amos's mind was as slow as his body, but Daniel knew Amos possessed one of the sharpest brains in all of industry. He'd built a massive fortune, reportedly from nothing, on copper mines in Montana. In business practices he was known to be precise, ruthless, and exacting.

He was also quite funny. And though most of society merely tolerated his wife, he seemed truly smitten with her. Part of how the Bradleys had climbed the social ladder so far, so fast, was by husbands badgering their wives into accepting Mrs. Bradley's invitations, as the men were keen to stay in Amos's good graces.

"Seems your friend will marry my daughter," Amos said, watching Daniel with assessing eyes.

He nodded in return. "I have heard so, yes."

Amos nodded back, moving the cigar from one corner of his mouth to the other. "I know he's penniless, despite that fancy title everyone's so impressed with." Daniel could not think of a suitable reply to this. Rupert kept up appearances, but since his father had died the year prior and his already-meager allowance had stopped, Daniel had taken over paying for much of his friend's wardrobe and his bachelor quarters at the Benedick, a lodging house frequented mainly by artists on Washington Square's east side.

"He'd better be good to her, or I'll rip his head off," Amos remarked, as if commenting on the flower arrangements. A frisson of unease settled between Daniel's shoulders. He knew, despite the casual delivery, that Amos Bradley was serious as death.

"Make sure he knows, will you?" Amos continued, allowing his lazy gaze to travel the ballroom.

"I shall," Daniel replied, just as neutrally. He did not want to make an enemy of Amos Bradley.

"Elmira's happy." Whether Amos meant with the engagement, the ball, or both was unclear.

"I'm pleased to hear it."

"What do you think of the old pile of bricks?" Amos gestured around the room with his cigar before firmly clamping it between his teeth again.

"It's impressive," Daniel replied honestly.

"Elmira wanted it to look like a French chateau."

Daniel made a noncommittal noise of assent.

"She's happy," Amos remarked again. "Once Esmie marries, she wants to put Rupert's family crest on the door." Daniel had noticed a crest upon his entrance and now realized it had been fabricated for the Bradleys. "Speaking of, there's your friend." Amos languidly gestured his grand head behind Daniel's shoulder. "Go tell him what I said, won't you."

It was a command rather than a suggestion.

Daniel obeyed, turning on his heel and making his way through the press of bodies toward Rupert, who pounced upon him gratefully.

"Daniel! I've been looking for you. Come, we need to speak." Daniel fought his way through the crowd again, following his friend out of the ballroom, across the grand entryway, and through a massive mahogany door into a hushed library.

Rupert shut the door firmly behind him and leaned his back against it. The library had walls of bookshelves that spanned floor to ceiling along all four walls, with what appeared to be recessed reading nooks carefully inserted halfway down each wall, and large, comfortable-looking leather armchairs arranged in the center of the room. As Rupert made his way to a sideboard and poured each of them a large snifter of brandy, Daniel inspected the books curiously. They were old, leather-bound volumes, but the shades of each binding had been carefully coordinated, and Daniel wondered whether they were actually read or simply for show.

Rupert handed Daniel his glass with a hefty sigh. "I had to get a moment of quiet."

Daniel accepted his drink. "How are you holding up?"

Rupert waved the air about him, dismissing the question. "How are *you*?"

He'd confided in Rupert about Genevieve, and Gerry Knox's body in the alley, and about his run-in with Tommy Meade. His old friend was perhaps the one person alive, with the exception of his cousin Kathleen, who knew his true origins.

Who knew how he'd inherited Jacob's fortune.

"I don't think she's here," Daniel replied, swirling his brandy. Rupert raised his brows.

"That's a stroke of luck. Do you think she's getting closer?"

"I'm not sure. I thought I'd put her off, but . . . I don't know. She's tenacious."

"At least your pursuer is attractive." Rupert snorted into his own glass. "Can't say the same for mine."

Daniel was shocked. Rupert was often flippant, but this unkindness was unlike him.

"Don't be an ass," he said shortly. "Where is your intended?"

"She's around here somewhere, buried under mountains of yellow shiny stuff." Rupert gestured wildly at the area around his neck and shoulders in an apparent attempt to visually describe the offending gown. "Looks like a pile of scrambled egg." He shot Daniel an accusing look. "Why is it that you Americans insist upon everything being so over-the-top?"

"We're inspired by the grandeur of our own landscape?" Daniel suggested, his reply falling on deaf ears as Rupert built his complaint into a tirade.

"God, man, the misery of it. You don't know the teas, the musicales, the luncheons I've had to endure these past weeks. Esmie's all right, I guess; I wouldn't know, the girl hardly says two words together. We're rarely without that shrew of a mother of hers, who talks enough for the whole city, and the both of them always decked out in the most garish of getups." Rupert closed his eyes briefly, jaw muscles clenching for a brief moment. When he opened his eyes again, he smiled brightly at Daniel. "But congratulate me, my good friend. She's now wearing my grandmother's diamond." Rupert stared into his drink for a moment, pondering. Daniel allowed the silence to unfold between them, letting Rupert gather his thoughts.

"We've nothing, mate, you know that, don't you?" Rupert glanced at Daniel inquisitively. "My family, I mean. Not a sodding farthing. Father squandered it all. The entire Milton fortune." Daniel, who had visited Rupert's crumbling family estate during school holidays, nodded somberly. "And if it was just me, I'd say blast it all and try my luck in the West, or take up some trade, or . . . I don't know." He looked at Daniel helplessly. "But I've got younger sisters. And a mother. And I'm the only one who can carry on the goddamn family name." Rupert's jaw muscles clenched again, and Daniel noticed his friend's knuckles whitening as he gripped his glass as well. Daniel tensed, wondering if he'd have to make his excuses and take Rupert home before his friend did something he'd regret. But even as he reached out to touch Rupert's elbow, suggest they find a quiet tavern where they could talk until he was calm, Rupert relaxed again, and offered Daniel a lazy half smile.

"And I'm a coward. And I like good food, and good champagne. So I'll marry the scrawny wench dressed in egg yolk, force myself to bed her a few times, and perhaps I'll get lucky and she'll insist upon spending a lot of time in the country, doing whatever it is she likes to do." With another bitter smile, Rupert tossed back his drink and headed toward the sideboard for another. "They do keep good liquor in the house, I'll give that . . ."

Rupert stopped abruptly, reddening in the face and looking over Daniel's shoulder in shock. Daniel turned and saw Esmie standing behind him, having just emerged from one of the shadowed reading nooks, and by the stricken look on her face, she'd overheard everything.

"Esmie," Rupert said in a harsh whisper, looking stricken himself. "Please, Esmie, I didn't mean . . ."

Esmie stood half in the nook and half out, her hand over her mouth and her face deathly pale. She held her hand out to stop him from speaking, then slowly straightened her spine and lifted her chin, some-how looking dignified under mounds of orange-yellow lace. She suddenly appeared much older than her twenty-four years.

"Yes, you did mean it, every word," she said in a low, halting voice. Tears pooled in her eyes and threatened to overflow. "You know, I don't particularly wish to marry you either. And you know, I . . . I don't pick out my own clothes," she blurted. The tears that had been threatening began to stream down her face, and Esmie turned on her heel and quickly but quietly left the room.

Cursing softly, Rupert followed her out the door, thrusting his half-poured glass at Daniel as he left. Daniel placed both their glasses on a nearby table and started after their retreating forms.

Rather than returning to the ballroom, Esmie turned right and hurried down the entryway, past the grand main staircase and towards the back of the house, Rupert hot on her heels. Daniel moved to follow but was blocked by a hand grasping his upper arm. He whirled, nearly colliding his nose with that of Genevieve Stewart, who jerked her face back the spare inches in barely enough time to avoid a painful impact.

"Leave them be," she said, eyes sliding past his face, appearing to assess the situation in one quick glance. "Let them work things out on their own. They'll have to get used to it, if they're to be married."

Daniel quashed the urge to rip his arm from her clasp and hurry after his friend. His loyalty to Rupert ran deep, but he knew Genevieve was right. She removed her hand of her own accord and stepped back, smoothing the front of her gown.

She looked beautiful. He made this observation begrudgingly, but it was the truth. Her moss-green gown perfectly suited her coloring. He liked that her skin had a slight duskiness to it, as if she spent time outdoors without a hat. And what was revealed of her arms above the long, cream-colored gloves she wore suggested strength, the muscles gently delineated.

Genevieve raised a gentle brow at his scrutiny, and Daniel felt a light flush on the back of his neck from being caught staring.

"I didn't think you'd be here," he said, overly gruff to cover his embarrassment.

"I came here to find you," she replied.

A small chuff escaped before he could stop it. He ought to be used to her bluntness by now.

"And why are you seeking me? Shouldn't you be following the money, as I recommended?"

"I'm not sure why you remain under the delusion that I have any obligation to heed your advice, Mr. McCaffrey. I go where my story leads me, and tonight it has led me, again, back to you."

He felt a smile begin to tug at the corner of his mouth. "And round and round we go."

"Indeed."

"What is today's lead, Miss Palmer? Has one of your sources revealed where I purchase my socks, and you believe this is front-page news?" Her shock showed on her face, and Daniel felt a quick pang for deliberately mocking the types of stories she was typically assigned.

Now who is being unkind? She was a good reporter and he knew it. But desperate times called for desperate measures, and he was—apparently—ungentlemanly enough to hit below the belt if needed.

Her chin raised a notch, and she set her gorgeous mouth into a firm line.

God, he admired her backbone.

"Theresa Dolan is my lead, in fact. You never told me Reginald Cotswold was a friend."

"You never asked."

"Nor that Jacob Van Joost paid for your education."

He remained silent. Seconds ticked into a full minute in the Bradleys' entryway, noise of the ongoing ball drifting through the walls.

It was she who broke the silence. "Mr. Cotswold wasn't happy with the committee," she admitted softly. *Interesting.* "That seems significant," she continued.

"It does."

"There's more." She was watching him carefully. "A valuable item was stolen the night of his death. A Russian box inlaid with rubies and diamonds, forming an Orthodox cross. And he didn't pass in his sleep, but in his study, where the box was kept."

Daniel was careful to keep his face an impassive mask. It did him no good to reveal how painful it was to hear about Reginald's death.

"Keep following the money, Genevieve," he said quietly, well aware only a doorway separated them from the majority of New York society.

Her brown eyes flared. "How is it all connected? Help me," she urged.

An unseen clock chimed the stroke of midnight, and the doors to the ballroom were abruptly flung open. Waves of chatter and music washed over them as partygoers began to spill into the entryway, packing around Genevieve and Daniel, jostling them until they were quite separated. He kept his eyes on hers across the crowded space, though. He could see her lovely bare collarbones rise and fall with her deepening breath, noted the tension that squared her jaw.

She stared back at him with an intensity that might have brought a lesser man to his knees.

Something kept drawing them together, some unseen strand of fate that intertwined her path with his. He wasn't sure to what purpose yet, or whether these entangled threads boded well or ill, but there was no longer any denying their presence. Secrets he had kept in the dark for decades were being teased out of him and into the light, and something about Genevieve Stewart was the reason. He'd given up on religion long ago but was Irish enough to believe he had a destiny to fulfill. And whatever it was, this woman was now part of it.

A hush drew over the crowd as Mr. and Mrs. Bradley, accompanied by Esmie and Rupert, descended partway down the vast staircase. The musicians in the adjacent ballroom ceased playing, and the crowd gazed at the party assembled on the stairs expectantly. Genevieve cut her eyes from his, turning her attention briefly to a young, dark-haired woman who emerged from the crowd at her elbow, then to the group assembled on the stairs. Daniel followed suit, noting that Esmie, while still pale, appeared composed. Daniel was probably the only person at the ball who could interpret the tightness around Rupert's eyes.

Amos launched into a speech welcoming the crowd, gearing up toward his formal announcement of the engagement. As Rupert had said, it was just what had to be done. His friend had, in essence, lived on the good graces of hostesses for years now, transforming himself from the gangly, awkward youth Daniel had first met at age thirteen into the suave, urbane party guest he was now. As Mrs. Bradley had hinted, there was a constant shortage of men at events, particularly during the winter season, and Rupert had gladly filled the role, exchanging his flirtations and wit for free food and drink. But his father had finally died, he'd inherited the earldom, and the weight of familial responsibility had come crashing down on his shoulders.

Daniel listened to Amos with half an ear, shifting his attention from the spectacle on the staircase to the young woman in the green dress, then back again. Genevieve's shoulders were set, her head was held high, and she appeared to be listening politely, but her eyes, too, discreetly drew across the crowd at the base of the stairs toward him again and again. During one of these glances, their gazes caught and held, broken only when the assembled crowd burst into applause.

Rupert managed a smile as the engagement was made official and reached down to clasp Esmie's gloved hand in his own. She looked at the hand wrapped around hers, then at Rupert's face. The tiniest, startled flash of a smile darted across her face in response, there and gone like the quicksilver of a tadpole glinting beneath a pond's surface. In that wink of a moment, her entire face changed. It seemed to light from within, illuminating a delicacy of features he hadn't previously noticed. She had a slender, slightly aquiline nose, and a sweetly rosy mouth set over a graceful jaw. In fact, for a split second the Bradley heiress appeared rather . . . beautiful. Daniel's breath caught unexpectedly, he was so surprised by the sudden shift.

But then her face collapsed into misery again, her cheeks flaring patches of red as she blushed furiously at the attention. She pulled her hand from Rupert's and clasped both hands in front of her, smiling uncertainly at the crowd. Rupert gently regained the lost hand and led her down the stairs, into throngs of waiting well-wishers.

Daniel wondered what had transpired between them after the incident in the library. Whatever was said, it appeared a fragile truce had been reached.

"Ladies and gentlemen, while we have you . . ." Amos's booming voice cut through the clamor, and the crowd quieted again. "You all know I'm not from these parts." A light laugh rose from the group, though to Daniel's ears it held an undercurrent of anxiety. Drawing attention to one's status as an outsider was usually the last thing people wanted. He saw a frown furrow Elmira's forehead.

"But I've been in New York long enough to know that this city's politics could use some fresh blood. Yes, Tweed was sent down some time ago, but there's still work to be done. And seeing as how it's the night of my daughter's engagement and you're all enjoying that champagne on me, I'll ask you to indulge me a moment and give a quick listen to mayoral candidate Thomas Meade."

Every hair on Daniel's arms seemed to stand at once, and he could feel the muscles in his face clench with anger.

Tommy was *here*? How on earth had he wrangled an invitation to a society ball?

The crowd appeared a bit confused, and Daniel saw some other angry faces—including that of William Vanderbilt, whose narrowed eyes betrayed how ambushed he felt—but most of the assembled guests offered polite applause as Tommy, in a surprisingly well-cut set of evening clothes, materialized from the throng and mounted a few steps, waving toward the guests in a practiced political way.

Daniel took a quick scan of the crowd, making sure to check the corners. Sure enough, the same henchman from the street was sulking against a far wall, staring straight at him. Daniel locked his eyes with the bodyguard's muddy brown ones until the man shifted his gaze back to Tommy. Daniel noticed the henchman catch Tommy's attention before nodding back in Daniel's direction. A slight smile played on the corners of Tommy's mouth when he saw him, and he gave Daniel a subtle nod of acknowledgment.

"I like Tommy," Amos said, allowing his gaze to sweep the crowd. "Like me, this isn't quite his world. I ask you give him a few minutes, and then we'll all keep dancing the night away."

The majority of the guests settled in, resigned to their fate. Daniel was trapped in the middle of the press of bodies; there was no way to fight his way out of the entryway without drawing attention to himself. As Tommy began spouting his drivel, Daniel shot a quick look toward Genevieve, unsurprised to find her watching him rather than Tommy. She made a face of concern toward him.

Is everything all right? the look clearly asked.

Damn, he must look angrier than he'd realized. Daniel softened his features and gave a quick headshake.

It's nothing, his gesture said in return.

Turning his attention toward the stairs, Daniel had the barest of moments to comprehend he had just partaken in an unspoken exchange with someone with whom he ought to be on the utmost guard, when a loud voice cut across Tommy's practiced political cadences.

Elmira Bradley's furrow of concern had changed to outright fury. "I think we've had enough lies, Mr. Meade. My husband is at least honest about being from Montana. Now why don't you share with everyone who you really are?"

CHAPTER 10

Tommy paused midsentence as the onlookers froze. He offered a thin smile at his hostess's query, but Daniel knew him well and could see fury matching Elmira's lurking behind his eyes.

He was not happy at being interrupted, and if Daniel guessed correctly, even less so about being challenged.

"I wasn't aware I was being duplicitous, madam. I'm very open about how I immigrated to this great nation from Ireland as a boy. This country has a long tradition of men making themselves from nothing. And while I wasn't born in a log cabin"—Tommy paused, offering a significant look to the crowd—"I do come from the more impoverished parts of this fair city."

"No shame in that," Elmira said, her mouth set in a thin line. "But I thought you should enlighten these good folks about your gang ties."

A collective gasp arose. Daniel stared at Elmira, thunderstruck, as she placed her hands on her hips and stared down the man known to New York's underworld as the Terror of the East Side.

God Almighty, what is this woman doing? How on earth would someone like her know about gang life in New York? And why was she publicly exposing Tommy? There were plenty of wealthy people who skimmed the surface of gang activity in the city—those with an addiction to opium, or unscrupulous businessmen hoping to make a quick dollar—but the bulk of the city's elite hadn't the faintest idea of the elaborate Byzantine hierarchy and affiliations that ruled the town's extensive gang network, nor of how so much of that network had a hand in the gears and cogs of industry that made the city run.

If not at the top of that network, Tommy was close. The men in his position almost always had unofficial ties with City Hall, but Tommy was the first to have actually tried to *occupy* City Hall. Publicly calling out his allegiance to the Oyster Knife gang was a dangerous business. Daniel would bet Elmira Bradley had no idea how dangerous, for if she had known she'd have run screaming from her own staircase.

Daniel felt a nudge at his elbow and found that Rupert had silently joined him, handing him a fresh brandy, which he gulped gratefully. The atmosphere in the entryway was thick with tension as Elmira and the majority of the city's upper crust waited breathlessly for Tommy to respond.

Tommy assumed a thoughtful expression. "The misdeeds of my youth, madam. Unfortunately, so many young boys from the less fortunate parts of town find themselves embroiled in similar circumstances. It's all long in my past now. After all, I am not the only one among us who is not from your ranks originally. Why, I remember when Danny McCaffrey there and I used to run barefoot like young heathens through the streets of the Lower East Side."

Tommy's sharp teeth glinted in the gaslight as he pretended to be oblivious to the shocked gasps that rose from the well-heeled guests. Elegantly coiffed and distinguished gray heads swung in seeming unison to stare at Daniel.

"There was a whole group of us that ran together right around the Draft Riots, weren't there, Danny?" Tommy chuckled and swept his arms open wide. "Did you ever think we'd wind up in a place like this? Only in America, right?"

So this was the game, was it? Expose his past, attempt to divert any questions about himself onto Daniel?

Daniel didn't really care if anyone knew where he originated; hell, his parents had had twice the integrity of most of the people in this room. But he'd promised the memory of his beloved sister Maggie never to tell how he had become heir to the Van Joost fortune, and his past and the inheritance were so intertwined it had been better to keep it quiet. All that had changed when he decided to reveal his origins to Genevieve at Delmonico's. Since then, he'd been prepared for whatever fallout might occur.

He hadn't, however, counted on his past being broadcast in this venue rather than in print. Daniel calculated his options.

The real question was, how much did Tommy know?

Two could play at this game.

He forced himself to keep his manner easy and maintain a calm smile, aware that the entire party was now watching him in fascination. Aware of Genevieve's anxious face turned his way. "Of course I remember running wild as a young boy; didn't we all?" He allowed a small frown to furrow his brow.

"But I don't particularly remember you and me associating that much as children. As I recall, your games and pursuits were not to my taste." He held Tommy's eyes, sending his own warning.

The heads whipped back to Tommy, standing on the stairs.

Tommy's smile tightened almost imperceptibly, but he rocked back on his heels and peered at the ceiling. "Maybe not," he allowed. "But here we are regardless. Of course, money helps. And you do have all that money. Jacob Van Joost took you in as a young boy, didn't he? You and your sister . . . Margaret, wasn't it?"

The heads turned back his way. Daniel nodded in studied nonchalance. "Yes, he did. Margaret and I had no family left. Jacob was very kind." The lies slid from his mouth as he continued to regard Tommy mildly, as if the secrets of his youth were not being spilled in front of half of New York society. If Tommy knew the truth, he would reveal it now.

But Tommy didn't. He simply widened his sharklike smile and turned back to the crowd of openmouthed spectators. "So you see, my friends, a man's origins have no bearing on his ability to *make* something of himself in this country. I ask you, what could be more American than that? And as mayor, I promise . . ."

Daniel discreetly glanced in both directions, and it was clear Tommy's gambit had worked. Wide, greedy eyes behind raised fans and astonished expressions kept sliding his way, then instantly retracting, then sliding back again. The general titter of whispers was so strong it nearly drowned out Tommy's speech.

This ball was done for him. Rather than face a thousand questions he wasn't ready to answer, Daniel began to politely move through the crowd toward the door. He could hear Rupert's voice over his left shoulder as his friend followed, casually answering some of the queries guests murmured in his ear as he passed.

"Of course I knew, didn't everyone? No, not that big a shock, not really. Yes, we'll speak later . . ."

Somehow Rupert conjured his belongings, and a footman held open his coat. As he turned slightly to facilitate its donning, he caught sight of Genevieve, who, like most of the party, wasn't even pretending to listen to Tommy now but was watching Daniel depart. The apology in her eyes was accompanied by a slight rolling of the shoulders and a slight head tilt toward the stairs.

I'm sorry it happened this way.

He gave the barest of shrugs back and felt the corner of his mouth tilt into a half smile.

It's not your fault. It will be fine.

Another silent exchange. Once again, he felt the intractable pull between them, its tug soft but insistent. The heavy door closed at his back, and he left the cloying, overly warm space of the mansion behind him, taking in a lungful of crisp, clean air.

All his ghosts, it seemed, were coming home to roost, leaving him partially flayed and aching. He just hoped he could corral them before a certain reporter exposed him to the bone.

★ ★ ★

The barest smattering of polite applause greeted the end of Mr. Meade's speech, as a good portion of the guests had already dispersed. Genevieve had felt herself quite unable to move after Daniel's departure, seemingly rooted to her own private square of carpet as the other partygoers flowed around her, eager to return to the music and the food. From the ballroom, the band struck up a quadrille.

Her mind was racing. She would send a telegram to her editor immediately tomorrow morning. Or later this morning, as the case was. It was Sunday, but Arthur would want this information about a mayoral candidate right away. It exposed Daniel, but half of New York now knew what he'd revealed in private to her at Delmonico's.

"Shall we go in? I believe the supper is to be served soon," Callie said, interrupting her thoughts. "Perhaps we can find a quiet corner to talk," she whispered.

Genevieve shook her head. "No, not here. And I'm not hungry. Let's find Eliza for you. I'm going home. I need to think."

"Don't worry about me, darling. I ought to go bat my lashes at some of these gentlemen. Eliza and I shall call tomorrow." Callie squeezed her hand once, then allowed herself to be swallowed by the remaining guests filtering toward the ballroom.

As she didn't see a readily available servant about to fetch her cloak, Genevieve went against the current of the few guests still drifting toward the festivities and ventured toward the back of the house, past the massive staircase. She poked her head into what turned out to be a water closet, then tried the ornate door across the hall, hearing voices within.

"Excuse me, I'd like my—" She stopped abruptly, feeling herself flush. Amos and Elmira Bradley turned in unison and glared at her from the confines of what looked like a private study. Amos's face was red as a beet, his thick finger a mere inch from his wife's nose as he towered over her menacingly. Elmira's chin was raised and her arms were folded in front of her chest defiantly.

"Do pardon me," she managed to whisper before yanking the door closed again. Mortified to have interrupted a domestic squabble, most certainly over Elmira's challenging Mr. Meade, Genevieve picked up her skirts and hurried deeper into the recesses of the mansion, not daring to open any more doors, simply hoping someone would appear to help her.

This house was *enormous*. She turned down a hallway lined with paintings, only to find it dead-end at a closed door. Backtracking, she retraced her steps and tried turning left instead. Here she had more luck:

a murmur of chatter emerged from a partially open set of double doors, mingling with the sound of rattling dishes. The kitchen must be back this way, and surely there she could find someone to retrieve her cloak.

A maid bustled out of an opposite door as Genevieve entered, and she found, instead, Esmie, who was leaning against a large, marble-topped work space in the center of the room. If the other girl was surprised by her sudden appearance, she didn't let on, instead dipping a spoon into a silver bowl she held, frosty with condensation.

"Genevieve." The spoon emerged, containing chocolate ice cream. "How may I help?"

"What are you doing back here?" Genevieve asked, confused. This had become Esmie's unofficial engagement ball, after all. The rules of etiquette were quite strict, and Genevieve was sure they didn't involve the bride-to-be hiding in a kitchen eating ice cream. "I'm sure everyone would like to congratulate you in person. And, congratulations."

Esmie shrugged, a slender shoulder briefly emerging from and then disappearing back into a mountain of truly horrid orangish lace. "I wanted some ice cream. And as Mother won't let me have any, I came here to be alone."

If anything, Genevieve was even more confused. "Why are you not to have ice cream?"

Esmie looked her straight in the eye. "Mother doesn't want me to gain weight," she deadpanned.

Genevieve regarded her dubiously. It would take gallons and gallons of ice cream, eaten every day straight for ten years, to make Esmie Bradley into anything close to plump, let along large. One could hardly tell what her body looked like under the layers of terrible clothes she typically wore, but it was obvious she was unfashionably slim, with seemingly no curves on her slight—one could almost label it skinny—frame.

Truth be told, the girl could stand to eat quite a bit of ice cream.

"Is she truly worried?" Genevieve asked delicately, not wishing to offend.

Esmie shrugged again. "I was a plump child. Mother didn't seem to care when we lived in Montana. But once we moved here, she became so concerned with fitting in . . . well, curvy is certainly fashionable, but being too plump is not." She took another bite and closed her eyes in apparent bliss. Keeping her eyes closed, she murmured around a mouthful, "Mother doesn't really do things in half measures."

"I've noticed," Genevieve responded, hiding her astonishment at the other girl's behavior. This was more than she'd ever heard Esmie say at one time since, well . . . ever. Esmie opened her eyes and resumed eating her ice cream in a slightly more restrained manner. "May I ask—why didn't Polly Palmer write about the theft of Sarah Huffington's ring? It would have made sense, seeing as how you were at the ball."

Genevieve's mouth dropped open. "How did you know I'm Polly Palmer?"

Esmie favored her with a glance just short of withering. "Everyone knows."

It wasn't scandalous, her job, nor secret—women had been writing for the magazines since the 1830s—but it was unconventional for someone of her social status, and it did cause gossip. Ah well, let them gossip. Genevieve realized Esmie was looking expectantly at her for an answer, spoon paused in waiting.

"My editor wouldn't let me," she admitted, still feeling the sting of being passed over for the job.

Esmie nodded sympathetically and turned her attention back to her bowl. "Did you see her parading about tonight? Wearing crimson, of all colors." She took another spoonful and kept the utensil in her mouth for a moment longer than was really polite.

Bewildered, Genevieve asked, "Who are we discussing?"

"Sarah Huffington, *of course*. She seems to be milking the attention around the theft for all it's worth, flirting with every gentleman present. Eligible or not." Esmie scraped her spoon against the bottom of the silver bowl, the sound causing Genevieve to wince.

Oh. Sarah Huffington and Rupert were friendly. Perhaps this was a display of jealousy?

"I thought Sarah was rather well entangled with Ernest Clark," Genevieve ventured. "That's what the Hood's letter said . . ."

Esmie nodded, tapping her spoon against her lips once. "Oh yes. For some months now. That was hardly news."

"I hadn't heard," Genevieve admitted. She refrained from mentioning that Eliza and Callie had seemed unaware of the affair as well.

"It was obvious to anyone who paid attention. You should get out more, Genevieve, if you wish to remain a journalist." As Genevieve reeled slightly from this sharp bit of advice, Esmie's manner softened. "I'm sorry, that was rude."

Esmie walked to the far end of the room, where a large steel sink sat, and began washing her bowl. "The benefits of being a wallflower," she explained over her shoulder, wiping the interior of the bowl with a cloth. "Nobody sees you. You blend in. But *you* see."

She turned, wiping her hands neatly on the cloth before hanging it on a peg and placing the bowl in an open cupboard above the sink. All evidence of the ice cream was erased.

"You see *everything.*" Esmie tilted her head and gave Genevieve a long, appraising look. "I know all kinds of secrets."

Unexpected gooseflesh suddenly prickled Genevieve's arms. She cleared her throat uncertainly. "My friend Callie said she saw you at Mrs. Brown's recently."

"Yes, I decided to get my own costume for the Porters' upcoming fancy dress ball." Esmie raised her chin a notch, unconsciously mimicking the stance Genevieve had seen her mother hold in the study a few moments prior. The gooseflesh intensified. "Are you planning to attend?"

"I hadn't planned on it, no."

"You should have seen the monstrosity Mother wanted me to wear. The costume of a kitten. Bands of white fur, some of it fashioned into a tail"—Esmie gestured toward her nether regions, blushing—"and a headdress consisting of an *actual* stuffed cat."

"Oh." There really wasn't anything Genevieve could add. It sounded horrific.

"I would be a bigger laughingstock than usual. I told Mother the bookstore was holding the new Stevenson novel for me, and I went to Mrs. Brown's instead." Her chin rose higher. "I wasn't sure they'd accommodate me, as I had no appointment. But Mrs. Brown was very kind."

Genevieve nodded, glad to hear the cat costume would not be making an appearance at the ball.

"Maybe you could accompany me to Mrs. Brown's sometime?" Emsie continued in a tentative voice. "I need new clothes. Mother has always picked them. Now that I'm to be a countess, I should like to choose my own. Different colors. Styles that allow for more movement. I should quite like to try a bicycle, come spring," Esmie's gaze drifted wistfully toward the large rectangular window set above the sink. Snow was swirling in the lamplight outside.

"I should like that," Genevieve replied politely, not sure if she would like it at all. She was trying hard to reconcile an image of Esmie Bradley, possibly the least graceful young lady in the Astor 400, on a bicycle. "But as for tonight, I do need to be off. I was just looking for my cloak."

"One more question, if I may. And then I'll fetch someone for your cloak. How well do you know Rupert?"

Genevieve hadn't thought the conversation could get any odder, but obviously she had been mistaken. "Not terribly well," she admitted, a bit taken aback. "We're friendly acquaintances. My friend Callie Maple knows him better. But surely you know him better than anyone now, Esmie."

The other girl rolled her eyes a bit ruefully, then leaned against the edge of the sink and began toying with her sash. "You know how it is. It's a marriage of convenience. I have the money, and Mother wants a title. *Mother.*" She bit the word off with surprising force. "Well, that's one good thing about this marriage: I'll be across the ocean from her, once Rupert and I move to England."

Esmie took a deep breath. "I can marry him, if I must, and it appears I must. But I do want to know . . ." She lifted her gaze to meet Genevieve's. "Is he a kind man?"

Genevieve's stomach dropped a notch at the thought of having to marry a man she barely knew. Sending a quick internal prayer of gratitude toward her lenient, eccentric parents, Genevieve pondered what she knew of Rupert Milton, the sixth Earl of Umberland. He liked parties. And pretty women. He liked champagne but not, so much as she'd heard, to excess. She believed he enjoyed pranks and silly, child-ish games somewhat; she recalled Callie telling her a long story—she'd only been half paying attention—about Rupert creating an entirely new version of lawn croquet at the DeWitts' house party in Newport last summer, some nonsense where all the players had to sing a line of verse from their favorite song if they lost their shot. It had been, by all accounts, ridiculous fun, and some of the gentlemen had turned to slightly bawdy songs, to the delighted shock of the ladies present. It had been a bit of a scandal, but a very mild one that only furthered Rupert's reputation as a delightful, if slightly unpredictable, guest. And that was Rupert to the core, Genevieve mused. Or at least what she knew about him. Delightful, slightly unpredictable, with a hint of benign scandal. And titled, of course.

Esmie nodded as Genevieve relayed this information. "And he needs a wife. A rich one."

"I believe so," she agreed, gently. She tried to visualize Esmie and Rupert living in the same house, eating breakfast together. Going for an evening stroll. Arguing in a friendly way over an article in the news-paper, as her parents often did. Try as she might—and she didn't want to try very hard—picturing Rupert and Esmie in any kind of embrace was nearly an impossible task, and her mind skittered away from the mere idea. "Perhaps the worst you might find him is"—Genevieve groped for the right word—"inattentive."

Esmie sighed deeply and unhappily. "I know," she replied, so qui-etly Genevieve could barely hear her. "He'll force himself to bed me a few times; then perhaps he'll get lucky and I'll insist upon spending a lot of time in the country, doing whatever it is I like to do." She appeared deep in thought for a moment, and Genevieve wondered if there was a polite way to inquire after her cloak again, but then Esmie drew herself up with such suddenness that Genevieve took an instinc-tive step backward. The other woman's eyes were hard, and the fury in her face was downright frightening.

"I like to do all *kinds* of things," Esmie said, drawing the sentence out so it suggested a mountain of innuendo. Genevieve resisted the urge to draw a hand to her throat, the change was so severe. Esmie drew back her shoulders and narrowed her eyes. "He can keep his silly songs," she spat.

Genevieve floundered for an appropriate response, stunned by Esmie's rage. Fortunately, Mrs. Bradley chose that moment to thunder into the kitchen.

"Esmie! I've been looking everywhere for you. People want to talk to you. What are you doing in the kitchen?" Elmira's inquisitive, bird-like gaze darted around the room, hovering with suspicion on the ice-box and then narrowing at Genevieve.

"I was looking for someone to find Genevieve's cloak. We fell to talking." Esmie's expression was once again bland as milk toast. She lied with a great deal of ease, it seemed.

"I'm glad to see Miss Stewart has found her way. Did you girls have a nice chat?" Elmira eyed them both. Despite being twenty-six years old and not the progeny of Mrs. Bradley, Genevieve shrank from the older woman's glare, feeling guilty by association about the ice cream and still slightly stunned by Esmie's wrath. She tried to look as innocent as possible and nodded enthusiastically, desperately wishing to be gone before any more Bradley family drama ensued.

Esmie looked mildly at her mother, as though she'd never even heard of ice cream. "Quite."

"I'll have our housekeeper retrieve your things, Miss Stewart." Elmira's lip curled a bit in distaste at the name. "Come along, both of you."

Elmira Bradley swept from her kitchen without a backward glance, confident that both young women would follow in her wake. And they did, Genevieve allowing Esmie to pass ahead of her and walk closer to her mother.

It was the last time she saw Elmira Bradley alive.

CHAPTER 11

Genevieve sullenly pressed the button for the fifth floor, huffing a frustrated breath as the elevator doors clanged close.

She had been sure, *sure* that Arthur would allow her to write the piece on Thomas Meade's gang ties, but her editor had assigned it to Clive. Again. Which, *again*, made no sense, as she had heard the entire exchange between Mr. Meade and Mrs. Bradley. There had already been a teaser piece penned by Clive in yesterday's evening edition.

Well, Arthur Horace was about to get a piece of her mind. He was going to know just who he was dealing—

The elevator doors clanged back open, and Genevieve stepped into chaos.

The newsroom was in an uproar. Secretaries were rushing from desk to desk, frantically gathering files, transferring them to the appropriate reporters, and delivering what appeared to be urgent telegrams. One journalist was shouting into the newspaper's telephone while others barked orders at their assistants. Genevieve walked in amazement to her desk, dodging newsboys and secretaries. Once there, she slowly removed her yellow gloves and surveyed the scene. A quick glance through the glass doors of Mr. Horace's office revealed that Clive was standing in front of the editor's desk, nodding while the older man gestured wildly.

To her surprise, Luther was in there as well.

What on earth was going on?

Genevieve grabbed the elbow of a secretary hurrying past, her arms full of files. "What happened?"

The shorter, bright-blonde woman looked at Genevieve in impatient excitement. "Robin Hood struck again. The letter arrived on Mr. Horace's desk not five minutes ago."

Genevieve gasped. "Who? Who did he rob this time?" she demanded, her eyes flying back to the door. Luther's presence in Arthur's office took on new meaning.

Luther covered homicide. Had someone been *killed*?

"The Bradleys. Miss, I've got to get these to Mr. Huxton . . ." The secretary pulled her elbow out of Genevieve's grasp and scuttled across the room, files precariously slipping.

A thousand possibilities, a thousand suspects, flashed in her mind's eye.

Anyone who had been at the ball could be the thief. Anyone.

Who had died?

She sat down with a clunk, keeping an eye on the door to Arthur's office. Both reporters with him were now nodding as Arthur pointed a finger first at one, then the other. She picked up a pencil and thrummed it against her desk out of sheer nerves.

Finally, the door opened. She turned to a stack of papers piled before her, pretending to be engrossed as Clive passed with a smirk, but looked up and caught Luther's attention with a little wave.

"Hey, toots." Her friend sat heavily on the edge of her desk. He removed a blue handkerchief from an inner pocket and mopped his brow.

"Robin Hood? At the Bradleys'?" It almost felt as though she should be whispering, even though the entire newsroom had heard.

"Yeah," confirmed Luther, looking at her somberly.

"But why were you in the meeting? Luther, has someone . . . ?" It was hard to form the question.

He nodded soundlessly.

Genevieve's breath caught in her throat. "Who?"

"Elmira Bradley." Luther blew out a breath and looked back toward Arthur's office. "This all just got a lot more serious, Genevieve."

"No," she gasped. Again, unbidden images from Saturday night popped into her head. Amos, shaking his finger in Elmira's face. Mr. Meade, narrowing his eyes at his hostess from the stairs. Esmie, spitting the word "*Mother*" in such contempt. Elmira's narrow back, peacock feathers bobbing, retreating down a long hallway toward the front entrance of the Bradley mansion. "*Murdered?*"

"Oh yeah." He did lower his voice to a whisper. "Her throat was slit. It's not public yet, so keep it quiet."

Genevieve stifled a second gasp. Unbelievable. Mrs. Bradley dead. She hadn't liked the woman, but she hadn't wished murder—a *cut throat*—upon her.

"When?"

"They found her early this morning and called the police."

A shudder passed through her. It was hard to shake the image of Elmira lying dead, her neck a gaping wound. "The ball was Saturday. The police think she was killed sometime Sunday night?"

"Or early this morning. The coroner will try to determine a more precise time of death."

The language of murder—*time of death, coroner, throat slit*—was making Genevieve's head spin. She knew that for Luther these terms were bread and butter, but they were a far cry from the hats and parasols in which she normally traded.

Genevieve straightened in her chair and removed her hand from her mouth, where it had flown of its own accord. If this was what she wanted to do, she had better get used to such language.

"But was Robin Hood involved? What does the letter say?"

Luther shrugged a bit. "The same. That's the weird thing. The sins of greed, ostentatiousness, you know. What the Hood always says. Doesn't say anything about killing anyone." He peered at Genevieve gravely.

Her mind instantly jumped to Reginald Cotswold. She thought of what her colleagues at the paper *didn't* know, and what the police had chosen to ignore as the rantings of a grief-stricken elderly lady. That something had been taken from his house. That Reginald had not died in bed but was found in the room where that something had been kept.

"What was stolen?"

He shook his head. "We don't know yet. The family reported the death, and I guess they're being questioned by the police at home right now. They didn't mention anything having been stolen, so far as we know. But we have the letter; the Hood says he was there."

"Do the police know yet?"

"They must by now. Arthur telegraphed as soon as the letter arrived."

As if on cue, the elevator doors opened noisily and silence hushed the office, the newspaper employees watching in unison as Commissioner Simons strode through the doors and marched between the desks toward Arthur's office, his face clenched in apparent rage. He slammed the door behind him so hard the glass panes seemed to tremble, and the wooden blinds within shut with a furious snap, blocking the workers' curious eyes. The muffled sounds of raised voices soon permeated the walls, and the noise in the office began to creep back toward its regular level.

"Blimey," Luther said, gazing at the closed door in awe. "He looked about to pop, he was so mad."

Genevieve exhaled, still trying to reconcile herself to this new reality. The one in which whoever was Robin Hood might be capable of *murder*.

And not just of Elmira Bradley, but perhaps of Reginald Cotswold also.

Perhaps, even, of an unfortunate man whose head had been smashed in an alley. She leaned forward and tugged her friend's sleeve.

"Luther, were you able to find out anything about that dead man? The one in Bottle Alley?"

He tore his attention from the arguing voices, which even through closed doors had noticeably risen in volume. "Yeah. His name was Gerald Knox, went by Gerry. He was pretty well known to the police, had a history of public drunkenness and petty theft. They're not changing their tune, mind," he warned, in response to her raised brows. "Cause of death is still the bottle."

Huh. Genevieve began to tap her pencil again, considering. Luther leaned forward, lowering his voice again.

"I did hear he somehow found out about that group the mayor put together. The one about housing conditions."

"The one that was never made public? How do you know about that?"

Luther rolled his eyes at her teasing. "Worst-kept secret in town. Anyway, on the day he died, your man Gerry showed up at City Hall, drunk as a lord, banging his fist on the reception desk and demanding to speak to the mayor about how cold his building was."

"*What?*"

"Yeah. The police had to physically eject him from the premises." Luther shrugged again. "Like I said, he had a history." He drew back his head and eyed her in a considering way. "What's all this about, Genevieve?"

Follow the money. The words echoed in her head, but outwardly she shook it.

"I don't know. Probably nothing. If it adds up to anything, you'll be the first to hear."

"Just be careful, toots." Luther hopped off her desk and fixed her with a concerned look. "Let me know if you need help with this nothing."

She smiled at him in return, a smile that sputtered out and faltered as he wove his way toward his own desk, no doubt to retrieve the things he needed before heading back to the police station in hopes of gleaning more information about Mrs. Bradley's death.

Genevieve heaved a worried sigh, then set her mouth with determination. As galling as the thought was, it was time to heed Daniel's advice.

★ ★ ★

Hours later, Genevieve looked up from her work at the small desk she had tucked herself into a back corner of the records room that held files relating to New York's most prominent members. She was dusty, tired, and disheartened.

Spread before her were files on several members of the elusive committee. As most of the men were old Knickerbockers, the paper had articles and journalists' notes on their respective subjects dating back decades. She frowned at the files, trying to puzzle out how Daniel's directive connected to the information contained in these dusty brown folders. *Of course* there were connections among the men, intricate spider webs of business and social ties that also stretched back decades; upper-class New York society was self-contained, the same families interacting and intermarrying for generations, hers included.

The only outlier in the group was Ernest Clark, the purported paramour of Sarah Huffington. Genevieve discontentedly flipped open his file, which was on top of the stack, and nudged the scant notes in there around again. A Wall Street *wunderkind*, Clark had become a begrudged favorite among many society hostesses: he was new money, to be sure, but he had plenty of it. He was also lively and charming, and possessed a slick sort of handsomeness that many of the season's new "buds," or debutantes, seemed to find attractive.

Flicking the folder shut, Genevieve leaned back in her chair and stretched. She idly wondered if Ernest would continue to be welcome at events, now that rumors of his affair with Sarah Huffington were public. And how those rumors would affect his dealings with Sarah's husband, Andrew. She sighed and plopped her chin in her hand. The machinations of society held as little interest for her now as they always had.

Ted Beekman. The file's label, written in an unknown secretary's neat, tidy script, slyly peeked out from underneath that of Ernest Clark. The handwritten name indicated it had been created some years ago, before the now-ubiquitous typewriters had begun occupying desktops with their collective squat presence.

She'd already looked within the file's dreary covers, had examined its contents, and had attempted to remain businesslike and dispassionate. But seeing the copious notes of Jackson Waglie, the late society reporter whose vicious, razor-sharp comments had made even the venerable Mrs. Astor quake in her slippers, on the details of her own defunct wedding had shaken her resolve. Waglie had been a stickler for decorum and tradition, and needless to say, the eccentricities of the Stewart clan had horrified him not a little. It was commonplace for society columns to build anticipation around an upcoming prominent wedding with articles detailing the plans and gifts. Upon Genevieve's insistence, her mother had dutifully supplied the particulars to Waglie and the *Globe*, though she'd claimed to have no idea why anyone would want to read about what the Winstons had gifted them.

Genevieve opened the folder and flipped backward in time to reread a few of the notes. The details she had fretted over, things that had seemed so important, such as the flowers, the color of the bridesmaids' gowns, the careful cataloging of presents, were all recorded in Ted's file. There was a copy of a telegraph from her mother—she presumed the original was in her own file, buried in its appropriate drawer—informing Waglie that the bride and her attendants would be carrying daisies. Memories arose of her feeling very strongly about these details, but they were distant, shrouded in haze. It seemed ridiculous to her now that she'd agonized, literally lost sleep, over the question of daisies (her choice; their sunny presence had always gladdened her) versus roses (the conventional choice, far more elegant, and what her almost-mother-in-law clearly expected—"But why *not* roses, dear? And daisies? They're little more than weeds"). She had stuck to her guns on the question of flowers and won the battle, but Jackson Waglie's preemptory notes on her then-impending nuptials made it clear she most certainly would have lost the war:

> *While perhaps the bride thought daisies would be a charming choice, reminiscent of carefree summer days, in practice their wilted, pedestrian numbers only served to reinforce our opinion that good taste can be neither bought nor inherited, but is always and only innate.*

Genevieve pushed her chair back, the scraping noise of the legs matching her harsh mood, and angrily stuffed Ted's file back into the drawer labeled "Be-Bo." The other files met similar fates. This was *useless*, and she directed her anger at Ted, his mother, and the now-deceased Waglie to Daniel, with his ridiculous directives. The money was so entangled it was impossible to follow. Reginald Cotswold and Peter Stuyvesant Senior had established not one but two charitable foundations together. Andrew Huffington's son from his first marriage was employed by Stuyvesant and was married to the deputy mayor's niece. Commissioner Simons had a side business venture with Huffington, Ted was a partner, and Stuyvesant Junior was on the advisory board. Indeed, the only name not entangled endlessly with all the other men's was Clark's, who seemed to be in league only with Huffington.

Genevieve paused, staring at the financier's name on the tab of his file before slipping it back into place with a thoughtful expression. She made a mental note to dig a little deeper into Ernest Clark's background, then turned her attention to the last file left on her table.

Daniel McCaffrey, the script read, in the same tidy hand as the others.

She'd combed through this file already in recent weeks but hoped to stumble across some tidbit that would make sense, particularly given what she now knew regarding his relationship with Reginald Cotswold. So far, Daniel was still her closest lead to Robin Hood. And now, with one confirmed murder and potentially another, the stakes of catching the thief were higher than ever.

Genevieve sighed, wiped her dirty hands on her skirt, and began to gather her things. She needed a break, and something to eat. Later that afternoon or tomorrow, she decided, she would peruse the contents of Daniel's file with more care.

The creak of the records room door stopped her in her tracks. Unable to see who might have entered due to the height of the file cabinets in front of her, Genevieve called out, "Hello? Who is there?"

No one replied, but the sound of footsteps grew closer.

"Alice? Verna? Is that you?" she asked. Images of the shadowy figures behind her on Fifth Avenue and Washington Square crowded her brain.

Stop it, she scolded herself, as she had every time the creepy mirages had arisen in the past few days. Her skin began to crawl at the memories. *You don't know that anyone was following you. Men walk on avenues all the time. And in parks.*

But while her head knew this logically, her gut told her something different.

And now someone was in here, with her, and not answering her calls.

Heart pounding, Genevieve looked frantically around her tiny corner of the records room. There were tall file cabinets on three sides of her, with only one narrow passage between them toward the door. The few windows in the room were partially blocked by the cabinets as well, not that they would have done her any good, since she was on the tenth floor.

Pulling herself up to her full height, Genevieve grabbed her notebooks and Daniel's file and held them in front of her protectively as a dark shape rounded the last file cabinet into her corner.

Clive.

Sagging a bit from relief, Genevieve felt her panic quickly turn to annoyance. It was just like Clive to follow her about to make sure she hadn't been given a better story than him—as if that ever happened.

"Why are you sneaking about, Clive?" she asked. "Why didn't you answer me?"

Ignoring her query, Clive glanced around the small space. "What are you researching?" he intoned nasally.

"None of your business," she said, exasperated, as she tried to walk around him.

He moved to block her path.

"Let me by. It's well past lunchtime, and I'm simply starved."

Clive didn't budge but continued to peer around the room. "You didn't answer my question."

Furrowing her brow in irritation, Genevieve thought quickly, then let out a fake sigh. "Arthur wants me to write a twenty-year history on the progression of ladies' footwear in Manhattan. How high did heels rise and fall? When did bows fall out of fashion? Buckles or no buckles? Must the slipper and dress color match? What about boots?"

"Okay, okay," interrupted Clive, his gaze finally settling on Genevieve. "Fine. Ladies' footwear, if you say so." He paused, idly swirling his diamond stickpin around in his lapel. Genevieve let out a small sneeze, overwhelmed by the scent of his cologne, and hoped he had bought her story. She really was hungry, and very much wanted to clear her head from the tangled accounts she'd been attempting to trace all morning. She moved to walk around him again, but Clive surprised her by asking, "Are you sure you aren't looking into the background of Daniel McCaffrey?"

Genevieve snapped her gaze toward Clive. "Mr. McCaffrey?" she repeated slowly. "Why on earth would I be researching him?"

Clive turned his attention to his stickpin, continuing to turn it again and again, and took another step toward her, making the small space seem much smaller. "Well, rumor has it you two have gotten quite close lately. You've been seen out with him quite a bit, you danced with him at the Huffingtons' ball—and it's well known Mr. McCaffrey never dances—and you had dinner together at Delmonico's."

Genevieve stared in amazement. How did Clive, who was not part of society, know all of these things?

He caught her stare and gave a short, bitter laugh. "Oh, just because I'm not invited to New York's exclusive drawing rooms doesn't mean I don't know what goes on in them, Miss Stewart." He fixed her with an oily gaze. "I make it my business to keep track of such things."

Clive took another step closer, making Genevieve wish she had space to back away farther, but the backs of her thighs were already pressing against the edge of the small desk she'd been using. Just thinking that Clive somehow knew of her whereabouts and movements made her feel slightly nauseous. He leaned in closer, causing her to shrink back, the smell of his cologne sickening.

"I know you, Miss Stewart." Clive narrowed his eyes at her, and Genevieve was startled by the utter hatred she saw glittering within them. "You may not think it, but I do. I know you're ambitious, and I also know, despite your being female, that you're actually a very, very good journalist. I know you're desperate to prove to Horace that you've got the chops to work on more serious stories. I also know how this town works. I know that because you're from old New York money"— he practically spit the words out—"old Horay would actually give you those serious stories you so long for, if he thought you could do it."

Clive abruptly straightened up again, and Genevieve exhaled in relief. "And I know you've been somehow nuzzling up to Daniel McCaffrey," Clive continued. "Who, it turns out, is from Five Points. Which tells me that either, one"—and here Clive held up a finger as if he were a teacher lecturing his class—"the two of you are actually romantically involved . . ." He snorted, letting his gaze audaciously roam up and down Genevieve's long, lean frame. "Which I highly doubt, you being an old-maid bluestocking, after all." Genevieve let out a shocked little gasp, wanting to remind Clive that quite recently *he'd* been desperate to have dinner with her old-maid, bluestocking self, but Clive went on before she could interrupt. "Or two"—here he held up a second finger—"that you're pursuing a story of some kind."

Clive pointed at Genevieve. "You think Mr. McCaffrey is Robin Hood, don't you?" Genevieve involuntarily gasped again. She should have known she wouldn't be the only person to make the connection between the mysterious Mr. McCaffrey and the mysterious Robin Hood. "And the bugger of it is, you're probably right. It makes perfect sense."

Genevieve's heart pounded. She still wasn't sure if Daniel was the thief or not, but she'd be damned if Clive was going to figure it out before her.

And on the slight chance that Daniel *was* Robin Hood . . . Clive could be dangerous to him. She wasn't sure why that thought was so unsettling.

The odious man hissed, "This is the biggest story of the decade, and I am not about to let a stuck-up, rich little girl who thinks she's too good for anyone else snatch it out from under my nose. Leave off whatever you're investigating, Genevieve. This story is *mine*."

Enough was enough. Genevieve pushed against Clive's chest with all her strength, surprising him into toppling backward against a file cabinet. She was shaking with anger.

"No, *you* leave off, Clive. For your information, I am not investigating Mr. McCaffrey, but I can and will research whatever and whomever I damn well please." Unable to stomach one more second in the cramped space with him, Genevieve marched past Clive and out of the records room.

Chapter 12

The door to the old Van Joost townhouse swung open, and Genevieve blinked in surprise.

Standing in the doorway was the largest and possibly least attractive man she had ever seen. He was a giant. Genevieve was tall, but this man loomed over her. His height was matched by his sheer physical girth, and it was obviously a powerful physique under his—oh, actually rather well-made and well-tailored—suit. Most alarming, however, was the man's face. Several rough scars crisscrossed his broad cheekbones, one running across his mouth and down his chin, and it was obvious that his nose had been broken and not reset properly. All in all, he looked a bit like Dr. Frankenstein's monster, albeit in a very nice suit. Dr. Frankenstein's monster, in a lovely suit, answering the door to what was now Daniel's home and place of business.

The monster spoke. "Yeah?" he asked in a gruff voice, thick with a Lower East Side accent.

She cleared her throat slightly and handed over her card. "I haven't an appointment, I'm afraid."

The large man glanced at her card impassively, then opened the door slightly wider to let her step in. "Wait here a minute," he commanded, then stomped down the hall toward the back of the house.

Genevieve nodded at his giant back. Though it was typically considered rude to leave a guest waiting in the hallway, there was no way she would budge from her assigned spot.

A scant moment later, the man thumped back down the hall, then led her to a large, well-appointed office with big sunny windows and a plush carpet from the Far East. "He's coming," the man grunted, closing the door behind him.

Genevieve took in the high shelves of books, the massive mahogany desk, and the deep-red leather chairs. She ran a finger over the back of one of the chairs facing the desk. Several neat stacks of paper and files resting on the desk's wide surface caught her eye.

She shouldn't. She really, truly, honestly shouldn't.

The files in question sat in perfect, well-lined piles, all in a tidy row. They were utterly tempting, begging to be opened. What if the secret to Robin Hood was *right here*? Though she was alone, Genevieve pretended a sudden, intense interest in the view from the window behind the desk. If she *happened* to catch a better look at the files on her way around the desk, well, that would just be coincidence, wouldn't it?

The window yielded a lovely view of the neat confines of the park on which the old Van Joost mansion—now the McCaffrey mansion, she supposed—was located. As the winter trees were still bare, she could see the well-ordered paths crisscrossing its expanse, lined with perfectly trimmed hedges. Unlike Washington Square Park, Gramercy Park was private, accessible only to the residents whose houses surrounded it. Casually turning her back on the window, Genevieve glanced at the desk. Frustratingly, the file surfaces themselves revealed nothing.

Unable to resist their siren song for another moment, Genevieve quickly flipped through the nearest stack. Legalese jumped off the pages: the document seemed like a motion to halt an eviction. The next pile was similarly fruitless, and the next.

Blowing a breath in frustration, Genevieve regarded the door warily and assessed her options. Deciding she was in for a penny, in for a pound, she lightly tugged on one of the massive desk's drawers. It slid open easily, though a slight poking of its contents revealed nothing more interesting than pencils and—wait, was that a *revolver*?

Genevieve knew a bit about guns. She couldn't have grown up around her brothers and *not* known. Not wanting to touch it, she peered into the depths of the drawer to get a better look. It gleamed evilly from its snug confines, almost daring her to test its weight in her hand. Ignoring the impulse, she noted it was a six-shooter, possibly Swiss in origin.

While this was interesting, none of the crimes thus far had involved a revolver. Genevieve made a mental note of the piece's existence, then shut the drawer carefully and opened another.

Ah, this was more like it—telegrams. Glancing furtively at the door, Genevieve grabbed one and began to unfold the paper.

She had ascertained that the note was in reference to the transferring of some funds when the office door opened. Starting guiltily, Genevieve dropped the telegram like it was on fire, but it was no use. There she was, behind Daniel's desk, drawer open.

And there was the owner of the desk in question, his cautious expression of welcome quickly changing to one of disbelief, followed by fury.

★ ★ ★

Outrage slammed into Daniel's gut, hot and explosive, at the sight of Genevieve pawing through his desk. He expressed it with a slam of the door, striding forward and grabbing her arm. He shoved closed the open drawer and resisted the urge to shake her silly.

Goddammit, he was such a fool. He'd felt an unexpected surge of gladness when Asher had told him Genevieve was waiting in his office, recalling their silent exchanges from the Bradleys' ball. And then he had rushed toward the room, pleasant curiosity about her visit welling up inside him, only to be confronted with—this.

How had he had forgotten? The damned press was all the same. They would all do anything for a story.

She stared up at him with big eyes, slightly shamefaced but unafraid. Her cheeks were flushed a delicate pink from embarrassment, and he could smell her clean, grassy scent.

"Are you only here to pry?" he ground out.

"Of course not," she retorted. "I'm here to . . . get answers." Her chin lifted in a now-familiar gesture of defiance. "So yes, in this instance, perhaps that meant prying."

Exasperated, Daniel let go of her arm and ran both hands through his hair. He had told his secretary to leave her, unattended, in his private office. When he knew she was a reporter who was deeply interested in his background.

He was suddenly struck by the ridiculousness of the situation. Unable to help himself, he started to chuckle.

Oh, but the fun Maggie would have poked at him. After all these years of avoiding attachment, after he'd built up a hell of a good wall, someone was finally prying away at the chinks in his armor. It had to be a girl who was determined to be a journalist, didn't it?

The girl who was now looking at him like he was crazy, even as his chuckles subsided. He held up his hands to show he was harmless.

"Pry all you want, Miss Palmer. You won't find much of interest." If she was looking for information on Robin Hood, it wasn't there. Just legal documents relating to tenement disputes and police corruption.

Her brow furrowed and for a moment she glanced back at the desk, like she was going to take him up on his offer and start rooting through his things again. This set him chuckling all over again, and he stepped back to let her pass by.

Genevieve still regarded him warily but moved past him toward one of the big red leather chairs, where he gestured for her to sit. She did, and glanced longingly at the decanters on the sideboard. Daniel followed her glance and gave a soft, amused snort. He poured a measure into a cut-crystal glass and offered it to her.

"Whiskey?"

She grasped the glass out of his hand and took a deep sip, making him smile again. He did enjoy a woman who could hold her liquor.

"Thank you," she said stiffly. "And I apologize for violating your privacy."

Daniel settled into a chair opposite her and swirled his whiskey a few times, leaving her apology be for now. "Perhaps you should tell me why you're here."

She nodded. "There have been new developments with Robin Hood."

He raised a brow at her. "I'm not sure why that is any concern of mine."

She set her glass down with a bit more force than necessary. "Because you're involved. You're . . . helping me."

"Am I?"

"Aren't you? Why else keep lobbing these cryptic tidbits at me, or, or, take me to dinner and tell me about your past?" She suddenly sat up straighter and eyed him with suspicion. "Or is it the opposite? Are you trying to obfuscate matters and keep me from the truth?"

"I have never maintained that I know *anything*, Miss Palmer, so I have no truth from which to keep you." It was only a partial lie. "*You* pursued *me*. I was simply going about the general business of living when you began appearing at my every turn, including showing up on my doorstep and pawing through my personal effects, seeming to think I am up to my eyeballs in nefariousness. Yes, I told you about my past, hoping it would appease you enough to leave me The. Hell. Alone." He punctuated the last word with a slamming down of his own glass and standing, causing a bit of the golden liquid to slosh onto the side table. Genevieve stood in response, eyes blazing. Several long moments passed as they eyed each other, and Daniel very seriously considered the ramifications of throwing her out of his house.

He knew, ultimately, it would do more harm than good, and draw more of her suspicion where none was needed.

And then there was that pull, that invisible cord that somehow bound them.

No, he was stuck with her. And she with him. To what end, he still wasn't sure.

"I don't believe you," she finally said, her words quiet.

Daniel picked up his glass and sipped, buying a few moments of time. He eyed her over the rim of his glass.

She met his gaze head on. "Robin Hood has struck the Bradleys. And Elmira Bradley was murdered."

Daniel held himself very still. Genevieve refused to release their eye contact, though he could hear her breath quickening.

"I need to know what you know," she said softly. "People are dying."

"I am being circumspect to prevent more from dying," he said, matching her tone. That was all he could say for now. Anything further could endanger her, and him.

He heard the catch in her breath. The atmosphere in the room thickened with tension. He could see her calculating her options, trying to decide how much to push. He allowed the silence to stretch out.

"Is Robin Hood a killer?" she finally asked.

"What do you think?"

She tilted her head ever so slightly, still not breaking eye contact. "I think not."

"Why?"

"His letters suggest no actual violence. They focus on greed, disingenuousness, hypocrisy. He brags that he gives the money from the stolen items to the impoverished. Robin Hood is about social embarrassment; nothing in the first three crimes suggests murder."

"And this most recent letter?"

"I haven't read it but have heard it follows the same pattern."

"Couldn't the thief escalate his crimes?"

Genevieve shook her head impatiently. The tension between them was shifting, morphing into something more collaborative and rhythmic.

"It just doesn't *feel* right," she said.

Daniel allowed a few moments to pass, digesting this. "No," he finally agreed. "It doesn't."

He sat, picking up his glass again and taking a thoughtful sip, then wiping at the wet spot on the table with his hand. After a beat or two, Genevieve sat as well, waiting for him to continue. He turned the matter round and round in his head, and saw no other option.

It was time to come clean.

Partially clean, at least.

"At the Bradleys, you asked me how it's all connected. The truth is, I don't know that it *is* connected. I honestly don't. I asked you to investigate the committee because it is related to my own work, and because I think it has potential to be more important than Robin Hood." She opened her mouth to speak, but Daniel held up a hand. "Please, let me finish. I'll admit I have suspicions about this committee. I believe it may be a sham. I am also willing to admit my suspicions might be a product of my own bias, as I've quietly been working on housing reform for years, on and off, and have seen how little interest the city's government has in the matter. But now, with what you've told me about Reginald's death . . . now I am thinking there might indeed be a connection to Robin Hood. But I don't know what it is. This may all be a wild-goose chase, Genevieve."

She leaned back in her chair and took another deep drink, looking as drained as he felt. Why was it that all of their interactions left him feeling as though he were swimming upstream, fighting the strong tides of the East River, as he'd done as a boy? He'd left those swims exhausted, wrung out, but also satisfied in some primal way. Wrangling with Genevieve Stewart had much the same effect on him.

Finally, she nodded again, slowly. "I understand. But I feel I have to do what I can to stop this. What can I do? What can *we* do?" She leaned forward, clasping her glass in both hands.

Again, that emphatic tug between them. It was undeniable, and strengthening.

He took a breath. "Did you look into the committee?"

"Yes." She favored him with a cross expression. "There are countless connections between the various members. I didn't find anything of significance."

"No financial entanglements? Nothing?"

Genevieve blew out a frustrated breath and looked even crosser. "On the contrary, there are plenty. Too many. It's like hunting for a needle in a haystack. Tell me what to look for."

Daniel thought for a moment. "Any kind of financial connections that seem unnecessary, or unwieldy, or anything that looks . . . off. Have you tried the municipal archives?"

"No, but those are open to the public. You can look there yourself, if you like." She leaned back again and took another drink.

"I'm not trying to shirk anything, Genevieve. It would be less suspicious if you went. Checking records is part of your job. If the need arises, I'll pick up a different unpleasant task."

She seemed inclined to argue for a moment, then nodded sulkily. "You're right. But Daniel . . ."

He waited. "What is it?"

Genevieve shook her head, declining to say whatever had been on her mind. Daniel decided not to press.

She stood, smoothing the front of her deep blue skirt. She held out her hand for him to shake. "So, partners?"

It was impossible not to take her hand, impossible not to feel that insistent pull. "Partners," he agreed. "For now."

Her mouth broadened into a smile. "Yes. For now."

Daniel had his housekeeper fetch Genevieve's jacket and gloves, and politely led her to the door.

"Daniel?" she asked, pulling on a yellow glove. She glanced around, seeming to want to make sure they were alone. "At what point do we go to the police?"

"We don't," he said, careful to keep his voice gentle. He ought to be frustrated with her naïvety, but he wasn't. She was a product of her world, after all, just as he was of his. She had never had call to think the police were anything other than trustworthy. "Commissioner Simons is on the committee, recall."

"Oh. Of course."

"Genevieve." He lowered his voice out of caution. "It's just the municipal archives. They're public records, in a public building. But do be careful."

Her return gaze was full of worry, but she nodded and turned to go.

"Wait." He stopped her. "Let's meet later tonight. Lüchow's? Ten PM?"

"Not Delmonico's?" Her expression had lightened to one of mild teasing, but he could still see the concern around her eyes.

"Let's mix it up," he shrugged.

"Lüchow's it is, then. And Daniel." She turned in the doorway, glancing back at him with wide eyes. "I'm always careful."

* * *

Satisfaction surged through Genevieve as the elevator doors opened with a noisy rattle. She stepped into the dark tenth-floor hallway of the *Globe*'s massive building and switched on one of the dim electric lights overhead. With just enough light to see, she bypassed the empty offices of the paper's foreign correspondents and made her way back toward the appropriate records room.

She *had* found something in the municipal archives, a filing of paperwork relating to the recent formation of a corporation called Lexington Industries by Huffington and Clark. If she wasn't mistaken, this venture was not listed among some of the other, more publicly known collaborations, in which Clark had financed some of Huffington's shipping interests. She had no idea if it was significant, but it pleased her to head into her late-supper appointment with something tangible from several frustrating hours of sifting. Perhaps Daniel could make heads or tails of it. She had made careful notes but wanted to double-check on whether the *Globe* had anything relating to Lexington Industries.

Genevieve consulted the timepiece pinned to her breast as she opened the door to the records room. Nine o'clock. She had just enough time to quickly scan the files of Huffington and Clark, and then in a different room she'd see if the corporation itself had merited a file yet, though she doubted it.

Glancing briefly though the records on both men, she found nothing. Retreating back down the hall, she fit her key to the offices into another room of files. The fifth floor, where her desk was located, was an open space, and there were probably several bleary-eyed journalists rattling around even at this late hour—she'd run into Verna, one of the secretaries, on the elevator tonight—putting the finishing touches on stories for the early edition. But the tenth floor was reserved mostly for the vast files of information reporters could access when they undertook research on a subject, as well as for the offices of journalists employed by the paper who were rarely in town.

Flicking on a light within the small space, Genevieve headed toward the appropriate drawer and hunted through the files. Sure enough, nothing on a corporation called Lexington Industries. She pondered the implications of this as she retraced her steps, turning the light back off and stepping into the hall to relock the door.

Just as a soft click informed her that the lock had hit home, the world around her plunged into blackness.

Someone had turned off the light at the far end of the hallway.

Her heart instantly sped to triple its usual rate. Pressing her back against the door she had just locked, Genevieve tried to make herself as small and quiet as possible.

This was no accident. Someone knew she was alone and wanted her afraid.

She listened.

From the opposite end of the hallway, near the elevator, came the barest scrape of a footstep. Trying to control the sound of her own rushing breath, she strained her ears.

Was that a slight rustling? Was it getting closer?

This standing and waiting wouldn't do. She wasn't about to allow herself to become victim to whoever was intent upon terrifying her. Despite how terrified she felt.

Moving as noiselessly as possible, Genevieve slipped across the pitch-black hallway and ran her hand along the wall until she felt the doorknob to the office opposite. She turned it, praying it would be silent. It was, but the door was locked, and she wasn't about to try her key when her vision was cloaked by darkness.

Another few careful steps, fingers running along the smooth coolness of the wall, and she came to the next doorknob. She tried again, wincing as the knob made a slight creaking noise. No luck; also locked.

Terrified that the noise of the knob had revealed her location, she felt an involuntary shaking begin to take hold of her hands. The feeling of exposure was almost more frightening than attempting to remain absolutely silent in the sightless hallway. She paused and listened again, her heart fluttering like a bird's.

Another scrape. Whoever was here, they were definitely closer.

Almost numb with panic, Genevieve rushed forward another few steps as quietly as she could until she found another doorknob. This one turned inaudibly in her hand as she stifled a sob of relief.

Now would the door creak on its hinges, or would she have another stroke of luck?

Genevieve bit her lip, waiting, hand on the turned knob. Another shuffling footstep sounded, even closer.

There was no time to wait. Holding her breath and whispering a quick prayer, she pushed the unknown door open as slowly as she could, desperately hoping it led into an office with a lock and not an overstuffed broom closet.

Her luck held, and she slipped into somebody's empty office. The blinds of the window were open, and scant light from the streetlamps below and moon above offered just enough illumination for shapes to coalesce into forms: a desk, a file cabinet, a chair slightly askew in a corner.

With shaking hands, Genevieve shut the door as quietly as she could and fumbled for the interior lock. She was almost safe.

Unless the intruder also had a key.

Rushing footsteps sounded outside the door. Panic leapt into her throat as she scrambled for the lock, but in her haste her fingers slipped on the slick metal.

The door burst open, banging against the side of her face with a painful thwack and sending her flying backward against the desk. A figure in dark, nondescript clothing lunged at her. She rolled to one side before scrambling to her feet. Running around the desk, she shoved the chair toward her attacker, causing him to stumble.

Losing no time, Genevieve scurried around the other side of the desk and toward the open door. If she could just get out of the cramped space of the office, she could run toward the stairs, begin to scream, and hope somebody heard her. She had seen Verna in the elevator; perhaps people knew she was here. Her fingers had just grazed the edge of the doorway when a strong arm wrapped around her waist and yanked her back, nearly forcing the breath out of her. She kicked with all her might, but it felt useless. She was spun around, and the man's body weight suddenly pinned her to the desk, a pair of hands wrapping around her throat. Screaming, she managed to wedge two fingers between the attacker's hands and her vulnerable neck, pushing against him with all her strength. The man's face hovered mere inches above hers, covered by the type of mask one might see at a society ball, a grotesque incongruity.

Light abruptly flooded the exterior hallway.

"Genevieve?" It was Luther's voice, thick with concern. "Genevieve!" There came another sound of footsteps rushing, only this time they were welcome, the noise of a savior.

The hands instantly released from her throat, and her attacker sped through the open door into the hallway.

"Hey! Stop!" A moment later, Luther's figure filled the open doorway. He rushed toward her. "Genevieve! Are you all right?"

Clutching her bruised throat, Genevieve frantically gestured that he should chase her assailant. "Go!" she creaked.

Luther dashed out the door again. She listened to his retreating steps as she shakily sat up on the desk, pushing her hair, which had come partially loose, behind her ears with hands that wouldn't stop trembling.

Shaking his head, Luther returned. "He was halfway down the fire escape outside Morgan's office; there's no way I could have caught up." He put an arm around her shoulders. "Jesus, Genevieve, what happened? Can you walk? We need to call the police."

"No." She winced; talking hurt. A lot. "No police."

"Are you crazy? Genevieve, someone just tried to kill you."

She shook her head, Daniel's reminder about Commissioner Simons ringing in her ears. "No police. I can't explain. Not yet."

"Then a hospital. We need that throat of yours looked at."

She shook her head again. "No. It will be fine. All I need is a cab."

There was only one place to go: Lüchow's. She needed to get to Daniel, and fast. Despite the numerous, swirling uncertainties, one thing now was certain: this was no wild-goose chase. She and Daniel were onto something, and somebody was desperate to stop them.

CHAPTER 13

Checking his gold pocket watch for the fifth time in seven minutes, Daniel swore lightly under his breath.

She was almost thirty minutes late.

A black-jacketed waiter arrived with the wine he had ordered, and Daniel allowed him to pour. He liked Lüchow's; it was slightly more casual than Delmonico's, and while the food wasn't the type that made one's eyes roll into the back of one's head in ecstasy, it was satisfying, solid German fare. The restaurant catered to the after-theater crowd, and it somehow managed to be both elegant and cozy, with the heads of taxidermied game set against deep golden walls. He nodded to a few acquaintances while he took a sip of the burgundy liquid, hopefully seeming to all the world like any man casually waiting for his dinner companion to arrive.

But he was in a turmoil of anxiety.

Dammit, he shouldn't have encouraged her to pursue any of this, not when he suspected it could be dangerous.

He tried to reassure himself that anything could be causing Genevieve's delay—a broken carriage wheel, a horse with a lost shoe, a traffic snarl, or even the unpleasant but not unrealistic possibility that she wanted nothing to do with him and had decided not to keep their appointment—but couldn't shake the foreboding feeling that something was amiss.

Daniel was getting ready to signal the waiter so he could pay for his half-drunk glass of wine, hop a cab downtown, and pound on the door to the Stewart townhouse until someone produced Genevieve whole and well, when he spotted Otto, the restaurant's unflappable maître d', leading the very cause of his worry toward his table. Relief caused his body to momentarily sag, before he composed himself and rose to do the honors of pulling back Genevieve's chair at the white-linen-covered table.

But another man was already there, helping Genevieve into her seat and glaring at Daniel with what appeared to be the force of a thousand suns, an expression that seemed out of place on the fellow's round, amiable face.

Confused by this stranger's appearance, Daniel looked to Genevieve for clarification, only to have his recent relief replaced by white-hot rage.

Something horrific had clearly transpired. Her lips were set but pale, and while she seemed composed, there was a slight tremor to her hands as she reached for the wineglass instantly filled by Otto. But what set every fiber in Daniel's being on edge was the beginnings of a bruise, at present delicately purple, along her right cheekbone. She had been struck, and hard.

His hands instantly clenched into fists, and he felt the muscles of his back tense. He was familiar with bruises and could tell hers would blossom into something truly spectacular by the following day.

"Will there be three?" Otto asked, having moved a discreet step back.

"No," Daniel ground out, staring down the newcomer, who stared back with equal force.

The maître d' bowed slightly and retreated, seeming to rightly read the sudden strain that enveloped the table.

"What happened?" he asked in a low voice, directing the question toward Genevieve but keeping his eyes on the other man, who still looked ready to pounce. "Are you quite all right?"

Genevieve nodded and opened her mouth to speak, but the stranger interjected. "What have you got her mixed up in?" the man growled.

"I got myself mixed up in it, Luther," Genevieve said. Daniel's rage went up a notch as he heard the harsh rasp of her voice and noticed the soft woolen scarf around her neck that she had failed to relinquish to Otto. "Mr. McCaffrey is helping me, and bears no responsibility for what happened tonight." Even as she said the words, she slanted Daniel a look with slightly narrowed eyes, as if she were still trying to decide if what she said was true.

If anything, the man's gaze hardened. "I thought that might be you, McCaffrey."

"Then you have the advantage of me," Daniel replied icily. He was in no mood for games.

"This is Luther Franklin, a colleague at the paper," Genevieve said. "He covers homicide, and is a friend." Something in the other man's demeanor shifted at this label, his gaze softening in obvious affection and gratitude, but his shoulders also falling slightly in defeat.

Luther tried to assert himself again, though. "I can't allow you to continue whatever put you in such danger tonight, Genevieve."

She looked incredulous. "It's not your place to allow or disallow me anything, Luther," she snapped in her new husky voice.

A look of genuine hurt crossed the man's face, and Genevieve instantly seemed sorry. She placed a hand on his arm.

"Thank you for your help," she said simply. "It meant the world, and possibly my life."

Her *life*? Alarm flared in Daniel, and he struggled to keep his face impassive. They were in public, after all, and with his and Luther's obvious standoff, they were already getting curious looks from the other diners.

"I'll be careful, I promise," Genevieve added. "But I can't tell you anything further, at least not now."

"But—" Luther started.

"I'm asking you to leave," she said gently. "I need to discuss matters with Mr. McCaffrey. I will see you tomorrow and tell you what I can. And please remember what I said: I tripped down the stairs. And no police."

Daniel watched the reporter wrestle with being dismissed, until he seemed to realize he had no choice in the matter.

"Fine," Luther relented. He shot one final, hard look at Daniel. "But know that I am here for you. And if anything further happens, I may have no choice but to speak to Arthur. And the police."

Genevieve did not respond to the threat but patted his hand gently. "I'll see you tomorrow," she repeated.

Luther looked on the verge of continuing, but instead nodded to both of them and took his leave. Genevieve heaved a weary sigh and picked up her wineglass again.

"Do sit down, people are staring."

Daniel did as he was told, barely able to keep his anger in check. He had nowhere to put it, and it clawed at his insides furiously, desperate to be unleashed. But upon whom? Not this Luther fellow, who really had no part in this, and certainly not Genevieve. It would have to wait until he learned who had caused that bruise; that person would feel the full force of his temper.

Of course, he could always turn it on himself. Whatever had happened to Genevieve, ultimately he was to blame.

The waiter reappeared, ready to take their orders, and Daniel winced internally as Genevieve requested only a bowl of turtle soup while briefly touching her scarf-covered throat. Once they were alone again, she favored him with a peevish look.

"Why is it all the gentlemen of my acquaintance continually try to tell me what I can and cannot do?"

"I believe they are trying to protect you." He sympathized mightily with the other men in her life—her father, whom he knew only by reputation, and her brothers, whom he'd met socially on and off throughout the years. This woman took risks with herself, and undoubtedly had been doing so since she could walk.

She blew out a raspy, exasperated sigh. "I neither need nor want anyone's protection."

"Apparently it was in order tonight," Daniel managed to say through clenched teeth. If within the next sixty seconds he didn't hear the particulars of what had happened, he might in fact lose the temper he was holding so closely in check.

Genevieve flushed slightly. "As would be the case with anyone, were someone trying to kill them. Male or female."

Daniel gripped the edge of the table. "Genevieve. For the love of Christ. Tell me what happened."

Thick, leathery wings of dread engulfed him as Genevieve quietly relayed her story, keeping her voice low to avoid being overheard. She paused once as the waiter returned with their food, resuming her tale once they were alone again. The schnitzel in front of him looked as perfectly prepared as usual, but Daniel's desire for food had fled. The telling of the story, however, seemed to strengthen both Genevieve's resolve and her appetite, as she dug into her soup heartily and then requested an ice cream parfait.

"My throat is already feeling better. This is helping," she said, gesturing with her spoon toward her now-empty bowl.

Daniel felt completely wrung out after hearing the particulars of the attack. There was no doubt that someone had attempted to murder Genevieve, and to do so at her place of work suggested three things to him, none of them reassuring: First, that whoever was trying to protect this information was getting desperate. Second, that he and Genevieve were getting closer to the truth. And third, most disturbingly, that somebody, or multiple somebodies, was watching them.

Or at least, they were watching Genevieve. Any of her interactions with him thus far could be written off as either social encounters or the routine work of a journalist intent upon a story. He may have escaped the unknown person's scrutiny thus far.

He glanced around the restaurant with new eyes. The room, which moments ago had seemed friendly and comforting, was suddenly full of unseen menace.

Daniel took another deep drink of wine and pushed his untouched schnitzel aside, relaying his conclusions.

Genevieve smiled at the waiter as he set down her parfait.

"Yes, I think you must be correct," she agreed, smile fading as soon as the waiter departed.

"All of which means," he said, pausing to take another sip to embolden himself, "is that your friend was right. This is getting too dangerous for you."

Her gaze snapped from the parfait to him, eyes full of fury. "Didn't we just have this conversation?"

"You are being *watched*, Genevieve. Which makes you a target. You cannot put yourself at risk any longer." She had opened her mouth to speak when a new thought jumped into his head, unbidden and shockingly appealing. "Unless . . ." he began, cutting off what was sure to be another protest.

"Unless what?"

Daniel drew himself up in his chair. "Unless whoever is watching you believes you are under someone's protection. My protection."

For a moment she simply blinked at him. "What would that entail?" she finally asked, slowly.

Daniel took a breath. She hadn't said no, which was a start. "If we spend more . . . physical time together. If they think we are courting."

He watched a series of emotions play across her face: confusion, understanding, followed by a slight flush of embarrassment.

"But how would that help? If we were to undertake such a scheme? When we're together, certainly, but what about times we're not together, like when I'm at work?"

Dipping his head in acknowledgment of her reservations, Daniel thought about how best to explain. "Do you recall how we met?"

Amusement flashed in her eyes. "I would be hard-pressed to forget."

"I have a reputation in certain quarters of this city as someone not to be trifled with, as do my associates. If word gets out that you are under my protection and a plot is afoot to do you harm, I may hear of it through certain channels."

Her mouth dropped open slightly, and she regarded him with fascination. "Well. Curiouser and curiouser."

He felt a small smile tug at his lips. "Down the rabbit hole we go."

A smile that likely matched his own twitched her mouth. "How would we make such information known? Take out an advertisement?"

"We've had dinner, in public, twice now. I can accompany you to a few other locations this week, and perhaps we ought to dance more than is seemly at an upcoming party. These will send the appropriate social signals."

Genevieve nodded slowly. "All right. Well, the Porters' costume ball is the next major event of the season."

Daniel groaned inwardly. It had to be a costume ball, didn't it? "That will do fine. We'll meet there, and I shall wait on you hand and foot."

"This arrangement is sounding better and better," she said wryly. "Are you planning to peel me a grape?"

"If you wish it. And in the meantime, please do me a favor: try not to be alone, especially after dark. Leave work when there is still plenty of traffic. Take cabs instead of walking. Conduct shopping trips with friends."

"Yes, yes, I know what it means not to be alone, Daniel."

"Good," he said, yielding to her obvious distaste for being lectured. "It's settled, then." The thought of showering Genevieve with attention in a public venue was absurdly, inexplicably pleasing. He would escort her home tonight, then go straight to Paddy and ask him to keep his ear to the ground.

That is, with greater urgency than he was already employing.

"A sham courtship," Genevieve mused. "Seems like the plot of a salacious novel, does it not?" she teased, scooping up the last of her parfait.

The tightness that had been squeezing Daniel's innards ever since he had seen her bruise eased the tiniest bit at the sight of her smile. But his eyes kept returning to that purple shadow on her cheekbone, already beginning to spread and darken, and the rage would bubble up again.

The man responsible had better pray that Daniel not find him.

★ ★ ★

"He said *what*?" squealed Callie, her voice floating up from behind the curtain at Mrs. Brown's. It was a week after the attack in her office building that had nearly killed her. A week since her agreement to start a sham courtship with Daniel. It was painful to lie to her friends and family, but she saw no other recourse.

Her parents had taken the news that she would be spending more time with Mr. McCaffrey with slightly confused caution. "I thought you were done with all that," her mother had said, frowning. "But of course, if you wish it." Her father peered at her bruise, which had mushroomed into something truly grotesque, with gravity. She could tell he was uncertain as to whether to believe her story about tripping on the staircase in their home.

Callie, of course, was over the moon with the whole idea. Eliza was more circumspect, looking at her thoughtfully when she believed Genevieve's attention was elsewhere.

Genevieve knew she wasn't looking well; the bruises on her neck had faded within days and she'd been able to forgo a scarf around her neck, but a week after the attack she still sported the one on her face, now morphing from a wretched greenish-purple into a milder but still appalling greenish-yellow, visible even under the powder she had applied. Its only saving grace was that it masked the horrid dark circles under her right eye, though those under her left eye were still vivid.

She wasn't getting much sleep. Every time she drifted off, the masked figure would appear above her in her mind, his hands on her throat, intent on squeezing the life from her.

In short, she hardly sported the glowing countenance of a young woman being courted by the city's most eligible bachelor.

A larger squeal erupted from behind the curtain.

"Miss Maple, you must remain still, or unfortunately you will suffer more pinpricks," came the steely, exasperated voice of Mrs. Brown, who was surely overwhelmed this week as all of New York society scrambled to get their costumes completed in time. Fancy-dress parties were all the rage, and society's ladies in particular competed to see who could come up with the most lavish costume.

Callie murmured apologies from behind the curtain. Eliza, standing on a pedestal and holding up her arms as a seamstress stitched up the last of her heavy velvet midnight-blue dress, rolled her eyes in Genevieve's direction. Genevieve, who had already been fitted for her costume, had changed back into her afternoon dress and was resting on a nearby pink-and-green-striped settee.

"Your costume is fabulous, Eliza. That blue matches your eyes perfectly," Genevieve said.

Eliza's cheeks pinkened with pleasure at the compliment. "Do you really think so? You don't think Ophelia is too literary a costume, or too depressing? The poor woman does drown."

Genevieve shook her head. "There have been plenty of Ophelias in past costume balls, I'm sure. I think Shakespearean outfits are quite common. It looks beautiful, Eliza; really it does." And it did.

"Well, it certainly can't surpass your costume, Genevieve. You might wind up being the belle of the ball."

"Mine?" Genevieve looked in surprise at the large box that lay next to her on the settee, containing her gown for the ball. "But it's so simple! Beautiful, of course," she hastened to add, hearing Mrs. Brown's muffled snort from behind the curtain. "And I am deeply appreciative of everyone's efforts to create such a gorgeous costume on very short notice," she called loudly.

She was grateful, very. After she and Daniel decided to pretend to be courting, Genevieve had sent notes to Callie and Eliza, asking if she could accompany them to their already-scheduled fittings. Callie and Eliza had been planning to attend the ball since they received the invitation and had put in their orders with Mrs. Brown weeks ago. Mrs. Brown, bless her, had thrown up her hands in dismay when Genevieve sheepishly trailed into the shop following her friends, but had come through like the professional she was.

"We do not have enough time to create anything truly complicated for you, Miss Stewart." The older woman had surveyed Genevieve's tall frame, clad only in her undergarments, with the eagle eye of a perfectionist. "But I think we can whip up something suitable." And so she had. Unearthing a bolt of bright-white silk, snapping orders at seamstresses who buzzed around her like worker bees to their queen, Mrs. Brown had draped, hung, wrapped, and pinned the silk around Genevieve's body until she was satisfied. Adding a few stitches here and there to secure the garment, she produced a long golden cord and wound it around Genevieve's bodice and waist. Finally, she turned Genevieve to face the full-length mirror that hung in the dressing room, Callie and Eliza hovering in various states of undress behind her, exclaiming over the rapid results.

"There," said Mrs. Brown in a satisfied voice. "Aphrodite. Make sure your maid dresses your hair high."

She had just as quickly unwrapped Genevieve from the white silk and handed it to one of her apprentices, who scurried away to sew the gown up properly. Now her costume lay neatly folded and ready in a box next to her.

Eliza rolled her eyes again, this time at Genevieve. "We shall see," she replied.

"Indeed we shall," added Callie, stepping out from behind the curtain with a tired-looking Mrs. Brown following. "Though I tend to agree with Eliza, Genevieve. I think your costume will create a sensation. Oh, Eliza! How lovely you look!"

Genevieve and Eliza gaped at their friend. "Oh no," murmured Genevieve in complete approval. "*You* will create the sensation."

"Isn't it just gorgeous? Mrs. Brown is a genius." Callie beamed at the seamstress, who grudgingly nodded in acknowledgment of the compliment.

"I enjoy a challenge," Mrs. Brown allowed, kneeling down to remove a trailing piece of thread from the gown's hem before gathering her seamstresses and shooing them into the next room.

Callie was dressed as the Little Mermaid from the Hans Christian Andersen fairy tale. Her gown, a deep emerald green that matched her eyes, was covered in a multitude of large, flat beads meant to resemble scales, which shimmered and flashed as she moved. There were no straps or sleeves on the dress, which hugged Callie's curvy frame. A deep V plunged between her breasts, forming a heart-shaped bodice that descended into a shockingly snug gown, revealing the swell of Callie's hips and derriere. Even more shocking, a slit was cut into the skirt that started just above her knees, widening in the front and eventually becoming two short, pointed trains of fabric that trailed behind her.

"See how clever? It's supposed to represent the moment the little mermaid's fish tail transforms into human legs. And I can secure the tail after the procession, fastening it to the back of the skirt so it's not in my way when I dance." Callie did a slow twirl so they could admire the costume from all angles. "Isn't it amazing?"

It was amazing. "You will have no trouble finding a husband in that outfit. I guarantee it."

"Callie, are you certain it's wise to show *quite* so much leg?" queried Eliza, ever practical. Genevieve had secretly been wondering this as well. While slightly shorter skirts were often worn for fancy-dress balls, they typically stopped midcalf. One could see Callie's rounded, creamy legs starting at her knees, a length unheard of for a grown woman.

"Desperate times call for desperate measures, my loves," Callie replied, gazing down at the gown. "You know my circumstances." She looked furtively around to make sure Mrs. Brown and the other seamstresses had left the small dressing room, then whispered, "I'm not quite sure how Grandmama is going to pay for this, but she assured me she'd find a way." Straightening back up, Callie turned a bit to the left to see the gown from a different angle, looking over her right shoulder. "I am terribly fond of this gown, though. It's going to look smashing with the diamonds."

"Your grandmother is really going to let you wear them?" Eliza asked.

"Oh yes. The necklace, earrings, and bracelet. The gown is really just a showpiece for the jewels, of course. Now, can we stop talking about boring matters such as jewels and gowns and turn our discussion back to the really interesting topic? Genevieve, repeat for us please, word for word, *exactly* what Mr. McCaffrey said to you about this ball."

"Yes," Eliza interjected. "The two of you have been spending an awful lot of time together lately."

"Has he taken you anywhere romantic?" Callie's gaze wandered dreamily at the thought.

"Well, a comic opera at the Casino Theatre, an exhibition of Dutch paintings at the Metropolitan, and we ate at Lüchow's in Union Square." Genevieve ticked off her recent activities with Daniel on her fingers, then wrinkled her nose at her friend. "Is German food considered romantic?"

Callie stamped her foot impatiently. "Did he kiss you on any of these outings?" she hissed in a stage whisper.

"No," Genevieve said firmly. "He has been the perfect gentleman." Callie appeared crestfallen.

"Genevieve, are you being quite honest with us?" Eliza asked. Callie glanced at her in surprise.

"Whatever do you mean?" she asked.

"Yes, Eliza," said Genevieve, tension suddenly coiling in the pit of her stomach. "Whatever do you mean?" She and her friend exchanged a long, considering look, while Callie's eyes snapped between them in confusion.

"What is going on?" Callie asked.

Genevieve held Eliza's gaze, silently daring her to voice her concerns. She knew her friend was in a hard spot, and on one hand felt guilty for exploiting it: there was no way Eliza could state that she believed the courtship was false without appearing wildly insulting. But on the other hand, Genevieve desperately needed her friend to accept the falsehood that she and Daniel were spreading.

The truth could endanger them. Endanger anyone she cared about.

It was Eliza who broke the silent standoff. "I just don't want Genevieve to get hurt," she said, sending a meaningful glance toward the fading bruise.

Genevieve swallowed. She was already nervous about attending the costume ball. She and Daniel had spent their recent outings discussing the best strategies for prying information from the relevant guests, a tricky position, as any one of them could be behind the masked man's attack. It was going to be a delicate dance all night, with them going their separate ways, each ferreting out what they could, rejoining, pretending to be romantically involved, and engaging in the same steps again.

It could all come to naught. Or she could find the answers she needed. The answers, it seemed, that could keep her alive.

CHAPTER 14

Days later, Genevieve's nervousness had not abated one bit, though her bruise, thankfully, had mellowed to a yellowy tinge.

Gnawing on her lower lip, Genevieve paced the front hall of her parents' house, waiting for the carriage that would take her, Callie, and Callie's grandmother to the Porters' costume ball. As usual, Genevieve's parents had declined to attend the ball but had given their typical absent-minded permission for Callie's grandmother to serve as the girls' chaperone, though chaperones weren't entirely necessary in New York society. Wearing a warm, silk-lined cloak, which hid her Aphrodite costume, Genevieve reviewed the plans for the coming evening in her head again. And again.

She checked out the window. Still no carriage.

"Blast," she muttered.

"Don't let Mother hear you swear," chuckled her brother's voice behind her.

Genevieve turned and regarded Charles with pleasure, grinning at him. "I'd just tell her I was having a moment of solidarity with the working class, and she'd probably start swearing too."

Charles grinned back. "That sounds like Mother, all right. You heading to the Porters' costume ball?"

Genevieve couldn't hide her surprise. "You knew it was tonight?"

Charles shrugged, looking down. "I still receive invitations, you know. Even though I never accept them."

Genevieve regarded her brother thoughtfully. When they'd been younger, all of her school friends had mooned over her older brothers terribly, angling for invitations to her house so they could bat their eyes in the boys' direction. Gavin had always flirted back, the scoundrel, but Charles would shrug it off and duck into another room, away from the girls' giggling attentions. As adults, their lives had progressed in much the same way, with outgoing Gavin, ever the romantic, skipping off to Egypt without a glance backward, and Charles staying put and avoiding public attention, despite the widespread praise for his architectural designs.

"Why don't you?" Before tonight, it had never occurred to Genevieve to ask. She had always assumed that Charles was simply uninterested in the machinations of New York high society, as she had been. She was realizing more and more, though, that her own disinterest had stemmed from insecurity about not fitting in and shame over her broken engagement.

"Society's always happy to have more eligible bachelors," she reminded him. And eligible he was. A successful—some even said brilliant—young architect with a promising future, he made plenty of money, and that didn't even count their family fortune. He was quite good-looking, with eyes that were a clear amber, darker than hers, and thick, light-brown hair. "You'd make some debutante very happy."

Charles smiled slightly. "Surely I'm too solitary and cranky for some bright young woman."

"But you go out when we're in Newport," Genevieve protested. Charles loved summers at their Rhode Island home, spending hours and hours on the water in his sailboat. He even ventured to the occasional picnic, lawn party, or evening soiree when there, though he typically sipped a drink in the corner or talked boating with his friends, still oblivious to the young ladies who batted their eyes in his direction. But at least he attended.

He shrugged. "It's different there. It seems . . . freer somehow." The slight smile returned. "Maybe it's the salt air."

Genevieve felt a surge of warmth toward her brother.

"You should get out more," Genevieve ventured. "Maybe try talking to some of the ladies who so obviously adore you. You might be surprised—some of them might share your interests. You could talk sailing, or architecture . . ." She trailed off, unsure of what else her older brother might like to do these days. He *was* rather solitary, she realized. He came to dinner at the house fairly often but didn't share that much about himself.

Charles smiled wider. "You see? I've not much to offer a girl."

"That's not true! You're handsome, and kind, and smart. Your buildings are changing the face of this city, and for the better. You'd be a catch for any girl," she said loyally, knowing it was true.

"Ah, enough about me. What's all this I hear about you and Daniel McCaffrey?" he asked softly.

The clatter of hooves and carriage wheels on cobblestones turned their heads. Callie and her grandmother had arrived.

Charles surprised Genevieve by folding her into a warm hug. "It'll keep, little sister. Just make sure he's worthy of you."

"Charles, may I ask a favor of you?"

He stepped back and regarded her quizzically. "Anything."

"Would you have any time to spare in the next day or so?"

"For you? Of course. What do you need?"

Genevieve quietly relayed her request, and Charles's eyebrows raised in alarm.

"Not unless you tell me why," he countered. "Does it have to do with this?" He gestured toward her eye.

Genevieve sighed with impatience. "Don't you trust me?"

Charles looked affronted. "Of course. But I also know you're the first person to wade into trouble if there's any about."

"Then surely you'll be comforted by my being as cautious as possible," she snapped.

Her brother shook his head at her slowly, and Genevieve knew she had won. Gavin would never have backed down, but Charles, she suspected, understood and respected the need for secrets. She believed he harbored more than a few of his own.

"We'll start tomorrow," he conceded, grudgingly accepting a kiss on the cheek. "Once you wake up. But Genevieve . . ." She paused on the threshold, waiting. "If you spot any trouble tonight, stay out of it, won't you?"

Her anxiety over the upcoming evening, which had lulled in response to their plans, awakened anew.

"I'll try," she promised. Charles didn't look particularly reassured, but it was the best she could manage, as well as being the truth. All she could do was try.

★   ★   ★

At long last, the blasted parade was starting.

Daniel tugged at the kerchief tied around his throat and scowled at nobody in particular. He felt ridiculous. An elbow dug into his right side.

"You certainly look the part, McCaffrey."

Daniel glowered at Rupert. "You're one to talk. I've seen fewer ruffles on ladies' gowns. What are you doing here, anyway? Aren't you in mourning?"

Rupert shrugged. "Amos insisted I come. Funny, he's become as obsessed with society as Elmira was. He's demanding a full report on how many condolences I receive." Rupert was dressed as a courtier from Louis XVI's court, in a lavish, deep-blue jacket with gold trim and lace protruding from the sleeves. He sported a long, curled wig, and had added a small patch to the upper left corner of his mouth. His one gesture toward his fiancée's mother's death was a black armband, stark against the blue velvet of his coat.

"What is that thing on your lip?"

"It's a beauty mark."

Daniel raised a sardonic brow at his friend.

Rupert drew himself up with dignity. "They were all the rage in the late eighteenth century. I was aiming for authenticity. I thought I'd best look wealthy, despite my reputation as a fortune hunter."

"You are a fortune hunter," Daniel remarked dryly.

Rupert tipped him a look. "Not anymore."

"How romantic of you."

Rupert snorted. "Now who's being a woman? There's no place for romance in a marriage like mine. It's a business transaction. You know it, I know it, and Esmie knows it."

"You deserve better," Daniel replied softly, keeping his gaze to the first of the guests, who were beginning to march across the stage, showing off their costumes.

"Esmie's not a bad sort," Rupert replied, just as softly. "She's actually quite sweet." Daniel looked at him sharply, wondering again what sort of truce the pair had formed.

"Won't there be services for Elmira?" Daniel asked quietly.

"Amos wants to wait until the police have figured out what happened."

"Aren't they looking at Tommy?" He kept his voice just above a whisper.

"Ironclad alibi, apparently." Rupert assumed a somber expression as Matilda Lemoyne, in a stiff black-and-white concoction meant to represent the Queen of Spades, paused and offered tearful condolences on the recent tragedy. "Thank you," he murmured, patting the society matron's hand. "Of course, I had to attend tonight. She would have wanted a representative from the family here." Mrs. Lemoyne nodded in understanding, her brow puckered in concern, but shot a more cautious look at Daniel, as if unsure how to relate to him now that it was known he hailed from Five Points.

He bared his teeth in response. Mrs. Lemoyne uttered a tiny shriek, mostly unheard in the din of the crowd, and hastily retreated.

Rupert gazed at Daniel incredulously. Daniel gave an irritated shrug in response.

"Quit scaring the locals," Rupert admonished. "*Your* future mother-in-law wasn't murdered, after all."

Daniel huffed, mightily wishing for a drink and tugging at the kerchief around his neck once more. He felt himself a more intense object of scrutiny than usual tonight. Some stared openly, but the majority only glanced his way as they whispered in small clumps. And no wonder: the revelation that he and Tommy Meade had been young ruffians from Five Points had been the topic of gossip columnists for days now. That and Elmira Bradley's grisly death, the details of which had somehow been leaked to the press. The fact that these two events had occurred in the same house, and in close proximity to each other, had set off a maelstrom of salacious, speculative articles.

It had been a busy, and Daniel guessed profitable, few days for the papers.

The results of the press's constant attention were apparent tonight: partygoers ebbed and flowed around him and Rupert as if there were an unseen barrier surrounding them, afraid to sully themselves with their presence; a few, like Mrs. Lemoyne, braved this boundary to approach Rupert, but otherwise it seemed society was collectively still deciding what to do with them.

Daniel scanned the stage for Genevieve, but so far she hadn't appeared. This damned parade was taking forever.

"Good costumes tonight. The ladies in particular have gone to great lengths, haven't they?" Rupert mused as a young woman dressed as a caged songbird paused on the stage to sing a few notes. The costume was an impressive construction of wire and feathers. "Such a shame I'm engaged. They don't even look at me now." He wistfully watched a petite redhead in a shepherdess outfit rush to join the parade, shaking his head in admiration. The audience clapped for the songbird, who made her way off the stage with some difficulty.

"But you, on the other hand." Rupert turned to his friend and assessed him. "You're garnering all *kinds* of attention. You don't have to try that hard to frighten anyone; you really do look the part. If only you could show your marks." He gestured to Daniel's upper arms, which underneath his white shirt and dark-red coat were covered with tattoos, evidence of his former gang affiliation.

Mostly former, that is.

"I've never been to one of these things before," Daniel replied irritably. "How was I to know what one wears?" It seemed his pirate costume was not quite the thing. Most of the other gentlemen in attendance were dressed, like Rupert, as historic courtiers, or as kings, emperors, or knights; in short, they were costumed as men of power, of intellect, and wealth. Daniel had been completely at a loss for how to dress, and had bellowed at Asher to find him something suitable. The resulting pirate costume had tight-fitting breeches with high leather boots, a sword strapped to his side, and a long red coat that flared over a simple, loose white cotton shirt. On Asher and Mrs. Kelly's direction, he hadn't shaved for two days, allowing his beard to partially grow in as if he'd spent days at sea. A loose kerchief was knotted around his neck, and they had set a tricornered hat on his head. Daniel had balked at wearing the eye-patch, but Mrs. Kelly had insisted. "It's the only way they'll know you're a pirate," she'd argued. "Otherwise you just look like a drunk on a three-day bender."

A murmur was growing throughout the crowd, tinged with an undercurrent of shock, and Daniel turned his attention to the stage, instantly spotting its cause. It was Genevieve's dark-haired friend, and she was clad in the slinkiest, sparkliest gown he'd ever seen, topped by simply enormous diamonds. She was practically bursting out of the bodice, and Daniel raised an eyebrow as she wriggled off the stage. If she was looking for male attention, she'd certainly get it in that outfit.

He eyed the diamonds in particular. A bold, and perhaps unwise, choice.

A second murmur rose from the crowd, distracting him from the giant stones. It was Sarah Huffington's turn, and she was slowly cross-ing the stage, head held high. She stopped in the center and turned in a lazy circle, her haughty gaze sweeping over the heads of those assem-bled, her disdain for their collective opinion obvious.

Half her costume was blindingly white, a soft, floating fabric that billowed around her left side. A great, nearly translucent wing grew from her back, and a semicircle of gold floated above the left side of her head. The other half of her costume was a deep, blazing red, with a low-cut bodice and a tight skirt encasing her right side. On this side, a single horn grew out of her elaborate hairstyle.

Half angel, half devil. Throwing another mocking look toward the audience, which had fallen into a rather shocked silence, Sarah glided toward the stage's stairs, making her exit.

Rupert sounded a low whistle. "She did tell me she had a cracker of a costume for the ball," he said. "I had no idea she had *that* planned."

An idea pinged inside Daniel's head. "May I ask a favor?"

Rupert glanced at him in surprise. "Anything."

Daniel quickly told him what he needed, finally catching sight of Genevieve's honey-colored head as she climbed the stairs for her turn to promenade across the stage.

"*Bloody hell,*" he swore, earning him a wary look from Rupert.

"You're in a mood tonight," his friend observed, though Daniel barely heard him. He had eyes only for Genevieve, who had dismounted from the stage and was looking around the room uncertainly. Sheer, diaphanous white silk hung off her shoulders, revealing bare arms. The fabric of her bodice was gathered and pleated in front, draping almost too low for public viewing, and a thick golden rope drew the fabric in at her waist. The gown had no bustle but hung naturally in soft folds to the ground. Gold bangles encircled her upper arms and wrists, and her thick hair was artfully piled on top of her head.

She looked stunning.

What she did not do, though they had specifically discussed it, was blend in. The people they planned to talk to tonight, their entire strategy,—it all depended on their both being part of the crowd, on *not* standing out.

With the way she looked, it would be impossible. He already saw young men cutting their eyes in her direction, gazes greedily roaming up and down her tall form.

Muttering curses under his breath, Daniel lifted his hat a bit and waved it, catching her attention. Genevieve nodded at him and then inclined her head toward one of the recessed areas that lined the edges of the ballroom.

And a grand, opulent ballroom it was. The Porters' costume ball was the one party of the season nobody dared miss, and this year it was cause for even more excitement. Rather than holding the ball in their Fifth Avenue mansion, the hosts had elected to make use of the facilities in the new Union Pinnacle Hotel, a giant, luxurious structure, to accommodate the vast number of guests.

"I'll find you later," Daniel murmured to Rupert, who flashed him a sardonic look but kept quiet. "You'll do as I asked?"

"Yes, yes." Rupert shooed him away impatiently. "You go on; I'm going to stand by the canapés and look sad, see if I can rack up more condolences for Amos."

Keeping an eye on Genevieve's massive pile of curls as she fought her way through the crowd toward the alcove, Daniel began to move in that direction too, though he had less fighting to do. Guests parted as he approached like the Red Sea before Moses, groups neatly sidestepping and then re-forming the moment he had passed. A few gentlemen nodded at him, sober faced: enough of an acknowledgment so as not to offend, but not an invitation to join their circle.

He wasn't offended. He wasn't even sure who half the guests *were*, their costumes were so elaborate. Masks of all kinds hid people's true identities: a commedia dell'arte Pulcinella chatted with a Harlequin, faces obscured by the traditional masks of their characters, and a portly gentleman costumed as a Pilgrim—Governor William Bradford, if Daniel had to guess—chuckled in low tones with someone dressed as a medieval king—William the Conqueror, perhaps?—both also wearing half masks.

Daniel frowned slightly as he nudged his way closer to the alcove. An unsettled feeling lingered in his chest as the covered faces and garish costumes began to blur together. The ballroom was densely packed, as the floor had yet to be cleared for dancing, and the prevailing mood seemed one of almost forced gaiety.

What would possess someone to throw a costume ball? It was hard enough to navigate the pitfalls of society when you knew who everyone was. When he was young, Jacob's butler had slipped him copies of visiting lists detailing who was who. He had studied these lists assiduously while at school, memorizing names and associations as determinedly as he had learned calculus and French. A mistake could be social suicide, and he had been determined to not make a mistake, determined not to waste Maggie's gift.

He saw Genevieve slip into the recessed space on the far side of the ballroom after glancing to make sure he was on his way. The giggling shepherdess he'd seen Rupert admire earlier ducked into a separate alcove, followed moments later by a grinning, masked toreador.

That was one appeal to a fancy-dress ball, he mused, pretending to adjust his sword to allow additional minutes to pass before joining Genevieve. The obfuscating costumes, combined with the increased crowd, provided cover for those who wished it.

The uneasy feeling in his chest intensified, and he glanced around, troubled by something he couldn't quite put a finger on, before ducking under the partial curtain into the alcove. People were constantly pretending to be something they weren't, him included. But on a night like this, those illusions could be taken to the extreme and used to cover any number of nefarious acts. He simply hoped he and Genevieve would be able to unmask their opponent before it was too late.

CHAPTER 15

"What the hell are you wearing?" Daniel demanded.

Genevieve's nerves, already wrangled and frayed, snapped to their breaking point.

"I thought it rather obvious," she bit out, raising her chin. His words stung; she had been feeling quite pretty. "And I thought I looked rather nice."

Daniel's jaw worked for a moment. Genevieve crossed her arms over her chest to mask her sudden insecurity. Did she, in fact, look ridiculous?

"You're radiant," he growled. A shy pleasure seeped through her, so unexpected was the compliment. "And therein lies the problem. You were meant to be inconspicuous."

"This was all the dressmaker could do on short notice," she protested.

"Bunch of fimble-famble," he muttered. "They could have thrown a sheet over your head, made a ghost of you."

"And *that* would have been less conspicuous? It's a fancy-dress ball, not Halloween. Besides, what are *you* wearing? Those breeches are so tight, you might as well be naked."

Her hand instantly clapped over her mouth as mortification washed through her, heat rushing to her face. Daniel looked as shocked as she felt. She had never said anything so wildly inappropriate in her life, *ever*.

A beat passed, where they simply stared at each other. She resolutely kept her eyes on his face, refusing to lower them anywhere near his trousers. "I apologize," Daniel finally said, a trifle stiffly. "You look lovely. I think we are both tense about this evening."

She accepted his apology with a nod of her head, her face cooling. "I apologize as well. You look . . . lovely too."

His mouth quirked into his cynical half smile at that. "Thank you," he said dryly. "How are you feeling? Ready to begin?"

Genevieve took a deep breath. Was she ready to wade among New York's elite, people she had known all her life, and attempt to ferret out a murderer?

The truth was, she didn't know. She didn't know if she would ever be ready for something like this.

At the same time, a thrum of excitement coursed through her, and part of her felt perfectly ready, even eager to begin. Part of her felt like this was exactly what she was meant to be doing with her life.

"It's a challenge," she admitted. "With the masks. Just like the one . . ." She bit her lip, pushing away the memories of the night she'd almost died. They would not do her any good tonight.

Daniel's gaze turned sharp. "The same mask? You've seen it?"

She shrugged. "Everywhere. Half the attendants are wearing that particular mask." She pulled back the curtain of the alcove slightly, searching the crowd. She pointed to a man dressed as Pulcinella. "Like that one."

He nodded slowly. "I saw him earlier. That's the mask?" She nodded back, then watched as Daniel scanned the revelers, undoubtedly noticing for the first time what had struck Genevieve instantly, like a blow to the gut: it was *everywhere*. The black half mask had downturned eyeholes and a long, almost sinister-looking nose. Deep grooves were cut into the forehead and cheeks of the mask, giving the wearer a weary yet macabre appearance.

Daniel glanced her way. Her heart had begun to pound in response to seeing the mask again, over and over, and she hoped her fear didn't show in her face.

"I'm sorry," he said softly. "Will this be too difficult for you?"

"No," she said instantly. "Whoever sent the masked person to kill me is probably here. We have to figure out who that is and how they're connected to Robin Hood."

Daniel glanced back at the crowd, and Genevieve followed his gaze. "Unless whoever sent the masked man works for the newspaper. They wouldn't be here."

"Perhaps," she said. She scrutinized the guests from afar, trying to ascertain who was who beneath their costumes. Some she could guess; others were more difficult. "Like Clive."

"Or your friend Luther."

She instantly shook her head. "Not him."

"Who else knew you would be on the tenth floor late at night? We have to keep all possibilities open, Genevieve, no matter how unpleasant."

"We've been over this," she retorted. And so they had, endlessly, it seemed. "Only a secretary named Verna saw me on the elevator that night. I told her where I was going, and I assume it was she who told Luther, who came to check on me."

"Awfully convenient."

"You sound jealous."

"You think very highly of yourself."

"Doth the gentleman protest too much?"

He snorted a laugh, and she felt some of the tension she had been carrying around for days begin to ease. It was good, this rapport between them. It made the coming task feel easier, more manageable.

"Even if someone from the paper did organize the attack," she continued, her breath catching slightly at the unbidden flash of memory of the masked face inches from hers, of the hands circling her throat, "they weren't working on their own. This goes deeper than one disgruntled newspaperman." She swallowed, willing the ghost of those fingers on her neck to dissipate.

"You're right," he conceded, then tipped his head toward the entrance. "Once more unto the breach?" Daniel's eyes gleamed in the dim light of the alcove. Her heart began to pound, in anticipation of the danger they were in, in excitement of what they might uncover. Without thinking, she grabbed his hand and squeezed it once, hard.

"We few, we happy few," she said, then dropped Daniel's hand, stepped past the curtain, and joined the fray.

★   ★   ★

Two hours later, Genevieve felt both wrung out and pleased with herself. Her costume might not have been as inconspicuous as Daniel would have liked, but she thought rather smugly that it certainly had been useful. She hadn't found herself the object of so much male attention since her debut, when the Stewart family fortune had brought suitors by the droves, despite her family's reputation for eccentricity.

The main objective of the evening had been to isolate and speak with all the members of the Committee on Housing Reform in hopes of gleaning further information. They had also hoped to ascertain who the mysterious investors in Lexington Industries were, as the company names listed in the filing at the municipal archives appeared in no other records. It had been no easy task, though, as one did not simply plunge into a conversation about a gentleman's business dealings in the middle of a ball, nor did young ladies usually make such inquiries; how and when to subtly insert such a topic into polite conversation required different tactics for different individuals. She and Daniel had divided up the list in their planning, based on which target might be more likely to be candid with whom, and had added a few other names that had come up in their research.

It made for an edgy, tense evening. Even as she engaged in acts as pedestrian as making a trip to the ladies' retiring room or sampling a truffled mushroom, she kept one eye on Daniel, who, she noticed, equally kept an eye on her. She was hyperaware of his movements around the ballroom, attuned to whether he was dancing or drinking or, she noted at least once with no small shock, flirting. A slight jolt reverberated through her body every time she confronted the black half mask, and the constant stress of keeping her face relaxed while her brain was on overdrive took its toll.

She was drained. She was exhilarated. The rush of the hunt was like nothing she had ever experienced before.

Ernest Clark, her first quarry, eagerly requested a dance at the slightest dropped hint. Like Sarah Huffington, he was wearing a rather ironic costume, that of a sandaled, hooded Capuchin monk. Unfortunately, his outfit did not negate his true nature, and she learned nothing other than that he was an unrepentant, socially ambitious flirt who couldn't keep his eyes off her décolletage. He sidestepped her tentative queries about his business relations so deftly that she wondered if she was being too obvious.

Or if he had much to hide.

She made marginally better progress with Peter Stuyvesant Senior, outfitted as King Lear in his right mind, over a glass of champagne. The old Knickerbocker was an acquaintance of her father's and was happy to chat with her about their mutual friends and his deep regret over Reginald Cotswold's passing. He too resisted discussing any business dealings, however, brushing aside her queries about the finances behind his and Cotswold's charitable organization for orphans. He was happy to talk about the orphans themselves and the ways she might make herself useful should she wish to volunteer, and in the process revealed his appalling lack of recognition of basic humanity in Italian and Eastern European immigrants. She hid her revulsion at his backward ideals and mentally filed away the information, noting that he did not, in fact, seem to be interested in seeing these populations receive better housing. She hoped Peter Stuyvesant Junior hadn't inherited his father's horrid beliefs.

Now Genevieve looked around the ballroom, but she couldn't spot the last person on her list. Daniel wasn't anywhere in sight either. Wondering if perhaps both men were in the gaming room on the second floor, she wandered toward where the punch was being served, suddenly ravenous. It would be best to speak with her final subject before the elaborate two AM supper was served, and she and Daniel really ought to have one more dance to keep up the illusion of courtship.

Her stomach grumbled with disappointment as she found that the earlier refreshments had been cleared away, undoubtedly so the guests could reserve their appetites for supper. Distracted by hunger, she stumbled right into the Holgrave twins, dressed as a pair of . . . hyenas? Alley cats? Some sort of mangy animal with ears—it was hard to say which. Callie caught her arm and pulled her out of the path of the affronted twins, one of whom pulled up her tail with a decided "Hrmph!" before stalking away.

"Genevieve!" Callie exclaimed, wiggling excitedly, her bosom barely contained in the sparkly outfit. She drew several appreciative glances from nearby gentlemen.

"Callie, stand still before you fall out of your dress," ordered Eliza, moving to stand strategically between her friend and the group of ogling men.

"Where have you been, Callie? I haven't seen you all night," Genevieve asked.

"On the dance floor." Callie's voice dropped conspiratorially. "On the *hunt*."

An involuntary wince hit Genevieve's body at the word "hunt," as it was so close to her own goals for the evening. Of course, Callie meant hunting for a husband, but it was still disquieting.

"And how goes it?" inquired Eliza.

Callie accepted a glass of punch from the footman behind the table and led the trio to a slightly more private area of the ballroom.

"Mixed results thus far," she admitted. "I danced the last quadrille with Richard Moore." She nodded toward a knight from the Crusades, who appeared quite overheated in his chain mail. Callie peered after his retreating form while absent-mindedly taking a sip of punch. "I don't know why they make dinner so late at these things. I'm simply famished. What do you both think of him?" She gestured with her glass toward where the knight had been swallowed by the crowd.

Eliza glanced in the direction Callie indicated. "I've heard he has gaming debts," she admitted.

"Blast." Callie pouted, taking another sip. "He actually had interesting things to say. Can you imagine being married to someone who had nothing interesting to say? What would you discuss at breakfast?"

"There's always the weather," Eliza remarked mildly, as Callie batted her eyes at a passing Henry VIII. He smiled back but made a regretful nod toward a trailing Anne Boleyn, made obvious by the severed head she carried under her arm.

Callie frowned. "Are there no single gentlemen at this party?"

Eliza smiled. "Callie, there are plenty of unattached men here. Isn't your dance card nearly full?"

Callie waved this away. "Oh, pish. None of them are rich enough for what Grandmama and I need. Now Genevieve, did I or did I not spy you and Mr. McCaffrey in an alcove earlier this evening? After the promenade?"

Feeling the color rise to her face, Genevieve nodded.

"And did he finally kiss you?" Callie demanded.

"No," she responded, cross. "Honestly, Callie, is that all you can think about?"

"Why would I want to think about anything else? Kissing is delightful. And speaking of, he's coming this way. Stalking, really. My, Genevieve, he does stalk well, your Mr. McCaffrey."

It was on the tip of her tongue to protest that Daniel wasn't *her* Mr. McCaffrey, but in the face of their pretend courtship, she held her tongue.

A brief spasm of longing passed through her, shocking in its unexpectedness. What if he *was* hers?

And then he was there, and Eliza was discreetly pulling a protesting Callie away to give them some privacy. She shoved the unruly thought away.

He followed her friends' retreat with an amused glance. "Do they believe it?" he asked in a quiet voice, as he gently retrieved and kissed her hand.

The feel of his lips on the back of her ungloved hand was unnerving. As was the way he gazed into her eyes, one corner of his mouth twitching upward. "They do," she said. "As will everyone else, the way you're behaving."

"We need the courtship to seem legitimate," he murmured, lowering her hand. "Now, I believe the next dance is mine, is it not?"

As Daniel led her onto the floor for the start of their waltz under the watchful eyes of half the Astor 400, Genevieve had a brief, strong flash of recollection of what it felt like to be fully accepted by society. To be the object of approving gazes rather than censorious ones. With her and Daniel's sham courtship, she could feel the societal tides shifting, away from their dour disappointment that she'd chosen a career over a husband and toward a self-righteous satisfaction that she was finally fulfilling her proper role, even if it was with someone currently under their collective suspicion. Anger welled within her, causing her jaw to clench, even as her body mechanically followed Daniel's in the graceful rhythms of the waltz.

Why must women fit into preordained molds? Why couldn't she be accepted and celebrated as a journalist rather than only as a fiancée or a wife? A turn around the dance floor brought Eliza, standing alone at the edge of the dance floor, into and then out of her line of sight. Eliza was a brilliant artist, but her skill and merit were never lauded as they should be, simply because of her sex. Another turn and there was Callie, dancing in the arms of Victor Fairstoke, a widowed banker twice her age, ridiculously dressed as Don Juan. The man was known for having a string of mistresses barely out of the schoolroom, and Genevieve's stomach knotted at the thought of Callie tied to the old leach. Her hand involuntarily tightened on Daniel's shoulder.

"Is my dancing that bad?"

She instantly relaxed her hold. "I'm sorry. No, of course not." And it wasn't. Daniel was a beautiful dancer.

"What have you learned?" The music, along with their constant rotations, was likely preventing anyone from overhearing, but he still kept his voice lowered.

"Not much," she admitted, relaying in equally muted tones her conversations with Ernest Clark and Peter Stuyvesant Senior. Daniel winced.

"The son is not much better." He shook his head in disapproval bordering on disgust. "And to think they are both tasked with improving housing for the impoverished immigrants they so hate. Impoverished due to circumstance and lack of education, not their own failings." She watched a range of emotions play across his face, realizing he was likely thinking of his own family.

Daniel gave his head a small shake again, though this time as if to clear it. "Enough. We're not finished yet, and I have one more person I'd like to approach before the night is through."

The waltz was winding down, and Genevieve caught sight of Felicity Holgrave, distinguishable from her twin Frances by eyes that were blue rather than brown, coquettishly smiling in Daniel's direction. "One of the Holgrave twins?" she asked, raising a brow as he led her back to the edge of the dance floor.

A look of alarm crossed his face. "Absolutely not. Do you know what one of them said to me earlier? I actually don't think I can repeat it to a lady, it was so salacious."

Genevieve surprised herself with a giggle. It felt good to laugh in the face of everything: the endless black masks, the ignorance of men like the Stuyvesants, the constant rumbling of fear in the pit of her belly.

"I told you those breeches were too tight."

"McCaffrey." A hand clapped Daniel on the back. Ted Beekman had joined them. Daniel stared at the hand for a beat, and Ted removed it, smiling a jovial smile. "Great minds think alike, eh?"

Genevieve stifled a gasp. To refer to their previous engagement via a double entendre, particularly in front of her, was horribly inappropriate. Daniel's gaze, which had already been quite neutral, turned chilly. "I beg your pardon?" he asked icily.

"I mean our costumes," Ted said, gesturing toward himself. He was clad in a blue satin jacket, almost to his knees, over gray tights. He sported no mask but instead a giant blue-tinged beard, and his head was topped with a jaunty hat adorned with blue and gray feathers. "I'm Bluebeard. We seem to be the only pirates in attendance tonight."

"Blackbeard was a pirate," Daniel clarified. "Bluebeard is a folktale about a man who killed his wives." His response was aimable enough, but Genevieve noticed that the coldness didn't leave Daniel's eyes.

"Bluebeard, Blackbeard." Ted shrugged and laughed heartily. "We'll just say I'm a pirate and be done with it, eh?"

Daniel turned toward her. "Champagne?"

"Yes, please." She actually didn't want champagne, but Ted was the final person on her list, and he was more likely to be candid without Daniel around.

It seemed as though half the ballroom watched as her ex-fiancé perfunctorily shook her hand and she inquired about his health, and the health of his wife.

"Oh, Amelia," Ted boomed heartily, referring to his seemingly absent wife. He had always been the sort of man who boomed; she wondered how she had ever tolerated it. "She's resting at home, of course. I am to be a father soon," he explained, correctly interpreting Genevieve's puzzled expression.

Genevieve paused a moment to digest this information, almost expecting small tendrils of pain to wrap themselves around her heart and squeeze; here it was, the life that had almost been hers. But the sting didn't arrive. It was akin to receiving news from a stranger.

"Congratulations," she said politely.

"Yes, yes. It's been hard on her, you know. She hasn't been feeling well for months."

"I am sorry to hear it," Genevieve replied. She took a breath, preparing to ask how his work was going, hoping to turn the conversation toward his role on the mayoral committee, but he interrupted.

"You're looking very well, though," he boomed again. Genevieve controlled the urge to wince. Couldn't he speak in a normal tone of voice? "Very well," he repeated, his gaze dropping down her body, a small, ugly smile playing on the corners of his lips.

The sudden urge to smack the smile off his face, to offer some kind of physical retribution for the shame he had caused her family, was so strong that she had to clench her fist for a moment to prevent her hand from swinging through the air. Over Ted's shoulder she caught sight of Daniel widening his eyes at her from where drinks were being served. She forced a smile to her lips.

"Business is good?" The smile felt brittle, but it was the best she could muster.

"Hmm?" Ted dragged his eyes away from her bare shoulders. "Oh, very, very."

Genevieve swallowed, glancing over his shoulder to Daniel again. Felicity Holgrave had indeed trapped him in conversation, but he met her eyes all the same, offering a quick, reassuring nod.

"I'm not surprised." She willed her smile to become sweeter and cast a look toward Ted through her lashes. "You always were poised for great success."

Ted's chest expanded a bit under the blue satin. "Well, if I may be allowed a moment to brag." He lowered his voice, his gaze sliding down her neck. It was hard not to shudder. "I am on the cusp of seeing a very healthy return on an investment. *Very*," he emphasized, finally returning his eyes to her face.

She let out a small, feigned gasp, operating on pure instinct. "Lexington Industries?" she asked in a hushed tone.

Ted's look turned shrewd. "Heard about it, have you? From whom?"

"I shouldn't like to say," Genevieve slid her eyes toward Ernest Clark's behooded figure, slipping out the door toward the grand staircase. Ted followed her eyes and gave a small grunt. "But I was asked if perhaps my brother Charles would be amenable to joining the venture."

Her heart pounded as the lies piled up. This was the closest she or Daniel had come to information about the mysterious Lexington Industries all night. And now the clock was starting to tick: as soon as Ted confronted Clark and the other investors—whoever they were—about speaking with Genevieve and discovered that in fact nobody had approached her, whoever hoped to do her harm would know she was getting closer to the truth.

They had to work fast now. And hope to get the information they needed.

"Tell Charles to come speak with me if he's interested." Ted looked thoughtful. "It would be a boon to have him on board. But I'm surprised you were not approached to invest."

"Me?" She didn't have to feign surprise this time.

"Why not? You've come into your money by now, have you not?" She had, the previous year. "We've other female investors. Could make quite a profit, you know." Ted leaned in close, so close she could smell the liquor on his breath. Her skin began to crawl. "Think about it, hmm? You know where to find me."

Ted tipped her a wink, running his hand on her bare arm for the briefest of moments before Daniel forcibly stepped between them. Ted gave a small bow and backed away, raising his hands. "Glad we had a chance to speak, Genevieve. I do hope you or Charles consider joining us. It would be ideal for our families to mend fences."

Genevieve managed a tight smile until he was gone, then gulped half her glass in one swallow. "Odious man," she muttered.

"Shall I knock out his front teeth?" Daniel asked, as if inquiring about the quality of the champagne.

"Much as I wish it, no," she said. Excitement began to edge out her exhaustion. "We need to talk privately, and fast."

CHAPTER 16

Daniel's pulse began to quicken. "All right. Let me think for a moment on the best way to handle that. But I have one more person to speak to first."

"I'm not sure we have time." Genevieve swallowed the rest of her champagne. "Ted thinks someone approached me about investing," she whispered as she leaned in to hand him her empty glass. "Once he speaks to the others and realizes it was a ruse . . ." Her wide eyes bored into his, conveying urgency.

He nodded quickly, understanding. Their time was limited now. "I'll be fast." Rupert sauntered by and gave him a casual nod, then continued past.

Good, everything was arranged. "Meet me back in the alcove in five minutes," he said.

"Not private enough," she murmured. "Get us a room."

Daniel couldn't help himself; he jerked back slightly in shock. "What?"

She laid a hand on his arm and smiled up at him, but he could see the growing frustration on her face. "Don't be such a namby-pamby. A hotel room, here. We haven't time to return to your house, and everywhere else is too public."

He patted the hand on his arm, keeping up the pretense of a besotted courting couple, and leaned in close again. "If anyone sees us, your reputation will be damaged irreparably," he said through clenched teeth. "It's too risky."

"We haven't any choice," she hissed back, then feigned a small laugh, as if they were sharing a private joke. "Do you know Eliza Lindsay, there in the blue?" He nodded shortly; they'd been introduced some years ago. "After you retain a room, meet her at the top of the staircase and tell her the room number. She will relay it to me, and I'll join you in fifteen minutes."

He tried to protest again. "But—"

She cut him off. "There's no time, Daniel. *Go.*" And with that, she patted his arm again, looking every inch the figure of a young lady in love, and made her way toward her friend.

Damn, damn, damn. She was right again, of course. Minutes, seconds, mattered now; they had to speak privately and compare notes as soon as possible. But *damn* if he didn't think this was a foolhardy plan all the same. He just didn't see a way around it.

Daniel elbowed through the crowd toward his own target.

Sarah Huffington appeared deep in conversation with Rupert on the peripheries of the dance floor. At Rupert's gesture, he joined them.

Head tilted, Sarah eyed him in consideration. "Daniel," she drawled. "Rupert says you might wish to join our little venture."

He smiled in return, exhilaration coursing through him. He'd had a hunch that Mrs. Huffington was more involved in her husband's dealings than either Huffington publicly acknowledged, and asked Rupert to place one or two discreet inquiries. It had paid off.

"I might. I've heard rumors of phenomenal potential returns."

"And you'd spot Rupert the funds until he gets his hands on the Bradley girl's dowry?" Rupert gave him a bright, innocent smile. Daniel hid his annoyance with difficulty. He didn't mind giving Rupert money, but he hadn't had time to tell his friend the entire story. There was no way he was getting in bed financially with the Huffingtons.

"Of course." He slid a look toward Rupert, who appeared to divine its meaning and instantly looked contrite. Sarah caught the exchange.

"Now, now, don't be cross with darling Rupert." She slid a hand up Rupert's arm. "The wedding's been delayed with this murder business, and the poor lad now has to wait for all that money. As his friends, it's our duty to help him. At least you get to socialize without that albatross of a girl around your neck for a few months." She leaned into Rupert's side while casting Daniel a flirtatious look from under her combined horn and halo. Rupert's mouth tightened at the disparagement of his fiancée, but he said nothing.

"You look ravishing, by the way." Sarah directed this toward Daniel, eyes moving to and lingering on his breeches. "You should have dressed as a B'hoy," she remarked, referring to the decades-old nickname given to Five Points toughs. "That would really have knocked off everyone's socks."

He affected a look of wry amusement, privately wishing the damn breeches weren't so tight. "I shall leave the knocking off of socks to you." He pretended to catch sight of the time on the large gilded clock visible on the wall just outside the grand ballroom's open double doors. "I have something else to attend to right now"—he glanced around as if wishing for discretion—"but let's be in touch soon about this opportunity."

The hallway clock began to chime, deep and sonorous. Two o'clock. In a moment, a servant would sound a gong, letting the guests know supper was served.

Sarah raised her brows. "Well, we all know what an appointment at this time of night means," she practically purred. "And as I can't imagine the righteous Miss Stewart would allow any such shenanigans, I'll have to resign myself to speculation on who the lucky lady could be. But mind you, don't ruin matters with the virginal Genevieve, Daniel; she's also in possession of quite a fortune. Could come in handy." She dropped him a wink before taking Rupert's arm and leading him toward the dining room.

Daniel wasted not a moment but casually began making his own way toward the hall, as if heading perhaps to the retiring room or downstairs to the gaming tables. He shared one quick look with Genevieve's friend Eliza, who gave him a single nod and paused by the door, where she would wait for his return.

★   ★   ★

Daniel paced the sumptuous hotel suite he had reserved, waiting. He stopped walking for a moment to pour a small glass of whiskey from a completely stocked side table and watched the door anxiously, hoping Genevieve could make it to the room unseen.

Hoping nothing had happened to her in the past fifteen minutes.

Twisting his mouth, Daniel took a sip of whiskey and swirled it around his tongue before swallowing. He restlessly unknotted the kerchief around his neck—he'd abandoned the ridiculous hat, sword, and eye-patch as soon as he'd entered the room—and resisted the urge to poke his head into the hallway.

A soft knock sounded at the door, and he leapt to open it.

Genevieve rushed in and quickly closed the door, the green-lined cloak thrown over her shoulders billowing behind her like a standard.

"Were you seen?"

"I don't think so."

Relief washed through him. "Good. I took the liberty of having some food sent up, as we're missing the supper." Daniel gestured toward some bread, cheese, and savory meat pastries set out on the sideboard, then poured a measure of whiskey into a separate glass and handed it to her.

"Thank gracious. I'm famished," Genevieve replied, accepting the glass after removing her cloak. He watched as she filled a plate, then took in the suite's rich surroundings as she nibbled: its heavy draperies, its gilded furniture, the ornate, overly large bed made up with crisp white sheets visible in the adjacent room beyond.

She settled on a love seat and set her plate on a low table, pulling the pins out of her hair, its honey-colored mass tumbling to her shoulders.

The moment was so startling in its intimacy that an involuntary swallow briefly clogged his throat.

"You don't mind, do you? My scalp aches from this hairstyle."

Daniel said nothing, ruthlessly quashing any improper thoughts brought on by the incomparable sight of all that hair piling around her bare shoulders, and chose the armchair opposite her.

"What did you find out?" he asked instead, pulling off his boots. Hell, if she was getting comfortable, he might as well be too. He noted

Genevieve's eyes following his motions and felt a grim satisfaction. Good, let *her* be thrown off guard by a partial disrobing. He nodded as she relayed what Ted had told her, clunking his second boot to the floor.

"Sarah Huffington also invited me to join," he said, leaning forward.

Her eyebrows shot up. "Ted did say there were other female investors." She took a cautious sip of whiskey. "This is good."

Daniel smiled. "It is."

"Show me the list of investors again."

He complied, pulling the notes she had made at the municipal archives out of his shirt pocket and handing it across. She frowned as she studied the list of corporation names.

"This only lists other businesses as investors. How are Ted and Sarah involved? I couldn't find anything on these corporations." Genevieve handed the list back. "And what does Lexington Industries even *do*? What are they protecting that they must resort to violence, to murder?"

Daniel studied the list in his hand for what felt like the thousandth time, taking a fortifying sip of his own whiskey. *Lexington Industries*, her notes read. *Andrew Huffington and Ernest Clark, chief operators. Investing entities* . . .

And suddenly he saw it. The answer was right there, right before his eyes. Daniel quickly switched seats so he was next to Genevieve on the love seat. He leaned into her, inhaling the fresh, almost grassy scent of her unbound hair. "Look," he said in excitement. "Look closely at the company names."

She puzzled at him for a moment, but did as he bade. He waited.

"Oh my god. How did we miss it?" She pointed to one of the companies listed: *Tiberius Point Beneficiaries, Inc.* "TPB," she said. "Theodore Paul Beekman." Genevieve's mouth slanted wryly as she took another sip from her glass. "He *would* name himself after a Roman emperor."

"And . . ." He pointed to another: *Syndicated American Hospitality Co.*

"Sarah Alston Huffington," she breathed.

Working quickly, they matched most of the remaining investor names to almost all the other members of the mayoral committee on housing reform: *Performance Standards Incorporated & Son* must be the senior and junior Peter Stuyvesants, and Deputy Mayor Giles Manfort was likely *Goode Manufacturing, Inc.*

"Not terribly creative, that one," Genevieve commented. "There's one member of the committee missing."

"No fictitious company with the initials R.C.," Daniel noted. "Reginald Cotswold." They shared a brief, grim look.

"And there is this one we haven't matched to a person," she said, tapping her finger on the page. "Tenfold Mercantile."

"Of course," he said. "Thomas Meade." A chill began to overtake him, and Daniel sighed, exhaustion suddenly swooping in and draining the brief burst of energy brought by puzzling out Lexington Industries' investors. He leaned back on the love seat and rubbed at his eyes.

Tommy. He could never, it seemed, be rid of the bastard. This was more dangerous than he'd feared.

"Why are the members of a governmental committee on housing reform using false names to support a seemingly nonexistent corporation?" Genevieve asked, more to the piece of paper laid on the table than to him.

"This is a mask," he answered. Daniel sat up and ran a hand through his hair. "It's a shell company, hiding the real business being done. A place to funnel the money."

"The real business of what?" she asked.

"I'm not sure yet. Something they don't want anyone to know about."

"Enough to kill for." It was a statement, not a question.

Daniel nodded. "Maybe not everyone on this list. Some of these people might be just innocent investors. But for some on this list, absolutely." His finger landed on Meade's name.

"They didn't seem to want Reginald to know," Genevieve said sadly. Her lips pursed in anger. "So how do we find out? How do we ascertain what they're up to?"

Daniel picked up the list and tapped it on the table a few times, thinking. "My guess is one of these company names is shared with the real business at hand, and the real company has the same initials as one of these." His eyes met hers. "We have to keep digging."

Genevieve's eyes flared with a brief moment of fear, quickly replaced by determination. "Back to the archives."

He nodded, his stomach twisting at the thought of her in yet more danger. But there was no other way. "Whatever they're hiding, they'll already know we're getting close by the time the archives reopen Monday morning. Go in broad daylight."

"It's fine." She straightened in her seat and finished her glass. "I can do it. I can even check whatever I find against the paper's records; I'll bring one of the secretaries with me if I must. Like you said, broad daylight."

Daniel noticed a worried look returning to her eye. "Only if you feel up to it. We're getting closer, though, and time is running out. This should be it."

Genevieve took a deep breath and nodded. "Reginald was on the committee, but why kill Elmira Bradley? And what does Robin Hood have to do with this?"

"I don't know," he said. "Perhaps Amos was approached and declined to be involved in whatever this is. My gut tells me Tommy is somehow involved. He's devious, Genevieve, and more dangerous than you can possibly imagine." Privately Daniel wondered if Tommy had ordered Elmira killed simply because she had embarrassed him at her ball, but he didn't see the need for alarming Genevieve further.

Genevieve's brow furrowed. "How do you know?"

He paused. "I've known Tommy a long time."

"Of course," she allowed. "But despite his past, the man *is* a mayoral candidate. Do you really think he's capable of murder?"

Daniel leaned back again and regarded her through tired eyes. "I don't just think it; I know it."

Genevieve's mouth opened a bit in shock.

He sighed a breath and unwound his limbs, which suddenly felt ten times their normal weight, from the love seat for a brief journey to the sideboard, where he refilled his glass with a generous splash of whiskey. He held up the bottle with an inquiring look, and Genevieve nodded, holding her glass up as well.

Daniel resumed his seat and took a deep breath. He'd never revealed as much about his past to anyone as he was about to share with her, with the exception of Rupert. And he'd told Rupert only after they'd gotten rip-roaring drunk one night at college in Boston, where they'd both been attending Harvard. He'd woken up the next morning, expecting his friend to have forgotten all about their mutual confessions the night before, or at least to be very British about the whole thing and pretend to forget. But as he cracked one eye open and tried to assess the damage to his pounding head, Rupert simply blinked up at him from the floor of Daniel's room where he'd collapsed, rubbed a hand through his wild hair, and said, "So, mate, if you're from Five Points, you must know where to get some very good opium. Let's go next weekend; what do you say?"

Daniel said no and convinced Rupert through stories from his youth that opium was a very bad idea indeed. But the casualness with which his friend had approached the topic opened something up in Daniel, something he hadn't even realized he needed before telling Rupert about his past. The secrets had been festering, and the strain of pretending to be someone and something he wasn't had been slowly killing him. Unburdening some of the darkest moments from his past—and only some of them; he hadn't told Rupert about Maggie— had eased his mind enough to allow him to continue on the path Jacob had set for him, but to simultaneously make that path his own.

"I do know Tommy from my youth," he said now. "We grew up together on Elizabeth Street. Tommy was just one of the kids we knew."

"Who is 'we'?" she asked.

"Just the kids I ran around with." Daniel shrugged, peering into his glass. "There came a time, in the 1860s, when if you lived in Five Points and you were male and you were of a certain age, you needed to declare your allegiance."

"Allegiance?"

"To a particular gang."

Genevieve nodded, seeming to take the information in stride, though he knew it was miles outside her lived experience. "And did you?"

"Of course. It was the only way to survive. Especially with my father gone. And it wasn't that bad. Your fellow gang members were like brothers. They protected you, and you protected them."

"Were you and Tommy in the same gang?"

"No, Tommy was in a different gang. I was a Bayard Tough; he was with the Oyster Knife boys. Our gangs were rivals. You must understand, gangs functioned something like social clubs, but of course violence and crime were—are—part of their nature. The Bayard Toughs traditionally worked the political angle of crime, fixing polls and the like, arranging repeat voting."

Genevieve's eyebrows shot up. "Did you participate in this as a child?"

Daniel shrugged. "Of course. I served as a lookout for the approach of the police, ran messages for whoever was in charge, that sort of thing. Tommy's gang, though, the Oyster Knife boys . . . they were harder. Tougher than us, actually. Despite our name." He smiled, lost in memory. "Don't get me wrong, the Bayard Toughs could hold their own in a street brawl—and brawl we did, quite often. Casual turf wars, that sort of thing."

"I see," she said faintly.

"The Oyster Knifers, now, they ran bars and brothels, could be hired out as muscle. As I said, they were harder, more vicious. I was invited to join their gang at first, as they are a more traditionally Irish gang, though there were Irish everywhere in Five Points, of course— did I tell you my parents immigrated from Lansdowne?" She shook her head. "They came in 1850. My mother was already pregnant with my older sister Maggie. It's a wonder they didn't starve on the boat. Or back in Ireland.

"But I didn't want to join up with them—even as a child I knew their reputation. It was just the sort of thing you knew if you lived in Five Points. Besides, my father had been a Bowery Boy, and the Toughs were a subset of the Boys, if you will."

"He had been?"

"Oh yes. Fought against the Dead Rabbits in that famous turf war in '57. And gang membership often stays in the family. The Toughs have traditionally been from a slightly more elevated social class than the Knifers—slightly." He smiled wryly in acknowledgment of the bare distinction. "Skilled tradesmen, butchers, mechanics, that sort of thing. My father had been a blacksmith. I meant to apprentice as one myself."

"But then you moved into the Van Joost house?" she guessed.

Daniel nodded slowly. "Yes, then we moved in with Jacob."

A thoughtful expression crossed her face. "Is that how you know Paddy and Billy from the alley the night I met you? From your youth?"

Daniel nodded ruefully and ran his hands through his hair. "Yes, that is how I know Paddy and Billy."

"You seemed to be the group's leader that night."

Daniel barked a short laugh. "Nobody leads Paddy and Billy. But I've offered legal assistance to them and to some of their associates in the past, helped them out of a jam or two, so sometimes they respect me enough to do as I ask. Within reason."

"So if you moved in with Jacob Van Joost in—what year?"

"Eighteen sixty-five."

"Eighteen sixty-five! Were you at all involved in the Draft Riots?"

"Yes, I was. This is when I first learned something was deeply wrong with Tommy. I snuck out of my house, joined some friends." They'd been wondering where to find some of the older gang members, he told her, looking for direction, boasting to each other about how brave they'd be if they ran across any rival gangs, when they rounded a corner and come across a group of similarly aged boys from the Oyster Knife gang, including Tommy.

"Normally there would have been a fight, but they ran past us and joined with a group of their older gang members." Daniel paused, struggling with the memory. "We followed them for a few blocks, but it soon became clear they were involved in, well, what the Draft Riots became known for." His stomach soured at the recollection.

Genevieve's hand drifted to her mouth. "They . . . killed someone?"

"Yes . . . hung him from a lamppost. I'd never seen anything so horrific, and I'd seen a lot. Tommy was in the thick of it, laughing like a loon."

"Oh my god," Genevieve breathed.

Daniel nodded. Jacob had sent him abroad when he was fourteen, but he still came home during the summers, and at night he'd join up with his old friends, like Asher, and roam the streets with fellow gang members. It was during this period that Daniel learned to exist in two worlds: the polished, mannered, and civilized ballrooms of Fifth Avenue and the summer houses of Newport, and the streets of the Lower East Side. As he grew older and went to university, he met up with his old friends less and less, apprenticing in the law after Harvard and becoming familiar with the city's courts. Even so, he retained the ability to slip back into gang life at will, at least on the surface. He still knew the streets and the alleys and kept up with the major players in his other, dirtier, world, and for a long time it was a world he often felt was more honest, and probably where he truly belonged.

"Of course, I don't really belong there anymore, and I haven't for many years," Daniel relayed. He eyed the sideboard but decided to hold off for the moment. Surely it would be dawn soon, and they'd have to get Genevieve home safely. "The money creates a barrier. My first few summers coming home from Harvard, after I inherited, I was challenged repeatedly, taunted, got into more fights than I'd ever been in before in my life. But that was to be expected—what wasn't expected was Tommy. At least once a year or so, he'd find me, or I'd find him, but not by chance, you understand? He'd figure out where I was going to be and be there too, and engage in some sort of . . . atrocity." Daniel shook his head, deeply lost in thought. "I really don't want to tell you the details, but suffice it to say I have pulled him off of countless others in the intervening years. It was always someone weaker than him, often women."

He fixed Genevieve with a hard stare. "Women who did not want to be with him. Do you understand what I'm saying?" She nodded slowly.

It was as if Tommy had wanted Daniel to find him, he explained. Had wanted him to intervene, so they could have an excuse to fight. It became a pattern: Daniel, with the help of his friends, would pull Tommy off whomever he was attacking. Tommy would then challenge Daniel and Daniel alone.

"You always need to save the day, don't you, Danny boy?" Tommy had panted, dancing around Daniel with his fists raised. The other boys, later young men, would draw back into the shadows, knowing this was not their fight but staying close. Sometimes other men, members of other gangs or additional members of theirs, would drift out of nearby taverns or whorehouses or tenement buildings to watch. And Daniel would raise his own fists, sometimes furiously, sometimes wearily, but always with resolve, and the two would proceed to fight until one of them was too incapacitated to move.

"I traveled the continent after I finished my apprenticeship, and when I began making intermittent returns a few years ago, it stopped. I never saw Tommy on the streets again—well, not those streets. I knew he'd become involved with politics, and I suppose he didn't want to risk being known as a street thug anymore."

"What a shock it must have been to find him in the Bradley mansion," Genevieve breathed, looking rather shocked herself. "How could such a horrible person be taken seriously as a candidate for mayor?" She flopped back on the love seat, looking drained.

Daniel didn't have an answer for this. He had thoughts about it, about the myths the wealthy liked to tell themselves about the ability of the deeply impoverished to pull themselves out of that poverty of their own volition, with no assistance, but now was not the time for such a discussion. They needed to think about getting Genevieve home before light.

"But what about Robin Hood?" Genevieve said slowly. "What does stealing from the Astor 400 have to do with this? Is it Meade, rubbing their noses in their wealth?"

He shook his head. "I don't think so. I have a theory about our Robin Hood, though."

This made her sit up tall again. "What?"

Uh-oh, Daniel thought. This wasn't going to go over well. He slid her a rueful, sideways look. "I can't tell you."

Sure enough, fury spread over her features. "I thought we were partners."

"We are partners, but this is dangerous enough. I can't endanger you any further."

"This is *my* investigation, remember? I dragged you into it, as you so often see fit to remind me. And now you know something you won't share?"

"I don't *know* anything."

"But you suspect something."

"I can't say. Yet."

Genevieve stood, hands clenched into fists at her sides. "You don't trust me, is that it? Or you don't believe I'm up to the task?"

Daniel stood too, the exhaustion temporarily wiped from his body. He was furious, *furious*, that she would continue to be so cavalier about her own safety.

"You were nearly killed! I won't risk you again!"

That made Genevieve draw back in surprise. He was equally surprised at himself.

"That is not your decision to make," she finally said in a low voice.

Frustrated, confused, Daniel turned from her and began to pace the room again. What had he even meant by that, that he didn't want to risk her? He stopped by the sideboard and stared at the decanters, less wanting a drink than needing a place to focus his eyes, gather his tumultuous thoughts.

She followed him a few steps, then stopped. "What don't you want me to know?" Genevieve breathed. "Was I right all along?" She advanced a few more steps.

"It's you, isn't it?" she said. "You're Robin Hood."

Daniel's heart pounded. He had to make this right. He turned back to her slowly.

"I can't tell you anything further about Robin Hood right now. But, to earn your trust back, I can tell you something else. I can tell you how I came to inherit the Van Joost fortune."

CHAPTER 17

He watched her fists unclench. "You . . . what?"

"You deserve to know the truth," he replied. "And you should know with whom you've partnered. I want you to know how I came to inherit Jacob's fortune."

This was it, then. This was the person to whom he was going to entrust all his secrets. A reporter outfitted as Aphrodite with the most glorious hair he'd ever seen. He gestured back to the love seat.

She took her seat again, eyeing him warily. "If you wish to tell me, then I'd like to hear about it."

He decided he did want more whiskey, retrieving his glass and adding a splash. He gestured toward Genevieve's, but she shook her head. He settled in on his half of the love seat.

Where to begin? It wasn't that atypical a story, not really. Not for immigrant families in the years immediately following the Civil War. Parents dead, children left on their own.

Daniel stared at the whiskey in his glass and swirled it slowly. He watched the amber liquid revolve around the cut-crystal glass, heavy and real in his hand, grounding him. "My father died in the war. I was seven. My mother died four years later, probably from cholera, though of course there was never any official diagnosis."

"You mentioned a sister," she said.

He put the whiskey down, kept his gaze on her instead. "Yes, my older sister. I also had three younger siblings. Maggie was fifteen when Mother died, and we were left on our own. She tried to play mother to all of us as best she could, but I was too wild, and the younger ones, well, she couldn't keep an eye on them all the time. Not with the constant battle of trying to find us food and keep us and the house clean." Here Daniel paused, gathering his thoughts.

This was the hard part to tell. It was the disappearance of his younger siblings, Mary, Connor, and little Stephen, that had pushed Maggie over the edge. When everything began to unravel.

"Disappear?" Genevieve asked quietly.

"As good as," Daniel replied. Maggie had been in the small shared courtyard of their tenement, washing the family's scant bedding. She had sent the younger children out to play in the street, as they were accustomed to do. It was understood that Mary, who was five, would watch over the littler ones. Daniel, eleven, desperately wounded by the recent death of his mother but determined to be a man and not show it, had refused his older sister's attempts to corral him as his parents had. On that particular day, he'd joined up with some local boys his age and wandered over to the piers on the city's west side, where they jumped off the docks and swam away the heat of the summer day in the dirty Hudson River. Daniel could still feel the cool water sluicing over his body, a blessed relief from the unrelenting, oppressive steam of the city's hemmed-in streets, as he plunged into the river's murky depths again and again. By the time he leisurely returned to Elizabeth Street, his hair dripping, his gnawing grief briefly sated from the hard exercise of jumping, swimming, and fighting the river's currents, Maggie was frantic. The little ones had been missing for over three hours, as far as anyone could tell. A neighbor woman offered the best clue: she had seen an older woman in a drab blue gown leaning down and talking to the children. At one point this woman had cupped little Stephen's chin so she could look into his mouth.

"Checking his teeth, we assumed," Daniel recounted, finding it hard to resist the waves of sadness that came over him whenever he talked about his long-lost younger siblings. "The woman in the blue dress was almost surely from the Children's Aid Society, you see."

Genevieve stiffened slightly on her side of the love seat. "The orphan trains?" she asked.

Daniel nodded at his glass. "Most likely. Even though Maggie was of an age to take care of us, to the Children's Aid Society we were parentless, and could be snatched up and shipped away at will to Ohio or the like to work on a farm. If I hadn't been swimming, I might have been taken as well—they often employed large men to take some of the older boys, like me. But children were fairly valuable, you see—good labor. It's still going on, you know." He glanced over at her. "They still take children."

"Did you try to find them?" she asked.

"We did," Daniel said, swallowing some more whiskey. "We tried. But who was going to listen to a pair of grubby street kids like us? To the authorities, the orphan trains were and are a godsend, getting unwanted children off the streets and into loving homes."

"But these children weren't unwanted," Genevieve finished for him.

"No. No, they were very much wanted." Another flash of memory, another pang: his little sister Mary, about one year old, toddling across the floor of their crowded apartment into his waiting arms as his parents and Maggie cheered. His father had been holding brand-new baby Connor. Irish twins, they'd called Mary and Connor, babies born within a year of each other. And little Stephen would follow about twelve months after that.

Daniel was distracted from his recollections as Genevieve grabbed his arm excitedly, almost knocking his glass out of his hand.

"We could find them," she said. "I, or Polly Palmer, she could find them. As a journalist I could get access to records, discover where they were sent . . ." She stopped short at the sight of his shaking head.

"Thank you," Daniel said, setting down his glass again. He should have known that Genevieve would pounce on this part of his tale like a dog on a juicy bone, that she would take it and worry it and try to fix it. It was part of her very nature, this desire to fix things, particularly any injustice. "Thank you," he repeated, "for saying that. But I have tried. I have been trying. Those records are sealed very tightly. I have people working on it, though, and I feel I'll have an answer soon."

Genevieve looked at him sadly. "Oh, Daniel. I do hope so. I can't imagine losing my brothers. I'm so sorry."

"Are you wondering what all this has to do with Jacob and the money?"

"I assumed you were getting there."

After the little ones were lost, Daniel continued, Maggie was utterly inconsolable. For days, she sat in the corner of their apartment, wrapped in an old dressing gown of their mother's, staring sightlessly out the window into the street. She could not be persuaded to either eat or drink and remained impervious to Daniel's pleas. Neighbor women would stop by and try to cajole her into taking a bite or sip or getting a few moments of sleep, but nothing roused her from her almost catatonic state. Daniel began to fear she would simply wither away and he would be left with no family at all. Word must have gotten out—it was a small, gossipy community—and even the gang leaders stopped by, standing in the doorway of their dim tenement rooms. Maggie was a great beauty, and her quick laugh and pretty ways, so similar to their mother's, were much admired. Even these gruff men tried to tell her, in their own way, that it wasn't her fault—children played alone in the streets all the time; the Children's Aid Society matrons were no better than predators—to no avail. Finally, one unlucky man said the unthinkable. As the leaders were taking their leave, having been given tea and soup by a kindly neighbor, one of the younger men paused in the doorway and looked over his shoulder at the once-lovely young girl slowly wasting away by a window.

"There, lass, don't take on so," he said, his accent revealing he was recently arrived from the old country, as they called it. "The wee ones are probably better off, headed to a clean life in the country." He had glanced around their two and a half rooms with distaste, Daniel remembered. Daniel also recalled the very unchildlike fury that rose within him, hot and bilious. He had wanted to fling himself at this stranger and rip out his throat for even daring to suggest that his siblings would be better off elsewhere. Adult Daniel understood better: the homesick, newly landed man had probably been thinking of the green pastures and open spaces he'd left behind in Ireland. All this man saw were the piles of unwashed dishes and clothes, the tight, mostly windowless rooms, and the accumulated dirt and soot in the corners and on the walls that no amount of his mother's or Maggie's washing and scrubbing had been able to alleviate.

But Daniel did not fling himself at the man. Instead he focused on his sister's pale, still-gorgeous face and silently implored her to take a sip of lukewarm tea, desperately wishing that all these people would leave his house. He was utterly astonished when, after almost a week of barely moving, Maggie's big green eyes slowly traveled to the doorway, taking in the strange man. Her mouth worked, as if she wanted to speak but couldn't quite form the words.

"Jesus, Mary, and Joseph," exclaimed the neighbor lady. What had her name been? Daniel couldn't recall, but he could clearly see the shocked expression on her careworn face, old before its time from too many children and too much poverty, as she crossed herself.

The gang leaders stopped in the doorway and looked back. They watched as Maggie began to unravel herself from the dressing gown she had been wearing like a shroud, her mouth still working. Her luminous, large eyes remained locked on the newcomer, their deep color accentuated by the dark circles underneath, stark in her pale skin.

"There, now, see?" smiled the newcomer. "She just needed to hear God's honest truth is all."

She moved so fast, later the men would swear she was part banshee. That no mortal girl, particularly one who had not eaten, drunk, or slept in almost a week, could descend on a man with the kind of ferocity Maggie inflicted on the newcomer. Given her weakened state, the others were able to pull her off fairly easily once they recovered from their shock, but the damage had been done. The young man, as it turned out a cousin of one of the most prominent members within the gang's leadership, had been blinded in one eye by Daniel's furious sister's outraged fingernails.

Temporarily driven mad by grief, they all agreed later. He could still see the neighbor lady's stunned and frozen expression, his sister's red hands clawing at air as two of the larger men held her back, and hear the young cousin's howls as his own hands covered his face, blood gushing in even, regular pulses through his clenched fingers.

There were no police called, no charges made, no lawyers, no trial. This was a community matter, to be dealt with by the community. Which meant dealt with by the gang leaders. Despite the injured man's being kin, it was decided that no punishment would be meted out—the girl had clearly been out of her head, and what the cousin said had been right insensitive to the wee lass. But still, it was thought best to get her out of the environment and into a new life. Daniel agreed—not that anyone asked his opinion. In the few weeks it took to make the arrangements, he noticed the injured cousin's one good eye making a bead on him, and more alarmingly, on Maggie, who had slowly recovered after her attack. She was still a pale and wan version of her former lively, chatty self, but at least she went through the motions of living: eating, sleeping, fetching water from the community well, mending one of Daniel's socks. She even talked a bit to him. Daniel's parents had been much beloved in the neighborhood, his father an admired member of the Bowery Boys. In honor of them, inquiries and introductions were made, strings were pulled, and before he knew it, Daniel found himself and Maggie bundled into a carriage, driven uptown, and deposited at the servants' entrance of the stately Gramercy Park mansion of Jacob Van Joost, Esq.

Maggie took one look at her new surroundings and nodded. This was safe, she decided. Daniel had become everything to her, and if she needed to be a maid to keep him from getting snatched away too, or to keep him from getting killed in a senseless gang brawl, then that is what she would do.

Daniel hated it. He rarely saw old Jacob, but from their first introduction the two loathed each other. He was eleven, fiercely missing his own mother after her recent death, overwhelmed with grief for her and for the loss of his younger siblings. *If only you hadn't gone swimming that day*, his brain would hammer at him incessantly. *If only you'd stayed and played with them, just that one afternoon, they would still be together. If only you hadn't gone swimming that day,* over and over, an endless loop of guilt. He'd watched his only remaining sister almost destroy herself with sorrow, and was old enough to know they had both narrowly escaped a worse fate than being sent uptown after Maggie's attack on the young Irishman. He wasn't a child, either, to be babied by his older sister; he was tough (a *Bayard Tough,* after all), a street kid, and wanted nothing to do with this namby-pamby, hoity-toity, uptown fancy world with its money and its arrogant, confusing ways.

But he could still see Maggie's haunted, wasted face in the weeks following the children's disappearance. He could still see her blood-stained hands clawing at nothing after she'd been pulled off the Irish cousin. So for his sister, he stayed. He learned the fancy confusing manners, he figured out which fork was which, he learned to change the way he talked. He allowed himself to be dressed in hot, uncomfortable clothes, and to gaze longingly at the cool depths of the river but never to swim in it again.

"Did you work for Jacob also?" Genevieve's brow furrowed.

Daniel shrugged uncomfortably. "It was Maggie who really worked for Jacob. As a maid. I . . ." Here Daniel paused. What exactly had he done for Jacob? Not much, actually. "I did the odd job or two, as required," he settled on. "But mostly no, I didn't work. Eventually I was sent to school, to Eton."

Genevieve looked even more confused at the name of the exclusive British institution. "That's right, Mrs. Dolan said Jacob paid for your education. But you weren't named his heir until later, correct?"

"Good memory, Miss Stewart. Correct, I inherited later, after Jacob's death."

"So why would Jacob send a servant boy to the most exclusive preparatory school in Britain? That's quite an expense. And not even a servant boy, but the brother of a servant girl . . ." Genevieve paused, coloring a bit. Daniel watched her expression change as the obvious explanation dawned on her. "Oh," she said uncomfortably. "Oh. Daniel, were they . . . together?" she asked delicately.

Daniel sighed. "As much as a man in his seventies can be with a teenage girl," he said wryly. "Jacob despised me. But he adored my sister from the second he laid eyes on her. At seventy-five, he was unwell, and somewhat frail, and wasn't in any shape to force himself on her, as he might have done twenty-five years prior."

Daniel recalled the day he began to suspect the pair's arrangement vividly: he had been halfheartedly shining a pair of Jacob's shoes in the townhouse's big, warm kitchen, under the watchful eye of Mr. Fallow, the butler, and thinking about how he would sneak out later to meet his friends, when a footman sent him into Jacob's study. It was an imposing, masculine room, with a giant mahogany desk and book-shelves that ran the length of the fifteen-foot walls, crammed with thick leather-bound tomes. Daniel was normally strictly forbidden from entering, as were the bulk of the staff. Jacob was sitting behind his desk, fingers steepled and looking like he'd just swallowed a lemon. To Daniel's surprise, his sister was standing nearby, primly dressed in her gray-and-white uniform, not a hair out of place.

"You are a very lucky boy," Jacob announced sourly. "I have decided I see potential in you," he continued, mouth twisting as he sneered down at Daniel, "and, after some tutoring to get you up to scratch, will be sending you to one of the most exclusive boys' schools in the world. I expect you to comport yourself with dignity."

Daniel stared wildly at his sister, who nodded to him. "It's a great opportunity, Danny," she said softly. "Mr. Van Joost is being very generous and kind." She turned to the old man. "He's really very grateful, sir, and I know will do you proud."

Jacob peered at Daniel doubtfully. "I will remain an anonymous benefactor for the time being, of course, until we see if he is as capable as you claim. Perhaps you will surprise me, boy." He turned dismissively back to the papers on his desk. "That is all," he muttered, not looking up.

Maggie ushered Daniel out of the room. He didn't see the inside of that study for another six years, returning only when Jacob had died to hear the shocking contents of his will read aloud. By then, of course, Maggie was gone.

Daniel had wanted to protest vehemently at being forced to go to some prissy school, but Maggie quelled that instinct with a look. "It really is a wonderful opportunity." Her jaw clenched as she added, "I'll not lose you too. You'll go to school, and you'll do well. You know you're smart enough." He had made good marks at the Lower East Side school he had briefly attended until Mam became ill, when he'd stopped to help Maggie care for her and the little ones, and to earn a little money working with the Toughs.

The next year was torturous. A tutor arrived, and it was immediately, painfully clear that Daniel was woefully behind in his studies. It was determined that he should work with the tutor ten hours a day, six days a week, learning Latin, math, literature, history, and French in preparation to attend Eton.

It also became clear that Maggie had entered into an arrangement of sorts with Jacob. The house was so large that Maggie and Daniel each had their own bedroom in the servants' area, a vast, unthinkable amount of space when their seven-person family had once lived in two and a half rooms. The empty bed unnerved Daniel, who had always slept with at least one other sibling. He and Maggie had kept up the practice once the little ones were gone, even though they had more room then, simply to stave off their lonely awareness of their once large, happy family reduced to two. Once they arrived uptown, Daniel would creep into Maggie's room late at night, after he'd returned from his nocturnal wanderings with the Toughs, to sleep on the floor of her room. One night soon after he'd started working with the tutor, she wasn't there. Daniel tried to wait up for her but instead awoke when she crept back into the room just before dawn and began to dress for the day's work.

"Where were you?" he demanded, though in his heart he knew the answer. Maggie refused to look at him as she buttoned up her uniform, her jaw set once again.

"Never you mind. You just attend to your studies." She struggled with the last button, high at her neck, then glanced briefly at Daniel, still curled under a blanket on the floor near her bed. Her jaw softened. "I'll not lose you too," she repeated softly, and slipped from the room.

Life on the Lower East Side was lived largely out of doors, as nobody had much room. Lovers' spats, quarrels, flirtations, and courtships were conducted mostly in public, for the world to see. Daniel knew what went on between grown men and women. The thought of the creepy, decrepit older man putting his hands on his young, once-vibrant but still-beautiful sister made his skin crawl. But Maggie would not be dissuaded. The two or three times he tried to protest, tried to broach the subject, she turned mulish and stubborn. "I'll not lose you too," was all she would say. And what could a twelve-year-old boy, especially one who had lost almost his entire family, say to that?

The weeks turned into a year. Daniel learned Latin, complicated mathematics, and how to sleep alone. He learned to live in two worlds: that of the privileged, which he half inhabited, and that of the city's slums and gang life, which he knew best. He wore the right clothes, after a year could say the right things, and finally figured out which spoon was meant for soup and which for pudding. Almost exactly one year to the day after they arrived at the Gramercy Park townhome, he reluctantly boarded a steamer for Britain and was thrust into the exclusive world of English public school.

At Eton, it became abundantly clear in minutes that his newfound knowledge of upper-class ways was utterly useless. To the English boys, he might as well still have been speaking with a Five Points accent; in their eyes, a Yank was a Yank. He had to relearn which fork to use all over again, as the rules of etiquette were different overseas, and had to bloody a few noses when the insults got out of hand. He was almost expelled for those, but suspected a generous donation from New York kept his place—for a time. After a few weeks, the other boys steered clear of him, leaving Daniel lonelier than anything he had ever experienced, until one day a thin blond boy plunked himself down next to Daniel at tea and began peppering him with questions about New York while eating Daniel's biscuits. Daniel didn't mind, and soon he and Rupert Milton were allies. He even began spending the Christmas holidays at the crumbling Umberland estate rather than returning to New York as he did for the summer. Even run-down, the house was larger and grander than anything Daniel had ever seen, putting the Van Joost mansion to shame.

Daniel felt as though he were living a half life during those years at Eton, mostly immersed in his studies, enjoying camaraderie with

Rupert and holidays with the Milton family, but once a year, during the summer months, he was thrust back into his old life in New York. He kept close to home during the long days, trying to see his sister when he could, and would slip out of the Van Joost mansion at night to roam with his childhood friends.

It was his graduation from Eton and his return to the States to attend Harvard that changed things. Nobody from New York had attended the actual ceremony in Britain, though Rupert's mother had given him a peck on the cheek and a small gift. Due to particular circumstances at Rupert's home, it was decided that he would attend Harvard as well, and Daniel set sail for New York after making plans to meet his friend in Cambridge later that summer. Once he was back, Maggie took him to dinner to celebrate, proud and lovely in a green silk dress purchased for the occasion. Despite being the mistress of one of the wealthiest men in New York, she did not live like one. Daniel didn't know if this was by choice or not, as they didn't talk about her relationship with Jacob, but he guessed it was. Even though he lived on the periphery of the household, it was clear that Jacob was besotted with his sister. Now an octogenarian, he watched Maggie like a hawk, loudly insisting she be the one to dust the Frederick MacMonnies sculpture in the drawing room, or be the one to bring him afternoon tea. The few times Daniel had glimpsed these interactions over the years, such as Maggie placing a pillow behind Jacob's back as he read the evening paper at his querulous request, the naked longing and devotion he witnessed on the old man's face had made his own face burn in response, as if he had walked in on the pair in an intimate act.

At the steakhouse Maggie had taken him to on the West side, Daniel felt awkward and tongue-tied, a stranger with his own flesh and blood. Maggie looked pale and drawn, though this only accentuated her beauty. Her deep green eyes and rich brown hair had drawn admiring glances all night, and Daniel had come to the uncomfortable realization that people assumed they were a couple.

"Off to college at summer's end," she marveled quietly, sipping on a glass of beer. "Mam and Da would have been so proud, Danny." Daniel shrugged silently, unsure of what to say. He was looking forward to going to Cambridge and leaving New York. It was growing increasingly difficult to reconcile his two selves, and he was ready to leave at least one of those halves in the past. Slipping out at night with the Toughs, involving himself in the turf wars and grievances of gang life, and avoiding the constant machinations of Tommy Meade had ceased to hold any appeal for him. He continued the practice only out of loyalty to his friends and his past. Harvard would be a different kind of challenge, but whether he liked to admit it or not, Jacob's gift of education had changed him irrevocably. He doubted he would spend the summers at home, even though Boston was a far cry closer than Eton had been.

He needed a break from his dual existence.

It had been a fine early summer night, and Maggie had slipped her arm through his on the walk home.

"I'll miss you, Danny," she said, breathing the night air deeply. She stopped a block short of the Van Joost mansion and fiercely met his eye. "You mustn't forget where you come from, ever. And you mustn't be ashamed of it, ever. Mam and Da were good people, decent people. You are too, Danny. Even though you still run with the Toughs." She shook her head at his half-articulated protest. "I know you do, though I wish you wouldn't. But I understand why."

They had reached the servants' entrance of the mansion.

Maggie laid a hand on his cheek and leaned in to kiss the other, soft as the early summer air. She held his gaze with those famous green eyes.

"Be good, Danny."

He gave her a lopsided smile. "Maggie, I won't be going away for at least a month."

Daniel remembered how sad she had looked, as she had for years. It was as if her sorrow had permeated her until there was nothing left. But she returned his smile. "Aye, but you'll be busy getting ready for Boston, and I might not see that much of ya. I love you, Danny."

Daniel told his last remaining sister he loved her too. They went to their respective rooms, and Daniel fell into a deep sleep, only to be woken some hours later by a housemaid's screams.

CHAPTER 18

Genevieve was silent, still taking in the story. How on earth had no one ever uncovered the connection between Daniel and one of Jacob's housemaids? She guessed his money must have bought considerable silence on the part of the remaining servants.

Remarkable, what money could buy.

"How did she do it?" she finally asked, her voice soft.

"She hung herself," he replied.

Her heart contracted. "I'm so sorry," she whispered.

"It was a long time ago."

"How did that make you Jacob's heir?" she asked, trying to piece the puzzle together. "With Maggie . . . gone, he didn't have to hold up his end of the bargain anymore, did he? How did you pay for Harvard?"

Daniel quirked a bitter half smile at her. "Would you believe, the old man actually seemed to love her? After her death, Jacob apparently changed his will, making me the sole heir to the entire fortune." He shook his head slowly. "He felt so guilt-ridden at her unhappiness, he completed in death the one thing she had asked for in life: to take care of me." He tossed the remaining whiskey back in one hard swallow.

"Despite what Maggie may have thought, I'm not ashamed," Daniel continued, his eyes suddenly fierce. "Not by my past, my family, or even what my sister did to survive. But I can't have her memory tarnished."

Surprised at his ferocity, she stammered, "Of course."

"This is not fodder for your career."

Genevieve leaned back, affronted. "Daniel. Have I written one word about anything you've ever told me? I wouldn't do that to you; we're partners."

His look softened. "I am trusting you with this information, as I am asking you to trust me about Robin Hood."

Genevieve huffed a small sigh. It was true: what Daniel had just divulged had been an extraordinary act of trust. She hadn't asked for it, but for now she felt she had no choice.

"Fine," she said, trying not to sound begrudging. "I'll trust you."

A look of relief washed over his face. "Thank you," he said, sounding exhausted. "Thank you. Give me a few days, and I ought to be able to tell you everything I know."

She nodded slowly. "How do I know more people won't get hurt in the meantime?"

"That I can't promise. I can only promise to work as fast as I can."

Pulling herself from the comfortable love seat, Genevieve crossed to the window and pulled open the heavy silk drapes covering the east-facing window. The sky was still dark, but a faint glow was just beginning to emanate from behind the buildings across the street. She turned back to Daniel and regarded him.

He looked a mess, his eyes half lidded and red from whiskey and staying up all night, with several days' growth of beard covering his cheeks and chin. At some point he had unfastened the top several buttons of his shirt, which billowed out from his tight breeches, almost completely untucked.

She knew she didn't look any better, with her rumpled costume and wild hair sticking out every which way. She had a brief memory of their meeting in the alley, of how she'd thought he was the most handsome man she had ever seen. Even though he exuded exhaustion, it held true.

It was time to go. If anyone saw either of them together, they would come to only one conclusion.

"That will have to be good enough, I suppose," she said, as she fastened her cloak around her shoulders and prepared to slip back into the hall. "I'll head to the archives first thing Monday and let you know what I find."

Daniel stood and moved toward the door. He stuck his head into the hallway. "All clear. Go quickly. And Genevieve—"

"I know," she interrupted. "I'll be careful."

★   ★   ★

Dawn was just starting to break as the cab pulled up in front of her house. Genevieve heaved a sigh of relief. The hallway outside Daniel's hotel room had been empty, and while a few party guests had still been stumbling around the lobby as the doorman hailed her a cab, she didn't think she'd seen anyone she knew. Also, the remaining attendees had been so inebriated that even if she *had* been seen, she doubted she would be remembered.

As she walked through her front door, extreme tiredness began to overtake her. It was hard to stay upright, and she had no thought other than tumbling into her soft, warm bed when a voice startled her back into wakefulness.

"Genevieve? Is that you?" Her mother, wrapped neck to toe in a violet dressing gown, came bustling out of the front drawing room. Genevieve winced; she had been hoping to sneak in while her parents were still abed. But the sight behind Anna's shoulder caused a gasp to escape her mouth.

"What's happened?" she asked wildly, all tiredness forgotten.

A police officer had trailed her mother into the hallway. And not any police officer, she realized with a start, but the same Officer Jackson who had stared at her so lewdly on the steps of Reginald Cotswold's house the day she went to speak to Mrs. Dolan. Genevieve wrapped her cloak tighter around her body, aware of her wrinkled gown, her disheveled hair.

"Come into the drawing room, dear." Her normally unflappable mother seemed shaken, and dread filled her.

"Please, tell me what it is," she implored, following her mother and the officer into her front drawing room

The sight that greeted her stopped her in her tracks.

Callie, wrapped in one of Genevieve's dressing gowns with a blanket over her shoulders for good measure, was huddled on the sofa, shaking hands clutching a cup of coffee. Genevieve rushed to her friend's side as Dr. Needler, their family physician, stood up from where he'd been kneeling beside Callie.

"Just a bump on the head, I believe. Shouldn't cause any lasting damage. But I'd like you to rest, young lady."

Callie nodded, looking small and vulnerable under the blanket. Genevieve wrapped her arms around her friend and squeezed her tight as her mother showed Dr. Needler to the door.

"What happened?" she asked, smoothing back Callie's hair.

"Robin Hood is what happened, miss," said a different officer, who was standing in the corner of the room with her father. Wilbur nodded gravely at her. Genevieve hugged Callie tighter.

"I came home from the ball around two thirty and went to bed," Callie explained, pulling back a bit to take a sip of coffee. "About an hour later I heard something fall downstairs. I went to check, as we've had, um, some problems with mice lately," she admitted, small patches of color flaring in her otherwise wan face. "The house was dark, but I saw the shadow of a figure in the front parlor." Genevieve could feel her friend begin to tremble. "When I turned to run away, I tripped over a piece of loose rug and struck my head on a table. I heard them run out the kitchen."

Genevieve's hand floated to her mouth, horrified. Then a new, more horrifying thought occurred. "Where is your grandmother?" she cried.

"Still asleep, hopefully." Callie took a deep breath and ventured another drink from her china cup. "She was when I left. I didn't have the heart to wake her. Once I saw she was fine, I ran over here as fast as I could. Woke up the whole house, I'm afraid." She gave Wilbur a watery smile, who moved closer to pat her shoulder.

"Think nothing of it, my dear," he murmured.

"An officer is guarding the front of the Maple house now, ma'am," the second officer noted.

"We've been waiting for you, Miss Stewart," Officer Jackson said, the gleam in his eye letting her know he hadn't missed her bedraggled appearance. "Miss Maple was quite surprised you weren't at home. She swore you left the ball hours ago."

Callie shot her a miserable look.

"I'm sure Miss Maple simply didn't see my daughter before she left," Anna said in a steely voice, daring the officer to voice his implication.

"Yes." Genevieve picked up the cue. "I was stuck in the ladies' retiring room for some time, helping Mrs. Stansfield with her costume." She turned to Callie. "You saw it, remember? She was outfitted as a skyscraper, complete with electric lights woven throughout. Quite cunning. But the lights began blinking erratically, and several of us spent at least forty-five minutes in there with her, trying to work out the wiring under her skirts—"

"That's fine, Miss Stewart," the other officer interrupted, looking pained.

"Are we sure it was Robin Hood?" Genevieve asked, wanting to move the subject away from her whereabouts for the past few hours. Officer Jackson said nothing but eyed her speculatively.

"It must be." Callie's eyes filled with tears. "The diamonds, Genevieve. They're gone."

★   ★   ★

"Once more unto the breach, indeed," Genevieve muttered to herself, wiping her filthy hands on her skirt. She frowned at the brown marks now marring the yellow wool, then at the indifferent facade of the last file cabinet she had to tackle.

A ball of pain was gathering at the base of her skull. It had been a long and tiring two days. The police had accompanied Callie, in a dress borrowed from Genevieve with its hem dragging in the mud, back to her own house, where they told her grandmother the distressing news about the theft. The older woman was so overcome that she collapsed on the spot and was taken to the hospital, where arrangements were made for the family to stay with Eliza and her father until the Maple women felt strong enough to return to their own home. Genevieve assisted in all of this, and once she ascertained that Callie was safely ensconced with Eliza (when she was not with her grand-mother at the hospital), she managed to meet up with her brother Charles for their appointment. Despite having had no sleep Saturday night and enduring an emotional and taxing Sunday, Genevieve found it almost impossible to fall asleep Sunday night, her anxious mind swirling with myriad theories about Robin Hood, Lexington Indus-tries, and Daniel. She supposed she finally drifted off to sleep some-time in the wee hours of the morning, for she woke at ten o'clock to a gray, wintry light suffusing her bedroom, the damp and foggy morn-ing matching her mood.

She'd spent hours painstakingly combing the files at the municipal archives, which felt like digging for the proverbial needle in a haystack. The clerk at the archives had handled her multiple requests profession-ally enough to begin with, but by her twelfth call slip she'd noticed a distinct tightening of the clerk's lips as the other woman tried and failed to hold in an aggrieved sigh. But Genevieve was glad she'd persevered, for it was in the final file that she had struck gold.

She knew who was funding Lexington Industries. She knew what they really did.

In the interest of thoroughness, she'd come to the newspaper's records room to double-check her information against the paper's files and see if she could ferret out anything new.

It was unnerving, to say the least, to be down the hall from where she had almost lost her life. And none of the secretaries had been able to accompany her, though Verna, who had been there the night she was attacked, had flashed her an understanding look and said she'd come up in an hour to check on her. To her relief, the tenth floor wasn't deserted today; one of the foreign correspondents was in his office, and the sound of his typewriter clacking away provided a reassuring, constant backdrop to her own tedious work. Despite this, a cold sweat continu-ally beaded between her shoulder blades, and several times she had to pause in her work for a deep, calming breath.

"Broad daylight," she muttered to herself, yanking open the last drawer she meant to check. "Broad daylight, broad daylight."

"Miss?"

A small shriek escaped before she could help it. It was Verna, standing in the doorway with a newspaper under her arm. A brief look of sympathy crossed the secretary's face, but it was quickly replaced by a different expression Genevieve couldn't quite interpret. It looked almost like . . . wariness.

"I'm sorry, Verna, I'm a bit jumpy today." She pressed a hand to her heart, hoping to calm its racing staccato.

"That's fine, Miss Stewart. I just wanted to check if you needed anything. I did say I would." The words were right enough, but the tone wasn't. Verna was normally the epitome of friendliness, a bubbly, fun young woman, the oldest of a pack of siblings, who often regaled Genevieve with stories of the younger children's antics, as well as her own with a seemingly never-ending list of potential suitors. Today, though, she seemed reserved, and was eyeing Genevieve with a look that bordered on distrust.

Genevieve's fear turned to bewilderment. When she'd seen Verna earlier, the other woman had been her usual warm self. What had transpired in the past hour?

"I don't need anything, and thank you for checking," she replied. Verna nodded once and turned to go. "Wait," Genevieve called, stopping the other woman. "Is everything all right? You seem . . ." She suddenly felt silly. Surely Verna's odd mood had nothing to do with her. Perhaps she had had a fight with her latest boyfriend, or maybe one of the other reporters, edgy about a deadline, had snapped at her.

Verna bit her lip, flushing, then thrust the paper under her arm toward Genevieve. "I'm glad you got a front-page story, Miss Stewart, I truly am. But, if you don't mind my saying, it does seem that you used Mr. McCaffrey rather hard, pretending to let him court you and all. The man's had a rough time." Genevieve took the paper, puzzled.

"My family's Irish too, you know," Verna concluded, then ducked her head and hurried down the hallway.

Genevieve barely noticed the other woman's departure. "No," she whispered, horror-struck, gazing at the blaring headline of the *Globe*. "No, no, no, no, no."

ROBIN HOOD UNMASKED! The paper trumpeted. And below, in smaller type, though no less compelling, DANIEL MCCAFFREY SOUGHT BY AUTHORITIES FOR QUESTIONING, and below that, most distressing of all, was *her own byline*, paired with Clive's.

The story below detailed, with sickening accuracy, much of what Daniel had revealed to her in that gorgeous hotel suite. The information he had *trusted* her with. Where he had lived as a boy, how his parents had died, how his younger siblings were taken by the Children's Aid Society, and how he and his older sister had come to be in Jacob Van Joost's employ. How Maggie had been the old man's mistress—of course, the word was never said outright, but it was implied in such a way that would leave readers with little doubt. How Maggie had taken her own life, and how a guilty Jacob had changed his will.

It was all there, in black and white. But how? Frantic, she rushed toward the stairs, not trusting the elevator would be fast enough, and dashed down five flights. Bursting into the newsroom, she ran toward Arthur's office, nearly pushing aside one of the secretaries, who yelled "Hey!" in her wake. She could just see the portly editor bustling toward his door. She glanced at the hands of the large, wrought-iron clock that hung on an upper wall of the offices: half past two. Arthur would be leaving to check on the final layout for the evening edition.

"Mr. Horace!" She breathlessly burst into the door of his glass-walled area, thrusting the paper in his face. "I must speak with you about this story on Robin Hood. There's been a terrible—"

"Not now, Genevieve, not now. I've got to see to the six o'clock." He absent-mindedly glanced at the paper Genevieve was holding and smiled. "Good work, that story; solid reporting. I wouldn't have given you the byline, but Clive insisted you'd done it together. Nice to see the two of you getting on. You make a good team."

Genevieve followed Arthur through the crowded office, her panic mounting.

"But I had nothing to do with this! Mr. Horace, please!" Genevieve grabbed her editor's arm. He stared at her hand on his sleeve in astonishment.

"Unhand me, Miss Stewart," he said sternly, shaking his arm a bit in an effort to dislodge her. She tightened her grip. "I haven't time for this foolishness."

"But Mr. Horace, *please*, listen," Genevieve shook the paper in his face again, causing the older man to blink and draw his head back like a turtle. "This is all lies. A fabrication. Do you hear me? Clive made this up, and I had nothing to do with it. You have to print a retraction."

Arthur stopped trying to swat the paper away from his face, regarding her owlishly from behind his glasses. "A fabrication? Lies? You're saying you did not collaborate with Mr. Huxton?"

"Yes," Genevieve gasped in relief, loosening her hold on his arm. "Yes, that is correct. Clive—Mr. Huxton—made this up. And I had nothing to do with it. Please, you must add a retraction to the evening paper."

"A retraction? To the evening edition?" Arthur's furry eyebrows climbed to his forehead and hung there like distressed caterpillars. "Miss Stewart, we can do no such thing. Mr. Huxton was quite clear. Even if there was a misunderstanding—"

Genevieve's heart fluttered wildly at the thought of Daniel reading the story. Of seeing his personal life and his sister's memory spread out in black and white for the whole world to read. Of thinking she had betrayed his trust.

"There was no misunderstanding!" she insisted. "This whole story is false! I don't know why he added my name, but I would never write such drivel!" With that, she flung the offending paper across the room.

By now, the entire office had fallen silent and still, watching their exchange. At the paper's flight across the crowded newsroom, a collective gasp arose. The pages sailed through the air, lazily drifting throughout the office.

Arthur watched its progress with mild bewilderment, as if he couldn't quite believe what he was seeing. Not a sound could be heard save the settling of falling pages, coming to rest on the surfaces of desks, files cabinets, the floor.

"These are grave accusations indeed, Miss Stewart. Most unprecedented. Yes, most unprecedented." The caterpillars on his forehead danced for a moment, then settled as he came to a decision. "But I can't print a retraction until I hear Mr. Huxton's side of the story. No," he said, holding up his hand and cutting her off as she began to protest. "Clive deserves his say in this matter."

He looked around the office again, taking in his staff, most standing with their mouths agape, and the strewn pages of newspaper. "Most unprecedented," he muttered again.

Genevieve knew this was as good as it was going to get. She would simply have to find Daniel and explain somehow. Explain that although she hadn't shared his confidences, somehow they had been printed in the paper for which she wrote.

"Though the authorities may find Mr. McCaffrey sooner rather than later," Arthur said regretfully, starting for the door. "They are most anxious to find out what has become of the Maple diamonds."

Genevieve was sure she hadn't heard correctly. "The Maple diamonds?" she repeated, starting after her employer again. She hadn't thought the theft was public knowledge yet. "What do you mean?"

"The Maple diamonds were stolen after the Porters' costume ball. Look, it's printed here." Luther was suddenly there, his face concerned. He turned a copy of the front page over, and under the fold was a continuation of the story she hadn't seen in her initial upset over the headline.

FAMED MAPLE DIAMONDS TAKEN! THE *GLOBE* AWAITS LETTER FROM ROBIN HOOD.

Quickly skimming the rest, Genevieve learned there had been no letter yet to the newspaper from Robin Hood, claiming responsibility for the theft, but the clear implication was that this was just another in the thief's long string of attacks on the city's wealthy.

Genevieve's mouth dried in renewed horror, even as tears pricked her eyes. She could not possibly imagine a worse scenario. Then it occurred to her, a thought so liberating she nearly laughed aloud for the joy of it.

Of course. Daniel was not the thief, and she could prove it.

Her editor was waiting at the creaky elevator doors, impatiently checking his pocket watch. Luther put a gentle hand on her arm, but she shook him off with impatience.

"Mr. Horace!" she cried. For the second time in ten minutes, Genevieve sped across the newsroom floor, dashing for her employer before he was swept away in the elevator.

Arthur looked distinctly alarmed at her rapid progress. The rest of the staff, who had resumed their usual bustle in the wake of her previous outburst, once again paused to watch whatever new spectacle was about to unfold.

"Wait, Mr. Horace! Mr. McCaffrey is not Robin Hood! He did not steal the Maple diamonds, please!" she protested, this time grabbing the older man's hand as he tried to quickly wedge himself into the opening elevator doors.

"Miss Stewart, this is unprecedented!" sputtered Arthur again, wildly looking around for help. Not a soul moved.

"But it's not true! He couldn't have stolen the diamonds, don't you see? They were taken at, what time?" Now it was Genevieve's turn to look around wildly, hoping someone nearby knew the answer.

"They were reported missing at four in the morning." It was Luther, who had rushed after her and was hovering anxiously.

"Four AM!" Genevieve cried triumphantly, turning back to Arthur and renewing her grip on his hand, which had begun to slacken. Arthur looked woeful as the elevator doors wheezed shut again, leaving him stranded.

"Nobody saw Mr. McCaffrey after about two in the morning, according to Mr. Huxton's report," Luther cautiously noted. He looked as though he knew how this would end and didn't like it. "Genevieve, let's go talk privately—"

"Yes," Arthur interrupted. "The theory is he was stealing the jewels from the Maple townhouse between three and four AM. It's all in Clive's article, and we'll discuss it tomorrow. Really, Genevieve, I must go see to the evening edition . . ." Arthur strained for the elevator, pushing the down button with his free hand.

"No, no, Mr. Horace, he wasn't anywhere near the Maple townhouse at that time. And I have proof." She gripped Arthur's hand fervently, willing him to believe her.

This stopped Arthur's straining. "Proof?" he asked cautiously. The color drained from Luther's face, and he shook his head at Genevieve sadly. A sudden look of realization hit Arthur's visage.

The caterpillars snapped together. "Come to my office, Miss Stewart."

Arthur barked orders about the evening edition at his two assistant editors as he led Genevieve toward his office. Otherwise the room was so quiet one could hear pigeons cooing on the windowsills outside. Once behind the glass door, Arthur snapped the blinds shut and wearily slumped into his chair.

"Out with it, Miss Stewart."

She steeled her courage, hoping what she was about to say wouldn't cost her her job. "Between two and five thirty AM on Sunday morning, Mr. McCaffrey was with me. In hotel room three sixteen." The caterpillars gave one brief, resigned wiggle, then settled again. "I'm sure the hotel staff can confirm the hiring of the room."

Butterflies coursed through her stomach, and she felt her face burn bright red. She swallowed, awaiting her fate. There was no use explaining that all they had done was talk. She, an unmarried young woman, had just admitted to her employer that she had spent the small hours of the morning in a hotel room with a man. Regardless of what had actually transpired in the hotel room, that fact alone was damning enough.

"Sit down, Genevieve," Arthur said, not unkindly.

Genevieve complied, suddenly feeling a bit faint.

"I will check with the hotel staff, and if they can confirm Mr. McCaffrey's rental of the room, I will print a retraction." He sighed, peering at her from under his bushy brows. "But I'm not sure I can keep you on staff. You all but admitted to this behavior in public."

Unbidden, tears pooled in her eyes. "I'm so sorry to have disappointed you," Genevieve said miserably, frantically blinking to keep the tears from spilling. Arthur was almost like a second father to her.

He now sat in the chair next to Genevieve and offered his handkerchief, which she gratefully accepted. "Oh child." Arthur comfortingly patted her back. "I'm not disappointed in you. You're young, but not fresh out of the schoolroom. You're old enough to know your own business. But the reputation of the paper, you understand, and the other young ladies employed here . . . let me think on it."

It was unfair, but Arthur was correct. If word got out, it would appear that he condoned such behavior, and the reputations of the secretaries and other women who worked at the paper would suffer.

"I do understand, Mr. Horace. And I want to thank you for all that you've done for me over the years," she said sincerely. She knew he hadn't wanted to give her a position originally but had been pressured to do so by her family's position.

The older man smiled gently. "You're a good reporter, Genevieve," he said, which made her start crying anew. "Take the rest of the day off," he suggested. "Get some rest. I know you're friends with Miss Maple, and I'm sure she needs you now. I'll let you know my decision."

Nodding unhappily, Genevieve went to her desk to retrieve some notes she'd locked in her desk the past Friday. It was more imperative than ever that the truth be revealed, but she needed Daniel's insights to help her patch together her discoveries about Lexington Industries. To figure out what it all meant.

To help her ascertain who Robin Hood *really* was.

Her stomach contracted. If he would even speak to her now, given the newspaper article.

Genevieve's heart caught in her throat as she slipped her key into her top desk drawer, only to have it slide open of its own volition. Someone had tampered with the lock. The drawer was open.

The cold sweat immediately reappeared, chilling her despite the well-heated room. She affected an air of casualness as she reached into the desk, well aware that whoever had broken into it might be watching. The previous week's notes on Lexington Industries were still there, but as she began to withdraw them, her fingers grazed something cold and metallic.

Puzzled, Genevieve clasped the object and pulled it out.

A small, glittering box sparkled in her palm. It was silver, its top encrusted with rubies and diamonds forming the shape of the Russian Orthodox cross.

Her heart pounded. She let her gaze slowly traverse the newsroom, but everyone was immersed in their own tasks. Clive was nowhere in sight and hadn't been all morning. Only Luther was glancing at her from where he was speaking on the telephone. He gestured that he would be off in a moment and then he would come to her desk.

She gazed back down at the small objet d'art in her hand. She recognized it, of course, from her childhood explorations at Reginald Cotswold's house. It was surprisingly heavy for such a small box.

It was a calling card. A message. Reginald's murderer was sending a clear threat: back off, or you'll meet the same fate.

Genevieve pocketed the box and grabbed her bag. Not caring who was looking, she dashed toward the stairs, once more not wishing to wait for the elevator. Past Luther, who put down the phone and called after her; past Verna, who jumped out of her path, startled; and past countless other reporters, stenographers, typesetters, and secretaries. Let whoever was working with a murderer see her run. She didn't care; she had only one thought: to get to Daniel before the killer did.

CHAPTER 19

"You haven't been able to find him?" Eliza asked sympathetically, cutting a slice of cake. It had been three days since Arthur ejected her from his office. Four since she had seen Daniel.

Genevieve shook her head, regarding the lovely piece of pastry on her plate. She loved cake. But today she couldn't seem to swallow a crumb. Her mind was swirling. She looked out the front window of Eliza's townhouse and gauged that she had about twenty minutes until the sun began its early, late-winter descent.

She would wait another ten minutes, then make her excuses and depart for home, where she would make her preparations for the night. A pang shot through her at the thought of leaving Callie, but Callie would be in Eliza's capable hands. Besides, hopefully she'd have good news for her friend by morning.

It was excruciating to see their typically laughing, lighthearted Callie in so much pain. She had deep circles under her eyes and stared, pale and drawn, at the newly budding trees in the park though the window of Eliza's family's sitting room, ignoring her friends' conversation.

Ever since the shock of losing the diamonds the previous weekend, which few knew constituted all that remained of the Maple family fortune, Eliza and Genevieve had been feverishly worried for Callie. Genevieve, setting aside her own anxiety about whether or not she had retained her job and about the fiendish newspaper article and equally fiendish Clive, had joined Eliza to think of amusements that might distract their friend, including a trip to the popular Elmsbury tearoom, which they had attempted that afternoon.

It had been an absolute disaster.

Rumors of Genevieve's scandalous behavior had spread.

She didn't know by whom. Maybe someone had seen her leave Daniel's hotel room after all. Maybe someone from the newsroom was spreading unsubstantiated gossip. Maybe Officer Jackson had placed a few well-timed remarks.

Regardless of how the rumors had begun, the fact that she might have spent time in a gentleman's hotel room in the middle of the night was clearly the topic of the day. The trio had been completely, utterly, and totally snubbed. Women whom Genevieve had known for years, girls she had gone to school with, cut her to the quick, refusing to say hello or even acknowledge their table's existence. Some even physically turned their backs when Genevieve tried to smile at them in greeting. It was as though the three women were stranded on an iceberg in the middle of the Elmsbury tearoom, floating along by themselves while society swirled and paraded around them as if they didn't exist.

"Maybe we should leave," Genevieve whispered miserably.

"Nonsense!" Eliza hissed back. "I am not about to be chased out of the Elmsbury tearoom, and neither are you." She looked for support from her comrades and found little. Callie was as deflated and gray as a glove left out in the rain, and Genevieve was so worn down she could barely muster the energy to hold her head high, let alone fight back.

This public humiliation was like nothing she had ever known. Her parents, who must have known the rumors to be true, given how late she had returned from the costume ball, had not broached the topic, but her mother, white-lipped, had barely spoken to her in days. In turn, Genevieve couldn't bear speaking to her father, who simply regarded her with kind, sad eyes. But the rest of society seemed to have made up its collective mind. Even after her broken engagement, people had talked to her sympathetically. It was excruciating and bewildering to be ignored by people she had thought were friends. She just wanted to hide under her covers until . . . when?

Until the next person was killed?

If someone else hadn't *already* been killed.

Because her biggest fear wasn't for her own reputation, as exhausting and disheartening as it was to be the topic of so much gossip.

In truth, she was terrified for Daniel.

She hadn't been able to find him.

At first she'd sent notes and telegrams to his house, pleading for a meeting so they could talk, saying she had been as surprised as anyone to see the story, saying she had a major lead in their investigations into Lexington Industries, even hinting at the discovery of the jeweled box, but from Daniel's direction—wherever that was—there had been only silence.

She had followed these attempts with a knock on his door, hoping he would relent if he saw her in person. Charles had insisted on accompanying her, reminding her that she was in enough trouble as it was and that showing up unannounced and unaccompanied on Mr. McCaffrey's doorstep was sure to set more tongues wagging. Dear, sweet Charles, who was normally so steady, was ready to find Daniel and knock the stuffing out of him for allowing rumors to circulate unchecked.

Daniel's housekeeper, Mrs. Kelly, only kept repeating that Mr. McCaffrey was not at home. It wasn't until Daniel's secretary Asher appeared at the door and reiterated this information with a look of pure hate that Genevieve fully understood.

Whether Daniel was truly home or not, he had seen the article and wasn't home to *her*.

Still, she was beyond worried. The paper had printed a retraction in Tuesday's edition, removing Genevieve's name from the previous article's byline and apologizing for labeling Mr. McCaffrey as Robin Hood. He should have made contact by now, if only to let her know he was safe.

"Please, let's *leave*," she had begged her friends at the tearoom.

Callie looked at her with dull eyes. Eliza sighed and began to gather her things.

"Good afternoon, Miss Stewart." It was Esmie, pinning back a length of heavy black veil that had been covering her face.

Shocked gasps and whispers arose around them—both because someone dared approach their table, Genevieve assumed, but also because Esmie was in a public place so soon after her mother's death. Esmie held her chin steady, her simple, slim-cut black dress contrasting quite beautifully with her pale hair and skin, which glowed like a pearl.

It was, frankly, the best Genevieve had ever seen Esmie look.

"Miss Maple, Miss Lindsay, hello," Esmie continued, taking a seat. She leaned forward and took Callie's two hands in hers, looking her in the eye sympathetically.

"I was so, so sorry to hear of your family's misfortune, Miss Maple. To have your home violated so." Genevieve could see the other woman's throat move as she swallowed. "I understand how you must be feeling."

Callie's eyes filled with tears. "Miss Bradley, please. You lost your mother. The situations are not comparable in the least. Do let me offer my condolences."

"Thank you," Esmie said. "But I have heard your grandmother is not well following the ordeal. Please know I am wishing for her speedy recovery." Callie seemed so overcome by the other woman's kindness that a sob burst from her, earning yet more censorious looks toward their table.

Eliza stood, flustered. "We really ought to leave." She put her arm around Callie, who had begun to cry in earnest, and led her out of the overstuffed pink room. Genevieve stood also, counting out a few bills to leave on the table, and hurried after her friends, but a hand stopped her at the door.

"Wait, Genevieve," said Esmie, who had followed her. Impatient, Genevieve paused, her hand on the doorknob of the restaurant. Esmie gestured her to one side.

Confusion joined her impatience as Genevieve stepped into a small recessed area of the entryway. Through the glass door, she saw her friends hail a cab.

"I should rejoin my companions, Esmie. It's quite cold outside." Adding insult to the injury of her dark mood, winter seemed to have decided to pay a return visit to their fair city. The temperature had been plummeting for days, the newly sprung crocuses dotting flower beds left bent and bewildered.

"This will only take a moment," Esmie said, her voice low. Her pale-gray eyes met Genevieve's, resolute. "I understand Miss Maple and her grandmother are staying with the Lindsay family at present?" she asked.

"Yes," Genevieve answered, even more confused. Eliza and her father were insisting that the women stay as their guests. Genevieve suspected that the Maple townhouse, which had been in the family for three generations, would soon be sold.

But how did Esmie know this? And why did she care?

"I believe if they return to their home tomorrow morning, they may find what was lost," the other woman said carefully. Her expression was perfectly neutral. "Good day to you."

Without another word, Esmie quickly brushed past Genevieve and was out the door, refastening her veil as she departed.

The shock of what Esmie had said froze Genevieve in place for a full five seconds as she struggled to wrap her mind around its implications. Willing herself to move, she yanked open the tearoom door, only to gape as the stiffly held back of the slender, black-clad figure turned a corner and disappeared like a wraith.

Speechless, Genevieve climbed into the cab with her friends. Thankfully, Callie had calmed somewhat, and even more thankfully, neither asked why she had been a few moments delayed.

They had now retreated to the Lindsay townhouse on the Square's west side, where Eliza had gamely tried to recreate the experience they might have had at the tearoom with cake, scones, and Darjeeling, but nobody felt much like eating anything.

Genevieve stared again at the cake on her plate, then glanced out the window. It was ridiculous, this sitting around. She stood, startling her friends, and began to spin a string of lies about why she must leave.

It was time for *action*. She feverishly hoped Daniel had not been harmed. But if he hadn't and was off somewhere ignoring her, licking his wounds, she was done trying to find him. Someone had to continue their investigation, and Esmie Bradley had made it clear that perhaps tonight, all their questions would be answered.

And if he had been harmed . . . well, then tonight would be the first step toward justice.

★ ★ ★

The bar's wooden surface was the most fascinating mixture of textures and color Daniel had ever seen. Different shades of brown swirled, expanded and contracted, merged with streaks of black and reemerged, in a mesmerizing pattern.

Just like Genevieve's hair. Warm, honey-hued strands, tumbling down her bare shoulders.

Daniel shook his head mightily to clear the image, and realized with a start that he was examining the bar's surface through the clear base of his glass.

His *empty* glass.

Well, that wouldn't do.

He blearily raised his head and looked for the bartender, tapping his glass on the wooden surface to signal he was ready for a refill. The barkeep, looking up from his paper at the far end of the bar, glanced toward one of the tables lining the wall behind Daniel. Daniel followed his gaze and noted Paddy's dispassionate nod.

Well, *that* wouldn't do either.

"I don't need his permission for more whiskey," Daniel protested, casting an accusing glance at Paddy, who turned back to his own drink without acknowledging the claim.

The bartender wordlessly tipped more of the amber liquid into Daniel's glass and returned to his side of the bar. Paddy and Billy nursed their drinks in silence. Daniel decided not to pursue the unjust arrangement—since when was *Paddy* his keeper, anyway?—and moodily sipped his fresh drink, enjoying the warm burn of the liquid coursing down his throat. He knew that soon the burn would stop and transform into a thin but necessary layer of fuzziness that would add to the existing layers of fuzziness, and all of these layers would pile up until they were the consistency of a thick blanket. The woolly kind. This woolly blanket would protect him. It would insulate him from the thoughts and memories that he couldn't stop from buzzing around his brain, stinging him with tiny, painful pricks.

Yes, the woolly blanket was his shield. But it also *itched*.

The memories pushed through despite his efforts, stinging and itching. His baby sister Mary, toddling across the room toward his parents. His father, picking up his five-months-pregnant mother as if she were a slight girl and swinging her round while their children laughed with delight. Maggie's sad face, telling him to be good in Boston.

Dammit, there wasn't enough whiskey in the world to build the blanket he needed. Nothing could insulate him. Not from his wretched, painful past, and not from the present, stinging betrayal.

He had *trusted* her.

Daniel hadn't allowed himself to trust anyone, not for years.

What he should have trusted was his gut. *Goddamn* the goddamn press. Anything for a story. And he had been taken in, had truly, honestly believed they were on the same side, that she'd keep his secrets.

He would never forget the sight of Asher, paper in hand, looking mildly stricken. That alone was cause for alarm, as typically an illustration of Asher's countenance could serve as the definition for *poker face* in Merriam-Webster. At first Daniel had been amused at the headline, wondering why it had taken one of the papers so long to accuse him of being Robin Hood after his origins were exposed by Tommy at the Bradleys' ball. Reading on, though, he found more intimate, private details of his life. There it was, words glaring at him from the page. The insinuation that Maggie had been Jacob's lover. The hint that her death had been self-induced. There was the usual suggestion of foul play that had accompanied Daniel since his teen years, but he was accustomed to that. It was having the sad details of his beloved sister's life and untimely death splashed about on the front page that cut him to ribbons and made him feel as though he were experiencing Maggie's death all over again.

All written under her byline: *Clive Huxton and Polly Palmer*. She must have rushed to this Clive person instantly, spilled all she knew.

This was *private*. It was nobody else's affair that poor Maggie had felt compelled to make the choices she had. His initial pain transformed to a hot, burning rage at the paper's intrusion.

The fire in his insides quickly turned to ice. He stared at the paper, disbelieving. All that time they'd spent together. All that time trying to solve the mystery of Reginald's death, of Elmira Bradley's. All the secrets he had shared. It had all been simply fodder for her career.

Daniel couldn't fully remember the details of the past—was it two or three?—days. They had turned into a blur of misery and recrimination directed both at himself and at her. First he'd gone to Kathleen's for a while, hiding out and getting drunk, but when he couldn't stand her *I told you so* look any longer, he had made his way to Five Points, hat pulled low. Once in the tangled den of back alleys and twisting side streets, he'd stumbled from one tavern to the next in his childhood neighborhood, sleeping for a few hours when necessary in one of the cheap boarding houses that littered this area of town. He'd needed to be away from the farcical lives of the wealthy, from their avid gazes and prying questions. He'd needed to be away from anything clean, anything fresh and bright. Anything that reminded him that he had let his guard down, been prepared to trust a wretched member of the press.

And a very convincing actress. A humorless bark of laughter escaped him, causing the bartender to shoot him a wary glance. She really ought to have pursued a career in theatre. He had fallen for her act like a rube from the sticks, like some new transplant from the cornfields. The toughened city boy in him should have known better. Somehow, he should have seen through her.

Why was his damn glass empty again?

"There you are." Rupert's cultured voice sliced through the fog encroaching on Daniel's brain. He'd gotten distracted by the wood grain in the bar again.

Daniel blinked at his friend. "What are you doing here?"

Rupert slid onto the stool next to him, eyeing the sticky surface of the bar with raised brows. "I'll assume the drink here surpasses the cleanliness. What's good?"

Daniel shrugged moodily, irritated. Couldn't a man get drunk alone? "It gets the job done."

"Ah. Very good, then." Rupert signaled to the barkeep, who came over grudgingly. "I'd like to get the job done, please." At the bartender's blank look, he pointed at Daniel's glass. "What he's having."

Rupert followed the bartender's glance back at Paddy and Billy, swiftly assessing the situation. "Your minders are here, I see."

Daniel slouched lower toward the bar. "Don't need anyone's permission to drink," he growled.

"Of course you don't," Rupert allowed, sniffing his newly arrived glass and grimacing slightly. "And although I'm certain I know the answer, I feel I must ask the obvious. Would you please tell me why we are in this fine establishment drinking what is fairly"—and he lowered his voice decorously, so as not to be overheard by the scowling barkeep—"substandard whiskey? You've much better stuff at home."

Daniel responded only by tightening his grip on his glass. He wished Rupert would go away. He needed to keep adding to the layers of insulation, building his woolly blanket, and his friend's voice was needling in his ears, making oblivion impossible.

Hell, it was probably impossible anyway. But he'd been trying to reach it for days, and he wasn't going to stop until he got there. Or at least devilishly close.

Dammit, there was that needling sound again.

"Shut up, Rupert."

"Well, if you want to drink yourself to death, be my guest. But surely we can do it somewhere more comfortable?"

"*We* are not doing anything," Daniel rasped. "*You* are leaving. *I* am staying here."

"Oh, I'm not leaving you." Rupert smiled cheerfully, throwing a little salute toward Paddy and Billy, who were watching the whole exchange. "I do wish you'd chosen a different watering hole, you know, one that actually cleans its glasses from time to time. But I'm sure this one has its charms," he amended hastily, catching the bartender's glare. Looking around the dank, dimly lit room, Rupert nodded at the dusty tin light fixtures, the dirty glasses piled behind the bar, the keep's soiled apron. "It's rustic," he murmured. "Yes, charmingly rustic."

Daniel wanted to swat at him like a nettlesome fly. "How did you find me, anyway?"

Rupert tilted his head toward the door, and Daniel saw the hulking form of Asher sitting at the far end of the bar. He scowled deeper. Traitors, the lot of them.

They sat in silence for a while. Daniel tried to lose himself in the patterns of wood again. Rupert ran his finger along the edge of his glass. Asher glowered by the door, and Paddy and Billy watched the pair at the bar. They made quite a contrast: one elegant and striking in an expensive, expertly tailored suit, the other rumpled, disheveled, and unshaven.

"She's ruined, you know," Rupert remarked conversationally.

Daniel raised his head from the bar's gummy surface, not quite sure when he'd needed to rest it. "What?"

"Genevieve. She's ruined." Rupert sipped his drink, grimaced again, and then looked thoughtful. "It does get better on the second try, doesn't it?"

"What do you mean, ruined?" Daniel was trying to pull together the pieces of his brain to make sense of what Rupert was saying. Why would Genevieve be ruined? There was nothing ruined about her.

"Well, everyone is gossiping that the two of you spent the night together, and now you've been gone for four days, leaving her to face the music alone. Everyone assumes you've had your way with her and then thrown her out like yesterday's scraps, moved back to Europe or something."

Daniel tried to process this information. Four days?

"That kind of thing tends to destroy a girl's reputation," Rupert said knowingly.

A few more moments passed as Daniel continued to absorb what he'd been told, willed the words to assemble themselves into an understandable picture.

"Hence the ruination," his friend added helpfully. Another beat or two went by. "She'll likely die an old maid," Rupert said, as if commenting on the weather.

"I have tried to quash the rumors," Rupert continued, holding up his glass and squinting at its contents, "insisting you were in the gaming room with me until five AM—everyone was so bloody drunk by then, nobody can remember anything properly. I think I've convinced a few folks. But it would be awfully helpful if you would emerge and say the same."

Daniel finally grasped what has been eluding him. "Rubbish," he declared. "Besides, she's got her precious *career*, hasn't she?"

"Probably not," Rupert said cheerfully. "Newspapers don't tend to employ ruined ladies. And you know she didn't write that article."

The words had the waking effect of an ice-cold glass of water in his face. Daniel was instantly alert. "Say that again, very carefully."

Rupert grew serious and looked his friend in the eye. "She didn't write the article, mate," he said gently.

"How do you know?" He signaled for a glass of water.

"The *Globe* printed a retraction on Tuesday." Rupert slid a folded page of newspaper across the bar at him. A corner of the paper instantly darkened with spilled liquid on the bar's sticky surface. Daniel snatched up the paper and read the retraction, including the apology for accusing him of being Robin Hood. He noted the *Globe*'s acknowledgment that authorial attribution of the piece had been given to Miss Polly Palmer in error. Everything clicked in an instant: Genevieve must have told her editor about their being in the hotel room together at the time of the Maple diamond theft, damning herself while exonerating him. And somehow word had leaked.

He ran a hand through his hair, amazed. He had trusted her and had been correct in that trust. Bile rose in his throat, which he quickly chased back down with a gulp of water.

"You have to make a decision, mate," Rupert said quietly. "Do you want to keep living in the past, with the dead? Or would you like to join us in the land of the living? Would Maggie really want to be a stone around your neck? Because that's what she's been to you, as long as we've been friends."

Daniel gripped his water glass and absorbed the words quietly, deep in thought.

"You've been set up," his friend continued softly. "As was Genevieve. Someone knew your vulnerability, your weak spot, and I'm sorry to say, they played you like a violin. Together, you two are a force, and whoever set this up was determined to drive you apart."

Rupert's words rang true. He felt like the most incredible bastard to walk the earth. How could he have been so blind? But his friend had hit the nail on the head: whoever had been out to trick him, they had indeed known how to find his emotional jugular. It was Maggie, had been Maggie since before her death. Really, since she had become Jacob's lover. Since she had, in essence, prostituted herself to an old man with gnarled hands so Daniel could have a better life.

He'd been carting that guilt around since he was twelve years old and hadn't realized what a weight it was until that very moment.

Daniel looked around the dingy bar, bemused. Who would have guessed he'd have the major epiphany of his life at McSorley's?

"So the question is"—Rupert's voice sliced through his memories, not buzzing this time but welcome—"who else knew about Maggie?"

Daniel shook his head. "Just you."

"Well, I can be an insufferable ass when I choose, but I do hope you know I'm not that much of an ass. You're my best friend," he concluded simply. "I would never betray you."

"It was Tommy," Daniel said, closing his eyes against both his own stupidity and the pounding headache that was beginning to encroach. He gestured to the bartender again. "He said as much at your engagement ball. And damn my eyes for not seeing it sooner."

This time, Daniel asked the barkeep if he could rustle up some coffee. He had barely slept, but that couldn't be helped. There was no time to waste, not if he was going to catch a killer.

Chapter 20

The darkness in the empty townhouse was not, after a time, utterly complete. The longer she sat, waiting, in the chair she had positioned in the corner of the drawing room, the more her eyes adjusted, and what had been mere shapes gradually transformed into furniture and objects she knew well: a credenza, a side table, a love seat. Familiar vases and bric-a-brac emerged from the shadows—though, Genevieve noted with a pang, there was less here than there had been.

Callie and her grandmother had sold quite a lot, it seemed.

Genevieve didn't allow her anger and grief over her friend's distressing financial woes to distract her. She remained still and silent, as immobile as any of the furniture. She'd chosen a plain chair from the kitchen for her wait, its hard seat and straight back keeping her alert and upright, rather than sinking into the plush comforts of one of the remaining armchairs.

Not that she could fathom falling asleep, even if she had been fully ensconced in the comfort of her own bed. No, tonight she was singularly focused.

It was time to end this.

The heating was turned off, and the cold was beginning to seep through the soft leather of her boots and the thick wool of her stockings. She wiggled her toes, waiting.

Patience had never been Genevieve's strong suit; all her life, it seemed, she'd been focused on what came next. This had particularly been true over the past few years, after her broken engagement. She had wanted to succeed in the newspaper business so badly, had been so desperate to prove her worth, that she'd almost completely removed herself from society, from all but a few close friends, and had barely even slowed down to enjoy the changing of the seasons.

Tonight, she had the patience of a cat. She could sit in this chair forever, the heavy, comforting weight of the revolver she held resting in her lap. Her ambitions seemed trivial at the moment; whether her actions tonight resulted in a story or not was of little consequence. What she really wanted was the truth.

That, and for the killing to stop.

The quiet creak of wood scraping on wood emerged from the back of the house. A kitchen window was being slid open. Genevieve sat taller, every sense in her body attuned to the noise.

She waited.

A few moments later, another creak, but this one of a foot gently landing on a slightly loose floorboard.

They were coming through the kitchen, then. Which way after that? She'd strategically placed herself where she could see the bottom of the stairs through the open French doors to her left, the dining room beyond, but could also see the entrance to the drawing room from the back of the house. Someone could come in that way, or loop through the dining room to the stairs.

Silent as a mouse, she raised her revolver, ready to point it which-ever way would be required. Her left hand held her right wrist steady. She deliberately slowed her breath.

No other sounds came. But a shadow suddenly filled the far door-way. Carefully and slowly, she shifted her shooting arm to the right.

The figure stilled.

She waited.

They began to move again, taking deliberate and quiet steps into the drawing room, with a pause of at least five seconds between each footfall. One, pause. Two, Pause. Three.

A blinding flash of light, coupled with the explosive sounds of a gun-shot and the splintering of wood, suddenly filled the quiet night. The acrid scent of Gun smoke instantly permeated the room. Keeping her hand steady and her eyes on her target, she simultaneously stood up and used her left hand to turn up a kerosene lamp she'd had waiting on the table next to her.

"Jaysus, woman, are you trying to kill me? Put that thing down!" In the gaslight, Daniel was still ducking, his arms around his head, gazing at her incredulously, his mouth a perfect O of surprise.

"If I had wanted to kill you, I would have. I shot exactly where I intended, directly over your left shoulder. Now don't move another muscle, or I'll direct my aim a bit more toward the right," Genevieve replied, pulling the hammer on the revolver back again. Her heart was pounding, but her hands still felt steady.

"Stop!" he yelled, hands in the air. "May I stand, at least?"

She considered the request, then nodded once.

Daniel's shoulders relaxed a bit as he unbent his long frame, still holding his hands in the air. She squinted through the sight of the gun. He took a step closer.

Another blast, and Daniel ducked again as a spray of woodwork from the wall behind his right shoulder rained over his head, accompanied this time by a shattering of ceramic. She'd shot a lovely little china shepherdess she knew the older Mrs. Maple had been fond of.

Well, it had been in her way. No helping it now.

"I always was an excellent shot, you know," Genevieve informed Daniel conversationally, pulling back the hammer a third time. He winced at the noise, carefully straightening again and still holding up his hands. "But I've been practicing with Charles out on Blackwell's Island for days now, as I was rusty. He says I'm quite gifted."

Daniel stilled completely. He blinked at her from across the Maple townhouse drawing room, his expression a curious mix of resignation, regret, and admiration. It angered her, that expression.

In truth, it angered her that she had been right. That she should have known, and listened to her gut from the beginning.

"You led me on a merry chase," she said softly. "And played me for a fool. It was you all along. I know now you had an accomplice, as you couldn't very well be spinning tales to me in the Union Pinnacle Hotel and here at the Maple home at the same time." Her jaw tightened as her anger intensified, thinking of the trauma Callie and her grandmother had endured in recent days. Her finger tightened too, pulling the trigger back a hairsbreadth. Daniel's eyes caught the tiny motion and flared.

If anything, he seemed to still further.

"Those diamonds were all they had left, you know. Half the furnishings in this house are gone; did that never cross your mind? Or your accomplice's mind? Or were you so focused on greed and revenge you were blind to their suffering, right under your nose?"

Daniel remained silent, his eyes locked on her trigger finger.

"I was blind, Genevieve. I'm trying to make it right."

From the doorframe behind Daniel, Rupert emerged, hands held high.

Genevieve shifted her aim to the right again, locking Rupert in her sights. "So you're the accomplice. I couldn't, in the end, work out whether it was you or your bride-to-be. I rather liked the idea of it being Esmie, but you were of course the most logical choice. Occam's razor and all that."

Rupert was shaking his head. "I'm not an accomplice. I am Robin Hood. Just me, and only me."

She shifted her gaze to Daniel. He had lowered his hands and was staring not at her anymore, but at his friend. Rupert lowered his hands too and shrugged.

"I guess the jig is up. Genevieve, can you please lower that thing? Unlike Daniel here, I'd never any doubt of your skill."

"Oh, I hadn't doubt. I just didn't expect to find myself on the receiving end," Daniel said.

She instantly pointed the gun back his way, causing him to raise his hands in alarm. "And why would you think that?"

"I thought you trusted me. Partners, remember?"

She huffed. "Yes, such close partners you failed to mention your best friend was responsible for stealing from half the Astor 400."

"I didn't know, not for sure," he said, eyeing the revolver nervously. "I suspected. Strongly. But why would I share that with a journalist?"

"Even after I was almost killed? So much for trust."

"Robin Hood and the murders are completely unrelated."

"So Reginald's death was a coincidence? As was Elmira Bradley's?"

"No. They were setups, meant to frame an innocent man." At this, Genevieve cocked an eyebrow. Even Rupert looked doubtful. "Fine, not entirely innocent. But Rupert did not kill anyone."

"I did not," Rupert reiterated. "Please, if you believe nothing else, Genevieve, you must believe that. I'm a thief. A wretched, twisted thief, who can't seem to stop. But I've never hurt anyone, and I never would."

"May we talk, Genevieve?" Daniel pleaded. "Can you please put down the gun?"

Genevieve waited a few moments. Her anger had not abated; if anything, it had risen. She *had* trusted him, and thought he trusted her. She had thought they had a true friendship, but he had turned tail at the first doubtful sign, not even bothering to ask if she'd written the damn article.

"Instead, I think you should give me one good reason I shouldn't shoot you both right now," she said, steadying the gun. "Robin Hood and accomplice, caught in the act. Self-defense. I'd write a cracker of a story, and it would really aid my career, don't you think, Daniel?"

He had the good grace to flush. "I'm sorry. I'm sorry I didn't reach out to you immediately. I should have known you would never betray my trust."

"Yes, you damn well should have," she shot back.

"I haven't had a lot of practice trusting people," Daniel said. "Please, put the gun down, and let's finish what we started."

Genevieve narrowed her eyes in suspicion. Despite all her talk of trust, she wasn't sure she could overcome her own feelings of betrayal. But her arm was getting a bit tired, as was she. Here, finally, was the opportunity for answers.

And she suspected she could fill in a few of the missing gaps to the story as well.

"You first," she finally said.

Daniel let out a relieved sigh, then reached underneath the back of his jacket and pulled a gun from his waistband. With the other hand still raised, he gently placed the revolver—she recognized it from his desk drawer—on the floor.

One down. "Rupert?" she asked.

Following Daniel's lead, Rupert kept one hand up and with the other extracted a long, thin blade from his left boot. He laid the knife next to Daniel's gun on the floor.

She raised a brow in query at him, and again, Rupert shrugged in response. "Quieter than a gun," he said. "Helpful in picking locks."

"Elmira Bradley's throat was slit," Genevieve observed. "That's quiet, all right." Truth be told, she had never thought Robin Hood had killed Elmira; it had never added up. She glanced back and forth between the two men, both of whom were returning her gaze warily, then lowered her gun. Didn't put it down, but lowered it.

Both men sagged in visible relief.

"Genevieve, I promise," Rupert began. "I didn't kill anyone. I take things. I . . . I've always taken things. For years. Tell her, Daniel."

"Not always," Daniel said quietly. "But for a long time now. I believe that when you are particularly concerned about finances, the urge is intensified."

Despite herself, Genevieve found her curiosity piqued. "Urge?"

Rupert nodded miserably, then plopped into a nearby armchair. "It's hard to describe. It's an almost physical sensation. This . . . *feeling* crawls up my spine and burrows into my brain. It's maddening, awful. But the only thing that sates it is to . . . take."

"Things that aren't yours," Genevieve supplemented.

"Yes, things that aren't mine," Rupert confirmed, gesturing around the room aimlessly. He looked exhausted and wrung out in the dim gaslight, his already pale face further bleached of color. "It started small. A silver-plated cigarette case here, a porcelain figurine there. I adore you Americans, you know, but sometimes the sheer *excess* of your money rankles." He frowned and shoved his hair back from his forehead. "Particularly if I'd just received another letter from my mother, again reminding me of the direness of our situation."

Daniel remained standing. "You can't solely blame America, Rupert. This began while we were at school."

Rupert nodded and blew a breath at the ceiling. "Yes. We'd always been genteelly impoverished, but that was when things really began to go south. I never meant any harm. It had been a lark, a bit of a gag, a subtle dig at the kids in school who made fun of my shabby jackets; at my father, who mismanaged and drank away our fortune; at the robber barons, whose overindulgences sometimes give even me pause." He closed his eyes and leaned his head back against his seat. "At this whole damned society with its vast cogs and wheels and my tiny place in it."

He opened his eyes and regarded Genevieve wearily. She realized she was probably seeing the real Rupert, without the social mask he continually wore, for the first time. "And eventually I couldn't control it anymore. I wasn't taking just to show I could. It became something I had to do. I've tried whiskey, women, swimming at the natatorium until I was so exhausted I could barely stand, but nothing worked. Nothing could replace the insatiable need."

Finally, Genevieve sat as well. She kept the gun in her lap, but the tiredness that had overcome her was so sudden and severe that her legs felt wobbly. It was partially the lateness of the hour and her continued lack of sleep, but it was also hearing Rupert's sad tale. This wasn't a mastermind criminal hell-bent on seeking revenge on a society he despised, as his letters suggested. It was a melancholy, disheartening story about the power of money and society and one man's broken way of attempting to cope.

"What do you do with all those things?" she asked. "Your letters never said, simply that the money was given to the poor. Which poor? How?"

Rupert allowed his head to roll to the side of the chair. "I sold them. I didn't *want* the teaspoons or earrings or snuffboxes I took. Couldn't stomach keeping them, in fact. Nor the money. I donated any profits to various charities I fancied. Anonymously, of course."

"But how could you sell something as recognizable as Sarah Huffington's ring? And what did you take from the Bradleys? The family never reported anything missing, but your letter indicated you took *something*," she asked.

He smiled cynically at her. "There's a buyer for anything in this town, Genevieve. Anything. You simply have to know who to ask. As for . . . Elmira, I took her ring as well. Big as a bird's egg, that thing."

"And you managed to find a buyer?" she asked skeptically.

Rupert shook his head. "Not for that, no. That I gave back."

Genevieve felt her eyes widen, suddenly feeling awake again. "Esmie."

The smile was softer now, less cynical. "Yes, Esmie. She figured out I was the thief and confronted me. Said she'd cancel the engagement and expose me unless I gave back her mother's ring and the Maple diamonds. She's clever, that girl. Far more clever than she lets on."

Genevieve's mind instantly flashed back to the night of Esmie's engagement ball. "*The benefits of being a wallflower*," Esmie had said. "*You see* everything. *I know all kinds of secrets.*" Genevieve made a mental note: what else did Esmie know?

"I had hoped being engaged would help," Rupert said dolefully. "Knowing I had money coming. I've read some books that described my . . . behavior, and some of these doctors, at least, seem to think a person like myself might get better in time. Maybe a fool's hope."

"But why steal from the Bradleys after your engagement was announced?" Genevieve asked, confused. "That seems a bit self-destructive."

Rupert sighed. "I don't know. It was . . . one final act of rebellion, I suppose. God rest her, but I never did care for Elmira. She spent the whole of the ball smirking, so pleased with herself to be aligned with our family." He barked a short, bitter laugh. "If only she knew what a mess poor Esmie will marry into."

"And then Elmira was killed, and the wedding was delayed," Genevieve guessed. "Another year with little funds."

"Yes," Rupert sighed. "Hence my taking these." He pulled the Maple diamonds out of his coat pocket, where they glistened and sparkled in the gaslight. All three were silent as he gently placed the jewels on a side table.

"It's done now," he said. "I've promised Esmie. I can't risk that marriage. Unbelievably, she seems willing to marry me regardless of what I've stolen, but she did make me promise to stop."

"Will you be able to?" It was Daniel, now leaning against the credenza with his hands shoved into his pockets, who asked the question.

Rupert looked at them both helplessly. "I don't know," he admitted.

Daniel met her eyes from across the room. "Well, Genevieve? Are you going to turn him in?"

She waited a few moments, considering. Turning over all the various angles in her head. "I don't know either," she said finally. "Not that I condone stealing. But I think you need help, and I'm not sure you'd get that in the Tombs." Rupert's faced blanched further at the mention of the notorious prison. "Let us put the matter of Rupert's crimes aside for now. If Robin Hood isn't a murderer, who killed Reginald Cotswold and Elmira Bradley? Who tried to kill *me*? And how do we keep them from killing again?"

CHAPTER 21

Daniel pushed himself away from the furniture he'd been leaning on and, after an inquiring look toward Genevieve—she still had that gun on her lap and obviously had an anxious trigger finger he did not care to startle—finally sat. His entire body, which he'd been holding tense for the past thirty minutes, seemed to sigh in relief.

"I have ideas about how to stop them. As to who they are, I think you have the answers to that, Genevieve."

He could tell that surprised her. "In one of your notes to me, you said you'd uncovered who was behind Lexington Industries," he continued.

Genevieve's eyes narrowed at him. "So pleased you finally read my missives, Daniel."

He hoped his expression betrayed exactly how sheepish he felt.

"Just this afternoon, yes. They were waiting for me."

"Where have you been?" she inquired with a curious expression. "Did you retreat to that brothel again?"

A half smile involuntarily tugged at the corner of his mouth. "For a time. It's owned by my cousin, you see."

"Ah," was her only reply. She didn't seem quite satisfied with that answer.

"He was drinking away his sorrows in the most rotten pit imaginable, Genevieve," Rupert chimed in, sounding more like himself again.

"Whiskey like rotgut. He was three sheets to the wind by the time I found him, possibly even drunker than he was the day we graduated Harvard; do you remember that, Daniel? You said you wanted to give Boston a proper send-off, but by three in the morning . . ." He trailed off, seeming to notice for the first time that they were both giving him singularly incredulous looks. "Well, he's come to his senses now," Rupert muttered, shrinking a bit in his chair.

Daniel turned his attention back to Genevieve and leaned toward her, resting his forearms on his knees. Gratifyingly, she didn't flinch back or tighten her grip on her weapon. "Tell me," he said simply.

He could see excitement replacing the anger in her eyes. "Recall 'Syndicated American Hospitality'?"

He sucked in a breath. "Sarah Alston Huffington."

Genevieve smiled triumphantly. "The very same. Syndicated American Hospitality Co. is the major investor and part owner of Sampson Affiliated Habitats, Incorporated."

"And their purpose?" He was sure he knew, but he needed the confirmation. All trace of tiredness was gone now, every sense on full alert.

Genevieve leaned forward, matching his pose. "Construction," she breathed. "And building management."

"And their profits?"

"Sky-high."

He smacked a fist into his open palm as the puzzle pieces dropped neatly into place. A huge weight he'd barely been aware of was suddenly lifted, and he stood, energized.

"*Stupid* of me not to see it. Of course, they were in on this together." He began to pace the width of the room, his mind working furiously.

Genevieve stood too, her eyes bright. "Andrew and Sarah," she said.

"They formed the company under her initials, making it less obvious. I bet she brought Clark into it."

"Her lover," began Genevieve, who had started to pace the room as well.

"Maybe. Maybe even with Andrew's encouragement, to get someone out of their direct sphere into the scheme."

There was that feeling again, that irrefutable connection between them. A strange, exhilarating symbiosis.

"So Sampson Affiliated Habitats is the real business, and they funnel the money made through Lexington Industries to hide its true origins." Genevieve ticked the points off on her fingers as she paced. Suddenly she stopped. "But why hide it? There's nothing illegal in having a building corporation."

"I'm sure this one is engaging in all kinds of activities that, if not illegal, are on the margins of ethical. Tenement construction, Genevieve. They're building and managing tenements. I'd bet my hat the buildings are substandard, with shoddy materials, and they're surely charging a fortune in rent. They'll all be making money hand over fist."

"And all the investors are on a committee devoted to tenement reform," Genevieve breathed, her eyes wide.

Daniel had stopped pacing too. They faced each other in the middle of the room. "Which is exactly what they don't want. Reform. The profits are too high. *That's* why Reginald was killed. We may never know for sure, but my guess is he figured out the committee's true purpose was to block reform rather than aid it, and had to be silenced."

Genevieve shook her head. "Just for money," she observed sadly.

"Greed is one of the most powerful motivators there is. And don't forget who else was involved: Tommy Meade. He would be the one to get builders on the cheap, know how to pay off inspectors, police officers . . ."

"Commissioner Simons," Genevieve said. "He was on the committee."

Daniel nodded. "And Deputy Mayor Manfort."

"And the others? Ted, the Stuyvesants? Did they know?"

"I don't know. The truth will out, though." Daniel ran his hands through his hair. "I have a hard time believing they'd condone murder, but money is a powerful drug. Reginald was a threat. Kill him, take the box, make it look like Robin Hood."

"This box," Genevieve said, removing a heavily jeweled object from her pocket. Rubies winked in the dim light. "It was left in my desk drawer, I believe as a warning."

Daniel shoved aside the spike of rage that erupted in his chest, both at the thought of Reginald's death and at continued threats to Genevieve.

"A letter about Reginald was never sent to the paper," Genevieve continued.

They both looked at Rupert. He'd been silent, watching them with a troubled expression.

"Exactly. The police refused to believe Mrs. Dolan that Reginald's death had anything to do with Robin Hood, but as it was deemed he died of natural causes, the killer didn't need to push the Robin Hood story."

Genevieve sat again, moving the revolver she'd left on the seat to the floor and shoving the box back in her pocket. "But Elmira? Were the Bradleys approached, perhaps?"

"Esmie says she has no idea who killed her mother," Rupert chimed in.

"My money's on Tommy," Daniel said. "He had that man you saw in the alley killed, Genevieve."

He saw her visibly swallow. "Gerry Knox. I heard he complained about the conditions in his building."

Daniel nodded. "And I'm sure, if we check, that building will have been constructed and managed by Sampson Affiliated Habitats. Gerry's grumblings could have been passed off as those of a drunk, and Tommy still had him killed. Elmira did far worse; she embarrassed him in front of society. Conveniently, Robin Hood struck that same night."

"Convenience?" Genevieve shook her head. "That seems too neat."

"It does," Daniel agreed. He leaned back against the credenza. Again, they both turned to Rupert, who if anything appeared distinctly alarmed.

"Someone else figured it out." Genevieve cocked her head at Rupert, considering. "That you're Robin Hood. They knew when you were going to steal from the Bradleys."

Daniel nodded. "And used *your* theft to cover up *their* murder."

"But who?" Rupert cried. "I never killed anyone." A sudden, ashy look came over him. "Esmie?" he whispered.

"I don't think so," Genevieve replied slowly. "If she wanted to frame you for her mother's murder, she wouldn't have confronted you about being the thief."

"Genevieve's right," Daniel agreed. "No, someone in league with Tommy. Esmie can't be the only one to have figured it out."

They were silent for a few breaths, thinking.

"It was Sarah," Rupert finally said. Daniel looked at him sharply. His friend looked utterly miserable. "I said something about how gaudy Elmira's ring was, and we laughed about it. She said what a pity it would be if Elmira lost it. The look on her face . . . I assumed she was joking, but if all you two are saying is true, then my guess is it was she." He blew out a breath.

"If she figured out you were Robin Hood, Rupert, she would have been quite angry," Genevieve observed. "After all, you stole from her too. You publicly exposed her affair with Ernest Clark. I'm sure she would have been perfectly happy for you to be blamed for Elmira's murder, were you ever caught."

"Another woman I've underestimated," Rupert muttered.

Daniel kept his mouth shut at that observation, though he slid a look toward Genevieve, who had pursed her lips in a telling fashion. In the end she chose to let the observation lie, and instead asked, "So what is our next step?"

"Rupert is going to lay low," Daniel said, with a stern look toward his friend, who nodded meekly. "And I am going to approach Mrs. Huffington. I'll tell Sarah I want to invest, but I need to meet somewhere private, and I will only meet with the principals of the firm. Tommy, Andrew, Sarah . . . such a meeting would be noticed. It will be somewhere out of the way, and I daresay I know where."

Genevieve stood and stretched. "That is a sound plan. I'll tell the same to Ted, and arrange a meeting as well."

Alarm reared within him. "You are doing no such thing. We don't know if Ted is aware of the underlying reason behind Lexington Industries, and there is no way you're meeting with Tommy Meade."

He watched Genevieve's face shift from satisfied to outraged in the course of his speaking. She planted her hands on her hips. "Haven't we had this conversation? You are not in a position to make any decisions regarding my actions. Besides, I've already almost been killed, I've been followed, I'd actually feel safer . . . what?"

His guilt must have shown on his face. Damn, he was tired, to have allowed that kind of mistake. Typically he had more self-control.

It was time to come clean, though he knew she would be furious.

"I had you followed," Daniel admitted.

He'd been right. Her outrage intensified.

"*What?*"

"The times you thought you were being followed, on Fifth Avenue, in the park . . . you were. But not by anyone involved with these crimes. By my associates."

Genevieve's face, which had paled at his first statement, was now marked by high spots of color on her cheeks. He instantly felt guilty but kept his head high and his shoulders back. Best to take the coming— and well-justified—torrent of anger like a man.

"How, how *dare* you," she sputtered, so angry, it seemed, that she could barely speak. "I was *terrified*. I thought I was losing my mind. I have lost weeks, *weeks* of sleep over this. What on earth possessed you to have me *followed?*"

"I was trying to keep you safe."

"By scaring me half to death?" she yelled.

"Frankly, my tactics were necessary," he replied, his own anger at her disregard for herself beginning to replace his guilt. "As one of the few places my associates couldn't keep an eye on you, your office, was where you *were* attacked."

Her mouth opened and shut a few times, but she didn't seem able to think of a suitable response. Daniel's rage burned bright as he thought, as he had so often over the past weeks, of the unknown assailant's hands closing on her vulnerable throat.

"This isn't over yet, Genevieve," he continued. "You are convinced of the danger Tommy Meade poses, aren't you?" Her breath was coming in fast, angry huffs. She clenched her jaw but nodded once.

"You've already been targeted not once, but twice," he reminded her. "You were physically attacked, and now someone has left that Russian box for you as a message."

"It has to be Clive," she muttered, letting out a deeper breath.

"My guess is Tommy has been cultivating Clive for some time," he said. "You know we can't go to the police, not yet. Commissioner Simons is involved, and we don't know which officers are corrupted. I need irrefutable proof I can take directly to the mayor. With what you've found, we're nearly there."

"Exactly, with what *I* found. It was *my* research, *my* hard work, and frankly, *my* neck, that got us here."

"I know that," he angrily replied. "And so do *they*. That's why it's not safe for you anymore. Dammit, woman, why can't you see that?" Daniel pushed himself away from the credenza and paced the room again, running his hands through his hair in frustration. "I thought perhaps the ruse of our courtship would be enough . . ." A sudden idea popped into his head. A crazy, wild idea, mostly in its unexpected, almost visceral appeal.

Before he could think too hard about it, he blurted, "Maybe we should get married."

As soon as the words were out of his mouth, he wished he could claw the air and take them back.

Not that he didn't want to marry Genevieve. It sounded, suddenly, like the most reasonable, tempting suggestion in the world. His brain snapped to a memory of her, languid on the love seat in a sumptuous hotel room, in a dress fit for a goddess, long tangles of honey-golden hair cascading past her bare shoulders.

But the look of complete shock on her face indicated that she felt otherwise.

Indeed, he would be hard-pressed to decide who looked more shocked, Genevieve or Rupert.

"I'll just step in here," Rupert murmured, giving Daniel a wide-eyed stare as he slid back toward the kitchen.

"Don't leave this house, Rupert," Genevieve snapped. He nodded at her wordlessly before disappearing into the darkness of the back of the house.

Genevieve crossed her arms over her chest. "You're already trying to curtail my activities. Why would I want more of that?"

"I'm trying to keep you alive," he said through gritted teeth.

"So your solution is to get married? To keep me under your thumb?"

"No," he protested, groping for the right words to say. "I understand word is circulating you spent the night in my hotel room. A marriage would end the gossip."

She waved a hand at this. "Gossip comes and goes. You're not really suggesting we marry only to stop a few tongues wagging?"

"That's not the only reason. Genevieve, I . . . I admire you," he finally admitted. A knot of feeling was pushing at his chest, one he couldn't quite untangle. This was either the best idea in creation, or the worst. "I find myself wanting to keep you . . . safe."

Her manner seemed to soften a bit. She uncrossed her arms and folded her hands in front of her waist instead.

He allowed a few beats to pass, waiting. Half fearful, half hopeful.

"But we don't love each other," she finally said. "Do we?"

The question froze him. His mind struggled to wrap around the concept. Genevieve Stewart was beautiful and witty and brave. He *did* admire her, as he had said. But did that equal love? He was so far removed from the notion of what love was, he wasn't sure.

In the wake of his silence, Genevieve smiled gently. He thought he caught a glint of some unnamed emotion in her amber eyes—regret? resignation?—but in the dim light of a single lamp, he couldn't be sure.

"I appreciate the offer, Daniel." Her voice was kind, but firm. "But I must decline."

★ ★ ★

The inky predawn darkness swallowed Daniel and Rupert as they retreated east into the park, undoubtedly either heading toward Rupert's bachelor quarters at the Benedick, on the Square's east side, or planning to walk uptown to Daniel's mansion on Gramercy.

No matter. She would wait fifteen minutes, then make her own way south. Genevieve dropped the dark-red damask drape on the window in her parent's front drawing room back into place and checked the time on the brass clock ticking away on the mantelpiece, just visible in the light of a single candle.

She had promised Daniel she would remove herself from the investigation henceforth, but had crossed her cold toes within her boots; it was never a promise she intended to keep. This was her story, and she would see it through until the end.

Both men had been anxious about whether she planned to turn Rupert over to the authorities, but Genevieve knew better than that. These crimes went deeper than Robin Hood, all the way to the very heart of the machinations that made the city tick. The story of a British earl suffering from some kind of mental illness that drove him to thieve was compelling, but nothing compared to that of the city's top officials scheming for riches at the expense of children's living conditions.

Besides, with Commissioner Simons's involvement in the Lexington Industries scheme, to whom could she turn with this news of Robin Hood? The police were not an option at present.

She chewed her lower lip and looked at the clock again. They were surely far enough away now.

As she slipped back into her warm cloak, Genevieve's mind returned, as it had repeatedly, restlessly, since she had been alone, to Daniel's proposal.

She paused, closing her eyes and pressing a hand to her chest. She couldn't seem to wipe the moment from her mind; he had looked so sincere.

He had also looked terrified.

A small, secret part of her had leapt in joy at the words. The life they could have together had passed through her mind in a flash: a true partnership, but enveloped in the type of love she'd never thought she'd be able to experience. Being with Daniel made her feel alive; Every sense was heightened when she was with him. She had dismissed the sensation as a reaction to their work together, to the thrill of the hunt, but at his proposal, she'd known in an instant it was also his presence that made her nerves tingle. Being with him made her feel as though the sun were shining especially and only for her.

But he didn't love her. His hesitation in the face of her question had been answer enough. He *admired* her, he'd said. After the heated looks he thought he'd hidden in the hotel room, she believed he was attracted to her as well. But if she had learned one thing since her near marriage to Ted, it was that if she ever came that close to matrimony again, it would be for love.

A cold, miserable rain had begun. Icy wind nipped at her nose and tugged the ends of her scarf as Genevieve slipped from her house, helping drive thoughts of Daniel's proposal from her mind. She began to cut diagonally southeast across the park—a cab might be hard to find at this hour, but surely if she walked along Broadway, one would pass sooner or later. It was imperative that she get to the offices of the *Globe* before it was too populated, to venture—once again—into the records room. Her employment status at the paper was still in question, but she was friendly enough with most of the staff that if there weren't many people about, she could go about her business with a friendly wave. Something niggled at the back of her brain; she *knew* she had read about a tavern in Five Points that was the Oyster Knife gang's stronghold. It was the only logical place Daniel's meeting could occur, and she planned to be there.

Lost in thought, she almost didn't notice the sound of heavy footsteps behind her. Gooseflesh prickled her arms as soon as they permeated her consciousness. Dawn was perhaps a half hour away, and while the sky was slightly less pitch-black than it had been before, the park, under its canopy of trees, was still deep in shadow. Risking a glance over her shoulder, Genevieve could just make out a shadowy figure, hat pulled low, about twenty paces behind her.

She now dearly wished she had walked due east along the park's north edge instead of following its wending paths in her haste to get to the office. The stately townhomes lining that side could have provided more than a measure of security. But it was too late: she was under the bare tree branches, which continuously rattled their saberlike branches in the cold March wind.

Foolish, foolish, foolish, she cursed herself. Her heart accelerated in time to her increased pace. The footsteps behind her, predictably, quickened as well.

Suddenly, a realization struck her so forcibly that she stopped in her tracks. Relief edged out her panic, and a short laugh escaped before she could stop it. Of course, this was one of *Daniel's* men, probably the same one who'd tailed her in the park earlier. Whoever this was, he could carry a very pointed message back to one overbearing Mr. Daniel McCaffrey. She was tired of being followed around the city, scared out of her wits.

She wiped the rain from her face and turned on her heel, ready to deliver a scathing setdown to Daniel's lackey, only to find the man mere inches from her, filling her entire field of vision. There was no time to scream, only a moment for shocked recognition as the blurred features under the hat resolved into those of someone she knew, before a blinding pain exploded on the left side of her head, and darkness descended.

CHAPTER 22

Low voices permeated the edge of Genevieve's consciousness, the tones strained. What were they saying? She couldn't quite make them out.

Her head was pounding. She was so tired and would happily go back to sleep if these men—and it would be men, wouldn't it? women were so much more considerate when others were trying to sleep—would just *stop talking*.

Who was it? Her father and Charles? It would have to be Charles; Gavin was abroad. That didn't seem right, though. Her family didn't quarrel like this, in quietly seething voices. They yelled properly when they argued.

Genevieve tried to swallow. Her mouth was horribly dry, an unpleasant accompaniment to her aching head. Had she had too much champagne at a function?

One of the voices became harsher midsentence: "Foolish to bring her here."

"What was I meant to do? It was starting to get light. I bundled her into the carriage and came to the only safe place I could think of."

"You were *meant* to get her out of the way."

"I didn't have time."

Memory flooded back, cruel and swift. She had been trying to get to the newspaper office. She had been followed. She had been hit on the head.

She moved her head gingerly, and pain radiated from the back of her skull and circled it in response. A low breath escaped before she could help it.

The voices abruptly stopped. The distinctive sound of a careful foot on a creaky floorboard rose in the air.

Genevieve kept her eyes closed, hoping she could feign continued unconsciousness and learn more. The light behind her eyelids shifted; someone was standing over her.

"She's awake," a voice said, in a tone of amused disgust. "Though she's pretending not to be." A hefty sigh from farther away followed.

"Well, what should we do with her?" the second voice whined.

"*You* are getting rid of her, as you were meant to do in the first place." The floorboard creaked again as the footsteps retreated, followed by the sound of a door shutting. Alarm reverberated through Genevieve's chest, accompanied by a brief, forceful wish that she could retreat to the comforting, dark stillness of oblivion from which she had so recently emerged.

Enough. Enough of that, you. If she was going to get out of this alive, she needed to see where she was and who she was up against. Gathering her courage, Genevieve peeled her eyes open.

A dirty, wooden ceiling greeted her vision. One old, dusty cobweb hanging from a rafter swayed gently in a draft, and a sudden chill shook her body. Wherever she was, it was not well insulated.

She tried turning her head to one side so she could further investigate her surroundings. The dull pounding sharpened to a lance of pain behind her left temple, and Genevieve closed her eyes for a moment, letting the pain pass. Moving more slowly, she tried again, looking first in one direction, then the other.

It appeared she was on the floor of a small, windowless space that was uniformly coated in grime. A rickety looking table, topped with a bottle and two dirty glasses, and a pair of rough wooden chairs squatted miserably in the center of the space. The only light came from a low-burning gas lamp hanging from a hook on one of the walls.

Distant laughter and an underlying hum of chatter floated in from somewhere nearby, and Genevieve had a sudden certainty that she knew where she was.

A dark amusement washed over her. She had left her house hoping to discover the name of the bar that served as the Oyster Knife gang headquarters and had a feeling she'd been brought to the exact place she had wanted to go.

Moving delicately to minimize the agony in her head, Genevieve pushed herself to a seated position. Once there, she leaned against the dirty wall and stilled, allowing the steady beat of pain to recede.

The door she'd heard shutting earlier reopened, the unmistakable raucous sounds of a tavern swelling. Clive's face twitched slightly at the sight of her awake and sitting, but he seemed to recover quickly, shutting the door behind him, again muffling the noise beyond.

A mixture of emotions arose: fear, certainly, as her unruly brain replayed the moment directly before she was struck on the head. It had been Clive following her in the park, Clive whose face loomed the moment before the blinding pain. But she also felt contempt. He had been a good journalist, and a successful one, but had allowed himself to get caught up in the games of the wealthy.

Underlying her dread, a sharp stab of hope jolted through her chest. If she could get to the noises of the tavern, could she find help?

Clive, keeping his eyes on her, sat at the table and poured himself a drink. He sipped, giving her a contemplative look.

"Well?" he prompted, taking a deep pull from his glass. Genevieve pressed her palms against the rough boards behind her. Ignoring the pangs that throbbed through her head, she slowly pushed herself upright, leaning back for support. Clive gestured with the glass toward the empty seat, but she elected to remain against the wall, taking a few deep breaths until the ache lessened.

"Well, what?" she finally responded. Her voice was unfamiliar to her own ears, scratchy and hoarse. She managed a swallow, desperately wishing for water.

"Anything to say? You've brought this on yourself, you know. If you'd just stayed out of it . . ."

Genevieve gaped at him. "It's my fault you hit me on the head and brought me to a dirty room to die? Is that really what you're saying?" she croaked.

An angry flush flooded Clive's face. "You were asking questions you shouldn't have. I tried to warn you away."

"Who brought you into this, Clive? It seemed you had a good life. Why get involved with all . . . this?" Genevieve waved a tired hand around the room.

His jaw tightened. "You wouldn't understand, having been born with that silver spoon in your mouth. Some of us have to make our own way in this world."

"But you had made your way."

Clive barked a short laugh. "Had I? You were nipping at my heels, as were others. Arthur would have listened to you sooner or later, begun to assign you some better bits. He'd already started."

Was it the blow to the head, or was Clive not making sense? What did story assignments at the newspaper have to do with corruption and murder? Her head was ratcheting up its pain, and she longed to slide down the wall and sit again, but another, deeper part of her knew that to do so would be tantamount to giving up. To death. "I don't understand," she said instead.

"Robin Hood, Genevieve. I told you it was my story. It was meant to make my career."

Her confusion deepened. "But you fingered the wrong man."

He gave a one-shouldered shrug. "Right, wrong, who cares? It was a damn good story."

Even with her sore head, Genevieve was starting to put together the pieces. "Someone approached you," she said. "Said they'd give you the identity of Robin Hood, the scoop of the year, in exchange for . . . what?"

He gave her a beady look and propped his legs up on the table, causing it to sway. "Never you mind what."

Her curiosity stirred. "But how were they planning on making the story stick? Daniel McCaffrey is not Robin Hood; I proved that. Arthur's already printed a retraction. And if I hadn't given Daniel an alibi, he would have had them for the other crimes . . ." It suddenly became clear. "Oh," she said faintly.

Clive smirked. "Catching on, are you?"

She was. They weren't planning on Daniel being alive to defend himself. "You'd kill an innocent man for a false story?"

"*I* wasn't going to kill anyone. But if others want Mr. McCaffrey out of the way, and I get the story of the decade out of it . . ." Clive spread his hands. "Everybody wins."

A wave of blackness crossed her vision, and Genevieve dug her palms into the rough wall behind her, willing herself to stay upright and conscious. "And you get money," she said, alarmed at how faint her own voice sounded. She willed it to be louder. "I'm sure they offered you lots of money."

He watched her dispassionately. "As I said, we weren't all born with a silver spoon. But yes, I'm about to become very wealthy, and Mr. McCaffrey is about to be very dead."

"How? How will they kill him?" Bouts of darkness continued to dance across her eyes. Genevieve dug her palms into the wall again, the pain of thick splinters gouging her hands forcing her consciousness back to alertness.

Clive shook his head. "Not my job, and I don't care. Once he's gone, other evidence will conveniently be found. We'll make the story stick, despite the retraction." He flashed a sour smile in her direction. "You should have accepted me when you had the chance."

Anger flared, hot and satisfying, temporarily blocking her fear and snapping her focus into place. "Is that what this is about? Are you still pouting because I wouldn't have dinner with you?"

Clive moved faster than she would have thought possible, pinning her against the wall and gripping her jaw roughly in his hand.

"Do not mock me, Miss Stewart," he gasped. "Your little stunt might have cost me my career, and I am not in a mood to be taunted."

"Your journalistic mistakes are not my fault," Genevieve managed, heart pounding.

He released her suddenly, shoving her to one side so that she lost her balance and stumbled. As she steadied herself, the strident noise of the tavern ballooned in again as the door opened.

Ernest Clark surveyed the scene with distaste. "Why is she still here?" he asked. It clicked for Genevieve: his had been the other voice she'd heard arguing with Clive earlier.

"Sometimes, Ernest, we must dirty our hands ourselves," a third voice sighed.

Tommy Meade wound his way around Ernest and smiled at Genevieve.

"I've dirtied my hands plenty," Ernest muttered, shutting the door. She bit her lip and tried to calculate whether she could somehow get past all three men and to the door. It didn't seem likely.

"Mr. Meade," Genevieve said, pushing herself off the wall. She wasn't going down without a fight. "How nice to see you again."

Tommy responded with an amused smirk. "Likewise, Miss Stewart." He advanced until she found herself backed against the same wall Clive had pinned her against earlier.

The rivulets of fear Genevieve felt expanded, though she did her best to maintain a brave facade.

Smiling his predatory smile, Tommy gently wagged his finger in Genevieve's face. "You've been a very naughty girl, Miss Stewart. Inconvenient. And I don't like to be inconvenienced, do I, Clive," Tommy continued, keeping Genevieve fixed in his unwavering stare.

"No, sir, not at all," drawled Clive lazily from behind the other man, clearly enjoying seeing Genevieve terrorized. She swallowed her fear and scanned the room for a weapon, gritting her teeth in frustration when nothing obvious presented itself. Perhaps the bottle?

"Your snooping was inconvenient," Tommy continued. "Your presence here right now is inconvenient. This fool was meant to have killed you weeks ago." His eyes flicked toward Clive, who ducked his head and looked away.

Fury arose anew in her. It was Clive who had attacked her in the records room.

"And Danny has been inconvenient for years," Tommy said, shaking his head in mock sadness. "He should have stayed abroad."

"How did you know Daniel had told me about his sister?" Genevieve managed to ask through her fear. It had been bothering her since the article came out.

A quick look of surprise crossed Tommy's face. "Told you, did he? Danny boy is more smitten than I thought. I've known for years, Miss

Stewart, and simply have been waiting for the right occasion to use the information." He shrugged. "Many in the old hood knew."

"It didn't matter whether McCaffrey had told you or not," Clive added with a nasty laugh. "What mattered was that he *thought* you betrayed him, *thought* you uncovered his past secrets. And it worked, didn't it? You both backed off your snooping, and I heard McCaffrey disappeared. All your precious retraction did was get you fired, and out of my hair for good."

Tommy sighed deeply, wrenching her attention back his way. His forearm suddenly blocked her windpipe as his body pressed against hers, holding her captive. Genevieve gasped for breath as he said, as casually as if he were ordering a cup of tea, "That's enough pleasant conversation. As I said, if one wants a job done right, sometimes one must do it oneself."

The crushing forearm was replaced by a thin knife, its cruel edge pressing against her throat. The blade was so sharp that she didn't feel the shallow cut, but the sensation of warm liquid trickling down her neck told her one had been made, and she knew Tommy wouldn't hesitate to slice her neck open and leave her to die in the back room of this tavern.

Tommy cut his eyes toward Clive, and with a quick shove she felt herself pushed into the chest of her former coworker, who pinned her arms behind her back. Struggling would only increase the pressure of the blade, which never left her vulnerable throat. Genevieve kept as still as she could, even breathing as shallowly as possible. Panic began to blur the edges of her vision.

"It may be a small consolation, Miss Stewart, but I've no doubt you'll be mourned," Tommy whispered again, almost tenderly. "Your family appears very loving. And for what it's worth, I've never seen Danny boy so taken with a woman. I'm sure he would have married you eventually. If there's one thing Danny is, it's honorable." He fairly spat the last word, increasing the force of the knife as Genevieve desperately shrank into Clive's chest in an effort to avoid its deepening push.

A bellow of pure rage rang through the thin walls of the tavern.

The trio froze, the knife a hair's edge away from ending Genevieve's life. Over Tommy's shoulder, she saw Ernest leap toward the door and open it.

Another bellow, and the noise in the tavern stopped abruptly. If it hadn't been for the blade pressed against her throat, Genevieve would have sagged in relief.

Daniel.

Tommy cocked his head, listening. A sliver of a smile emerged on his thin, hard face.

"Danny boy," he said quietly. "I wasn't sure he'd get here in time. Frankly, I wasn't sure he'd come at all. Thought he might have stayed drunk for a month after that article." He turned the smile on Genevieve, who tried to shrink back farther, to no avail.

"That sister was always his weak spot. I knew it would come in handy someday," Tommy remarked in a conversational tone. He pointed the knife at Genevieve's face, a mere fraction of an inch from her left eye. She could suddenly, barely breath. "The secret to surviving, Miss Stewart, is to have no weak spots. To *not* care. Because if one cares, that can be exploited, don't you see?"

Their eyes locked. Genevieve held her breath, not daring to speak. One couldn't reason with a madman.

The knife moved away from her eye and pointed at Clive. "You, finish your job," Tommy instructed. The knife then pointed at Ernest. "And you, take care of our new guest."

"And what will you be taking care of?" she spat in Tommy's direction.

Condescending amusement washed over Tommy's face. "Matters more important than you, dearie. I've got a mayoral campaign to continue, and how would it look for a candidate to be found slumming at the Eagle Head Tavern?"

The knife disappeared somewhere in the folds of Tommy's coat as he cast a significant look at both Ernest and Clive, and then he slipped out the door, Ernest following closely behind.

Clive's hold on Genevieve's arms tightened as he shoved her up against the wall again, this time turning her around so her cheek pushed into its rough surface. He used the force of his body to keep her pinned against the wall but said nothing. He was pressed so close into her that Genevieve could smell his rank body odor rising from underneath fading layers of cologne. She fought to keep from gagging but also remained quiet, mind working frantically. Their ragged breath mingled, and each stilled as they listened to what sounded like gathering commotion outside the tavern. After what seemed like an eternity but was likely less than a minute, all noise from the outside ceased, and an eerie silence settled.

They waited. The quiet swelled until it became almost oppressive. It was worse, far worse, than the cries and jeers Genevieve had faintly made out earlier through the thin tavern walls.

What on earth was going on?

Where was Daniel? Was he injured? She had to get out of there and help him. She thought of Tommy's knife and Ernest's cold eyes and shuddered. Daniel needed to be warned.

She eyed the half-empty bottle on the table behind Clive, then risked a glance at her captor. His face was still inches from hers, but his gaze was riveted toward the door to the outer room of the tavern. His jaw worked and sweat dripped from his brow, despite the steadily dropping temperature. He appeared completely focused on trying to decipher what was happening outside. Suddenly, a loud cheer rose from the street. Clive started slightly, straining toward the door instinctively and relaxing his hold a fraction. Genevieve didn't waste a second. Using all of her considerable strength, she thrust herself backward into Clive's chest, ignoring the waves of pain that exploded in her head. Her unexpected movement caught him off-balance, and he stumbled backward, mouth open in shock, falling into the small table behind him. The rickety piece of furniture couldn't hold the force of his weight and collapsed underneath him, smashing the whiskey bottle as well. Clive gave his own bellow of surprise and pain; the bottle's shards must have pierced his back.

Quick as a flash, Genevieve darted for the door and dashed into the outer room of the tavern. It was empty save for a crowd of men gathered at the front door, straining to see what was happening on the street. They were four or five deep, at least, and Genevieve knew she'd never be able to push through them to safety before Clive reached her. She could already hear him scraping along the floor and cursing at the glass stuck in his back. He would be on her momentarily. Seeing a stairway that snaked upward behind the bar, she dashed for it, not knowing where it would lead.

Taking the stairs two at a time, Genevieve found herself in a long hallway lined with closed doors. She heard Clive's roar of rage as he stumbled up behind her, followed by another cheer from the crowd gathered on the street. She had a fleeting moment to wish for Daniel's safety as she tried several locked doors in vain, before one opened underneath her sweaty grasp to reveal a second flight of stairs. A quick glance over her shoulder showed Clive emerging, red-faced, bloody and furious, at the end of the hall behind her. Seeing no other option, she went for the stairs and slammed the door shut behind her, knowing that without a lock it wouldn't keep him out long.

The winds had picked up, the icy rain shifting to wet, heavy snow, the first few flakes swirling in an ever-darkening sky. Genevieve staggered onto the rooftop of the three-story building and immediately sought a way down other than the staircase she'd just ascended. She knew how to throw a punch, but casual boxing with her brothers in the park was a far cry from fighting for her life on an icy rooftop with a deranged man, particularly when she was weak and injured. It was better to run, run to safety if she could find it. Usually these rooftops connected and she could simply transverse the buildings until she found a way down, but this appeared to be a stand-alone . . . *there*! Genevieve spied where the building did not connect to its neighbor, but there was a foot or so between them—that would be an easy enough distance to navigate. She sped in that direction but was stopped before arriving by Clive, who was suddenly looming in front of her.

Genevieve's heart pounded as she slowly backed toward the edge of the roof. There was a drop to the courtyard at the back of the building behind her.

"I'll finish the job, all right," Clive snarled. He lunged for her, and reacting on pure instinct built from a childhood spent sparring with boys, Genevieve ducked and dodged to her right, simultaneously swinging with her right fist. She clipped Clive in the side, inadvertently adding to the momentum he'd already gained from his dive in her direction.

"No!" Genevieve yelled, horrified, as for one heart-stopping moment Clive teetered on the roof's edge. She reached forward, but it was too late; his balance tipped and there was a sickening thud as his body hit the pavement three stories below. Shaking, Genevieve risked a glance over the edge of the roof, shuddering deeper as she saw Clive's mangled and broken form twisted in an impossible position.

A shout from the opposite side of the building wrenched her thoughts back to Daniel and what must be an altercation with Ernest. Leaving Clive's corpse to whatever fate might befall it, she raced down the stairs again and toward the sounds of fighting.

CHAPTER 23

"Meade!" Daniel bellowed again, growing hoarse. He stood in front of the Eagle Head Tavern as a few flakes of snow began to fall. Except for the crowd that had clustered at the door of the bar, most of whom had emerged from its depths at his first cry, the small triangle-shaped square was nearly empty. Any passerby had either joined the crowd or hurried inside to safety.

He waited. Genevieve was inside. He would see her safe, and he would end this. *Now.*

Billy had been cutting across the park in the early morning hours, ready to take up his post outside the Stewart house as previously arranged, when he had become distracted by a cat's mournful cry. After extricating the cold creature from underneath a shrub, he spied two figures far down the path, and watched the man strike the woman and carry her away. Instantly understanding that he had failed at his task, Billy rushed to find Daniel at the Gramercy mansion and mournfully relayed the tale, still holding the shivering cat.

Daniel realized that he should have known Genevieve wouldn't stay put, despite her promise. Rupert was already with him, as they had retreated to his house to plan their next steps, but Daniel knew he would need more muscle than that to take on Tommy. He gathered Asher, Billy, and Paddy and set off for the Eagle Head Tavern.

Daniel was prepared to wait all day. He knew Meade was in there, knew the tavern was an Oyster Knife stronghold of old. Sure enough, he recognized more than half the men—and a few women—who had gathered and watched him in silence.

They weren't watching just Daniel. He would have come alone and torn the wretched place apart plank by plank to find Genevieve, but as he, Rupert, and Asher had made their way across town, Paddy and Billy had silently peeled away, and by the time he had reached the intersection where the tavern stood, a gathering of Bayard Toughs were waiting. Word had gotten out: Daniel McCaffrey needed help, and Daniel was one of their own. The Toughs had answered the call and now stood assembled behind him, some with weapons, some armed only with their fists, all ready to fight.

They waited. A wooden sign of a neighboring druggist squeaked as it swung in the growing wind. The noise from the sign was joined by another creak, this time from the tavern door slowly opening.

The crowd parted, and Daniel started in surprise, as it wasn't Tommy who emerged but Ernest Clark. Clark impassively surveyed the situation, making note of the four dozen or so Bayard Toughs standing motionless behind Daniel, and doubtless equally aware of Tommy's numbers gathered around the entrance of the bar.

It would be a fairly even fight, if it came to that.

Despite the wet cold, Daniel had removed his jacket and rolled his shirt-sleeves high on his upper arms, exposing the tattoos that identified him as a Tough. His shirt was plastered to his skin from rain and the beginning of wet snow, but he wasn't going to hide who he was anymore. He was a Bayard Tough from Five Points. He was the son of Irish immigrants. He was also a Harvard-educated lawyer and in possession of one of the largest fortunes in the city, indeed in the country. He was a member of the Astor 400 who knew which fork to use, which suit of evening clothes to wear, and which architect to employ to design his summer cottage in Newport.

He was all of these things at once. He belonged to both worlds.

Daniel faced Clark, tense and ready, jaw clenched. "Where's Meade?" he growled.

Clark eyed him with disdain. "I don't know what you're talking about," he replied. "Mr. Meade wouldn't patronize an establishment such as this."

It took every ounce of control Daniel possessed not to pounce on the other man and immediately begin beating him to a bloody pulp.

"It's all going to come crashing down, Clark," he warned. "Meade won't save you. He has no loyalty to anyone but himself. Do you really want to take the fall for these others? Meade, Andrew Huffington?"

Ernest's coat was already off, and he began to casually roll up his shirt-sleeves as well. "We're really not that different, you know," he remarked. "I came up in Chicago instead of New York, but like you, I'm not really one of them. The swells. Of course, you inherited your fortune. I made mine." Ernest began to walk in a half circle toward him, and Daniel took a few steps in the opposite direction. Not retreating. Assessing. He knew how to fight Tommy, knew that man's weaknesses and tricks. He wasn't sure what to expect from Clark.

"And why risk that fortune?" Daniel asked. The crowd surrounding them was silent, watching. Ernest changed direction. He appeared to be doing his own assessing.

The other man barked a short laugh. "Taking risks is how I got where I am. I'm willing to risk everything for her."

Daniel understood in an instant. "Sarah Huffington." The words emerged on a cloud of white air, but he barely felt the cold.

"She's too good for that ancient husband of hers. But the money she'll have as a widow, combined with what we're making . . . we'll rule this town." Ernest stopped, and Daniel could see the other man readying his body to fight. He followed suit, bending his knees slightly and tightening his fists.

"I wasn't aware her husband had passed on," Daniel remarked, his light tone at odds with his tense body.

Ernest smiled. "All in good time."

Quick as a wink, Ernest slid forward, a sudden knife slashing in his hand. Daniel had seen the slight hitch of Ernest's shoulders and correctly guessed that it signaled his readiness to move. Despite his being prepared for the lunge, though, the sharp edge of the knife nicked Daniel's left bicep. Blood seeped through the linen of his shirt and down his arm, mingling with the inked dragons and Celtic signs that adorned his muscled flesh. He barely felt the cut, he was so intent on besting his opponent. He made his own lunge, pure rage driving his head into the other man's midriff, knocking the breath out of Ernest and forcing him to the snowy street. Daniel quickly wrested the knife out of Ernest's suddenly unclenched fist and sent it skittering across the cobblestones. But Ernest recovered quickly and surprised Daniel with a sharp uppercut to his jaw. Pain exploded in his mouth.

The two men's ragged breath joined the creak of the wooden sign as the fight continued, sometimes giving Daniel the upper hand, sometimes Ernest. An occasional brief cheer arose from one side or the other if a particularly good punch was landed, but for the most part the crowd was quiet, watching. They knew, as the two main opponents did, that this could be a fight to the death.

A clattering sound broke through Daniel's focus, and he saw Ernest lunge in its direction. Someone had kicked the knife back toward the men. In one smooth motion, Ernest swooped it up and jumped toward Daniel. Reacting instinctively, Daniel jerked to the right. The snow had been falling steadily, making the cobblestones under their feet wet and slick. Ernest's foot slid out from underneath him when he landed, and he fell forward with a grunt, his left palm extended to brace his fall.

It didn't help. The other man's hand slipped as well, and he crashed onto his own face, where he lay, not moving.

Daniel waited a moment, panting, wondering if the stillness was a ruse. He approached the body cautiously, and with his foot turned the figure over.

Ernest had fallen on his own knife. It must have twisted toward his stomach as he fell, and the force of his own body weight had driven it deep, for now it was buried in the man's belly to halfway up the hilt. Blood pooled on his shirtfront and stained the snow, while a small trickle ran from the corner of his mouth. Ernest's mouth opened and closed a few times, a gurgling sound emerging.

"Daniel!" The voice, clear as a mountain stream he had once seen in the Swiss Alps, cut through his haze of disbelief. Genevieve pushed through the crowd and ran to him. He pulled her close in relief, before holding her at arm's length to make sure she was unhurt. At the sight of her neck and bodice covered in blood, he hissed, turning again toward Clark's still form, but she pulled him back.

"It was just a scratch. I'm fine. Please, look at me. I'm fine." Daniel turned back and examined her neck carefully. The small cut had crusted over.

Some of the men who had gathered in front of the tavern began to approach Ernest's limp body. The horrible gurgling sounds had stopped; Ernest Clark was dead.

A hand fell on his shoulder. "We should leave," Rupert said. "They're coming," Daniel heard clanging bells in the distance and nodded. Someone had called the police, and he didn't want to be there when they arrived. With Police Commissioner Simons's involvement, he needed to get to the press before the police and allow the *Globe* to report on the tangled web of corruption they had uncovered.

The Oyster Knifers melted into the shadows from whence they'd come, drifting back into the Eagle Head or slipping away down side streets. Some Bayard Toughs stayed to assist Daniel, should help be needed, but most dispersed, satisfied at the outcome of the fight. Several nodded to Daniel as they casually made their way into the evening, and Daniel nodded back.

Rupert handed Daniel his coat, and he realized Genevieve must be freezing. The wind had picked up even more, and the snow was swirling around them. He draped his jacket around Genevieve's shoulders and frowned at its thinness.

"We have to get her home," he instructed Asher, who was waiting nearby.

"Clive . . ." Genevieve swallowed, and Daniel followed her glance toward the back of the building. "Daniel, he fell . . ." She gestured, and he quickly dispatched Paddy and Billy to investigate.

"And I don't want to go home," she continued.

"Genevieve, you can't stay here—"

"We should go to the *Globe*," she said. "Right away. Daniel, Tommy is still out there."

The sirens were growing louder. Ernest's body was already covered by a quarter inch of snow.

"Let's go," he said. Paddy and Billy returned, confirming Genevieve's story with a single look. "Get out of here, boys," Daniel directed, glancing at the ever-darkening sky. "I think this storm is gearing up to be something rather memorable. I don't want any of you caught in it."

Daniel and Asher led Genevieve toward a carriage they had waiting around the corner, trailed by Rupert, while Paddy and Billy disappeared into the swirling white mists. Daniel glanced over his shoulder once, shuddering slightly at the scene. The square was eerily empty, save for the lumpen shape of Ernest Clark's dead body, the bright red of his blood gradually becoming muted and pale under the accumulating snow.

★ ★ ★

The next twenty-four hours, Genevieve would later reflect, were simultaneously the oddest and the most satisfying she had ever spent in her life.

Luckily, the *Globe*'s offices were only a few blocks farther downtown from Five Points, and it was quickly decided in the carriage that Rupert should not accompany Genevieve and Daniel to see her editor. Asher dropped them in front of the building on Park Row and assured them he would go only a few blocks more, taking himself, Rupert, and the horses to a boarding house nearby where they could hole up until the storm passed.

Gale-force winds whipped Genevieve's skirts and the flying snow sideways, and she and Daniel struggled their way across the sidewalk and into the building, clutching one another for support, once inside finding it nearly deserted.

Nearly, but not entirely.

"Miss Stewart." A confused-looking Arthur emerged from his office at the sound of the elevator doors opening. It was a miracle the building still had power. "I told everyone to go home." He blinked at what must have been an outrageous sight: Genevieve, bedraggled, exhausted, and bloodstained, accompanied by Daniel, splattered in blood, hatless, a dark bruise blossoming around his left eye.

"What has happened? Sit, sit." Arthur urged them toward some desk chairs while looking worriedly out the window at the blowing gusts. "I daresay you'll be here all day, perhaps even all night, at this point."

He would prove to be correct. They were able to dispatch a telegram to Genevieve's family and Daniel's household, letting them know of their whereabouts, right before the lines succumbed to the winds and the weight of the heavy March snow. The power followed soon thereafter, and Arthur fired up a coal stove he had fitted specially into the corner of his office and made them all strong coffee. As they drank, warming themselves before the stove, Arthur produced some muffins from a cupboard.

The muffins toasted, filling the empty, darkening space with a cozy fragrance, as Genevieve spun her tale. She felt a bit like Scheherazade, enchanting Arthur with partial fact, partial fiction. Daniel remained mostly silent but interjected the occasional comment.

"Ernest Clark?" Arthur sputtered, nearly dropping his muffin. "The financier? And Clive Huxton? Together *they* are Robin Hood, you say?"

Across Arthur's office, she saw shock, relief, and gratitude sweep across Daniel's face, before he resumed a more neutral expression.

"They are. This is why Clive tried to frame Mr. McCaffrey, you see. To protect himself."

Daniel shook his head at her, infinitesimally. She dipped her head a tiny bit in acknowledgment of his unspoken thanks. Truth be told, she hadn't been sure whether she would tell the truth about Rupert being Robin Hood or not until she'd begun speaking.

But Ernest Clark was dead, and Clive was dead. They had committed murder, even if it was at Tommy's behest; let them take the blame for the thefts as well. Enough damage had been done; let the living forge on as best they could.

Arthur removed his glasses and rubbed them on his shirt. "Most extraordinary."

"We believe the thefts started as just thefts," Daniel said, picking up her thread. "A way to thumb their nose at the rich. But once Ernest became involved with the Huffingtons' building scheme, he was able to use the thefts to cover up his additional crimes, such as keeping Reginald Cotswold quiet."

"Ernest killed Mr. Cotswold, as he discovered the mayoral committee on housing reform was working to actually profit from the construction of slums rather than improve them," Genevieve said softly, sadness returning anew at Reginald's senseless death.

Arthur peered at them, seeming to take all this in. He passed Daniel another muffin and scratched his face, looking out the window again. "This storm is making for the oddest bedfellows," he remarked, more to himself than to either of them. Turning his attention back to Genevieve, eyes sharp, he asked, "And Andrew Huffington's involvement?"

With his free hand, Daniel dug into his trousers pocket and pulled out the list he and Genevieve had compiled, the one that cross-listed the names of the mayoral committee with those of the people who had invested in Lexington Industries. Genevieve explained about the shell company.

Her editor looked at the list and sighed deeply. Placing his half-eaten muffin on the corner of his desk, he picked up a telegram and wordlessly handed it to her. Genevieve gasped as she read the contents, passing it to Daniel.

"That arrived just before you did," Arthur said, his eyebrows rising. "The suicide death of one of our leaders of industry is major news."

Genevieve and Daniel exchanged a look. The telegram stated that Andrew Huffington had shot himself that morning, but Genevieve wondered.

Who got to him first? Tommy or Sarah?

"Give me everything else you have," Arthur ordered. Daniel willingly handed over the rest of their notes, which he had buried deep in various pockets. One was water-stained, and blood had seeped through his shirt onto the corner of another. Arthur took them all with a fussy expression, smoothing out wrinkled pages and arranging them around his desk. Genevieve stood, anxious to be of use.

He waved her off. "Let me have a look first. I'll need to confirm all this. Now," he continued, peering at her from behind his glasses, "when I write this up, you'll share the byline?"

Something hot burst in the center of Genevieve's chest. "You'll give me credit?"

Arthur frowned. "Of course. I'd prefer to do the writing for a story this big—my, my, Giles Manfort, the deputy mayor," he murmured, looking at their notes, "but it's your research."

The hot thing fluttered, and she could barely stop herself from jumping up and down and clapping her hands like a child. "I . . . I get to keep my job?" she breathed.

"What? Oh yes. Yes. That talk will die down soon. Besides, I've heard from several reliable sources that Mr. McCaffrey was in the gaming room until the wee hours." He fixed Daniel with a beady look. "Is that not correct, sir?"

Daniel nodded mutely, looking as surprised as Genevieve felt.

"Then that's settled," Arthur said. "Let me get started, and the two of you get some rest. You both look dead on your feet. You may be able to find a cushion or two in someone's office, but stay within my sight." Arthur eyed them both sternly. "I'm your chaperone, I suppose. The last thing we want is a resurgence of the unseemly rumors we're about to put to bed. Here, Genevieve, take my coat." He handed over a thick wool coat, redolent of pipe smoke and snow.

The exhaustion she had been fighting for hours came flooding back in a rush, and she had to clasp Daniel's arm to keep from falling down. They arranged themselves on the floor outside the glass windows encasing Arthur's office. Daniel hunted around and found her someone's shawl to use as a pillow and spread Arthur's heavy coat over her body. Along with weariness, her aches and pains came roaring back, and she had to fight to keep her eyes open. Still, the overwhelming emotion she felt was gratitude: she was grateful to be safe, she was grateful to be warm, and she was grateful to be prone, even if it was on the hard wooden floor of her office.

Through heavy eyelids, she watched Daniel set up about ten feet across from her, using his own coat as a pillow. He lay on his side, facing her. She felt herself slipping toward sleep but smiled in his direction, a secret smile, one she hoped conveyed the gratitude she felt toward him as well. No matter what happened next, they were connected now, forever. He smiled back, blue eyes twinkling at her from across the wood floor. It was the last thing she saw before sleep overtook her.

When she woke up hours later, the worst of the storm had passed and the space on the wooden floor ten feet away was empty. Genevieve pushed herself up and blinked around the still-empty newsroom.

"He's gone," Arthur said, emerging from his office and handing her a steaming mug.

The cold air assaulted Genevieve's shoulders as Arthur's heavy coat slid down and pooled in her lap. She sipped at the mug, wondering why the short statement was causing such a pain in her heart.

"Is he coming back?" she asked, attempting to sound casual.

Her editor leaned against the doorframe of his office and looked at her with sympathy. "I don't believe so. He left when the winds quieted. Frankly, I was surprised he got out of the building at all. I can see drifts as high as third-story windows out there."

Genevieve nodded.

"Come," Arthur said, approaching and holding out his hand to help her stand. "Let's get to work."

Work. Genevieve applied herself to the task, reading what Arthur had written, making corrections, adding sentences. The sun emerged and shone through the large rectangular windows that lined the room, warming the space, its bright light glinting off the piles of blinding white snow without. It was satisfying in a deep, primal way, this work, this ordering of weeks of toil and investigation into an orderly, neat narrative.

Genevieve's pleasure in the task, though, did not keep her from glancing toward the doors into the room every few moments, hoping that one of the times she looked up, a tall, dark-haired figure would frame the empty space.

But it never did, not that day, nor the next. She didn't see Daniel again for almost a year.

EPILOGUE

One Year Later

June 1889

It was a fine day to set sail.

The sky overhead was that cocky blue unique to early summer, with barely a cloud in the sky. The spring winds had passed—thankfully without another blizzard this year—and the dog days of July and August had yet to trap the city in their oppressive heat. It was one of the rare days the New York air felt fresh and invigorating, even at the docks, and Daniel savored a deep breath of it, hands shoved into the pockets of his light-gray suit.

He stopped short at the sight of Genevieve.

She was summer personified, wearing a dress of pale green sprigged with white flowers and a straw hat with matching green ribbons. She was squinting toward the vast ocean liner, her hand held over her forehead to shield her eyes from the sun.

It had been over a year since the blizzard. Over a year since he had fallen asleep on the floor of a newspaper office, her bruised, beautiful face, peaceful in its slumber, the last thing he saw before his eyes closed.

Over a year since he had forced open the door in the *Globe*'s main lobby, shoving aside a two-foot snow drift, squinting in the harsh sunshine.

Their paths hadn't crossed in the intervening months until recently. At first he'd wrestled with whether or not to pay a call, but he would recall the shock on her face in the gaslight of the Maple townhouse following his impulsive proposal and find a reason to put it off again. He'd soon read in the gossip pages that their brief courtship appeared to have ended, and he'd folded up the unexpected pain that accompanied this news and carefully hid it among other, older pains.

Still, he'd debated paying a call. But then she had sailed to Europe with her parents just before Easter and departed almost immediately for Newport on her return. Another winter season had come and gone, but he hadn't participated much, mostly avoiding the parties and balls this year. His earlier desire to be social had faded.

Genevieve, though, seemed to have attended every single one.

Or at least, her column indicated that she had. She was now writing the society column for the *Globe*, the position for which had been vacant since the previous columnist, Jackson Waglie, had died some years ago. Rupert had done a good job of convincing several gentlemen that he and Daniel had gambled with them until daylight at the Porters' costume ball, to the point that one of them even paid Daniel a decent-sized sum he swore he owed. The brief scandal of his and Genevieve's supposed night in a hotel room had vanished, forgotten in the wake of larger, more important scandals.

Of course, they had both been at the wedding the week before. Indeed, they had both been in the wedding party. But even amid the festivities, they had managed to avoid each other.

Or she had avoided him, it seemed. He had kept hoping a reasonable opportunity to approach her would arise, but every time she was free and he took a step in her direction, something or someone else would occupy her attention.

This time, he approached. She turned as he stepped closer, and he was disheartened to see a flash of wariness cross her face before she smiled politely, extending her hand.

"Mr. McCaffrey." Ah, they were back on formal terms, then.

"Miss Stewart," he said, picking up her cue and shaking her hand. "I did not get a chance to say, but you looked beautiful at the wedding."

Her nose wrinkled, some of the old familiarity between them emerging. "Really? I don't think peach is quite my color, but it is nice for a June wedding."

Privately, he disagreed. Not about which colors suited a summer wedding—he didn't give a hang about weddings—but about how she had looked. She had glowed like the rising sun in her bridesmaid's dress.

"The bride certainly looked beautiful," he said, switching to a safer topic. And Esmie had, in a gown of icy-blue satin that suited her pale coloring perfectly. "I hear from Rupert she has you to thank for it."

Genevieve smiled. "Some time ago, she asked for my help in choosing new clothes. We've spent quite a bit of time at the dressmaker's this past year."

"I quite liked your recent article as well," he ventured, referring to her column on Rupert and Esmie's wedding.

Genevieve's mouth tightened. "The behavior of this city was a disgrace. It was the least I could do."

"I quite agree. You handled it well. I suppose it's for the best they're off to the continent now, though I will miss Rupert," he said. And he would. Rupert's imminent departure was making him realize how few friends he had. "Do you plan to visit once they're settled in England?"

"Perhaps. In time," she replied, glancing toward the ship again. "I hope Esmie likes England. She deserves some happiness."

"Rupert will be good to her."

Genevieve narrowed her eyes. "He'd better be."

"I daresay she'll enjoy Italy."

"Everyone enjoys Italy."

"Yes."

Was this all there was between them now? Awkwardness and polite conversation? Was that cord that had once existed between them severed, torn apart by the weight of what they had endured together the previous winter?

We helped people. The thought was sudden and fierce. Helped people, and seen—some, at least—justice done.

Not enough, of course. It would never be enough. The article Arthur and Genevieve had written based on what she and Daniel had discovered had reverberated through the Astor 400 with the force of a bomb. Andrew Huffington, dead, a bullet to the skull, and whether he or someone else had pulled the trigger was a secret he had carried to the grave. Sarah had tearfully pleaded that she was simply an investor, with no idea of the true nefariousness of the organization. It seemed that Andrew and Ernest were the only ones who could have contradicted her, and with both gone, the investigation had yielded nothing incriminating and she was never charged. The Stuyvesants and Ted Beekman, by all accounts, really had been innocent of knowledge of the true purpose of Lexington Industries and were now regarded with sympathy by much of society.

Though people still whispered behind their hands, as they would.

Deputy Mayor Manfort and Commissioner Simons had both stood trial, a lengthy, histrionic affair the press dubbed the "case of the century." Daniel wished the papers would come up with a more creative moniker; it seemed they were labeling at least one trial a decade as such. Both men had been convicted, but Commissioner Simons had chosen to follow Andrew Huffington's lead, though he'd opted for the rope instead of the pistol.

Tommy Meade had maintained his innocence in the whole affair, claiming that he was also simply an investor with no knowledge of the real scheme to thwart housing reform. But due to his background, the whispers around him had been louder, and he had eventually been forced to abandon his mayoral bid. Neither Deputy Mayor Manfort nor Commissioner Simons had ever implicated Meade, but Daniel suspected that this was due solely to the fact that they knew what fate would await them if they did. Indeed, Daniel was far from convinced that Simons's death by hanging was a suicide, just as he was suspicious of Huffington's gunshot to the head.

Still, some justice had been served.

But both he and Genevieve, he knew, bore scars. How could they not?

"There they are," Genevieve said suddenly, pointing to the upper deck of the ocean liner and waving. Rupert and Esmie waved back enthusiastically.

"I think they're pleased to be leaving," Daniel murmured. Genevieve did not respond but shot him an enigmatic smile.

Rupert pointed downward, then held up a finger, indicating that they were going below momentarily but would return in a moment. Daniel and Genevieve nodded dramatically to show that they understood.

A silence stretched between them. Daniel stole a look at Genevieve's clear, expressive profile as she continued to scan the decks of the giant boat, waiting for their friends to return. An emotion he couldn't quite place gnawed at his insides, making him want to huff impatiently. Suddenly it hit him: he'd *missed* her.

Could they not, perhaps, be friends again? It was summer, after all. Daniel thought of warm nights and the pleasures of a soft breeze and cool drink in one of the city's many rooftop bars. Perhaps she would agree to accompany him. Tonight. Just for a glass of champagne, to toast Rupert and Esmie's sendoff. He drew a breath.

"Genevieve," he began, but was interrupted by a resounding scream coming from the liner.

She looked at him with wide, startled eyes. "I think that was Esmie," she said, sounding shocked.

From a lower deck, Rupert's head suddenly popped up. Even at their distance it was obvious that his face was drained of color, his expression frantic.

"Daniel!" he yelled. "Come quickly!"

Without pausing to think, Daniel grasped Genevieve's hand and began to run toward the gangplank. The sounds of more shouting emerged from the boat. Passengers about to ascend halted, looking worried.

He shoved around them, causing someone to yell, "Watch it, man!" in their wake, but he kept running, tugging Genevieve behind. And a second realization hit him: her hand in his felt exactly right. The connection between them, the odd synchronicity they had sometimes shared, *that* is what he had missed, and just by holding her hand, it was back, as if it had never left.

Halfway up the gangplank, he paused for the barest of moments to glance back at her.

Did she feel it too?

Genevieve's face was full of determination and courage, her amber eyes blazing, and underneath it all lay an undeniable hint of excitement.

"What are you waiting for? Go," she urged, gesturing with her head up the narrow gangplank.

It was all Daniel needed. He began to run again, her hand still securely in his, not needing to turn back again. He knew she could keep up.

Acknowledgments

Though this is a work of fiction, certain characters and events were inspired by real historical figures. My heroine Genevieve Stewart is loosely based on Elizabeth Cochran Seaman, better known by her pen name Nellie Bly, largely considered to be the first female investigative journalist in America. Though Bly was a native of Pittsburgh and not New York, she was groundbreaking in her field, opening doors for other women in the industry. The pairing of Rupert Milton and Emsie Bradley was inspired by the phenomenon of the so-called "dollar brides" in the late nineteenth century, or American heiresses who brought much-needed revenue to England by marrying British royalty. Esmie and Rupert are based on the couple Cornelia Martin and William George Robert, fourth Earl of Craven and Viscount of Uffington, whose 1893 wedding is described in M. H. Dunlop's book *Gilded City: Scandal and Sensation in Turn of the Century New York* (Perennial, 2000). And of course the blizzard at the end of the book is modeled on the Great Blizzard of 1888, a horrific storm that crippled the east coast for days.

This book would not have come to fruition without the intense efforts and faith of my tenacious agent, Danielle Egan-Miller of Browne and Miller Literary Associates. Danielle has been a fierce champion of this book since the day she first read it, and I am grateful for her confidence in my work, particularly when I have none, and for her continued guidance through the murky waters of publishing. I am also grateful to her team, past and present, whose vigilance and thorough reads of the manuscript made it stronger, and to Eleanor Roth for being so helpful with all logistical matters. My editor at Crooked Lane Press, Faith Black Ross, expertly polished the manuscript, and I am also thankful for her enthusiasm and support of this book. I have much gratitude also to the entire team at Crooked Lane, especially for the hard work of Melissa Rechter, and to Nicole Lecht for the gorgeous cover design.

Early readers of this book included Juli Ann Patty and Christina LaFontaine, and I remain thankful for their astute comments—the book is better for their suggestions. My entire family has been nothing but supportive during this endeavor, and their cheerleading has meant the world. My sister Christine Gillespie in particular has offered commiseration, advice, and endless encouragement at all hours. She has read countless drafts and been a champion of this project from the beginning; everyone should be blessed with such a sister. My husband Marc has been the ultimate hero throughout this process, from designing my website to giving me time and space to write when I needed it. Finally, the arrival of my son five years ago was the impetus to finish my long-tinkered with manuscript. I am eternally grateful to both my guys; they are the reason this book exists.